I0823496

THE SKY OF SACRIFICE

BOOKS BY
ROSALIA AGUILAR SOLACE

THE BOOK OF WISDOM TRILOGY

The Great Library of Tomorrow

The Sky of Sacrifice

THE SKY OF SACRIFICE

ROSALIA AGUILAR SOLACE

Published in 2025 by Blackstone Publishing
Interior art and cover image and design by TL International BV/Tomorrowland
Typesetting by Blackstone Publishing

Printed in the United States of America

First edition: 2025
ISBN 979-8-212-53792-6
Fiction / Fantasy / Epic

Version 1

Blackstone Publishing
31 Mistletoe Rd.
Ashland, OR 97520

www.BlackstonePublishing.com

ADSCENDO
Realm Of The Birds

The Shimmering
Tree
The High
Eyrie
The
Fountain
Mount
Nest
The Aviary
Arcadiana

The Maiden
Atmosphere
Jaele's Mount
Centonis
ADSCENDO
The Great Islands

THE STORY SO FAR

A deadly attack on the Rose Garden in the realm of Silvyra leaves the Rose Garden and its magical flower, the Cerulean Rose, destroyed. Worse still, Perennia, the Garden's dragon protector, is missing.

Having been caught in the onslaught, visiting Sages Helia and Xavier of Earth's Great Library of Tomorrow are both wounded, Xavier mortally so. Though it broke her heart, and suffering from head trauma, Helia and the Sages' two Orb companions flee back to the Great Library on the back of Amare, a magical bird capable of transporting a person anywhere in reality.

Once back at the Great Library—a magical repository of knowledge hidden on an island somewhere on Earth—Helia confides in Mwamba, the Sage of Knowledge, that the attack came from Suttaru, a figure from the Library's ancient past. They call a council of the Sages, each of whom represents and is sworn to protect one of the ten core values of humanity, to discuss the threat.

For Nu, a young woman living in the Library, the day starts as usual as she heads excitedly to her role as a welcomer to visitors of the Library. Today it is Arturo, a middle-aged man from Mexico City, dissatisfied with his job as a marketing copywriter, who discovers an implausible bookshop, within which is a gateway to the Great Library. As Nu escorts him into the Library, she locates Xavier's Orb, which has rolled away from Helia in its grief. Robin, the Sage of Love, encounters them, and almost by accident, they attend the Council of Sages.

Back in Silvyra, where news of the attack has yet to spread to Mother, Dzin, a student Runner at the Botanical Education School, prepares for his final examination by creating his unique formula for the Elixir of Life. As the students prepare, however, they are attacked and murdered, with Dzin being the only survivor. Framed for the murders, Dzin and his brother, Yantuz, flee from the Great Tree, across the First Forest, and toward the Maze, which protects their community from those who are not pure of heart.

Helia, suffering gaps in her memory that can't be helped even by the vast knowledge of the Great Library, consults the Book of Wisdom, the guiding consciousness of the Library. However, the Book is worryingly silent, so Helia travels back to Silvyra using the magical Portal to get a sample of the Elixir, which can reportedly cure almost any physical ailment. Nu, now looking after Xavier's Orb, is encouraged to go as well.

Veer, the Sage of Strength, volunteers to go to the Silvyran town of Aedela in the land of Bloom to support them against Suttaru's forces, while Sage Robin hosts Arturo, who begins to develop strange magical powers.

Helia and Nu arrive at the Great Tree to find it in chaos. The attack on the students, as well as attacks on their fleet of airships and Elixir itself, have sent the Great Tree community into a state of turmoil. Worse still, the remaining stores of the Elixir seem to be inert, and with the Runner students dead and their formulas destroyed, they realize Dzin may have the only valid formula left for the Elixir.

Helia and Nu set off to find Dzin and his brother, rescuing them from the hazardous Maze that protects the First Forest. They then join forces to find what might be the last surviving seed of the Cerulean Rose in the collection of the Raptor Prince, ruler of the Clockwork Mountain.

They travel to Undergrowth, a town to the north of the Great Tree, where they meet former Runner and airship crew member Rascal, who agrees to help them. After a death-defying descent, they find passage aboard the *Golden Oriole*, an airship bound for the Mountain.

Once at their destination, they seek an audience with the Raptor Prince, but he proves to be fickle and refuses to help, forcing Helia and her companions to steal the seed while the forces of Suttaru launch an attack.

Meanwhile, Veer, the Sage of Strength, joins forces with the Petal Queen, ruler of the land of Bloom on Silvyra, to try and stop the enemy from destroying the capital, Aedela. Despite their combined skills, the best they can do is safely evacuate most of the citizens while Suttaru's forces decimate the land.

At the Great Library, Arturo and Sage Robin hunt through the oldest parts of the Library to find a clue to where the dragon, Perennia, might be. While exploring, they find references to a place called the City of Forever.

Their search is interrupted, however, when Edwin Payne, the Rogue Sage, launches an attack on the Library with an army of Suttaru's Unwritten. As Nu, Helia, and their friends head for the City of Forever on the *Golden Oriole*, Dzin creates a fresh batch of the Elixir of Life using the seed captured from the Clockwork Mountain city, which Helia later, using her powers, transforms into a living Cerulean Rose. Arturo joins the fight to defend the Great Library, using a unique power to write things into reality using just his creative imagination.

Arriving at the realm containing the City of Forever, Helia, Nu and their companions find themselves in a vast, sophisticated, and yet deserted place. They see their memories come alive in the gardens around the city and discover that Perennia is one of those memories, killed by Suttaru back in the Rose Garden on Silvyra.

As Suttaru arrives at the City of Forever, all seems lost. While her companions fight off his Unwritten forces, Helia sees hope in the image of Perennia, and using her magic, amplified by her Orb, Vega, she manages to bring the dragon back to life. Nu watches as Helia and Vega give their lives to resurrect Perennia. As the dragon engages Suttaru in combat, Nu comes into her power as the new Sage of Truth, revealing Suttaru to be his true self—a small and jealous man—consumed with hate and dark powers. As he realizes his own truth, the combined powers of Nu and Perennia vanquish Suttaru, and he turns to smoke and dust.

While Nu and her companions grieve for Helia and Vega, they are joined via the Portal from the Great Library by Mwamba, Robin, and Arturo, who defeated Edwin Payne. However, Payne escaped, fleeing in the final stages of the battle. Reunited, the Sages and their companions return home.

After a celebration to formally recognize Nu as the new Sage of Truth, the Great Library celebrates and then bids goodbye to Arturo, who wishes to return home to his daughter, Rosa. Despite knowing that the Library's magic will remove his memories of this magical place and the events he has witnessed, Arturo knows his renewed sense of creativity and purpose will live on so long as the Great Library is there to protect humanity's values.

After the celebrations, Dzin, back on Silvyra, finds traces of rot in the roots of Mother, the Great Tree . . .

PROLOGUE

The halls of the Great Library of Tomorrow were a hive of activity. Construction, masonry work, carpentry, and yes, though it seemed hardly possible, scholarly research.

Fairen moved through the halls in a daze. There was so much happening, and only she and her most trusted companions knew about her recent discovery of the astonishing shimmering *portal*—for what else could it be?—in the depths of the Library. The Founder had closed off the area and was studying it himself—even she was denied access—and now this new mystery heralding from the slopes of their mountain home.

Adi had sent a messenger to call Fairen back from the oldest of the stacks, and his scribbled hand both excited and troubled her.

> *Fairen, come with haste. An artifact has been unearthed, and it's like nothing we've ever seen!*
>
> *—Adi*

They'd found many things during the extensive excavation and exploration of the deep underground vaults in the twin mountain island they now called home. But this was the first time Adi had seemed excited.

Fairen crossed over the growing Main Concourse and into their reading room, and found Adi pacing, gesticulating widely at the workers moving a huge carbon and metal object through the room.

"Steady! Steady, you oafs! This is priceless! Priceless!" Adi said to the groans and muttering of the workers.

"It might go easier, Scholar Adi, if you lend them a hand rather than waving your arms around like a madman," Fairen said, a playful edge to her voice that caused Adi to first scowl, then grin. His lanky form was dressed in a crumpled scholar's robe, his dark, wavy hair unkempt and billowing.

"Fairen! What took you so long?" Adi said, mock outrage on his face, combined with a dash of genuine vexation. "These fellows have taken hours to move our find here. Hours! Lost time to begin the examination!"

"Of what? A hunk of metal? We're not blacksmiths, Adi. What need have we for all this ore?" She was serious now. *What did this rock matter, when the portal was denied to her?* she thought.

"I think it may be a fallen star, Fairen. It was buried in the side of this very mountain, long covered by dirt and other detritus, according to the diggers working on the surveys of the island, but it had cut a furrow in the rock a dozen lengths of you or I." He was animated, although she feared he might be heading into one of his more manic phases.

"Patience, Adi," she said, resting her hand on his shoulder, which seemed to calm him. He reached up to lay his hand on hers, and she allowed it but felt guilty. They had almost been more than colleagues not that long ago, but her heart was elsewhere these last few months.

She smiled at the thought and didn't begrudge Adi the warmth and calm her touch brought him. He must have realized she had met someone. Her friends knew, including the third member of Adi and Fairen's scholar group.

Adi pulled away. "Look closer, Fairen—the burning, the glint of gold and silver in the sheen of the visible metal. But it is not one or the other, I believe. I think this may have come from the heavens!"

"Let me look closer, Adi." She moved toward the object and felt a tingle in her fingers as she touched the misshapen boulder. The metallic glints seemed to shift and change in the light. Adi was right: It was silver and gold and brass, mixed with starlight. Could they have discovered a new metal? Impressive, but hardly comparable to the portal she herself found just days before. Unless . . .

"Adi, when was this discovered?" she asked.

"Oh, a few days back. A little before your"—he looked around with exaggerated caution—"own discovery," he said in a lower voice.

She looked at the large silver-and-gray mass before her and wondered how it could possibly be connected to her own discovery.

"Adi, do you think—"

"That revealing the one caused the other?" He practically beamed at her.

Could it be? she thought. How would this affect her life and the Great Library? She had a lot of decisions to make, and her greatest fear was it would require her to make a choice between the portal and the captain who stole her heart.

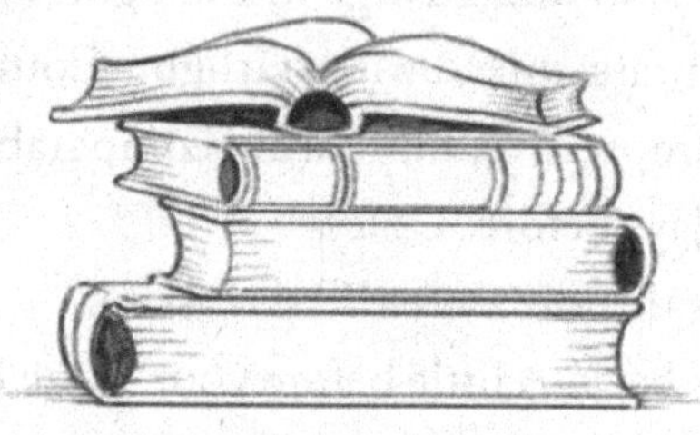

CHAPTER ONE
THE CHOOSING

Nu woke to the pulsing rhythm of Antares's golden lights, the Orb's excitement pushing at the boundaries of her consciousness until she woke. The complex patterns—a mixture of swirling fractal crystals and strobing lights—showed the Orb's joy at what must be a special event. It seemed the signs had been right: The selection of the new Sage of Hope was at hand.

Nu looked over at the still-sleeping form of Triss, her hair a golden cascade over the pillows as she slept. It was difficult to balance her job and spend time with Triss, and it didn't look like it was going to settle down anytime soon. Being chosen as a Sage was an amazing honor, but her position—its rewards and challenges—were difficult to balance while also starting a new relationship. It wasn't uncommon for Sages to find romance in the Library, but the obstacles existed for both her and Triss. Nu had and would continue to travel to Paperworld, especially in the current uncertain times. She knew the truth of it better than anyone: The demands of her position would always take priority. Not to mention the unspoken reality that Nu might live several lifetimes, while Triss was destined for a normal lifespan. But those were problems for another day.

Nu slipped from the covers with the grace of a dancer—a pastime she had enjoyed since childhood—her bare feet welcoming the reliable warmth of the floor of her quarters, carved from the living rock of the mountain's interior. The Sage of Truth was still amazed she had been given this suite of rooms. Understated yet refined, and befitting her position as the Sage of Truth, they had belonged to her predecessors going back centuries. A portrait of Xavier hung on one wall, a reminder of the last Sage, whom she'd seen in life but never had the chance to meet. The picture was her way of honoring his sacrifice, no less than he deserved.

A rolled-up piece of paper struck her on the head. The blow was soft and not entirely unprecedented. Triss was awake. The page torn from her notebook rolled to the floor as Nu turned to face her, a grin already forming on her face as she saw Triss's exasperated expression and dutifully signed an apology to her.

"I'm sorry, my love. I should have woken you. I just wanted a moment to consider what today will bring." Like most people born in the Library, Nu had been brought up learning to sign.

"You promised we'd go together," Triss signed back, a playful expression on her face. "That is if her Sageship is happy to be seen with a mere scholar-apprentice and not gallivanting off around Paperworld without me."

Nu looked at her lover thoughtfully for a moment, then ruthlessly yanked the covers from the bed.

"Better get a move on, then. Antares is almost vibrating apart to get to the Observatory. It must be close if she's getting this excited. Maïa will likely already be waiting for us."

Triss grinned, rose languidly from the bed, and dashed for the shower like a raptor after game. Nu shook her head and followed her lead.

The Concourse teemed with activity as they looked out through the windows of their streetcar. Its upholstered seats were lush and comfortable, lovingly maintained through their generations of use, and the silent mechanisms, powered by esoteric steam engines—designed by the great Leonardo himself, some said—made swift but not excessive passage along the great length of the Library. Its passengers—mostly the elderly, children, and those in an unusually urgent hurry—buzzed in conversation, and Nu wished Triss could hear their excitement. Triss, however, had one hand pressed to the glass, feeling the vibrations passing through them, and she knew Triss could read those as well as any book in the Library.

Her other hand held Nu's, and the Sage of Truth felt her contentment and saw the truth of her own feelings. Love, desire, respect, and contentedness. It had taken time to get there, and Nu didn't want to waste a moment of it. It was a time of uncertainty; their love was a truth she had come to rely on.

Antares rotated at her shoulder, the Orb's attention once again pulsing into her mind, and Nu turned to look at the Orb.

What is it? she asked.

You seem . . . unsettled? The lines and patterns on Antares's surface were once again a maze of possibilities that Nu instantly understood.

It's nothing. A dream. I'm just nervous about today.

Antares flashed a rainbow of colors, a wordless expression of love and acceptance. Nu felt Triss squeeze her hand and looked back to see her partner staring at the Orb with an expression of wonder mixed with wistful regret. No one but the Sages and the Book of Wisdom could fully understand the language of the Orbs, but their raw emotional feelings were there for all to see. Antares was celebrating. And why not? The Sages' ranks were about to be restored. The new Sage of Hope would be chosen shortly, and the Library would be whole. Nu, for one, was thankful the search was finally over.

Maïa was waiting for them at the terminal near the Observatory. The elegant, crimson-haired woman stood patiently, her cloak rustling slightly in the breeze created by the streetcar's movement.

Nu felt the corners of her lips twitch, trying to contain her excited smile. Nu barely glanced up at the older Sage and simply nodded. Antares hovered at her shoulder, her golden leaves all a flurry across her silver surface as though caught in a breeze. The little Orb shared Nu's anticipation over this big event.

"We've been waiting so long for this moment," Nu said to the Sage of Integrity. "The Great Library needs its champion of hope back. But, more importantly, so does Earth. A world without someone to fight for hope is one that's vulnerable. That goes for Paperworld too. On my last few journeys beyond the Great Library, it's been like a knot in my stomach, a gut feeling that something isn't quite right. Had we gone on much longer without a champion of hope, I fear we might have crossed a line beyond which the world might not recover." Nu breathed and smiled broadly. "And it goes without saying that it will be a privilege to see the Sages united once more. A full complement of the guardians of the Great Library! I cannot wait to welcome our newest member. I think we're *all* ready for this."

Triss started to sign. "We all felt it when the Orb was gifted with life, but why did it take so long?"

Maïa looked at Triss for a long while before replying, and Nu worried Triss had committed some sort of faux pas.

"The making of a Sage's Orb is a rare thing. As we're taught, the designs go back to Fairen herself, after she built the Book of Wisdom. Even our greatest scholars and Sages have yet to unlock the mysteries of how her magic works, or what determines its pace."

Nu was amused. It was difficult for any Sage to resist the temptation to lecture people on the Library's origins, despite the fact all the children of the Great Library learned of its history in school. And yet Triss was captivated, Nu thought, which made her all the more adorable.

Maïa carried on. "The Author must meticulously build each component, from the rare to the impossible, and weave them together, using the very magic of the Library itself, through her connection to Paperworld, to bring life to inanimate objects. No scholar or Sage is capable of this feat."

Triss signed her appreciation, caught up in the excitement of the day.

"Triss, Mwamba tells us endlessly of your endeavors as his new protégé. There are scholars twice your age who would be humbled to take your place, and yet you are more skilled in working with the Codex and the labyrinthian records of the former Sages that he's trying to catalog."

Triss looked excited. Nu was proud of her. Only the very best scholars were chosen to be mentored by Mwamba, as only the very best could keep up with his astounding intellect.

Turning back to the Sage of Truth, Maïa said, "Nu, you are right. This has been the longest I've ever known us without a full complement of Sages, and I've been here since the Belle Époque. Of course, waiting for the new Orb to grow takes care and patience. But now that Eltanin has been brought into being, we shall see this destiny fulfilled. Even in my second century, it is good to see there are things that can surprise and delight us. And, as you say, it is hope restored, yes?"

Antares buzzed at Nu and showed a beam of light, copying Vega's signature image of leaves in her own unique golden patterns, an homage to the fallen Orb and Sage. *Helia would be proud!*

Nu grinned at her little companion's enthusiasm. Though she had wondered how she might feel in such a bittersweet moment, coming to terms with her mentor's loss, she was beyond excited. The future was positive. Hopeful. Exactly as Helia would have wanted.

She tilted her head to lean against the Orb for just a second. "I think she would be, little one. And Vega, for that matter. They would both enjoy this." Triss leaned into Nu from behind and gave her a quick hug, the simple act raising Nu's spirits even higher.

The three of them continued watching the party in the images around them. There was a large crowd gathered around a DJ on the beach, and people were dancing, drinks in hand, lost in the beat. Others watched the action from the sidelines, lovers and friends hugging each other, some just enjoying the vibe.

The pictures here in the Observatory were so real that if Nu zoomed in close enough, she could almost see the grains of sand move as the bass thumped, and she could feel the ocean breeze on her face and the sand beneath her feet. Had she not known better, she might have started dancing along with the other people under the moonlight, before heading to the bar for a cold drink. It all felt so real, yet it was all an illusion of sorts, another one of the Great Library's wondrous tricks. Set within a globe-shaped room where—thanks to a combination of technology and magic—the screens surrounding you could show you almost any moment happening anywhere on Earth and place you right in the scene itself.

Right now, for Nu and Maïa, it was as though they really *were* on a beach in Venezuela in the midst of a party, about to witness one of the most important moments in some time.

The selection of the new Sage of Hope.

Orb!

Maïa's Orb, Thebe, and Antares both noted the visitor to the party at the same time. Nu peered closely and saw the glimmer of silver hovering over the ocean.

"Discreet and quiet. Just a glint of moonlight off the waves." Maïa nodded as if expecting nothing less. "Very good, Eltanin."

"Do you think our prospective Sage is paying attention though?" Nu asked.

"That's a good question, Nu. Our new Sage is in the midst of a party, surrounded by his friends and family. I can imagine under normal circumstances his thoughts would be on his immediate surroundings! Yet the arrival of an Orb comes at precisely the moment a new Sage requires it."

Nu smiled. "So what you're saying is we should just watch and wait?"

"I am indeed. See? The Orb is moving inland, further down the beach so as not to cause a stir, as she should. Yet I believe that any moment now . . . *there*! Did you both see that?"

Nu had, and her smile widened as she shared a glance with Triss. "He looked up and did a double take, didn't he? Oh, and now he's moving toward her!"

She felt a shiver of excitement as the smiling, happy young man,

Densi, moved away from the party, lured by curiosity toward the floating sphere along the beach. There was also an underlying sense of . . . something else. Nervous anticipation, possibly?

She looked to Antares, but her Orb was transfixed on the scene unfolding before them, and Nu tried to shut out any worries and focus. This was too important and historic to miss. While her own choosing had been unique, undertaken under difficult circumstances, the others said the choosing of a new Sage on Earth was often a magical and magnificent experience, and one not to be missed.

She felt honored to be given the chance to witness it now. Special. Which was funny, because no matter how much she thought she had grown used to life as the Sage of Truth—one of the protectors of Paperworld—there was always another moment sitting around the corner of her journey to surprise her.

There was another tug of the knot in her stomach. She shifted uncomfortably.

"Antares, move us closer to the meeting, please," she asked.

The Orb's surface grew warm with rivulets of gold as it communicated directly with the Great Library, and the Observatory screen around them flickered before relocating them further along the beach. Nu's knees almost buckled with the sudden transition, and both Maïa and Triss moved to steady her.

"I find it's good to close your eyes before doing such a thing in here, my dear," Maïa said with a wry smile. "Your evolution as a Sage has been truly remarkable, and to witness you blossom into your role has been a joy. Yet still . . . for all our powers, Sages are not immune to motion sickness!"

Nu pursed her lips together, trying to hold back the onset of nausea. Triss nodded encouragingly at her, and Nu smiled back, slightly jealous that her lover seemed immune to the effects of the transition—if that was all it was. Something lingered, though, at the edge of her mind. More than just simple nausea.

"Breathe and center yourself. It'll pass quickly; trust me."

Nu felt her foreboding flicker and grow. She let her gaze drift from one end of the beach to the other and saw nothing untoward. Just the party to one side and Densi following the Orb in the opposite direction. But still the feeling held.

"Nu, are you okay?" Triss signed, her worried expression growing.

"I'm not sure. I think I just had a *knowing*."

Maïa grew tense. She straightened and looked around too.

"I see. Was there a vision to go along with it?"

"Not yet, no."

If Nu's powers were trying to talk to her, they weren't being that obvious. But she wasn't about to let on to Maïa that this part of her truth-telling abilities was sometimes out of her hands.

"Good, then just try to relax." Maïa's soft French accent gave her words a musical quality, and she smiled with the patience that came with being much older than she looked. Two hundred years older, to be precise. "It is likely just nerves. But really, there should be none here. This boy, Densi, is a worthy Sage-in-waiting. A skilled paramedic, with preternatural skills and a tenacious spirit. He has saved many lives, including those his colleagues have admitted to themselves they would have let slip away, but not him. Densi saw things they didn't—made choices they couldn't. He has already spent his life offering hope to those who had none. Now he will champion it across the realms." Maïa lifted her long fingers to the skies, toward the pinpricks of light, gesturing to the stars in other galaxies, in other times. "This is all as it's meant to be, Nu. And it shall be a wonderful experience, as the choosing of a new Sage should be. We may not be on that beach in person, but this is almost as good. Breathe it in. Revel in the magic."

Maïa reached for Nu's free arm, Triss already at her other side, and squeezed it reassuringly, before all three went back to watching Densi step calmly across the beach as though in a daze, skirting the gently lapping waves, to where the new Orb was waiting for him.

The sheer joy on the man's face gave Nu a mix of emotions. Chief among them was excitement for him and what was about to happen.

Yet there was also a little sadness there, too, as she imagined was to be expected. Densi had no idea what events had come to pass in order for his life to change. He would never know the beauty and kindness of his predecessor, Helia, and her charming Orb, Vega. Only Nu would remember the moment they had all been put onto this path—how it came to pass in a flash of fire and ash, in the midst of a battle in a city of memories, in an entirely different realm of existence.

There was another tug in Nu's stomach, stronger this time.

Densi had reached the Orb, and the little being was pulsating in glorious navy hues. The man seemed to realize he was being spoken to and was speaking back. Then he reached out a hand and touched the Orb, and there was a crackle of energy between them, a spark of the purest connection that could only be present between a creation of the Great Library and its chosen Sage.

This was the moment.

"Oh, it's beautiful," Nu whispered, forgetting the uncomfortable feeling deep in her gut for a moment, unable to take her eyes off the glow surrounding the pair. "Eltanin has chosen well."

She kept watching, thinking back to her own connection with Antares. It had been less traditional, more of a slow-burn connection built over time and through necessity. She sometimes wondered what it might have been like under normal circumstances rather than in the aftermath of Xavier's death, and now she had her answer.

But as she glanced at her Orb, she knew she wouldn't have had it any other way. Theirs was a stronger bond for their experience—she was sure of it.

"Is this done now, Maïa?" she asked. "Do we have a new Sage of Hope?"

But Maïa didn't get the chance to respond. There was an urgent vibration from both their Orbs as something horrific emerged before them: a shape scrambling on all fours from the ocean right behind Densi. It looked like a man, yet one who had been in the water a long time, bloated and bedraggled in seaweed, with all too familiar markings carved into his puffy blue skin.

"An Unwritten," Nu breathed, before watching in horror as the figure pulled something from his belt and leaped at Densi.

The wet, jagged edge glinted in the moonlight before it found the new Sage's midsection and buried itself deep. Densi's anguished cry was muffled as a bloodied, soggy hand slapped over his mouth, and his entire form seemed to harden outward from the wound.

Maïa swore in French and pulled Nu after her. Nu looked back at Triss, who gave her a tight smile and a small wave. A simple gesture to most, but Nu saw the worry in her face and the tension in her small, nimble hands. Then the screens in the Observatory went dark as the two Sages and their Orbs rushed out, heading for the portal to try to save the new Sage of Hope.

CHAPTER TWO

AN OLD FOE

Nu and Maïa arrived on the Venezuelan beach within only a minute or two—an incredibly short amount of time to travel from the Great Library all the way to this paradise.

But Nu immediately understood they were too late.

Densi was standing alone beneath the moonlight in the same place they'd watched him. A solitary figure, unmoving, as the waves continued lapping at the shore.

The boy had been made a statue, transformed entirely into sand.

The Orb, Eltanin, still hovered before him, flashing weak messages Nu could barely make out. Antares and Thebe flew immediately to their companion and swirled around her, communicating in bursts of light to find out what had happened.

Maïa bent down to the sand to retrieve a piece of driftwood and lifted it to the light. She turned it over, revealing its jagged and blackened edges.

"This has been imbued with some kind of poison," Maïa said, her lips twisting into a grimace, looking back up at Densi. "And there is nothing on Earth that can do *that* to a person. This has surely been tainted with magic not of this world. I can feel the darkness on it. Sticky and acidic." She glanced to one side. "Nu, you said that creature was one of the Unwritten?"

"I think so," Nu replied. "It didn't look much like the others I saw before, but I recognized the lettering carved into its skin. I think it had been in the water for a while."

Maïa looked around the beach. "Where did he go, Eltanin?"

It was Thebe who answered.

Returned to the water.

Nu didn't even have time to blink before Maïa had slipped the poisoned wood into her belt and started loping toward the ocean. "Don't leave the Orb," she called back to Nu before throwing herself into the breaking waves and disappearing into the gloom. The water churned for a moment, then the surface returned to its glistening sheen beneath the moonlight.

Densi.

It was Antares who "spoke" this time, her little patterns muted in their soft golden glow, forming words in her mind as she flew before Nu. Antares nudged her attention back to the poor man who was still standing here. Nu turned and witnessed the figure begin to crumble away. The warm evening breeze coming in off the ocean eroded his beautiful features, erasing him from existence—slowly at first, as though he was fading from a dream. Then, suddenly, he collapsed all at once and became one with the beach. His clothes fell in a heap.

He was gone.

Nu's insides were chaos. The heat of anger and frustration battled against a burst of ice-cold fear at what had just happened to Densi. She couldn't stop staring at the echo of his figure beneath the moonlight. The look on his face was burned into her mind. How could something so horrific happen so easily? Why hadn't she seen a vision of such an event that would allow her to stop it?

Her hair was blowing across her face, and as she pushed it behind her ear, she realized her hands were trembling. As well they should. Densi had been on the verge of a brilliant and bright new stage of his life. An adventure the likes of which most could not imagine. And now he had been wiped clean from the world.

She took a breath to steady herself. Antares nudged her shoulder.

I'm here.

"Thank you," she said, nudging back. She turned to the vast, empty ocean, knowing she had to focus on the next step rather than the ramifications of what had just occurred. There would be time for that later. Right now, her concern needed to be with the other Sage.

"Should we go after Maïa?"

Maïa is in control, Antares said.

"I feel helpless, Antares. I can't just stand here doing nothing!"

You cannot help down there.

"But what if she needs me?"

You?

Antares flashed a ring of light on her surface. While the Orbs could communicate through intricate geometric patterns, shades of their unique color, and levels of vibration, combining to create complex speech that only their own Sage could fully understand, they had their own "shorthand" that all the Sages instinctively understood.

In this case, it consisted of three words communicated in as close to an admonishment as Nu had ever received from her Orb.

Truth. Not swimming.

Nu's eyes narrowed, but she tried not to take it to heart. Even though it felt like the pair of them had grown into their roles together, she often forgot that Antares was incredibly old, and there was so much experience contained within her tiny form. Right now, she was reminding Nu her Sage's powers did not include holding her breath.

"Right as always," Nu said, her gaze flitting across the undulating ocean. "Let's stick to what I know best, eh?"

She lifted her left hand, palm outward. She didn't know if it was part of her power or a ritual she'd become used to, but either way, the movement helped her focus, to gain control of her search for the truth in a moment. Antares instantly drew closer, and she felt the Orb's warm energy begin to flow through her, increasing her power and allowing it to flourish as it was meant.

Nu tried to fix her gaze beyond the water, beyond this realm, beyond everything. She was no longer looking at what was in front of her. She gazed into the universe itself, searching for that feeling she knew all too well. That *knowing* she should never have doubted, even for a second.

Then it came.

There was a knot in the fabric of being. In the ocean, in the gentle beings swimming through it, in the atoms that made them up, and the magic that existed in the divide between the atoms.

Nu pulled on the knot, and it unraveled a little in her mind. Not completely, but enough to come loose and let her feel the knowing that it held.

Maïa was still there. Under the water, but okay.

She couldn't feel more than that, but it was enough to allow her a sigh of relief and to wrench her eyes from the ocean.

Eltanin, who had been forgotten in all this, was hovering low over the patch of sand where Densi had last stood. Her solemn patterns were so dark they were almost shadows across her surface. Antares drifted down to accompany her sibling, offering colors of a warm autumn glow in solidarity with the Sage-less Orb.

"I'm so sorry," Nu said to Eltanin. She crouched beside the pair of Orbs and lightly touched her hand to the sand. "Densi was a wonderful choice and would have made a fine Sage of Hope."

The sound of laughter split the melodies of the music in the evening air. The party was still in full swing nearby, and no alarm had been raised yet. Only later would they realize Densi was missing and then find his clothes here on the beach. Nu's heart felt heavy at the thought and wondered if there was something that could be done to ease the pain for his family and friends.

But then there was a splash close by, and Maïa slipped from the water, struggling with a heavy bundle wrapped in seaweed and kelp. Her Orb, Thebe, followed close behind her.

"Got him," Maïa said. "Although he didn't come without a little fight. Isn't that right, my friend?"

Her jaw set, and her eyes steely, Maïa threw the bound mess of a person against a boulder. As the bloated figure slapped uselessly against his bonds, writhing to free himself, Maïa's fingers shot out and clamped around the monster's throat, while her other hand pulled the poisoned driftwood from her belt, holding it up to the thing's face.

"You didn't account for me being able to hold my breath like a pearl diver, did you? I'm afraid you underestimated who you were dealing with. And now you will answer some questions."

Nu stared in horror at the abomination before them. One of the Unwritten. A reminder of what she'd faced in the City of Forever, although this one was even less pleasant, given his time underwater had left his face swollen, and his eyes were long since missing. His stinking mouth sloshed and spat watery obscenities at them, while his skin was as she remembered: covered in carved letters and words that burned now with the hatred spilling out of him. A language of pain and hate that they had, so far, been unable to decipher.

"Who sent you?" Nu demanded, drawing closer to the man. A coldness took her as the answer to her own question presented itself in her mind.

A flash of a memory blinded her. She shuddered, blinking it away, but it refused to leave. The image was stuck fast now, burned into her eyes. A scene from a dream she'd had only the other night. The same kind of nightmarish—perhaps prescient—dream she'd been having far too often recently.

She looked to Antares, who seemed to be thinking the same thing.

We killed Suttaru . . . didn't we?

Taking advantage of the distraction, an arm unfurled in her direction, trying to grasp her face. Had she been with any other Sage, she might have been in trouble, but such was Maïa's power. Even here on Earth, she was quicker. Maïa slipped her hand from the creature's throat and pinned his arm against the boulder, while simultaneously pressing the jagged edge of the weapon as close as possible against the creature's throat without breaking the slick, sickly skin.

The Unwritten man stopped squirming and glared at the pair of them.

"Answer her," Maïa insisted, her lips curling in a grimace. "What are you, and what did you just do to that man who was here?"

"Denssssssi," the creature hissed. His breath was foul, like sewage pouring over his toothless gums. His tongue flapped within, like a fish gasping for breath. "He is gone. He has become one with the Earth. Sand. Drifting along the beach. Beyond even your powerssss."

Antares buzzed angrily around Nu's head, feeding off her emotions. The Orb flashed an array of symbols.

Unwritten. Same as before.

"Yes, but this is Earth, not Paperworld. He shouldn't be here! Where did he come from? Who sent him?"

Antares said something else, but Nu took her eyes off the Orb as the creature choked, water spilling over his bloated lips with what must have been laughter.

"Helpless. Hopeless. *Good*!"

Maïa growled and twisted the driftwood at his throat some more. The man struggled backward against the rock, trying to get away. Another movement and the corrupted abomination would likely go the same way as poor Densi. And from the squirming it was doing to avoid the driftwood, it at least recognized that.

"Why are you here?"

The laughter faded. "I have been waiting."

"For what?"

"For now."

Nu shook her head, confused and angry. How was it possible this *thing* had known, but she had not, despite her powers?

"But who made you wait? And how did you know the choosing would happen here? Tell us now!"

"There are many of *usssss*. We are legion."

"That answers nothing, murderer," Maïa said.

"It does not," the man admitted, grinning again. He was baiting them. Wasting their time. "And soon the others will steal more than just your new Sage. Soon your *friend* will be gone too."

Nu's insides went cold. "What friend?"

Before he could answer, the abomination's eyes went wide. He convulsed and shook as though something was trying to explode out of him. It was so violent even Maïa was pushed back as his limbs flailed outward, though she held the wooden dagger at him as protection.

It wasn't needed.

The man's skin burned fiercely as all the words lit up at once, as if a fire within him had been stoked.

Then his mouth pulled unnaturally wide, and a voice that was not his spoke. A voice that Nu couldn't help but recognize.

"The end is coming, Sages," it said in a cold, clipped English accent. "It cannot be stopped. It cannot be diverted. No matter what you heard here tonight, it is too late to change things. Say your goodbyes to all you have known—to your Library, to your Book of so-called *Wisdom*, to your precious *writer*. This is the end of all you hold dear. A new age will soon be ushered in."

The words scrawled across the slick skin of the man suddenly caught flame with such intensity the thing didn't even have a chance to cry out. Light poured from his throat and his eye sockets as the heat consumed the assassin so quickly that he became a brief beacon in the night sky, creating a glow of pure white as the evil words carved into his skin became one flaming mass, until the skin itself cracked and burst, scattering charred chunks of the creature into the sand to join his victim.

The driftwood knife in Maïa's hands caught fire. She tossed it away as it burned to nothing, leaving the world quiet and calm again. The stars shone above, and the waves lapped at the shoreline, and the Sages were alone once more.

"What just happened?" Maïa asked. "Was something speaking through him? Did it do this to him?"

"Not something but some*one*," Nu said.

She looked to Antares, and the Orb shared her disturbance. It had been the very same cold, sneering voice they'd last heard with Helia at the Great Tree, having an argument with the Chief Scientist. A man they later discovered had been masquerading as the Chief Scientist's Advisor, hiding in plain sight after falling from grace many years earlier.

The disgraced Rogue Sage known as Edwin Payne.

He was back, and the implications for what *any* of this meant froze Nu to the spot beneath that moonlit sky.

Your friend. The writer.

The words stuck in her head. Nu had made several friends during her last adventure, but there was only one writer she had met.

Arturo.

"We need to go," she said, but Maïa was already ahead of her.

The end of the Unwritten assassin had roused the attention of some partygoers nearby. There were raised voices on the other side of the palm tree. Voices getting closer, Maïa tugged at Nu's arm and gestured for them to head back toward the portal. Hurrying across the sand, they barely got a few yards before Antares flashed wildly.

We can't. The portal has gone.

Nu drew to a halt. "What do you mean the portal's gone?"

Maïa sighed. "They're glitching again, I assume? Ever since the Book of Wisdom was poisoned, the portals have been erratic. We can't count on finding it again quickly if it's moved, and who knows if it'll even stay put. Come on. We must find another way."

The older Sage changed direction and led them farther down the beach. Nu felt the chill of the evening air creep into her lungs with every breath. As they moved behind another outcrop of trees, the raised voices behind them became cries for help as someone stumbled across Densi's clothes and the remnants of the assassin. The sound of confused anguish pulled at Nu's insides. She looked to the Orb accompanying them, who by rights should have been guiding a new Sage of Hope back to the Great Library of Tomorrow. The small being was colorless, barely a shadow, except for the moonlight that occasionally reflected on its surface as it floated along.

"We have to get back to the Great Library."

Eltanin gave a weak glow of agreement.

"Antares, contact the Book of Wisdom. Explain what's happened and ask if she can locate Arturo through the Observatory. If there are any Sages present, tell their Orbs we want them waiting at the Haven for us. We're on our way."

The Orb's symbols swam across her surface to confirm she was already doing just that.

Maïa glanced over at Nu. "Arturo is the one you think is in danger? Do you think Edwin Payne would have been able to discover who he was? Even then, Payne would know Arturo's memory had been wiped on his return to his normal life. What value would there be in targeting him?"

"I think it must be. Robin was keeping an eye on Arturo via the Observatory, though the enemy shouldn't be able to track him back on Earth. I can *feel* the truth that the assassin was referring to Arturo though. We need to get back either way. Antares, can you find us another portal? A natural portal, like our visitors use when they find us by chance or by fate. Those, at least, have been steady and shouldn't disappear on us."

Understood. Locating . . .

Nu continued running along the sand. "Anything?"

Patience is a virtue.

Nu gave her companion the side-eye. "It isn't mine, Antares. You've already reminded me of that tonight," she said evenly, knowing the Orb's comment to be true.

True. And located.

"Where?"

Ahead, then down.

"Down?"

"Sometimes the portals on Earth that lead to the Library aren't quite what you expect," Maïa said, sensing Nu's confusion. "They can be found in the most unlikely places and in the most unlikely forms."

Nu had experienced the Earth-side portals before, of course. It was how she'd first met Arturo. Yet that had been during her time welcoming visitors to the Library. This was her first time using one herself. She looked around at the beach, the ocean. Her life had been one of service to the Library, and yet . . . One day she wished to explore more of Earth, as she had Paperworld.

Thebe and Antares continued leading the way, pulsing lightly as they hovered above the sand, flanking Eltanin. The combined lights of the two lead Orbs illuminated the dark as the moonlight overhead slipped beyond some clouds hanging over the coast. It was enough to hide them from the partygoers behind them, but they still needed the low Orb light to show them where to walk between the sharp shells and the occasional stranded jellyfish strewn across the beach.

The light fractalized as they rose up over some coastal rocks, and the two women had to tread more carefully as they clambered up the slippery stone, before reaching an oval henge of seaweed-covered stone filled with unnaturally still water.

A rock pool.

"Here?" Nu asked as the three Orbs came to a stop overhead.

The water looked dark, cold, and uninviting at first glance. But as she stared at it, and the clouds parted to reveal a ray of moonlight, Nu saw the surface catch the light and shimmer with a strange and enticing gold gleam. Beyond it, she could almost see and hear the hustle and bustle of the Library Foyer.

Told you, Antares flashed at her.

Nu raised her eyebrows, then looked to Maïa, who nodded.

Without hesitation, Nu stepped off the rock and slipped through the surface of the water.

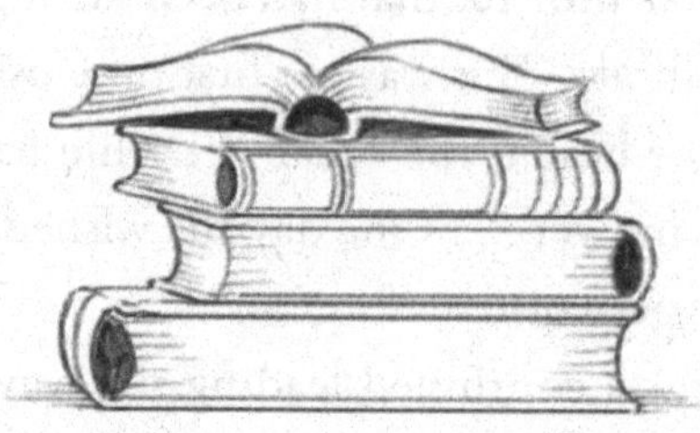

CHAPTER THREE
THE OTHER AUTHOR

Nu and Maïa ran into the Foyer, the three Orbs following close behind, startling several visitors who had only just arrived in the Great Library. Across the hall they went, before rushing out through the towering, reverent stacks of the Main Concourse and slipping under the viaducts. Nu heard the rush of water passing overhead and the rickety wheels of a streetcar passing on a bridge. It reminded her of when she'd greeted Arturo and let him into the Great Library.

It seemed like both yesterday and a lifetime ago.

She glanced over to the three Orbs, hoping her little companions had got a message through to the other Sages already. The words rasped by the assassin moments before his death were fresh in her mind.

If Arturo was truly in danger, she needed to get him protection, and quickly. The charming man with a wry sense of humor had been brought to them by the Book of Wisdom and the essence of the Author contained therein. And the man had made an impact on their lives at a time when they'd needed him most.

They'd checked on him discreetly, through the Observatory, after his departure. Robin said he had been doing well, despite losing the memory of his time here. As with most visitors to the Great Library, he'd left inspired. Apparently, he'd almost immediately embarked on finding a new job more suited to his passions, finally creating a sense of purpose for himself.

Why would the forces of evil target him now? Arturo could remember no secrets of the Great Library or the Sages. His memory had been wiped clean of such things.

As Nu and Maïa continued through the Great Library, from the vaulted ceilings of the outer halls into the network of finely carpeted corridors weaving around the cozy Sages' reading rooms, she remembered Robin telling her about Arturo's power.

The power none of them could really explain.

"Thebe," Maïa said as they neared the Haven. "Have they located the writer yet?"

White fractals fell like a blizzard across the Orb's surface.

"That was fast! Where is he?"

The Orb spoke again, and Maïa relayed the information.

"They found him in Cairo, Egypt. It's early morning; he's attending some event that's about to get underway; and from what we're hearing, there's quite a crowd—so chances are he's safe enough for the moment. The enemy wouldn't dare touch him in broad daylight." Her eyebrows twitched and pinched together. "Would they?"

Nu could hear the Dark Sage, Edwin Payne's, voice in her mind, speaking through that Unwritten foot soldier. "Yes, I'm afraid they would. Payne wouldn't shy away from a public display of power. Did you feel the evil in his words on that beach, Maïa? They were sticky with it. We need to reach Arturo quickly."

The two Sages burst through the double doors into the Haven—the carved rock chamber at the center of the island that held the Great Library of Tomorrow. An immense, airy space, it was as large as one of the grand theaters on Earth Nu had read about in books, and it encouraged reverence in any who visited.

This was where the magic had first been discovered all those years ago, when the Scholar Fairen first discovered the portal. It was also the home of the Book of Wisdom, the tome that held the Author, which was currently resting on a grand pedestal in the center of the chamber, a location fitting for watching over the portal that allowed the Sages and their Orbs to travel from this fantastical city to the realms beyond—and, in this case, back to Earth and to Cairo.

If the portals were working again.

Nu slowed, seeing the frame was already filled with light. "Did the Book prepare the portal for us already?" she asked Antares.

Not quite.

Nu shot her Orb a look of confusion. "Is that Egypt on the other side or not?"

It is.

"Well then?"

It was Maïa who answered. "Someone else has already gone ahead. Another Sage."

CHAPTER FOUR
THE ELECTRIC MUSE

The sky was like tar, black and sticky, with a wet and foreboding sense that if you touched it, it might just swallow you up. Edwin Payne gazed up from a ruined tower in the heart of an ancient and ruined city. This place never ceased to amaze him, with its menacing aura and warped natural features. He knew it was once a shining realm of light and plenty before its fall to Discordia, and long before the people of his own world even knew how to write their stories down. Now it was a broken husk, the scorched remnants of a sophisticated magical society laid to waste by the hubris of a few.

"A cautionary story, Myrtilus," he said to the Orb hovering at his side. Smoky white patterns were its only reply. "Those who meddle in things they don't understand are destined to end in failure . . . or destruction."

"Well, we've led those simpletons from the Great Library on a merry dance since our *master* fell to them at the City of Forever, but I've finally cracked the code in his—Adi's—journal."

But why do it? Why bring him back? Edwin could almost taste the question from the swirling patterns his Orb used to communicate, like a combination of chalk and ash.

"Because the nightmares are getting worse again since Suttaru fell! Once he disposes of my nightmares, I shall be able to rebuild the realms to true order and function."

As you wish. The white lights danced in the darkness of the world they stood in. Payne nodded his thanks as his mind flashed back to the previous night. The wracking chills and sweat he'd woken to from the nightmare followed him through the night, like a tiger stalking its prey.

It had started centuries ago, before he'd even heard of the Great Library. As an officer in His Majesty's Army, Edwin had fought in many of wars, starting with the Seven Years' War and ending with the ignominious defeat in the American War of Independence. He was a scientist at heart, but the army had given him a place when no one else wanted to hear about his outlandish ideas, and he'd shown himself to be a skilled commander. Loyal, and, he liked to think, honorable. But his younger self had dreamed of following in the footsteps of Ewald Georg von Kleist and Pieter van Musschenbroek to harness the power of electricity.

That Benjamin Franklin—that traitor—had so flamboyantly proved the existence of electricity with what seemed to be a mere child's trick had been both inspiring and frustrating.

The nightmares, the flashes of lightning in his missing eye, burned in a way no physical pain could. With it came the faces of the dead he'd seen in battle, forcing him to return to being a seeker of knowledge, an advocate of peace. The loss of his eye in combat had seemed like the worst that could happen to him, but then came the nightmares, the darkness, the lightning flashes, and the faces of the dead.

We should go, Myrtilus said through the pulsating patterns of white light, hauntingly similar to his nightmare, but the price of swapping his allegiance from the Great Library to Discordia meant many changes. Myrtilus had been bright and vibrant, a soothing lavender until they had betrayed the Book of Wisdom. Then the Orb had turned smoke white and cold.

Edwin had deliberately led the Sages astray across the many realms of Paperworld, aware that they would want him captured and, despite their squeamishness over taking life, likely have him punished in some way. Perhaps turn him over to the Silvyrans, whose Great Tree he had conspired to desecrate with their precious Elixir.

It had been almost too easy to infiltrate the Silvyran society, gain their trust as an advisor, corrupt one of their own instructors, and then sabotage them from within.

Perverting their Elixir had been a pleasure. It had not worked for him back when he was a Sage. He'd been told it could heal almost anything, yet their precious concoction had seemed to reject him, leaving him with the night terrors.

They might choose to lock him away in some dark corner of that cursed Library, and he'd never be seen again; they were too weak to kill him themselves, but nothing could be worse than his current life and the horrors of sleep. Suttaru, at least, had lessened the effects with his dark magic, muting them into softer stories. Not a cure, but a welcome salve. Despite his own growing powers, Edwin still did not possess the skill to apply them to his own mind.

And for Myrtilus, his one true companion, capture might be even worse. Would they dismantle him and use him for parts? Take the precious metals that allow safe passage through the realms? Wipe the Orb's mind like a chalkboard and rewrite his personality?

No, they would pay. For their false promises and their potential punishments. Their fellowship that never cured his tortured nights. Their foolish meddling in things they did not understand. Things that threatened the very Earth their precious Library hid itself from. Their arrogance in meddling in the affairs of Paperworld, an entirely different reality to their own, one that even he had struggled to understand.

And yet . . . he had been chosen, hadn't he? Myrtilus had found him and brought him to the Great Library, a place where his creativity was honored and his values seen as unique. At least for a while. But those days were done. Their inability to cure his nightmares, or refusal to, had made him look beyond the motto of the Library. His life was a ruin, denying him the joy of true love or peace, and robbing him of any sense of unity. Instead, he had found a new patron: Discordia, the realm of dark stories itself, was now his source of power and opportunity.

Myrtilus hovered beside him, then moved toward the broken staircase, and Edwin followed.

"We've led them on a merry chase, old friend. Now that their precious Sage of Hope is lost to them, the cracks in their resolve and power will show."

He paused before reaching the stairs and looked back one last time at the broken world before him. "But I will not become another Suttaru in the process. No . . . I will keep my humanity, such as it is, until I can set things right, the way they should have been before this magic cursed our world."

Myrtilus said nothing, but bobbed up and down in agreement, paused to let his fallen Sage pass, and followed silently behind as Edwin Payne began the long walk to their next destination.

CHAPTER FIVE
MEANING

Arturo stood in the sliver of early-morning sunshine at the back of the museum hall, clutching his notepad and pen, on the verge of writing something that he hoped might become meaningful.

"Can I *please* go now?" Rosa asked, rolling her eyes with the disappointment only a child could have for her father.

His daughter's fingers were tapping impatiently on the grip of her camera, a vintage Leica M6 his father had owned, which he in turn had learned to shoot film on. She looked around the exquisite hall with hunger in her eyes. Arturo felt a swell of pride. Rosa was actually excited to be here and present in the moment.

"These ancient artifacts aren't going anywhere, daughter," he said with mock exasperation. "They've been here a while already. Surely you can wait until I've finished my interviews, and I can come with you?"

"Papa, I know this is your climate science event, but we're in standing in one of the best museums in one of the oldest cities on the planet, and there is so much cool stuff here! Please? I just, like, want to go and take a few pictures."

"Okay, fine. Go get some good pictures, and we'll develop them later, together? Just don't wander far. I'm sorry I have to work, but these important scientists aren't going to interview themselves."

"I can develop them myself now, you know," Rosa said.

"I know, but you wouldn't begrudge your old man helping out, would you?"

Rosa looked at him, calculating her response. "I *suppose* that would be okay. Can we get ice cream on the way home first though?"

"Sure, baby girl," Arturo said, knowing it would drive her mildly insane.

As she threw her arms up in protest at the pet name, she surprised him by giving him a quick squeeze of a hug. Slightly shocked, he couldn't help but add, "Just remember to take a few photos of this event, too, please. I had to be at my most charming to convince the magazine to fly you here as my assistant, and it'll be good to have some evidence to prove I put you to work."

"*Okay*, Papa. *Jeez*, you know I will."

Arturo watched his daughter move around a Noble Prize–winning climate scientist and immediately made for the nearest statue and carefully composed a shot, before snapping off a picture and heading for the next artifact. He couldn't help but grin with pride. Rosa was getting older, more confident, and way more independent. An attitude came with it, of course, but such was the way with kids this age.

The marble floor of the hall rang with the footsteps of the fifty or so people gathered. Some were in suits; a few others were a little more casual in a shirt and trousers, like Arturo; while the rest were dressed in saris, dishdashas, and other styles from around the world. It was a true melting pot of humanity. It felt perfectly apt, considering the scientists and journalists alike were all here to celebrate the unveiling of a new humanitarian organization—one he was covering for the magazine he now wrote for.

"You all right, Papa?" Rosa asked a few minutes later as she breezed past, heading toward the other side of the hall. Her camera was half raised, and he pulled a face. She snapped the shot.

"Just soaking it all in, Rosa. This is a big day for the future of Earth. These people are real heroes of the world. They keep hope alive as the world rolls from one disaster to another." She was about to move off again when he grabbed her sleeve. "See that woman with the short, cool hair, Rosa? That's Dr. Lombarg, an expert in volcanology. Make sure you get a shot of her if you can. She's been studying the recent tectonic activity and ash cloud emissions—you know, with all those volcanoes that nearly simultaneously erupted." He paused. "It's such an honor to be here, hearing their stories and telling the world about them. Maybe it'll make some kind of difference."

Rosa wriggled from his fatherly grasp, embarrassed once again. He grinned. He knew it drove her mad. "I'm on it!" she said, before zigzagging through the crowd again.

He stood there a moment longer, hoping there was truth to his words. He'd always been a big believer in the power of stories, and he definitely felt there was more meaning in his current writing work. It was only a shame he'd not had the inspiration to change direction in his career sooner.

Annoyingly, he still couldn't really remember what exactly had inspired him. He vaguely recalled a bookstore. He'd been browsing, maybe? And when he'd left, the creative spark had hit him. Within a couple of weeks, he'd quit his job in advertising and landed a new one working as a journalist with an international magazine specializing in humanitarian and environmental efforts around the globe. How? He still wasn't sure. All he'd done was sent off an article he'd written in the wake of the volcanic event, which discussed using it as a wake-up call for positive action. Not only did the magazine then offer to publish the piece, but they happened to have a full-time position open—and they wanted to bring him in!

After years of feeling like his work wasn't making a difference, he finally was, and in a big way. It made him feel alive. A surge of purpose he got just from waking up every day and getting to do this work. A gut feeling that this was his path. He *loved* it.

And yet he still felt a nagging sensation. A whisper that he wasn't quite there yet, that he needed to be doing more.

That perhaps he wasn't just meant to be telling stories of other's heroics. He needed to take action of his own.

"Stop with your delusions of grandeur," he said quietly to himself. A passing dignitary in a turban gave him a polite but wary smile and hurried past a little faster than he had been. Arturo blew out his cheeks and gripped his notepad and pen a little tighter. "And also, stop scaring your interview subjects."

He was about to get to work, when he caught the gaze of a woman hustling through the crowd, and he remained where he was, bemused, confused, and a little awestruck.

Arturo didn't know her. At least, he didn't *think* he did. But there was something about her face that was immediately familiar, with waves of black hair framing warm copper skin and brown eyes that held his in a way that suggested she was both delighted and concerned to see him.

Disconcertingly, the concern was the most prevalent. She was pushing firmly past people as she headed for him, and the closer she got, the stronger the familiar feeling became. He found himself mouthing something, feeling the familiar taste of a name on his lips. But that didn't make sense. He didn't know anybody named Rob—

He realized she was mouthing something back.

"Watch out!"

An arm reached around his neck and dragged him backward.

CHAPTER SIX
LOVE CONQUERS ALL

In hindsight, Arturo knew it had been a mistake to stand at the back of the room.

He had noticed the door to the research room when he'd chosen to stand in front of it upon arrival at the museum. He didn't think much of it at the time, assuming it was locked and a good place to situate himself to survey the room while keeping out of the way. He often liked to do that at events. To pause on the fringes of the ebb and flow, to gauge the mood, and to spot the cliques and the loners. It helped him identify who to speak to, and when and where.

Unfortunately, the door wasn't locked. Which he only discovered when the foul-smelling, tattered gray arm stretched out from it, clasped around his neck, and dragged him into the room beyond, out of sight of the main gathering.

As the door slammed shut, he was thrown against the wall. His shoulder blades crunched into the plaster, knocking the wind out of him so hard his eyesight went blurry for a moment.

When he looked up to his assailant, he wondered if he was seeing things. Because it resembled a corpse, all dead eyes and gray skin, on the verge of decay. It seemed as though the life had been sucked out of it. Its soul and any humanity it might have had was pulled clean from it and left it a husk of a figure.

Written across every inch of skin Arturo could see beneath the man's tattered clothing—at least, it looked like it had once been a man—were furious scrawls that looked like words carved with a worn blade. Down the arm, across the sunken chest, up the neck, and all across the face.

It was the most horrifying thing he could remember seeing.

And yet there was a level of dread curdling deep inside him that spoke of familiarity.

I've seen this before.

As the monstrosity looked at him with its dead eyes, very fiber of Arturo's being went cold. The words carved into the being's skin began to glow a bright, hellish crimson, as though he was about to catch fire from the inside out. The toothy grin became a howl of rage.

Arturo fell backward, collapsing on his backside. He tried scrambling back, but his feet couldn't find purchase on the floor.

And then he felt the most peculiar sensation. One that began flowing around him, as though he'd fallen into a river of pure sunshine.

Love, he thought with a strange sense of confusion. *I think it's love?*

"Die!" the creature growled at him as it leaped. "Di—"

Through the haze of his delirium, Arturo saw long ribbons of golden light flowing through the air from the left, past his head. They caught the attacker and wrapped around its limbs, slithering around its body, holding it mid-leap.

"What's going on?" Arturo said, staring up in confusion as the light bent and pulled tight, holding the creature where it was. He could see the hatred in the thing's face start to fade. The gray patches began disappearing, and in its place was clean, healthy skin, unmarked by the letters and words scrawled across the rest of it.

Arturo turned his head to see where the light was coming from.

The black-haired woman he'd seen hurrying toward him in the main hall stood in the doorway, hands raised, fingers extended as the light poured forth from her. There was an added glow from a little round shimmer above her shoulder, as though there was something hiding in the air there—an energy that seemed to feed into the woman's own ribbons of love.

He felt a touch on his arm. A light, ethereal touch that brought with it a sense of timeless magic and a great many other sensations he couldn't quite comprehend. It flowed *into* him, through his body, filling him up. He was so surprised by the power of it that he struggled to turn his head to see what was happening.

At which point he looked directly into the deep brown eyes of the woman, who had reached his side.

"Hello, Arturo," she said in a soft English accent.

He didn't know what to say. What *could* he say? Who was she, and how did she know his name? And what exactly was happening right now?

"Uh-huh," was all he could say in reply, still reeling from the outpouring of love flowing into him from her touch.

She laughed cheerfully, a melodious and mischievous sound that failed to contain an undercurrent of relief. "You still have a wonderful way with words, I see. It's quite incredible you made it as a writer, really."

The teasing grin she gave tugged at parts of his being he hadn't felt in some time, though her gaze was now reserved for the man-beast. She was in control of it somehow.

"Do I . . . I'm sorry, but do I know you?" he asked, his mouth increasingly dry as her fingers drifted slowly down his arm until they reached his hand.

She grasped it in hers and slid her palm against his in a more official greeting.

Her skin felt warm against his. The light grew around their handshake.

"I'm Robin," she said. "And as much as I'd love to explain all this, it's important that you simply trust that I have your best interests at heart and try not to call for help or anything. Would that be okay?"

"Um, sure, of course."

She went back to studying the increasingly human-looking creature wrapped up in her light. Its eyes blinked through the translucent glow, looking confused at finding itself here. "Curious," she said. "What do you make of this, Centauri? My powers have dulled the Unwritten's words."

The shimmer above her shoulder grew more intense.

"Yes, I agree. We should report this to the others when we get back."

Arturo looked around him.

"Who exactly are you speaking to?"

"Oh, well, Arturo, *that* is a story we don't have time for right now." Robin tilted her head toward the exit. "Again, you need to trust me on this. We should go. I am not sure how long my power will hold it, and I don't want to risk it getting loose again while you're still here."

The touch on his arm was firmer now as she pulled him after her. Yet even as he contemplated arguing that he couldn't leave his daughter here, Rosa appeared in the doorway, staring in disbelief at the scene before her.

"Papa?"

Arturo wanted to tell her to run, to call for help, to get as far away from the creature hanging in the air as possible. But it was Robin who turned to the girl with a reassuring grin.

"And this is Rosa, I assume? It's lovely to meet you! Please don't be alarmed. Everything is under control, but you, me, and your dad need to be going now. Is that okay?"

Rosa's mouth remained open as she looked from the weird creature to her father and then back to Robin.

"How do you know—"

"Your name? Oh, there's a lot about me that you'll discover soon enough. For now, though, I can say that your dad and I used to be very good friends, and as soon as we get out of here and back to the Great Library, I'm sure he'll tell you all about it. Come on now. Let's not dally any longer."

"The Great Library?" Arturo repeated.

Those three words. They tasted different on his lips than any others he had spoken. Familiar, important, yet in a way he couldn't quite understand.

Robin noted his double take as she pulled him along. "Keep moving—both of you, please. As soon as we're safe, I'll explain all the things you need to know, but it's best we do it in a place where you're less likely to be attacked. Sound good?"

"Um, sure?"

Robin made some movement with her hands that tied off some of the ribbons flowing from her. It left the monster bound and floating in the center of the room as she led them away, still trailing light behind her. Arturo grabbed Rosa's hand as they ran.

Nobody in the main hall gave them a second glance as they wove through the crowd. Arturo wondered if he should do or say something, but Robin's warm hand on his was enough to quell the worry he might otherwise have felt in these strange circumstances. He didn't even question that following her was the right thing to do. This was someone he could trust. Somehow he just knew.

They left the museum and raced down the steps, through the ticket barrier, and into the courtyard bathed in the morning light, only to run into two women hurrying past the fountains toward them.

The pair skidded to a stop as they saw Robin. One of the women was tall and lithe, like an athlete, with red hair and dazzling green eyes. But it was the shorter woman who caught Arturo's attention. Younger than the others, her long, straight hair flowed over her shoulders like a dark waterfall, while her tilted eyes betrayed both her youth and the shadows of experience.

Those eyes widened as she looked from Robin to him. A look of recognition, which he felt was likely mirrored in his own. Because just like Robin before her, he felt instantly like he'd met this person before.

It was like being inside a dream filled with friends he knew but couldn't quite place.

What is happening to me?

"Arturo!" the young woman said, slightly out of breath. Then, as if realizing they hadn't been properly introduced yet, her gaze quickly returned to Robin. "You found him, then? And it looks like just in time too. I take it there was trouble?"

"Yes, and there may be again imminently. I've tied the thing up, but I'm not strong enough to hold it at a distance. Not here. In fact . . ."

Robin's shoulders sagged a little, and the ribbons of light emanating from her finally disappeared. It was an incredible sensation of loss. Like sitting next to a roaring fire on a snow-filled night, only for the fire to be extinguished by someone opening a window. The air around them was suddenly empty, a vacuum into which a variety of different emotions rushed to fill the void.

Chief among them was fear.

Arturo tightened his grip on his daughter as the three strangers looked back toward the museum, from which screaming had begun. The young woman stepped forward to slip her arm under the now tired-looking Robin, then fixed Arturo with a look.

"Arturo, my name is Nu. I know you're confused and want to know what's going on, and I would love to tell you, but we probably can't right now."

"That's what Robin said," he replied warily. Had he met these people before? Why couldn't he remember? He turned to the woman who had saved his life. "Are these friends of yours?"

"They are, yes. And you can trust them as you have me. We're here to protect you."

"From what? That thing back there?"

"That and more," Nu said, interrupting. "Now, we need to get you out of here in case anything else shows up."

Arturo didn't know what to think, but he knew what he was feeling. In a choice between dealing with another decaying monster and trusting these people, there was only one choice.

He nodded. "Of course."

The red-haired woman now spoke in a low French accent to the young woman. Arturo knew enough of the language to understand what she was asking.

"Are we taking the girl too?"

"I think we should, Maïa. For her safety and his peace of mind."

Arturo glanced at Rosa, who despite their predicament was actually grinning. She was enjoying this far too much!

"We should go with them, Papa," Rosa said, clearly trusting her instincts too. Her hand slipped into Robin's, who took it and smiled. Arturo felt something snap into place, like he'd been outvoted and outmaneuvered. Yet he didn't seem to mind.

"I think you and I are going to get on great," Robin said to her, whispering conspiratorially. "Now tell your dad to hurry up and come with us, or else I'm going to have to wrap him up in my power and carry him over my shoulder. Do you think he would like that?"

Rosa laughed. Arturo's cheeks grew flush.

"There will be no need for that," he said firmly. "I can walk fine."

There was crashing in the museum behind them. Maïa gestured for them all to move and flexed her fingers.

"I suggest you run, don't walk. And go now. I will deal with whatever we have in there."

"He is Unwritten," Robin called over her shoulder, pulling Rosa and Arturo after Nu. "Remember, Maïa: There is someone underneath the darkness. My power revealed glimpses of who he had been, so please don't hurt him unless you have to. There is still hope."

"I understand," Maïa responded, already on her way to the museum.

With that, Nu led Robin, Rosa, and Arturo across the courtyard and through the gates, out into the Cairo streets, through alleyways and side streets, past sleepy cafes and a labyrinth of bazaars, until Arturo was quite sure he was lost and could never find his way back to his hotel again.

He maintained his grip on Rosa throughout, though saw her wide-eyed exuberance merely grow stronger as they let the two women lead their escape. *Kids*, he thought, slightly envious of her excitement.

Nu tapped the bracelet on her wrist. The polished metal sphere set into the gold band lit up in response, and Arturo noted her mouthing to it, before she immediately stopped, turned a corner, and led them down what amounted to a space between two crooked houses that hadn't quite been built properly.

"Down this alley," she said. "Almost there."

"Almost where?" Arturo said, turning himself sideways to squeeze past a particularly narrow gap between the brick walls. The four then stepped into a sandstone courtyard with a central fountain and an ivy-covered arch set into one wall.

Bathed in the glorious sunlight overhead, and with the highly decorative scrollwork of waves and carved mythological figures detailed in relief around the high walls, it was as though they had stepped back in time. Had it not been for the phone lines and rusted satellite dishes decorating the nearby rooftops, he might have thought they had journeyed back to the early days of this fine city.

"We're here!" Nu said brightly. She tapped a finger to her wrist again and turned to Arturo. "Please just trust me that everything you're about to see is fine and normal, and you're safe."

Arturo didn't know what that meant. He supposed he should be worried, but there was just something about these two women he couldn't help but like.

Nu's bracelet began to glow again. Once again he could feel a warmth pulse around them, through them, weaving through the fiber of his being and back out into the world.

The archway beneath the vines suddenly shimmered and changed. Not in any perceivable way that Arturo could see—he could only feel it. There was something more than just leaves and vines there now.

He pulled them aside to take a closer look.

"What is happening?" he muttered to himself.

A hand found his shoulder.

"Do you trust me?" Robin asked.

He burst into laughter at the ridiculousness of the question. "You're asking a lot of me, Robin. A complete stranger has enticed me and my daughter into running from monsters, and now you want us to walk through a wall? You did save my life back there, I think, but really . . . I'm beginning to wonder if I had something bad to eat at the museum, and maybe now I'm hallucinating?"

Rosa tugged at his hand. “Papa, I think we can trust them.”

Arturo scratched his beard. “Yes, I think we can too.”

Robin and Nu shared a glance, then gestured to the vine-covered archway.

“All you need to do is take the first step,” Robin said, that mischievous smile playing at her lips again. “Don’t be afraid. Not everything is as it seems.”

He stared at the wall, blinked, and watched as it began to change.

The golden stone was growing more translucent, losing its tangibility, until soon there was nothing beyond the foliage. There was just a half-hidden open arch, a doorway full of possibilities, waiting for travelers.

Arturo looked to Rosa, and they both nodded. Then, holding tightly to her hand, they pushed aside the vines and stepped through.

CHAPTER SEVEN
A MEMORY OF HOME

It was like stepping into a long-ago dream.

Arturo's boots clicked against the marble floor as he found himself in an aisle of bookshelves. Cool, fragrant air hit him—a strange and pleasant sensation after the intense heat of the Cairo morning. He paused to breathe it in, looking around in awe, unable to help touching the shelves and along the spines as he continued walking forward, taking Rosa with him, toward the light and noise.

With each step, the unseen fog shrouding his brain began to lift, slowly dissipating, until suddenly he emerged from the bookshelves into a grand circular hall, one filled with people and surrounded by magnificent frescoes that rose several stories high. And whatever dam shoring up his memories now broke. They rushed back into his head, splashing against the insides of his mind as he circled and took in the view.

It was as familiar as the day he had left.

"The Great Library of Tomorrow," he whispered to himself. That mystical, magical place of enlightenment he'd discovered quite by accident. A city that stood at the edges of Earth's reality, on the boundary between his world and an endless plane of other realms.

He was back.

Around him there were multitudes of people from all over the world, some going about their daily business, others stumbling in here for the first time and gawking in amazement at the stunning paintings wrapping around the walls and those laid out beneath his feet. Meanwhile, the Volare Machina were buzzing overhead, carrying messages, books, and information, darting this way and that as they flew with purpose.

He stopped and breathed it all in with a sense of relief and palpable joy he hadn't known he'd been missing since he'd left.

"Welcome home," a voice said cheerfully.

Arturo gasped and spun, remembering the guides who had led him here. Not just two strange women who had saved his life but Nu and Robin, two old friends.

He let go of Rosa for a moment and wrapped them up in a sudden hug. "Oh, I've missed you both. Even if I didn't know it!"

"You too, Arturo," Robin said.

Rosa tugged at his arm. "Papa, where are we?"

Arturo let his friends go and gave his daughter's shoulders a squeeze of reassurance. "We're somewhere safe. With friends."

"Are you saying you remember all this, Arturo?" Robin asked, seeming confused.

"Should I not?" he asked. "Isn't this how it works? Now that I have returned to the Great Library, so have my memories of my time here?" He laughed. "It is strange, but now I even remember *not* remembering while I was gone! How wonderfully bizarre."

Robin and Nu shared a glance.

"Actually, no, this isn't how it works at all, Arturo," Robin replied. "The few times any visitors to the Great Library come back—and it's rare, if they do—they don't usually remember much of any previous visits. Typically, only those born to the Library—and the Sages with our connection to the Book of Wisdom—retain our memories as we pop back and forth between the Great Library and our lives back on Earth. For returning visitors like yourself, we would expect your memories to return, but the process can be disorienting."

The shimmer over Robin's shoulder suddenly materialized into a small silver ball. Rosa yelped and dove behind her father. Arturo laughed again.

"Centauri! How have you been? You're looking not a day older than whatever ancient age you are!"

The Orb's surface swirled with intricate designs, too complex for him to understand, although he thought he felt the warmth of friendship through the web of patterns. Arturo held out his fist, against which the Orb bumped itself gently in greeting.

"It's good to see you too, my little friend. I mean that, truly."

Meanwhile, Nu's Orb, Antares, had lifted itself out of her bracelet, returned to her normal size, and was slowly floating toward Rosa. Arturo held his hand on her shoulder, feeling her tremble with nervous excitement.

"Shhhh, my girl, it's okay. I know this is all very strange. But these are our friends, I promise. We're in a very safe place, along with some marvelous people who will look after us. You have no need to worry. Trust me."

Nu crouched down until she was face-to-face with the girl and held out her hands. Rosa hesitated only for a moment, before reaching out and taking them.

"Rosa, this is Antares. She's my Orb."

"An . . . Orb?"

"Yes. Think of her like a floating ball of magic and technology. She's my friend and companion who connects me to the Library and the wider universe."

Rosa stared for a moment, then held out her fist to the Orb as her father had done. Antares bumped her, then spun a pattern of amber circles.

"She's happy to meet you," Nu said.

"It's nice to meet her too," Rosa replied.

Arturo wasn't surprised to see that his daughter's attention had already moved away from the Orb again, back to their general surroundings.

She stared in amazement as a couple of inhabitants dressed in Library tunics wandered past, engaged in a passionate discussion about floating islands. A flock of twenty Volare of strange and wonderful designs whizzed overhead. And in the distance, a train sounded.

"You said something about a library?" Rosa said. "You mean, is that where we are right now? A library? But where are all the books?"

Nu laughed lightly and gave a little nod as she pulled the girl to her feet. Her clothes had transformed on the journey through the portal, so she was back in her Sage's tunic and looked as regal as any of the Sages he had met on his first visit. Arturo stared at her, surprised by just how confident this young woman had become since he'd last seen her. Being a Sage had clearly given her a sense of responsibility and calm.

"Oh, we have books," Nu replied. "You would have seen a few on the shelves we brushed past as we came through the portal. But this isn't just any library, you know. It's a place unlike any other that exists on this world or those beyond. You could say it is *the* Library. Those of us who consider it home call it the Great Library of Tomorrow. Because that is who it is for: the people of the future. The people of tomorrow. It's a place to educate and inspire, to help the growth of the individual and the collective. It has been here for centuries and will be here for centuries more, protected by those who live and work here, and the ten Sages who were chosen to be its appointed guardians."

"Sages who we really should gather and meet," Robin said pointedly as Arturo caught her glancing at him again. She looked away quickly as Centauri said something in that secret language of his. Robin glared at the Orb, then brushed some invisible fluff from her own Sage's tunic and stood tall. "Nu?"

"I've already had Antares send word ahead. We'll need to wait for Maïa, of course, but I get the sense she won't be much longer. Now, to the next matter at hand, because we should really go and discuss why you were in trouble in the first place, Arturo. Would you and Rosa mind accompanying us? I think it's important you be present as we talk; it's only fair to you to understand what lies behind the attack. There is clearly more to all this—and your part in it—than any of us know, but together we can figure it out. And while we talk, Rosa can hang out with Antares and perhaps read a book or two? I know some good ones that you might like!"

Rosa smiled and nodded eagerly. "Yes, I'd love that! Can we, Papa?" She gave him the big eyes, like a cat that claimed it had never been fed.

Arturo looked at his daughter, then to Nu, then finally to Robin. Her slightly raised eyebrow suggested he had little choice in the matter.

"Let's see what you Sages have in store for me this time," he said, gesturing for them to lead the way.

CHAPTER EIGHT
VISIONS AND JOURNALS

Nu sat up as straight as she could in the tall-backed chair, feeling the weight of the occasion settle on her shoulders. They had moved to the Assembly Room; the largest reading room in the Library, reserved entirely for the gathering of the ten Sages and their Orbs. Her first time there had been when she was newly brought into the fold, and they had sat to discuss the events in the City of Forever.

This time the mood was heavier, more fraught with tension. The Sages had found themselves meeting more frequently on the urgent matters relating to Suttaru's attacks on Paperworld and the Library itself. They'd relaxed the rules about all ten Sages needing to be present—how could they without a Sage of Hope—and scholars could be seen coming and going at all times of the day. It had become a hub for their ongoing efforts to reverse the effects of the deadly attacks. Not so much a meeting room now, but more of a crisis management center.

The room itself was elegant, with high-arched windows at one end, through which collected starlight beamed across a large table, around which the rest of the space was focused. It was large and circular and sat in the center of the room, its intertwined legs were like the branches of a tree polished to a high shine, and the tabletop itself was multicolored glass patterned like the wings of a dragonfly. Ten matching chairs traditionally surrounded the table, one for each Sage, but they were now reenforced with others pulled from the nearby rooms. Nu saw Triss sitting in one to the right of Mwamba. All around them were walls bound by fine bookshelves, with cast-iron balconies serving as galleries higher up and several spiral staircases leading up.

It was charming and warm, yet there was an air of importance to it too. It was like a smaller version of the Concourse, a place she knew all too well, and the familiarity helped her now to bear up under the pressure she felt—a responsibility not to let down her colleagues or friends.

"United once more," Veer boomed from beside her with forced good cheer, before adding, "Almost."

Nu had always considered the Sage of Strength as something of a bear of a man—at least a foot taller than her, with wide shoulders and a thick mustache that was even bushier than the wild scruff of brown hair atop his head. Yet if Veer was a bear, he was most certainly a friendly one. A friend she had come to love being around, thanks to his unwavering sense of cheer and good fun.

Almost unwavering, anyway. Even he couldn't hide the undercurrent of frustration at play today. His mustache twitched as he continued. "I would say gladly, but clearly we are meeting under more difficult circumstances than we had expected. More's the pity. I had hoped to spend tonight celebrating."

The eight other faces around the table, including Nu's, gave a solemn nod. Even the companion Orbs, floating above the table, having their own brief communications, seemed subdued. There were momentary bursts of patterns across their surfaces, but nothing too colorful.

"We should not dwell on what happened, Veer. It will serve us no good."

The woman who had spoken had short, spiky hair and unusual golden eyes that dazzled above a smile that was never not infectious. Even now, Nu felt herself feeling emboldened by her presence. Paix, the Sage of Joy, was originally a pianist from Brazil. She had been at the

Library as a Sage since the early 1900s, but she often visited Earth for months at a time every decade or so to collaborate and play with different orchestras around the world, just for the fun of it. Some of the others often joked she and Veer must be related somehow, such was the positivity of the pair. Yet Nu could sense even Paix wasn't able to convince Veer to stop dwelling.

"We should have been there, even as just a precaution. To oversee matters. It was too important, and I should have gone," Veer said.

"You have been busy leading your investigation, Veer," Maïa said. "Give yourself a break. It's been months of traveling realms looking for that rogue, Payne, and you and the others have barely taken any time off. We were not about to send you off to a midnight beach party."

He gave a gruff sigh, and his cheeks grew a little flushed, but he did not argue. Nu could feel his frustration. The Sage of Strength wasn't used to being in a position where his power couldn't help him.

"Besides, in the end, there was nothing either of us would have been able to do," Maïa added. "Nobody here is faster than me, yet I was unable to prevent Densi's loss. It was instant and beyond stopping, short of having foresight. And even with Nu's abilities, we were unprepared."

Nu held her face steady as all eyes turned to her. She thought again to the dreams she'd been having in recent weeks. Were they dreams? She wasn't so sure now.

"Our powers do not always manifest as we might wish they would," Mwamba, the Sage of Knowledge, said kindly, addressing the table without letting his gaze rest on any one of them, but Nu understood he was speaking to her. "We have all experienced the journey that comes with learning about our abilities, and it can take decades to truly harness them. Yet, even so, sometimes the destiny of others lies beyond even our long-honed skills and experience. I believe there is little any of you could have done today."

Nu and the others inclined their heads, glad of his words. Mwamba rested his elbows on the table and clasped his fingers together, his penetrating gaze sweeping once more around the first gathering of Sages they'd had in weeks. A gathering that was still one Sage short.

United once more. Almost.

As Mwamba took in the empty chair where Helia would normally have sat—and where Densi should now be sitting—his brow creased.

"It is no lie to say that the loss of our new Sage of Hope is significant," he said, his voice low and solemn, with a hint of weariness to it. The growing of the new Orb had required a lot of his care and attention. "The world lost a beautiful and promising young man today, who I'm sure would have been with us for many years to come. Yet the impact of his loss stretches beyond the bounds of the Earth. It also means that our strength as Sages remains incomplete. And it leaves the world without a champion of hope for even longer than we could have imagined, at a time when Earth needs hope more than ever."

His solemn eyes found the Sage of Creativity. "Jin, would you like to elaborate for us on what you told me earlier?"

Jin was a Chinese woman who looked to be in her thirties, with a red stripe diagonally through her closely cropped hair and black-framed glasses. Originally from a small town near Beijing, Jin had always been an activist and champion for good. She had started out designing and building inventions to help mitigate her country's water crisis and then graduated into a climate scientist of much renown around the world. Such was her commitment to helping solve the environmental problems facing the world, she was the Sage who spent the most time on Earth.

Which was where she had been spending most of her time since Suttaru upset the delicate balance between Earth and many realms of Paperworld.

Jin's usually soft features grew hard and troubled. *This can't be good,* Nu thought as the woman's multicolored nails tapped the table slowly, as though trying to work up to revealing what she knew.

"My friends, I've alerted you previously to the Earth's suffering. We already knew that climate disruption has been having significant effects in my country and everywhere else too. As we say in my community, the whale song grows weak. And we know that if the song disappears forever, we will all become silent. That we are in trouble and have work ahead of us, there is no doubt. And yet"—she stopped tapping and looked up at her friends—"whatever evil Suttaru unleashed is still impacting Earth, and it will only get worse."

Above the table, the nine hovering Orbs grew still, sensing the solemn mood descend upon the room. Even Robin's Orb, Centauri, prone to making remarks when he possibly shouldn't, let his surface shine a silent silver as he listened.

Jin continued. "Volcanic activity of that magnitude, that widespread, was a scientifically impossible occurrence. Even months later, my colleagues—the smartest minds in the world—still cannot begin to put reasons beneath what happened. And yet, thankfully, I suppose, the people of Earth are not yet questioning what they saw. So much in the world has been unprecedented lately; tolerance for such things is at an all-time high. The volcanic activity was a big story in the media for only a few weeks before attention waned and fell elsewhere."

Veer shifted in his chair, before saying, "Is it good they're still ignoring what's happening to the planet?"

"It gives us time to try and stem the taint that's bleeding through from here, before full-blown panic sets in," she replied, then looked around the table. "Unfortunately, what happened six months ago is still having an impact. The community of experts confirm there is increased activity still present beneath the Earth's crust. And reports have been coming in from various Sages while traveling that we are also seeing effects across a wider array of realms in Paperworld than we first thought."

The Sage of Loyalty, Amin, clasped his fingers together on the table before him. "It's amazing, really, despite the seriousness of the situation, to see physical evidence of the link between our home on Earth and Paperworld. To know it is one thing, but to see it on such a difficult level . . . Cause and effect; one affects the other. All the stories on Earth are the foundation of Paperworld, so it follows that such events would impact the realms beyond the Great Library. It gives new gravity to what we all learned upon our arrival as Sages."

"It seems pretty conclusive now," Jin said with a nod.

Paix spoke up. "At least there are positives to all of this. Silver linings of the clouds that may gather. We have the power to contain what's happening here, and a lack of panic on Earth means we still have time to resolve what is happening before things become really problematic."

"But what *is* happening?" Robin asked, although Nu could tell by the tone of her voice that it was a rhetorical question. She already knew the answer and simply wanted to bring it into the light now—a point made clear when she looked to Nu with an encouraging smile. "I think this is the right time to discuss what we all face, and I think Nu has some guidance for us here. Because from what I know, an old enemy has returned. Hasn't he, Nu?"

Nu felt the attention of the eight other Sages fix upon her. Even Arturo, until now sitting quietly and listening in with alternating looks of awe and horror, was staring at her with the expectation he was about to get answers as to his own predicament.

She sat up straighter, clasping her hands in her lap away from everyone's gaze so they wouldn't see her hands shake. She had a feeling Robin wasn't just referring to the return of the Rogue Sage. Had Antares communicated her dreams to Centauri? Or had her friend simply picked up on the weight of worry Nu had been trying to suppress lately?

It didn't matter either way. She had the spotlight now and the opportunity to address her concerns. And she was grateful to Robin for that.

"There are two parts to what I'm about to tell you," she said, trying to keep her voice level as she looked at each of the Sages in turn. "After the attack on Earth, Maïa was able to apprehend the assassin." She turned to the redheaded Sage, waiting for her to pick up the story.

Maïa continued. "Before he died—or rather, was killed—he seemed possessed in some way. His body became a shell for communication, by someone I had met in my early years as a Sage, and who I know all of you are familiar with in deed, if not in person. The same person Veer has been looking for. The former Sage known as Edwin Payne."

There was a mixture of nods and horrified looks. Veer muttered something under his breath, sitting up straighter and staring her way. Nu understood that Antares would have communicated some of what had happened on the beach back to the Great Library, but not every Sage would have been here then. Or perhaps they had just not believed it possible.

"What I'd like to know is how Payne knew to send his assassin at that time and that place," Veer said. "It seems an incredible coincidence he had someone there at that exact moment. That he knew who the Orb had chosen. Is it possible he infiltrated the Great Library somehow?"

Maïa frowned. "You think he was able to access the Book of Wisdom to track our Orbs?"

"I'm not saying it's possible, but it would at least explain how he orchestrated Densi's murder."

Nu saw Mwamba shaking his head.

"I cannot believe that to be true. For one, the Author would have alerted us to any external interference, even if it were possible to infiltrate the Book. But how would Payne have the ability to even attempt it?"

Arturo finally spoke up. "Isn't Payne the man who led the attack on the Great Library when I was last here? Are you saying he's come back?"

Veer's mustache blew out with his low chuckle. "He never really went away, I'm afraid. We've been seeking him, following what few clues we've been able to find. A glitch has been noticed in recent years in the Orrery, which became more overt around the attacks on the Rose Garden and the Library itself. But at first the scholars of the Orrery thought it was just a simple error. After all, only the Book herself understands the mechanics of the system—but now seems to have been the ghostly trace of an Orb. It must have been Edwin Payne, the former Sage of Creativity. It seems his Orb was not entirely severed from its connection with the Book of Wisdom and the Great Library. But we haven't seen it since his disappearance after the attack."

Canopus began swirling colors above the table, and Mwamba raised his hand to acknowledge his Orb's excitement.

"That much was true until this incident, Veer," said Mwamba. "The Book alerted us to the return of the glitch around the same time as Nu says Payne talked to them."

Veer sat up straighter in his chair. "His use of magic to speak through the Unwritten must have put him back on our radar. Well, I'll be damned. Can I—"

"The scholars are working to locate the signal, to give us an idea of where he was speaking from. Where he has been hiding. After we're done here, perhaps you could go to the Orrery and see if they have found him yet. For now, though, I think we'd all agree we need you here. There is still much to discuss," Mwamba said.

Veer nodded, glancing over to Nu. "And you were sure it was him?"

"I'm afraid so. And his ability to wield dark magic remotely is something I feel we need to try to understand. How is it possible he can do this, when it is not something we Sages can do from too far even within the same realm, let alone in between them? Unless . . ."

Nu's words drifted into the quiet of the chamber as the gathering considered this. Robin gave her another look, and Nu took a breath, steeling herself for what she knew she needed to say next.

"Unless *what*, Nu?" Mwamba asked gently.

"Well, the second part of what I had to tell you may offer some explanation behind Payne's heightened abilities. In that I don't think he is working alone."

"What do you mean?" Jin asked.

"I've been having dreams. Well, nightmares, really. That's how they presented themselves, and until now that's all I thought they were. Just nightmares that the darkness we faced not so long ago has returned. That the one responsible for the destruction in the Rose Garden, Aedela, the City of Forever . . . that Suttaru has somehow returned."

"Suttaru? Can it be possible?" Mwamba said.

Nu nodded. "Perhaps. I don't yet know the truth of it, but it would seem a possibility we must consider."

The silence in the chamber fell heavy upon them all. Even Paix looked perturbed.

Nu felt her mouth go dry. She licked her lips as best she could and continued. "I'd assumed I was simply having nightmares because . . ." She let her voice trail off for a moment, lost in memory. Then she straightened. "Because I saw Suttaru die in his battle with Perennia. And there has been no connection, no response at all, to my presence in any nightmares I've had of him. Not like there was before when he witnessed me *in* my vision, and I could feel him reaching into my head."

She looked around the table, trying to bury her guilt at letting the villain insinuate himself into her thoughts, allowing him to learn of the Sages' plans in the process. She'd not been in control of her powers back then, of course. Robin had been quick to remind her of that when Nu had brought it up. Yet still she bore the burden.

"You are having visions of him returning?" Amin asked, frowning.

"Yes."

"But there has been no sense that he has actually returned? You have not felt him try to establish a connection with you?" Nu shook her head, and Amin continued. "Could it be a vision of the future?"

"I don't know," Nu replied honestly. "But knowing Payne is back and actively working against us once more, I fear they might be. He died—I have no doubt of that. But somehow Suttaru may still be a threat. And I think we need to counter him before he wreaks even more death than he and the Rogue Sage already have."

That was quite enough information for the gathering. Perhaps too much, for some of them, Nu could see. Amin looked troubled, and so did Jin. Paix had lost a shade of the glow of positivity you could almost see around her most days. Even Maïa, who had witnessed the assassination of Densi, looked as though she was having trouble believing what they were facing.

"We should consult the Book of Wisdom," Maïa said.

Veer waved a bear-size hand around dismissively. "The Book and her Orbs appointed us as protectors of the Library, the Earth, and Paperworld. Shouldn't we at least try to find out more about what's going on before we speak to the Author?"

"Veer, my darling, will you not believe it even when coming directly from the Sage of Truth herself?"

He had the decency to look a little embarrassed by that. "No offense, Nu," he said with a nod, "but the sheer improbability of a dead man returning warrants some caution, don't we think?"

"The dragon was brought back to life," Nu said simply.

And that was enough to end the argument. She might not have been sure about the meaning of her nightmares or visions or whatever they would turn out to be. But Nu had witnessed the dragon's rebirth. She had been a part of bringing Perennia back to life.

Nu shifted uncomfortably in her chair, staying quiet as the discussion moved ahead without her. The other Sages soon came to the conclusion that the Author would need to be consulted as soon as possible. Nu sat silently, considering the weight of what she hadn't told them.

Was it being truthful if you said nothing and withheld all you knew? It wasn't a lie. Yet it felt duplicitous and unlike her.

What could she rightly say though? That aside from the darkness returning and the sense of Suttaru being alive in her visions, she'd also seen another figure in there too? Not a Sage but a mortal man from Earth who had reminded her of the writer sitting with them now. A man of good and honor, who would stand and face the darkness in their time of need. And although his actions would save them—perhaps save everything—she knew deep in her heart it would come at great cost.

The images in Nu's nightmares hadn't been very detailed. Her visions weren't always tangible like that. Sometimes there were a collection of sights and feelings. But Nu had the terrible feeling that if these visions of the truth played out as she had experienced them, someone she cared about was going to die.

A price paid for the greater good.

Was that a truth worth keeping to herself for the time being to ensure it came to pass?

She watched Arturo as the discussion returned to the involvement of Payne. Arturo had been growing more concerned with every revelation, as well he should, but now a confused frown broke over his face as if he had suddenly remembered something.

He leaned over to Robin and whispered something.

She looked surprised, thought for a moment, then gestured to her Orb to join her and whispered something back to Arturo.

Nu watched with interest as the writer discreetly got up, mumbled that he needed to step out for a moment, then followed the bobbing Centauri away from the table and out of the room.

Robin's gaze returned to the table and the ensuing discussion, though she was clearly deep in thought. Nu wondered what might have transpired between her and Arturo; only a few minutes later, the door creaked open again, and he slipped back in. Centauri floated back up to join his companions above the table, while Arturo took his seat again, taking a few brown pieces of paper from a notebook he now held, placing them in front of him.

At the next break in conversation, Arturo then spoke up. "I have something to add," he said.

Mwamba's eyebrow arched as he nodded. "Certainly, Arturo. Speak freely."

"Thank you. I was obviously here before, with Robin, when the Great Library was attacked. And with all this talk of that man, Payne, I realized that the last time I was here, when he happened upon us at the First Cave, I had taken something from him—ripped pages of a book he had been holding—as I tried to stop him getting away. They fell to the floor, but I picked them up and shoved them into my pocket as I gave chase. After the chaos of that whole attack was over, I placed them into my notebook, ready to look at them later . . . only to forget about them, until now. I'm embarrassed to say I got caught up in all the celebrations of Nu becoming a Sage, and I left my notebook in the room I stayed in. I'm sorry. I've only just remembered about them."

"But knowing that Payne came back for the book the pages were taken from, maybe me leaving them here was fortuitous. Perhaps they can give us some insight into what he was looking for. I looked them over at the time, but I couldn't read the language."

The papers eventually passed into the possession of Mwamba, where they stopped. Nu understood there were no leaders among the Sages. They were unified and equals. But Mwamba was the elder Sage and the wisest. As befitting his position as the Sage of Knowledge, it was only logical that such things would pass to him first for his careful, experienced eye and his unparalleled ability to absorb and understand information.

The Sage stretched out his fingers as if reaching for something incredibly delicate . . . or dangerous. Picking it up, he slowly unfolded the paper. From the other side of the table, Nu could see it appeared to be four sheets, all with a ragged side where Arturo had torn them free. Mwamba's face darkened as he read the scrawled ink marks she could see through the back of the pages.

"I do not believe this was left here fortuitously," he said, finally. "It is possible the Great Library had you leave your notebook here with the pages inside for just this moment. Had you taken them home, you might have lost them. But now . . ."

"Do you know what they are?" Arturo asked.

"Why, yes, I think I might." Mwamba looked up, a glint in his eyes. "But you will have to excuse me before I say any more. These will need some time to read closely and translate accurately. If we meet back here in two hours, that should suffice? Triss, perhaps you could accompany me. This may require your excellent penmanship to draft copies while I translate."

He stood, but not before Nu asked, "What do you think it is?"

Mwamba looked at her, then around the table.

"I think this is Suttaru's journal," he said.

CHAPTER NINE
THE MYSTERY OF THE SPHERE

Mwamba was met with an audible silence around the table upon his return, Triss attentively at his side. He could almost feel the shock rippling out from his confirmation that these pages were indeed written by their enemy.

"Suttaru kept a journal?" Veer asked. The usually cheerful Sage looked concerned, and he wasn't the only one. "And you have some of his writing there?"

Mwamba bowed his head in acknowledgment. He was sure. As sure as he could be. The shock his colleagues were feeling now was the same he had suffered as he'd translated the scribblings. The pages were ancient, incomplete, and written in a language he had not seen in centuries. It had taken him the entire couple of hours to translate the pages. But the messages the ink revealed were enough for him to identify the source.

His eyes returned to the four pages before him. "Yes, Veer. Although, as we all know, Suttaru once went by the name of Adi, long ago, and I can tell that these pages can be dated to the era before he turned." He turned them over in his hands, studying each one. They were each filled with scribbles. Mostly notes, but a few equations and a couple of drawings in the corners. "They are journal entries, each one written in the first person, like a diary. And while of course they could be anybody's from that time, I see here there is mention of the Author herself. At least, the person she used to be."

"Fairen?" Robin asked.

"Yes. She's mentioned by name here a few times."

That was an understatement. The passages were unhinged, the thoughts of a man consumed with purpose and madness and jealousy. Yet Mwamba could also tell there were details within the scribbles that shone like glints of gold in the fissures of a rock face. There were clues here.

As the Sages listened, he read a passage aloud:

And now Haruto, my friend, has turned against me too. I caught him looking over my experiment yesterday, or perhaps this morning. Who can tell anymore. Time does not exist down here in my laboratory, away from the hustle and bustle of the rest of our Library. Haruto claims he was looking for inspiration to help Fairen with the Book, but I don't believe him. I think he has nefarious intentions with my work.

"Perhaps Adi was already corrupted by this point? We know from the records of the time that something—Discordia—corrupted him. The tone suggests he was becoming paranoid. It may be he was already too far gone," Veer said, and nobody disagreed.

"To hear a contemporary account of the making of the Book of Wisdom though. What a waste, to think we had this book all along, and no one knew where it was," Robin said, and the others nodded their agreement.

Then Nu spoke up. "Who is this Haruto?"

The younger Sage looked around the table as if expecting an explanation.

"I haven't heard the name before, at least not in our histories," Mwamba said. "But it is a name of great significance in the Japanese culture, one that goes back to ancient Japan. It was and is an auspicious name, often given to those with strong connections to the natural world and the accomplishment of great deeds. That he could have been forgotten seems . . . incomprehensible." A quick glance to Canopus confirmed it. The Orb flashed flame orange, a series of quick patterns that Mwamba understood as frustration and confusion. Canopus didn't know who it was either.

"We'll look into who that might be, although it is telling that such a potentially pivotal friend to Adi and Fairen has been left out of the records," Mwamba replied, returning to the pages. He looked for the next passage that he had marked as being useful and began reading again:

> *I have been working with the artifact for months now, yet it continues to astound me with its intricacies. It is beyond the creative abilities of humanity or any nature we know of. A gleaming black-and-ruby ball, much like a blend of obsidian and lava, only there is a fire within the stone itself. I swear I can see it growing in power, certainly more so since my encounter with the darkness. Almost as though the two are connected somehow.*
>
> *Ah yes. The darkness still calls from Discordia. How I know that name, I do not entirely understand. I suspect it left its taint on me when it beckoned, and I foolishly listened. Yet the encounter also provided another title, a whisper through the tear in time and space that I believe the artifact traveled through to reach us.*
>
> *The Maksus Stone. That is the name I have begun calling the artifact. Fairen and Haruto have not pursued reasons as to my naming, and I have not offered them. She is too busy with creating her precious "Book" anyway. Haruto continues helping her. They would not understand the leaps I am making with my work through that meeting with the darkness. They would be concerned, I think, especially since the disappearance of the Founder. They would warn me away from my experiments lest the same happen to me.*

Yet Maksus is the name of the fire within the stone. The source of it. The darkness whispered its name. It was a whisper of mocking, though, of hatred. I think it fears the Maksus Stone.

Such horrors are fascinating. I yearn to learn more.

The Sages around the table were captivated, held silent by the words reaching out to them from an age in the past, from the hand of the very man who would now seek to kill them all. Thus, it was left to Arturo to articulate what they were probably all thinking.

"This Maksus Stone sounds like a reason for Payne to want the journal. I'm stating the obvious, I can see, but this seems to be more than just some diary from the early days of your Library."

Mwamba held up his finger as he turned the pages over and prepared to read part of the final entry. "Yes, I think you're right. But it is your Library, too, now, Arturo." Arturo nodded his thanks to the elder Sage, who continued. "And this part is particularly fascinating. It's part of the final entry of the pages you ripped from the journal." He cleared his throat and continued:

My laboratory . . . ruined. The Maksus Stone is destroyed; the flame has gone out.

Our opportunity to fight back has gone.

Haruto has ruined it. Fairen must have sent him to sabotage my work, yet the fool did not know what he was doing. The explosion broke two fragments from the stone. One buried itself in Haruto's chest. I found him bleeding, with the fragment embedded close to his heart. Yet, even as I prepared to watch him die, I saw the wound around the fragment healing. The blood stopped; the skin puckered around the stone as if holding on to it, yet was unmarked.

Haruto recovered sufficiently quickly to take advantage of my shock and push me away, running like the coward I now know he is. It is unfortunate that Fairen stopped me chasing him. Even more unfortunate that the sphere disappeared in the event—I could find no trace of it afterward. Only the second fragment remains.

I suspect Fairen. She has finally shown her colors and turned against me.

The darkness beyond the portal was right.

Mwamba sat for a moment to ponder this last passage. There was so much of interest here, not least the healing properties of the stone, yet the crucial information was the breaking of the Maksus Stone.

It was clearly of importance to Adi, and the implications in these scribbles were significant—the stone could fight the darkness. Yet it had been shattered into three pieces, a fragment of which Haruto had run off. Where had he gone? And where were the other pieces?

Looking up, he realized the Sages were waiting for his response, an indication of what they should do with this information.

Pushing his chair back, he stood.

"There are questions here that even I cannot answer, despite my accrued knowledge; however, there is one possible source of knowledge here we can always turn to in times of need."

"We must consult the Book of Wisdom," Nu said.

"Indeed, for there we may find the truths we need to make sense of this. Lead on, young Sage. It is time for us to consult the Author herself."

Mwamba waited as Nu, who had yet to perform the auspicious act of talking directly to the Author, knocked on the door to the Haven and waited only a moment before walking into the grand chamber alongside his protégé, Triss, the two young women standing close to one another. He smiled, then followed them in with his fellow Sages, save Robin, who had gone with Arturo and Rosa to observe him after the return of his memories. While technically Triss wasn't permitted in the Haven,

Mwamba knew this would be an important moment for her, decorum be damned. There was little enough to be cheerful for these last few days.

As the door swung closed silently behind them, he nodded for Triss to take a table nearby to undertake the task of making copies of the journal, while he headed for the lectern that held the Book of Wisdom. Nu and Triss drifted apart, their attachment clear, as the Sages formed an imperfect circle around the Book. It was not just Robin who was missing; the glaring gap in their number was driven home once again.

The others gestured for him to take the lead, the combination of his age and experience, not to mention the practicality of his perfect recall, making him the obvious choice, and he began his ritual—first a pause for respect, then stretching out his hands and offering the words that would call forth the Author.

When she finally appeared, she hung above the Book of Wisdom, all light and purpose, a gift of inspiration for those who looked upon her, and often a source of wisdom—even for the Sage of Knowledge himself.

"Author, we have questions of great importance. Questions whose answers, we think, only you can give."

"Ask, Sage of Knowledge, and we will try to find you the answers you seek."

"Thank you, Author. We have discovered pages from a journal once belonging to Adi, your former companion, about something called the Maksus Stone and a man called Haruto. Can you shed light on these matters?"

A light came down from the great ceiling, a Volare Machina, poised above them, which darted swiftly to where Triss was making copies of Mwamba's translation of the pages. She sat back, and the machine hovered over the originals, its small wings holding steady as a beam of blue light captured the text and transmitted it to the Book herself.

Mwamba and the others waited patiently for the wisdom of the Book. It took her mere seconds to access the most ancient information in the Library, and in times of great need, relay the necessary answers.

Usually.

Not today though.

"I can confirm this is indeed the handwriting of Adi. Presumably written before he was lost to Discordia. A cipher of his own making, I believe, but complex none the less." She looked at Mwamba and nodded in acknowledgment of his skills. "It would take our finest cryptographic scholar weeks to decipher this, but thankfully it is child's play for our longest-serving Sage of Knowledge." Even at his great age, Mwamba felt the warmth of a blush at the Author's praise. In truth, his abilities as the Sage of knowledge to read and understand almost any text were so much a part of him now, being praised for it seemed unusually embarrassing.

"All records of his early work were copied for historical preservation, and the original destroyed, so deep was the pain of his betrayal. But this is his handwriting. Here all this time, yet unnoticed even by me. I recognize his handwriting; there can be no doubt of its authenticity. And yet, while there are extensive references to individuals known as 'Haruto' in the Library's archives, these are celebrated individuals from Earth. Poets, artists, even footballers and baseball players, even literary characters, but there is nothing from the time of Adi, although the name feels familiar to me, from my former life. As does this Maksus Stone."

"Forgive me, Author," Mwamba said, pressing fingers into his brow and pushing them outward, trying to massage away the thick knot of confusion forming behind his eyes. He moved over to where Triss was still working and picked up and waved the ragged, aging pages again as if doing so might dislodge some kind of clarity from the ink upon them. "You've confirmed this is the writing of your once–colleague and friend Adi. Yet you are saying you won't provide us with any context to these pages, despite you being mentioned in these pages and clearly knowing of his work with this *Maksus Stone* described by Adi himself?"

The Author eyed him with an air of regret and perhaps also sadness. It was an unusual emotion for him to witness within her visage, even in the long years he had known her. That the same emotion had only ever accompanied talk of her old friend. She told Mwamba there had been more to their relationship than perhaps he'd ever considered. Yet it had been her business and none of his. Until now.

"It is not that I won't, Mwamba," she said, her words like butterflies in a breeze. "It is that I cannot."

"We have spoken of Adi before though."

"We have. And there is much about him I can talk upon and remember as though they are memories of only moments ago. I have told you about the first time he attacked the Great Library and how he was subsequently banished to the darkest corner of Paperworld. I have spoken of the fact we were good friends once upon a time. But those pages you carry are from a different time, before the darkness took and twisted him. I am afraid I no longer have access to those memories."

"Do you think this is an effect of the poison you endured at Payne's hands?"

Her face swung from side to side. "No, it is not. This is something else. A protection I recognize as my own doing."

"You have purposefully destroyed your own memories?"

The note of shock in his voice reverberated around the room. It was enough for his Orb, Canopus, to react with incredulous flashes of flaming light, which caught the eye of Triss nearby, who had moved from her desk to stand near Nu, as she and the other Sages waited respectfully for the Author to continue.

"All okay?" she signed, looking from the Orb to Mwamba.

He smiled reassuringly and nodded.

"The memories are not destroyed," the Author said patiently. "I have searched my archives and can tell the records are still there. Yet they are locked. Inaccessible to me, hidden by my own design, it seems. I recognize the protection as something I have enacted myself. And although the reason why eludes me, I believe it must have been important to do such a thing."

"Could it have anything to do with this Haruto?" Mwamba asked, wafting the papers again. "It has long been known among the Sages that you and Adi were friends, scholarly colleagues in the blossoming of the

Great Library. But there were only ever two scholars mentioned in the history of this city. Only two scholars known to those who've studied the history of the Founder and the discovery of the evil of Discordia. There were whispers of others, but they were never named. This is a third, isn't it? This Haruto? He was one of your colleagues too?"

"He was, yes. The name sounds familiar, at least. But—" The Author's face glitched as she struggled to pull more data. Once more she came up short. "But I cannot determine much more than that. The memories are cast in a haze. I can tell you that I knew him once, but that is all. I'm sorry, Mwamba."

He stared with frustration at the journal entries in his hand. Haruto, whoever he might be, was clearly a key piece of this puzzle.

"Then what of the Maksus Stone? You clearly knew of it, and by these accounts, it could be of great importance to us all. Is the location of that locked in your memory vault as well?" Despite his devotion to the Book, Mwamba felt himself growing frustrated. Why—*how*—could she withhold such information from them?

Mwamba saw the faintest hint of something flash across her eyes, but the Author said nothing. *She knows something*, he thought. There was an uncomfortable knot inside his chest that was never present before when talking with her. The Author had been a constant his entire life as a Sage. He had never felt as though she was anything but open and honest with him. For a moment now, though, he could almost feel her wariness.

"Author?" he said gently.

"Mwamba," she replied. "What I'm about to reveal to you I have kept hidden since the beginning: an artifact that lies within my very foundation and has done so without context or story. I've had no reason to mention it until now. Although I locked myself away from the memories that explained it, clearly it was important enough to hide close to me. Thus, I have kept it secret all this time. But it seems the artifact I hold must finally play its part in the story of the Great Library. By the description in that journal, I think it may well be the Maksus Stone. No living person has seen this in centuries.

"Behold, outside the Portal, this is the first truly magical element to come into the possession of the Great Library!"

Mwamba felt a sudden charge in the air, akin to the sensation he felt when the portal activated for the Sages to travel. He felt the hairs on his arms stand up, and a burst of static cascaded around the chamber. His eyes widened, and he took a step back from the cascading colors. There was a sudden whirring and clicking as the cover of the Book of Wisdom seemed to warp and glow at the center, then took on a shifting, pulsating form, alternating between solid and translucent.

Mwamba longed to reach out and touch the book, to reassure himself it was still there, but he knew better than to mess with the primordial magic of the Great Library. There was still so much they didn't fully understand about the magic, but he knew better than to interfere. He glanced around and saw his companions in similar states of shock and awe, their Orbs all flashing intense excitement as the chamber lit up with magical energy.

The Book quickly gained density as the simple gold oval decoration at its center suddenly became a focal point that shone with an intense light. The gold filigree fell away, and the dome grew and emerged from the front of the Book.

As he peered closer, his breath caught as he saw glimpses in the light of ruby swirling within a blackened stone.

This is it. The Maksus Stone that Adi wrote about.

"How?!" he said as he studied the impossible coexistence between the Book and an object that would clearly not fit within the covers.

"The Portal holds many mysteries, Mwamba. While here in the Haven, I have been able to keep this relic safe from view. In modern terms, think of it as a pocket universe generated using the exotic metal that lines my very bindings, which once transported this artifact to our island untold ages ago."

Mwamba was the oldest person in the Great Library—had been here for centuries—yet he awed at an artifact that existed from the very beginning. An artifact that predated the Book of Wisdom itself.

One that had been present when the Author had been a scholar named Fairen, Suttaru had not yet turned to evil, and the Founder himself had not yet been lost. His mind, the keenest in all the Library, started thinking of the implications, about the possibilities of the connections between this stone, the Portal, and Paperworld. But there would be time for that later. For now, they had more immediate concerns.

"May I?" Mwamba asked, reaching for the piece.

"I think it's best you examine it, yes," the Author replied.

He brought it out and held it up in the palm of his hand. Canopus hovered close by, his surface silent and watchful. Mwamba beckoned Triss over to come and have a look too.

It was an incredible object. A sphere of stone, a little larger than his fist, and cold to the touch, but in a way that felt like it had once contained great warmth. Like an unlit fire on a winter's night. The stone itself gleamed as the journal described, with swirls of ruby running through the purest black.

"It's incomplete," Veer said, echoing Mwamba's own thoughts.

"So it is," Mwamba said, running his fingers lightly on the jagged edges on one side of the sphere, which had been blown out, just as Adi had written.

"The explosion broke two fragments from the stone," Mwamba said, quoting the words from the journal. "One buried itself in Haruto's chest . . ."

He looked up to the Author, who was herself peering down intently, as if seeing the artifact for the first time. Given she had barred herself from those memories, perhaps she was.

"This appears to be the Maksus Stone described in the journal," Mwamba said. "That's what you've been keeping safe this whole time. The same artifact that your friend Adi was working on when you knew him, before he was twisted by the darkness."

The Author nodded. "It seems so. The journal was right. I did take it and hide it from him."

"And it is good that you did. Yet it remains incomplete." Mwamba turned it over in the light, admiring it. "Adi seemed to place a lot of importance on this stone in the battle against Discordia. We have this piece, and we know he has another. Yet the third, I assume, remains with Haruto, wherever he went."

"I cannot answer what you are about to ask," the Author said. "I cannot recall where he may have gone. All I know is what the journal has revealed."

"Why hide the man, Haruto, but allow access to the stone? There is more to this mystery still."

"That I cannot answer, my Sages. But if anyone can find the truth of it, it is you." Mwamba saw Nu straighten at those words. A simple enough comment, but he saw the steel in their youngest member's eyes, her mouth hardened into determination. *Good*, he thought. *I'll wager we will have need of that steel before this is all over.*

But before he could respond, Triss caught Mwamba's eyes and began to sign. "We could consult the historical archive. It will hold the records of the comings and goings from the Great Library at the time. Even if he is not mentioned by name, it may narrow things down."

Mwamba smiled. The young woman had spent her entire life in these hallowed halls, and although her years were short compared to the epochs he himself had lived through—nearly five hundred years in the Library—she was proving capable and smart, as he knew she would. By asking her to accompany him and bringing her into his and the council of Sages' confidence, he was rewarding her previous assistance during Arturo's first visit to the Library. He was also seeking to open her mind to the magnitude of the Great Library, its true place in the myriad realities they were sworn to protect, and set her on the path to the brilliant scholar she was destined to become.

Clever, Canopus swirled approvingly.

"That's a very good idea," Mwamba said to Triss. He knelt and placed the Maksus Stone back on the surface of the Book's cover and watched in amazement as it again disappeared into the Book itself. This time, as the Book and the air around them reacted, he was lost in wonder at the larger revelations. As the Author absorbed the stone once more, the Haven returned to its normal serenity, though this time Mwamba noticed that the gilt layer over the visible part of the stone was no longer present on the Book, the decoration having been destroyed during its emergence. He paused before he stood and bowed his head. "Thank you, Author. This has been most remarkable, and helpful. We should perhaps have the disguise replaced until we need the stone again."

"You're welcome, Mwamba, and my machines are already crafting a replacement."

He then turned to his companions. "We have much to discuss. But first Nu, Triss, and I must go on a little adventure."

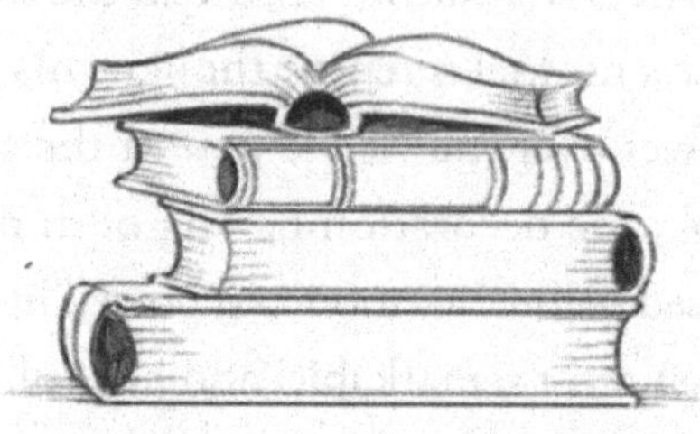

CHAPTER TEN
THE HIDDEN RECORD

Mwamba, Nu, and Triss hurried along the pristine floor at the rear of the Concourse, back toward the streetcar that would quickly take them to where they needed to go.

It had been a long time since he'd needed to visit the historical records—after all, there were perks to being the Sage of Knowledge, and perfect recall was just one of them—and he hadn't ventured as far back into the archives as the age of Fairen and Adi for centuries. He knew the Great Library held such information. Nothing was ever discarded entirely; even Adi's original notes had apparently been transcribed before the originals were disposed of, for all details great and small were valued here. But these were the oldest records and were surely buried deep in the mountain city.

They moved from the Concourse into the Quiet Quarter—where the scholar-archivists lived—then took a left halfway through and entered the domain of the Special Collections, famed for their vast rows of movable bookcases and shelves containing everything from the rarest of scrolls to the most precious artifacts of Earth's stories. A fountain pen from a famous author; an original manuscript of a celebrated novel; declarations of war and peace; a child's first hand painting, an early sign of some artistic genius.

"Remember when you got lost down here?" Triss signed to Nu.

"It's happened to us all at some point, Nu," Mwamba said, continuing to follow Canopus and Antares through the shifting gaps in the stacks as one collection closed to make room for access to another, ensuring they wasted no time losing themselves today. "My first time down here, a scholar-apprentice began to close off the row I was walking down. He hadn't bothered to check it was unoccupied. I barely made it out in one piece." He chuckled at the memory, seeing the two young women relax a little with his lightening of the tone.

Out the other side, they took the stairs two levels down, where they began to hit the rockier, earlier tunnels, filled with walls of books. The sense of going back in time was much like Mwamba remembered of his trip to the First Cave a few months ago—a place not too distant from where they were now. Except these tunnels were wider and better lit, more frequently used by those studying the history of the Great Library.

Triss had been down here before on a few occasions, fetching records for Mwamba and doing her own research. She was an incredible protégé, tenacious and trustworthy, and right now he could tell she was having trouble containing her excitement from this unusual little adventure. She was the start of something new here in the Great Library. It was a plan to hand over the day-to-day running of this city-size repository of knowledge. He'd asked his peers, and they had agreed unanimously: They needed a Principle Scholar and committee to take the place of the Sages as the governing body of this magical place. It would take years—maybe decades—to train a new cadre of scholars. Triss was one of the first.

"And here's where I had to come for the research into the original gardens at the Great Library," Triss signed, taking great delight in discussing her work with Nu. She gestured to the endless bookshelves they were walking past. "It took me a while to dig it out."

Mwamba answered, "And yet you found exactly what was needed in the end, despite the endless records kept here. It is incredible, is it not, that we're not even halfway back in our history? Such wonders never fail to astound me."

Nu looked around thoughtfully. "And the archive we're looking for is along here?"

"Close," Mwamba replied. "We'll find it ahead."

The corridor of books eventually came to a halt in a large room. It was much the same with bookshelves lining the walls, floor to ceiling, except the ceiling was a little higher than it had been previously. Mwamba could see Nu craning her neck to look up.

"How do you reach the books up there?" she asked Triss. "There are no ladders here."

"I always have one of the Volare Machina with me. I tell them what era I need and what I'm looking for, and they usually find the records pretty quickly."

Nu looked to Mwamba. "What I know of the ancient archive is that it's hidden. Few know of its existence beyond us Sages. And the occasional protégé, of course." She flashed a smile at Triss. "So where exactly is this collection of the earliest writings of the Great Library's history? Because this is a dead end."

"Ah! Well, these are the earliest writings of the Great Library *after* the Book of Wisdom was created. All these records were written and preserved by the scholars and Sages of the library once the first Sages were appointed, then stored here as part of the living history of the Library. Yet there was a time *before* the Book. Years of history when the Author was Fairen have also been preserved."

"Further?" Triss signed, gesturing around. "There's nowhere else to go, Mwamba."

With a stride to the far wall, he let his fingers drift across the rows of gold-bound spines before finding the one he needed. Hooking his finger over the top of the hard cover, he pulled it out of the shelf, opened it up, and placed his palm on one of the pages.

"Canopus," he said.

His Orb drifted from overhead, closer to his Sage's hand, before he began to vibrate. Mwamba closed his eyes, feeling the energy through the Orb's bond, pouring through him and into the book.

Except it wasn't just a book.

With a click, the entire wall of books came alive. Multiple books now slid from their shelves beside and above him, as if pulled by invisible hands. They were huge bound volumes that might otherwise have held grand drawings and images of days gone, yet these were meant for something different.

When the books looked like they might fall from the bookcase, they stopped and then spun as one until they were all horizontal.

"That was a key?" Nu said as Mwamba closed and replaced the book he'd been holding back onto the shelf.

"One specially made for the Sage of Knowledge," Mwamba replied. "Only I have access to these archives, and only I have seen them in my time as Sage. Until now. Come, follow me."

Taking care, he led them up the wall, stepping from book to book, until his head was nearing the ceiling. He turned again to the bookshelf, found the other volume of the book he'd pulled below, and did the same. This time a section of the bookshelf swung backward in front of him.

"A secret door," Nu said, unable to help the grin she wore. Antares flashed something at her, and she nodded. "Yes, this is very much in keeping with the mysteries of the Great Library."

Mwamba let her go through it first, before Triss brought up the rear, looking awestruck.

"You Sages and your secrets," she signed.

He laughed and gestured for her to go next, following behind afterward.

They eventually came across a well. A gigantic, circular wall about waist high and filled with water in the middle of a domed cave in the rock.

His companions stared at him, puzzled.

"Where are the records?" Nu asked.

Mwamba said nothing, wanting to give the Sage a chance to figure it out for herself. Nu understood and began walking around the room, first looking at the wall for more hidden levers, then she returned to the lip of the well and looked into its depths.

"You're kidding," she said. "Down there?"

"Down there," he confirmed.

Canopus hovered beside his head.

Tell me when.

Mwamba gave his Orb a grateful nod. "Go."

His companion went still for a moment, communicating with the Book of Wisdom, per procedure. There weren't many areas of the Great Library that required a direct request of the Author herself, but this wasn't one of the usual areas. This archive hadn't been seen in centuries, and Mwamba was the only Sage to have ever visited. He'd questioned at the time the need for such lengths to protect the records held here and had never been given a satisfactory answer. Knowing what he did about the Author's self-protective block on her own memories, he could imagine this had something to do with it.

Within moments, the water began to recede. There was no dramatic rush or whirlpool; it was as gentle as the tide going out. Slowly the outer walls of the well were revealed, and Triss gasped to see it was lined with more books. These looked much older than they'd seen previously.

"How are they not damaged?" she asked.

"The magic of the Great Library takes many forms," Mwamba replied, climbing over the small stone wall and onto a silver platform that had floated to the surface. He motioned for Nu and Triss to join him. "In this case, the water isn't entirely water but is a special concoction created specifically to ensure the protection from the atmosphere of these ancient tomes. Canopus has asked the Book for permission to visit a particular record." As the water dropped, so did the platform. "We'll have to be quick though. The liquid isn't held back for long to prevent the oxygen deteriorating the pages. Once we find the book, I will use my powers to draw out the information we are searching for."

"And why am I needed?" Nu asked.

"The Author had locked down her memories of this era. For whatever reason she did that, it must have been important enough to do the same here in some way. I fear the information won't be in its original form. I may need your help to pull out the truth."

They descended in silence, accompanied by the gentle splash of the watery substance lapping against the platform. As the light disappeared above, the two Orbs both began to glow and cast the well in an astonishing array of light as the titles of thousands of book spines glistened around them.

Mwamba had forgotten how beautiful it was down here. But there was no time to stare and take in the sight. They were almost there.

He began to draw on his power from Canopus just as the platform stopped descending.

"Quickly now," he urged.

Canopus sped through the air directly to the books at the left of Mwamba. There was one there with green leaves up the spine that sparkled like emeralds.

That one.

Mwamba reached and tried to extract it from the shelf, but it wouldn't budge. For a moment he wondered if he'd done something wrong, then he realized the books were held in place. One last fail-safe mechanism to unlock.

"Mwamba?" Nu asked.

"It's still bound to the bookshelf," he responded, kneeling down to concentrate. He ran his fingers over the top of it, feeling for the catch, stretching deep into the recess.

Hurry, Canopus told him.

Mwamba could almost hear the ticking of the clock in the back of his mind as time ran against them. Finally, his finger found what it was looking for. A small metal clasp at the back of the book. Not one that you had to release but one designed to respond to him and him alone.

He pressed the tip of his finger to it and held for a second.

The clasp warmed and then unlocked.

"Got it," Mwamba said, pulling the book out. He balanced it on his knee, then carefully opened the cover and placed his fingers over the first page.

His powers were not physical. They did not manifest in the same ways as the other Sages, and there was nothing Nu or Triss could see now that would indicate he was doing anything. Yet even without touching the paper, he was able to reach into the book with his mind and sort through the information contained upon the pages. He could read the words and parse the details and construct the big picture of whatever the book was about in his head, like placing puzzle pieces in his mind. This power had allowed him to read incredible amounts of books in the Great Library over the time he'd been here, more than any other visitor combined. And yet he'd still not read them all.

Including this one.

"Anything?" Triss signed beside him.

"I've . . ." He paused with a frown. "I've got something. Records of an explosion in the old scholar rooms. The name Haruto appears here too. This is of the time of the incident the journal describes. Yet . . ."

"What?" Nu asked.

"Subsequent mentions in the days following the incident have been erased. I don't know if maybe there is a page missing or something has been rewritten. There is ink upon ink, a jumbled mess. It's been deliberately tampered with."

Triss looked at him with concern. "The Author?"

"I think so. Nu, this is where I'm going to need your help. The original information is still in here somewhere, even if it's just an imprint of the original writing on the following page. I need your power to reveal the truth of what should be here."

Nu was already reaching over, placing her hand over Mwamba's. Antares dropped beside her, and Mwamba could feel the energy pour through them, as it was from Canopus to him.

"How's this?" she said, pushing her power through his and into the book.

It was like rain falling down a window, washing it clean. Quickly the obfuscation of ink was cleared, and the original words were revealed, floating to the surface in his mind:

> *Haruto left suddenly today. He had been speaking to me about following the Founder, and although nobody saw him leave through the portal, the Book of Wisdom showed signs of being used. I must surmise he used it to guide him safely into the realms beyond. Where? That I do not know. All I can say is that I will miss Haruto desperately, but for now I have bigger issues to attend to.*
>
> *Adi is furious. He says Haruto has stolen something . . .*

The platform jolted Mwamba from the story unspooling in his head. The water was beginning to rise again.

"Did you get it?" Nu asked.

Mwamba closed the book and slipped it back onto the shelf again, just as the platform was carried over it. He stood as they were taken back up to the top of the well of records.

"I got it," he said, though there was no jubilation in the confirmation.

Haruto—and the missing piece of the Maksus Stone—disappeared into the infinite possibilities of Paperworld, and there was no indication of where they might have gone. Trying to locate him would be like searching for one grain of sand within an entire continental coastline.

The Sages stood, leaned, or sat around Mwamba's reading room, their frowns lit by the flickering flames of the fireplace behind him. He regarded his friends and colleagues solemnly, making it clear he understood the nature of their predicament and what may be asked of them.

"We don't know where he is?" Veer asked, confused. "But if he used the portal, surely the Book of Wisdom would have known where he'd gone."

"The Book was in the early stages of development," Mwamba said.

"Which means?"

Nu tapped her fingers on the arms of the chair she was sitting in. "The Book didn't record everything back then. It was only later that Fairen gave it the ability to track directly into Paperworld. Before then, I don't think it had the ability."

"That's correct." Mwamba pushed down the sigh forming in his chest and straightened instead. This was going to be a challenge, but they were Sages. No challenge was insurmountable, if they worked together. "So we have some difficulties ahead of us. Now, you have heard all the information we have been able to ascertain. What do you say to our next steps?"

Maïa looked around the group. "We need to unify the stone."

"Maïa's right," Veer said. "You've told us that Adi said there was some kind of connection between that object and the darkness. I assume he meant Discordia?" Mwamba nodded, and Veer continued. "We know what happened to Discordia, and how the barrier that kept it separate from the rest of Paperworld broke down and allowed it to spill forth. Maybe this Stone has something to do with that. Perhaps it's some kind of weapon. Regardless, Adi himself said the darkness feared it. And that it might allow them to fight back."

Jin was nodding along. "It definitely sounds like something we need on our side. That and the journal. There has got to be more information in there that could help us. For example, this." She was carrying a copy of the journal pages with her and placed them on the table in front of her. As she ran her finger down one of the pages, she reached the passage she was looking for and read it aloud:

I've placed the fragment around my neck and taken to wearing it as a charm of sorts. A ward against my enemies. The dark world through the portal continues to haunt me. I hear it calling, beckoning still. Yet it is clear I must be careful of those in the Great Library too. Fairen says I am paranoid, but I know I cannot trust her, not after what happened. I will continue to wear my amulet as I must.

Jin looked up to Nu. "So the question is: Do you remember seeing it on him?"

Nu looked troubled as she stared into the distance of her mind.

"I do, unfortunately. I remember all too clearly that he wore something around his neck. Both in the times I saw him in visions and . . . at the end. In the City of Forever."

"He was wearing it when he died?" Amin asked.

"Yes."

Mwamba leaned forward, elbows on his knees, hands clasped together as he regarded the group before him. Passionate, talented, kind. They were exemplary humans and a better group of Sages than he could have hoped for. All they were missing . . . was hope itself.

"My friends," he began. "The death of our newest Sage of Hope has set in motion events that have led us to this point. We remain only nine Sages, yet I know we can handle the tasks we must set ourselves now."

Eldra, standing beside Veer and a clear foot shorter, stuck his chest out proudly. "We are ready, Mwamba."

"I'm glad to hear it, because I fear this will not be easy. As we have discussed, the Maksus Stone may well be of importance in our battle with Discordia, and we would do well to unite it. We have the sphere itself here, kept safe by the Author. Two fragments remain missing. We need to find them."

Jin frowned. "But one is on the body of Suttaru though. Nu just said so. All we need to do is—"

Mwamba shook his head, stopping her. "We have already checked. Eldra and his Orb could find nothing left at the City of Forever. Even if his body was burned to cinders by the dragon, the fragment of Stone he carried would have been left. Adi's notes made it clear it was impervious to great heat. Yet there was no sign of man nor amulet."

"Payne," Veer said, his voice a low growl. "He went back and retrieved it. He must have. Damn him. I'm sorry, friends. I should have caught him before now, but I swear to you: I will get back on his trail and find the traitor."

"Yes, I believe Payne is to blame. And I think we need to redouble our efforts to capture and neutralize him. Not only to prevent any further attacks on us or the Great Library, but because he still has the rest of the journal and now may also have one of the missing fragments of Maksus Stone—or at least may know where it is." Mwamba rose from the chair. The others who had been seated now rose too. The time for action was at hand. "Veer, return to the Orrery and see if the scholars have identified the location of the portal. From our study of the journal, we know Adi saw a dark realm beyond the portal, one that called to him. I believe that wretched place may be a base of the evil that escaped Discordia, the starting point for all the trouble. I also believe that's where the glitch is appearing, in the dark heart of Paperworld that the Author once had to seal off. Between the map and the Book of Wisdom, you should be able to find where Payne put his head above the parapet, so to speak."

Veer nodded in agreement, turned, and hurried out of the room, followed by Lynx at his shoulder. The other Sages watched him leave, then turned back to the table.

"And what of Haruto?" Nu asked. "We need to find him and that other fragment of the Maksus Stone, too, don't we?"

He took a breath and nodded. Of course she would be the one to ask. The young woman who had grown up in the Great Library was now growing before them all as a confident, purposeful Sage. Helia would have been proud of her.

"How might we do that?" Eldra asked. The Sage of Harmony looked around the room. "We don't know where he went in Paperworld, and it is vast. Among all the infinite realms, we cannot possibly hope to happen upon news of him. Especially as he traveled there so long ago."

"There is a way," Mwamba said.

"Of course you would say that," Paix said with a growing grin. "What aren't you telling us?"

"There is a myth in the realm of Silvyra of a hidden source of knowledge. A place of stored records, of a sort, that might know of the comings and goings of visitors to Paperworld. It's rumored to exist within the Great Tree that connects to the roots that extend beyond that realm to all others. It is known as the Rings of History. If there is a way to find our missing Haruto and give us a starting point to track him down, that will be where we find it."

As the Sages pondered this, Mwamba caught Nu's eye. She wasn't the tallest of the Sages, but the way she carried herself in this moment had her standing head and shoulders above the others. She was growing in confidence. And he knew what she was about to say.

"I'll go," she said.

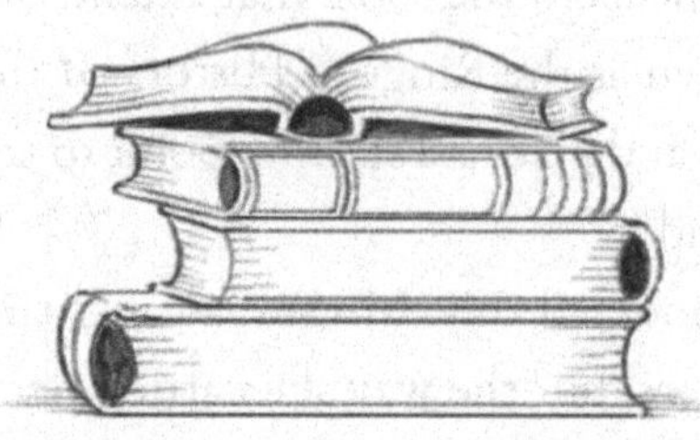

CHAPTER ELEVEN
REFLECTIONS

Arturo sat at a bright, speckled fungi table in a cavern with Robin, watching Rosa explore. He felt the shock of the day and the tension in his broad shoulders relax and let go. Watching his daughter's innocent sense of wonder was a salve to his troubled mind. He looked back around, catching a glance at Robin, a surge of memories coming back from their time in the Library. *She was intoxicating*, he thought without embarrassment. He'd been drawn to her from the first time they met, and he remembered standing close to her, searching for lost manuscripts, fighting, and fleeing from monsters trying to take over the Library. He saw her looking at him on occasion and imagined, had things been different, less life-and-death, there might have been something there. He grinned inwardly, chiding himself for thinking of such things while, apparently, the fate of the world—or worlds—hung in the balance. But still, his eyes lingered on her, enjoying her company.

It was well lit in the cavern, although there was no discernible lighting, and it had taken him a few minutes upon arriving to realize that the subtle and varied colors were pouring out of the thermal pools scattered in the rock floor all around them.

"The Pantulan Pools," Robin explained as they ate, "were discovered during the initial building of the Great Library. They were so beautiful that they built around this area, leaving it untouched while ensuring the inhabitants had access to it to bathe in its wonder. Each pool contains a unique array of bioluminescent water plants that feed on the thermal vents and light up this place."

"Not a bad place for hanging out so you can . . . What was it you called it? Check that my memories are reintegrating properly?" Arturo gave her his most-winning smile, pressing his fingers into the squidgy surface of their "table." He looked around at the other seating arrangements. All different. All natural.

"How do you feel, being here?" she asked, studying him carefully.

He met her gaze and nodded. "Fine. Good. Wonderful, in fact." He tapped his head. "All my memories seem to have returned and aren't fudging my brain. Did I pass?"

She laughed. It was like music to his ears. "The jury is still out. But yes, I've always loved this old cavern. It's near where the magic of the Great Library is strongest and has become a bit of a haven for those residents and visitors who need to rest and regather themselves. It's a quiet location, but it was never meant to be a place of solitude. I'm a big believer that one of the important ways people embolden their spirit is through connection, companionship, good conversation, and great food!"

"Well, we certainly have that," he said, gesturing to the varied bowls of fresh- and healthy-looking foods the servers had been almost constantly bringing in and replacing for the last hour.

A bakery's worth of breads, various flavored rice, at least seven different styles of potatoes, succulent herbed dips, oil-drizzled roasted leaves and stalks, and some truly bizarre, bat-shaped nuts. There was also a platter of plant cheeses Robin assured him were all grown here in the Great Library.

She helped herself to a spoonful of rice and sprinkled the rain of reds, greens, and oranges onto her plate. "Originally, this was all just rock and pools, but some visiting botanical specialists decided to help create a more natural seating area. Working with some of the research brought back from Silvyra, they utilized the thermal currents and guided the growth of the fauna and . . . Well, as you can see, it's a little unconventional. But I think you'll find you've never had a more comfortable dining experience."

Arturo let out a happy chuckle of agreement, then went back to the mouth-wateringly good flatbread he'd just dipped into the emerald-green hummus. It was hours since he'd eaten, and this veritable feast was second only to the company. This place might be underground, but it felt like home.

He ate the piece of bread, wiped his mouth with the provided linen napkin, then went in for another piece, much to the apparent amusement of Centauri, who said something to Robin.

"Hey, it's just too good to pass up." He paused, then passed the basket of bread to Robin, who took a piece herself.

"Oh, let us eat, you curmudgeonly Orb," she said. "Who knows when we'll have a moment of calm again like this."

"Not to worry, Centauri. I think I've reached my limit for one day," Arturo said. He gazed off into the distance, lost again for a moment in his recently recovered memories. Things he'd not had time to process the first time he was here but had been lingering somewhere at the back of his subconscious.

"Robin, can I ask—"

The Orb interrupted, flashing another slightly more pointed message in a variety of shapes like lightning bolts, darting in a short burst to one side.

His daughter came ambling back to the table, a flush of excitement in her cheeks. Clearly, the Great Library was more interesting than Rosa could resist.

"What did you want to ask?" Robin said.

"Nothing. It can wait."

"I think I saw another one," Rosa said.

Robin leaned forward on her elbows with interest. "Okay, and what fish did you see this time?"

Arturo didn't think she had children of her own, but he knew she was a teacher back on Earth, and clearly she had a natural talent for interacting with kids. Her relationship with Rosa these last couple of days had been a joy to see.

"It was multicolored but long, like a snake. And it had fins like horns!"

"Ah, you found the bull eel. Very good! You clearly have an eye for these things. A regular David Attenborough. Now, see if you can spot the singing fish in there. You've never seen anything like them, I promise you. They are in one of these pools somewhere, and if you find them and stare hard enough, they might just allow you to feel some of the Zen they are famous for. Trust me—it's a heck of an experience."

Rosa grinned, intrigued, and wandered off again a little faster this time.

Robin turned to Arturo. "Not everyone can see the singing fish. They take a lot of patience to find. But I bet Rosa will surprise me. As the kids probably don't say anymore, she's pretty cool. You should be proud, Papa Arturo."

"I'm just glad she's not too affected by this. I think the wonders of this place were exactly what she needed," Arturo said. He stared at the last piece of the salty and ever so slightly sweet bread on the plate in front of them and found his appetite gone. "But yes, she's amazing. A strong spirit and stubborn, yet there is goodness in her heart, and curiosity. For that, I'm grateful and proud. There is a lot of trouble in the normal world—terrible events and people. I'm proud that she is already one of the good ones."

"We hadn't intended to bring her here with you, but on reflection, I'm glad she was able to see the Great Library. She fits in. Just like you do."

He nodded, understanding what she was getting at.

"I can't explain it, but it's like coming home, Robin. Like a return to family. To the embrace of the familiar and extraordinary. Of course, that's not to say that life wasn't going well out in the world. Since my last visit, I forged a new direction in life. Found my path, so to speak. I think I owe all that to the Great Library. Without you all, I'm not sure

I'd have found the inspiration to live my life as it was intended. So, please believe me—anything I can do to help you Sages, please let me know. I have my . . . strange abilities." He grinned at the thought of his notebook and the things he'd brought to life through simply writing words. "And it would be my honor to assist in any way I can. This place, these people, it's how humanity should be back home. A world of inspiration, with champions of the positive in life. I want this for Rosa and her generation. I will fight to protect it for them. I won't stand by and let them hurt my little girl, or deny her the life she deserves."

They both watched Rosa lean over pool after pool, moving a little more quickly now from one to the next. She had her camera out, pausing with great deliberation before taking each shot, clearly fascinated by what she was seeing. He turned to Robin and said, "I hope it's okay for her to take so many pictures. I can't imagine you'd want a twelve-year-old's photo montage circulating around outside the Library."

"She's fine, Arturo. She's lucky. There's something about the Library that resists digital photography. Think of it as the Library's own security software. But film cameras are used here all the time. We probably single-handedly kept Kodak in business through the digital transition years. Polaroids are very popular here."

"Really! I can't believe you pop down to the local supermarket for film, and I bet there's no online delivery service to this island." He grinned, teasing gently in a way he knew could sometimes infuriate people. Something he inherited from his father.

"We're not completely cut off from the outside world, you know," she replied, a twinkle in her eyes as she looked back at him. "We even have movie night in the auditorium."

"Really?"

"Yes, really. All stories are of interest to the Library. Drama, both written and performed, are all part of the stories that we are sworn to preserve and protect. We even make our own popcorn . . ."

Arturo laughed. "Well, perhaps before we return home, we can take Rosa to see something." He paused, looking again at his daughter, then back to Robin. The levity disappeared from his tone. "Thank you again for saving us, Robin," he said quietly. "I think we might have been in real trouble if you hadn't arrived when you did. It's a hard thing to reconcile, as a parent, that you might not be able to protect your own daughter from the normal dangers of the world. But this . . . this is something I don't think I'd have known how to fight without these memories. I don't even know if my . . . abilities . . . would work in what I'm struggling to think of as the 'real' world."

She brushed the hair from her face, a move he found at once unconscious and captivating, and gave him a grim smile. "You would have been, yes. We've seen that Payne doesn't mess around, as the new Sage of Hope found to his cost."

"Do you know yet why Payne would want to come after me? Would he not have known I didn't remember anything about him while I was back on Earth? How could I be a threat?"

"I wish I knew, Arturo. When the message came through to Centauri from Nu and Maïa that you might be a target, I didn't stop to think. Which is good, because it meant I reached you just in time. Yet what we saw, the Unwritten man who was after you . . . It doesn't make sense. It was a blunt assault. Not like the assassination of the Sage of Hope, where dark magic was used to corrupt the weapon that killed him."

"Lucky for me?"

"Perhaps. Though I'd argue inconsistent is closer to the truth."

"Perhaps they were just hoping to draw you out or distract you somehow." They both fell quiet, thinking about the possibilities. Arturo looked back to Rosa, and he realized the reason didn't matter. Edwin Payne had threatened his little girl. He didn't get to do that. No one did. Not without consequences. He felt the anger then, the frustration and helplessness. He thought of his father and mother, and what they had sacrificed to give him food, shelter, and education. He would do the same for his child.

Two figures drew up beside the table and took the empty stools next to them. Arturo noted that both Mwamba and Nu looked pensive and weary, despite their smiles of greeting.

"The time to act is upon us," Mwamba said. "Robin, how is our visitor here?"

"His memories are settled; there's nothing untoward I can determine. I think he's fine."

"Good!" Mwamba smiled at Arturo. "Then we can proceed with deciding upon a plan. The pages you ripped from the journal, Arturo, have been authenticated as being from the journal of Adi, a scholar in the early days of the Great Library who was twisted by the darkness to become Suttaru—the same infamous figure Nu faced in the City of Forever. They have acted as a catalyst to uncover more information than we could have imagined, and they give us direction in our current dilemma. Perhaps even a possible way to defeat Suttaru and his accomplice, Payne, and the evil that drives them. So, we must thank you once again. You have been a boon to the cause of good."

"You're welcome," Arturo replied with a slight nod of gratitude. "As I was saying to Robin, I'm here to help in any way I can. I'm glad the discovery of those pages is good news."

"It is. In a way."

"Did the Author tell you more about what had happened?" Robin asked.

"She told us enough of what she could, and it's become clear that we need to recover the fragments of the broken artifact known as the Maksus Stone. That may yet be of great use to us in the coming fight against the darkness. We know it has been driving Suttaru and Payne all this time, so it is imperative we reunite the pieces and try to fix it."

"We don't know much about this darkness," Nu added. She'd been a little quiet so far, unwilling to meet Arturo's gaze. He wondered why. "But we know that it twisted Adi into becoming Suttaru and drove him to attack the Great Library . . . not once, but twice. It may be corrupting Payne as well. And there is every reason to believe that its taint is seeping through Paperworld, as we can see it impacting Earth."

"There has been a lot of climate disruption on the news," Arturo said. He glanced to where his daughter was still investigating the thermal pools, and he frowned. "And nobody can explain the sudden activity of so many volcanoes around the world. Would that have anything to do with this?"

Robin joined in now. "We were thinking that ourselves," she said. "We've been keeping a close eye on events through the Observatory, and the consensus is that the two are related."

Nu continued. "And presuming they are, it's all the more reason we need to recover the missing pieces of this Maksus Stone, as well as the rest of the journal that alerted us to its existence. There could be far more information in there that may help us use it. Workings, theories, equations. Even a sense of what this enemy has planned."

"I assume you've sent someone after them already?" Robin asked.

Mwamba gave a little nod. "The scholars located the glitch we believe was Payne using his magic. Veer, Paix, and Maïa left immediately to find him and recover the journal and the fragment of Maksus Stone he might have. We felt there was no time to lose, and with any hope, they will be back soon."

Arturo sat up straight. Here was his chance to act. For his daughter, for his world. He realized—now that he had his memories back—that this was where he was meant to be. Here, in this moment, in this strange yet wonderful place, with family and new friends.

"What can I do to help? They have threatened my daughter. I'll help in whatever way I can."

"Well, Arturo, as you heard, Veer is leading a team to recover one of the missing fragments of the Maksus Stone. We believe an old scholar named Haruto has the second."

"So we have to go find him, yes?"

"We do."

"Do you know where he went?"

The look on Mwamba's face was less enthusiastic than Arturo would have liked. "He went through the portal into Paperworld. That is as much as we know from the historical records. Nobody knows more than that, not even the Author. Where he went and what he did with the stone is what we need to uncover. Nu will be heading into Paperworld, to a realm known as Silvyra. She has been there before, and given her experience with what we face, she has volunteered to take a team." Arturo noted the look of pride on Robin's face at hearing this, and he felt the warmth of it too. Mwamba continued. "They will head to the Great Tree to find a unique source of information that could help us locate the man we need."

"So that's all good, but I'm assuming you're not just telling me for the sake of it? What of me and Rosa?"

Arturo looked to his daughter, still moving from pool to pool. Every now and then, Rosa would help herself to snacks from the bowls of food laid out on all the tables, free for anyone to partake in. She wore a smile and was even chatting with some of the other children who were observing the reflections with their families, pointing out some interesting things she'd clearly seen. There were still signs of his little girl here, beneath the surface of this growing young woman.

Which was wonderful to see . . . if not for the sense of foreboding creeping over him.

"Arturo," Mwamba said gently. "It is an unusual request, but we would like you to accompany Nu on her journey."

There it is, Arturo thought, looking between them.

Nu held his gaze in a way that slightly unnerved him. It was as if she wanted to look away, but she wouldn't let herself.

"I think we've all felt that your presence here is no accident," Nu said. "I also believe you may yet have a part to play in helping us hold back the darkness, though I cannot really explain how. I know you were brought to the Great Library in the first place by the Book of Wisdom for a reason, and that reason was to save us, which you did with your special talent. There is every chance you have returned to us now, not simply for your own safety, but because this is your path. And as much of a break from tradition as this will be, I have a feeling your path extends beyond the Great Library this time. I might have need of you on my journey. I believe it is of great importance."

Arturo blinked, equal parts excited and nervous about what was being suggested. Was he really being asked to travel to an entirely different realm beyond the one he knew to help save the world? He looked again to his daughter, then back to Nu, then to Robin.

"And Rosa?" he said.

She smiled reassuringly. "You needn't worry, Arturo. Rosa will be safe in the Great Library in the care of the Sages while you're away."

He wiped his fingers across his brow. It was a humbling request, but one he welcomed. He didn't want to leave his daughter, but there was also the matter of the darkness, the problems on Earth, and the deep-seated instinct that he couldn't pass up the chance to do more to help, as he'd felt from the moment he got his memories back. This was where he was meant to be. This was how he could help keep his daughter safe.

"Have you had one of your visions that maybe I should come?" he asked Nu. There was a brief shroud of something clouding her eyes, then she nodded.

"Something like that, yes. It's a knowing I have. We stand a better chance of doing what must be done with you there."

Robin harrumphed. "Well, I hate to be the metaphorical stick in the mud, but rest assured, *neither* of you are going anywhere without me. This isn't a mission for one Sage alone, Nu."

"I didn't think it would be," Nu said with a grin. "You and I have been traveling together for months now. I was assuming you would join me again."

"Good. I'm glad that's settled. The two of us will go and find this fragment, and we'll bring it back."

"And Arturo here, if he agrees . . ."

They all turned to Arturo now.

"Well?" Mwamba asked.

Arturo felt a shift of energy within him as he made his decision. Nu was right. This was his path.

"I'm in," he said.

Rosa's head tilted with intrigue as Arturo sat down with her on a bench.

"You're leaving me here?"

There was a touch of accusation to her tone, but for the most part, it was a simple question. One that he felt she'd appreciate a direct answer to.

"Yes. Is that okay?"

"I guess." She looked down at her shoes. "I don't mind it here. There's a lot to do, and everyone is nice. And I guess I'm going to be safe here, right?"

"You will be. I trust these people with my life."

"When will you be back?"

"Not long. Maybe a day or so?"

"What about Mom? I was supposed to call and let her know how the trip went—and start planning for my next visit to California."

"Your mom will be fine. It's safer for you here than in California. They have the means for me to call her and explain I'm taking you on another assignment, and cell coverage will be spotty. This will be hard for you, though, Rosa. We can't tell her what's happening, and even if we did, she might not understand. We're in a good place now, the best since we broke up, so let's not do anything to worry her now."

"Okay, Papa."

They were in an aisle of books just off the Main Concourse. It made Arturo feel a little anxious. The last time he'd been down here Payne had been trying to invade, and only Arturo and his notepad had stood in the way. He kept looking up at the books, half expecting a portal to open up and snapping evil faces to appear within it.

"You're going to other worlds, aren't you."

It was spoken without any kind of questioning. A statement. Arturo was suddenly very proud of her for being so readily accepting of the fantastical elements of this whole experience. It had taken him far longer on his initial visit.

"They call them realms, but yes. My friends Nu and Robin say I need to help them find somebody who can give us some information. It will help keep the Great Library safe. And Earth too. We need to make sure your mother and all your friends are protected from the bad guys. Right?"

"Can't I come too?"

He blew out his cheeks, wishing it were possible.

"I'd rather you stay here, if that's okay. Keep an eye on the place for me."

"But I want to come and see the other realms, Papa! Why do you get to go, and I don't?"

It seemed no matter the location, whether on Earth or in some mystical, magical Great Library, parenting was still fraught with guilt.

"I can't take you with me, Rosa. I don't know what lies out there, but I do know what Nu went through last time I was here. She lost a dear friend. She had to fight an army of crazed, soulless people. I believe there were also giant spiders . . ."

"Oh." Rosa visibly shivered and she took a step back. "Yeah, no thanks. I'll stay here."

Arturo nodded approvingly, the guilt growing by the second. She hated spiders, and he hated drawing on her fear to convince her to stay. But they had little time to do this, and it's not like he was lying. As much as he wanted to keep his daughter by his side, it would have been selfish to take her, putting her in harm's way. Wouldn't it?

Yes. He knew this was how it had to be.

"I promise I won't be long, Rosa. And, in the meantime, you can explore this place more and let me know of any cool things we should see when I get back. Deal?"

"Deal."

Pulling her close, he kissed her forehead, gave her a squeeze of a hug, and then stood up. At the end of the aisle, Robin was waiting, and she'd now been joined by a man with a beaming, youthful face beneath scruffy, graying hair.

Arturo led her over, and Robin made the introductions.

"Rosa, this is Sage Eldra. He and Mwamba and the other Sages are going to look after you while me and your dad are away. Nu's partner,

Triss, will also be around, too, so there will be plenty of people to entertain you. Is that all right?"

Rosa gave an enthusiastic nod.

Eldra's smiled widened as he held out his hand. "Lovely to meet you, Rosa. Robin has told me a lot about you, and I'm looking forward to showing you more of the Great Library. We're going to go and meet Mwamba and Triss now and then perhaps take a trip on the streetcar. Would you like that?"

"Sure!"

Arturo barely had a chance to ruffle her hair before Eldra gave both the adults a nod, turned on his heels, and led Rosa across the Concourse.

"You promise me she's going to be okay here?" he said quietly to Robin. "She can't get lost or wander anywhere she shouldn't?"

"This is the Great Library, Arturo, and she's in good hands. Eldra had to look after five younger brothers and sisters back on Earth. Raise them after his parents died. I might be good with kids, but if there's anybody better than him at caring for and entertaining children, I've yet to meet them." She turned to him now. "Now, are you ready for an adventure?"

CHAPTER TWELVE
A SEEKER OF REVENGE

Edwin Payne jolted awake with a start.

Suttaru's journal fell from his lap as he pulled himself upright, wincing as the ruined stone of the pillar dug into his back. The pain was nothing compared to the unavoidable sojourn into the hell of unconsciousness he'd just experienced, however. The screams still rang in his ears as he blinked away the images burned into his mind and reacquainted himself with the corrupted realm to which he'd returned.

As always, Myrtilus hovered in the air before him. The blank metallic surface made it seem like the Orb, too, was resting, but Edwin knew better. The silence from his companion was likely an accusation of weakness. Orbs were not grown to experience truly human emotions, but they had their own version. Edwin thought they should have been created only to compensate for the frailty of the Sages they accompanied. That is how he would have done it. Another sign, he thought, of the failure the Book of Wisdom and her Sages.

To him, Myrtilus seemed to actively resent Edwin for the flaw in his consciousness that allowed it to terrorize him in his sleep. Only a human would replay memories in their subconscious that would detract from their ability to function. It was a design flaw. One that had led Edwin Payne, the then Sage of Creativity, to head down this path in the first place. He stared at the Orb as he got up. They'd been together a long time; he considered them companions, even, if not actually friends, but he found himself resenting the judgment that lay beneath its metal surface.

That Edwin had only been asleep a few minutes didn't matter. Waking was always a mercy from the nightmares that had plagued him since his days on Earth. Terrors that had only grown worse with time, their roots burrowing through his thoughts and entangling themselves in his very essence.

The wife, her arm across her dying husband.

The boy crying out behind her.

His soldiers calmly raising their rifles again and again, taking lives that could have been spared.

Sweeping an arm across his brow, he wiped away the sweat that was half the dank humidity of this realm and half the essence of his own fear. Images were still burned into his mind, those of the suffering he'd witnessed in the midst of war . . . and sometimes was responsible for. It wasn't the fault of those who had been sent to war. They'd just been born in the wrong place at the wrong time, obstacles to be overcome in the name of King and Country. Some of them were passive, pleading for mercy. Others less so, fighting against their attackers, even when they were outmatched and outgunned.

It didn't matter who was who. They all ended up bloodied and dead.

Justified acts of war, old boy, is what he'd been told leaving each battlefield, returning from the fog of war to tea and medals. It was a mantra his commanding officers, who never once got their own hands dirty, had lived by. Thus, it became ingrained in his own approach, after he was given responsibility for guiding others into the fight.

Everything Edwin Payne had done for the British Empire was justified as part of the larger fight. His waking self made his peace with that long ago. Unfortunately, to his chagrin, his subconscious had disagreed. And, ever since, nightmares had tormented him whenever he closed his eyes. And ever more frequently he was also plagued by flashes of lightning in the dark spaces of his ruined eye. It came with the haunting dead, setting his nerves on fire in what felt like physical pain. A cruel taunting of his own desire to harness electricity.

All the more reason to stay awake, then, he thought, staring up at the broken towers of the city stabbing into the murky twilight skies. He wiped the perspiration from his brow and pulled his now damp shirt away from his skin. This had once been a place of collaboration and unity. Now it stood as a powerful reminder of the strength of the darkness that had been set free. A place of death.

That was the beauty of such things, Edwin considered, picking up the journal he had been rereading, trying to make sense of all it. It had not been the book of magic he had thought it might be—a charmed artifact he could wield in some way for his benefit. Instead, after months of learning to read the ancient language it had been written in—with the help of his Orb teaching him how to translate it—the revealed journal was more mundane, but hopefully no less helpful. The pages were crammed full of diary entries, reports on experiments, scribbled notes in the margins, diagrams, hypotheses, and scientific theories written by Adi—before he became Suttaru—as he'd embarked upon his fateful journey long ago and sought to harness the power of the Maksus Stone.

The latter held the most interest for Payne now. Certainly more than the troubling personal entries jotted in between the science, detailing his friendships and worries.

One passage in particular kept drawing him back. Enough that it was now burned into his mind and had led him to recover Suttaru's body, his pendant, and begin preparing a ritual in this forsaken realm.

The artifact has another property. One vastly more important than the others. I stumbled across it after testing for organic compounds, and while the results for those were negative, I discovered something altogether unprecedented.

A base energy matter within the material.

Haruto suggests it could be some form of inner spirit, a Zen-like awareness or connection with the universe. He and I have studied the same alchemic texts, and while I do not yet concur wholeheartedly, I am open to the possibilities.

Meanwhile, Fairen has suggested it could be a form of magic. Her knowledge of the religious beliefs of northern Europe show clearly here.

Still. The scientific evidence is sound. Tests and retests have shown the energy exists, dormant but tangible. If this energy can be harnessed in some way, I wonder what form that might take. What if Haruto is correct? What if this is some form of spirit energy, a building block of life, and if used in a particular way, could it actually create *life itself?*

Wouldn't that be something?

"It *will* be something," Payne said aloud, letting the theories settle again in his mind, mulling them over, assuring himself he was on the right track.

He slipped the journal inside his military-style tunic, the one he'd brought with him from Earth. He was no longer in hiding, so there was no need to blend in. Besides, it made him feel strong, reminded him of who he was.

It tightened comfortingly around his torso as he strode to the growing circle of writhing bodies in the middle of the city. So many wide, dead eyes, scratching fingers, and teeth gnashing against the shadow vines that bound them against one another. At least a hundred of them, with more being brought and added every day. The sight of their torment inspired no fear in him. Suffering was very much a part of life, perhaps the core of it. The reason. Edwin had always thought death should be celebrated more.

In Penumbris, it was.

The bridge city that sat at the heart of this realm had once been a dazzling sight. It had been built into a vast structure that connected the two very distinct hemispheres—the bridge itself had been made entirely of the purest crystals. They were now blemished, cloudy, and cracked. The city itself was also grown, the giant crystalline structures cultivated and then hollowed out and turned into buildings and towers.

Rising up and over the furious ocean waves below, the city provided a constant reminder of collaboration between humans and nature in this realm. A place for the cultures on either side to come together for trade and commerce. And this was how they existed for generations, living in peace and harmony with one another. A template for paradise, some once said, corrupted now, yet still standing.

Edwin appreciated the irony, knowing that this would be the place pure darkness would rise again.

Another one comes, Myrtilus said. *More fuel for the fire.*

Without response, Edwin turned at the sound of footsteps through the din. Another Unwritten—a giant of a man, well over seven feet tall and seemingly half as wide—with two more of his kin bound and struggling under his arms. Edwin nodded and watched as his helper thrust them down into a place in the circle that wasn't quite as full of bodies, tying them to the others and smacking away their attempts to fight his actions.

"We are close," Edwin said to his Orb. "Can you feel it?"

I do not feel. Are you sure this will work?

"It will have to, Myrtilus. This is the only way forward now. Suttaru himself has shown us the way with his writings, and now we will follow to rectify the grave injustice done to me by that infernal Book and her Library of fools."

"You witnessed it—when my nightmares grew, they did nothing." The Orb shook back and forth in the affirmative. "What, I ask, is the point in the Book of Wisdom, if it couldn't solve such a simple issue? 'You need time, and peace,' Mwamba had said—that upstart fool. As if living a long time made him wise. As though being a master of accumulated knowledge can compare to the power of creativity!" He was letting his anger get the better of him. They'd tried to help him, of course. Meditation, physical and phycological therapies that wouldn't become popular in the mundane world until the twentieth century. He hadn't needed to talk through his problems; he'd needed *magic*. And they had demurred.

Oh, they'd had their reasons, which seemed very sensible and thoughtful. But Edwin had seen through it. They were weak.

Bringing Suttaru back was a calculated risk. In the short term, it would mean the nightmares would recede, and in the long term . . . Well, they would see. Suttaru was a terrifying force, to be sure, but Edwin wondered just how much spark was left in the husk of a man left behind after a millennium or more of torment by the full force of Discordia. Suttaru had become a weapon, and nothing like the earlier voice of Adi in the pages of the journal. Adi's had been a mind on the cusp of greatness. Not as gifted as himself, Edwin thought, but close. No, hopefully, Suttaru would be the weapon he required to fulfil his own designs.

He looked back to the Orb, and they both studied the scene of bodies before them.

Using the Unwritten like this was a means to an end. Edwin had no feelings toward them one way or another. There were plenty of them still and plenty more he could craft should the need arise—there were enough desperate survivors in this realm he could turn them with empty promises of food and water.

He walked over and knelt beside the new additions. He reached out and ran a finger down the sallow cheek of one of them. A woman. Although how much of who she had once been remained, he didn't know.

"You should consider yourselves honored to be a part of this moment," he said, as though gently admonishing one of the soldiers he remembered being in his charge, long ago. "This is the turning of history and the future. A chance to regain what we lost and make it whole again."

He felt hope at the thought and had to smile at the irony of it.

Edwin felt Myrtilus bobbing impatiently at his shoulder. He rose again and tapped the bottom of his hollow left eye. The Orb obeyed, shrinking before him until it was the right size to embed itself into his empty socket. The cold of the metal bit against his skull, delicious with its agony, reminding Edwin that he was alive. Powerful. And nearing the completion of his goal.

The Unwritten woman at his feet suddenly stretched out to grab his leg, but he saw that her arm ended in a ragged stump, long lost to one of the many creatures that roamed these wastelands.

"I think not," he said, kicking her away.

In the months since his attack on the Library had failed, he had sought to experiment with his powers to expand his army. To secure his own safety in the absence of Suttaru.

He had long ago learned to push his magic outward a little, putting the strain on his Orb to create a field of exposure that allowed him to transform others. It had worked well on that sniveling lacky, Tywich, in Silvyra. He'd also employed it on some of the corrupted, turning them into hounds, transforming them in a similar way to his own abilities. They were subpar versions of his own flaming alter ego, of course, but it still made them more useful, and more dangerous, when needed.

Yet it wasn't enough. And so he'd looked to Suttaru's journal for information to help enhance his ability. It had been while studying these ancient texts that he had not only discovered he may have a chance of resurrecting his mentor, but he had also discovered passing mentions of other magic he could call upon and wield—such as the ability to speak through any being he had corrupted, from whatever distance.

That had worked well for the assassin who ended up dispatching the new Sage of Hope. It disintegrated the host, but that was a meaningless price to pay to be able to let him taunt the other Sages and let them know the Mexican writer would be next. To lure them into his trap.

This was war now. The Library knew they were under attack. All that mattered now was that Edwin could fulfil the next part of his plan: not only expanding the army that right now were bringing him the subjects he needed for the ritual but to resurrect the man who had come so close to destroying the do-gooder Sages before.

The man—the thing—who would do it properly, next time.

It was evil's will. And Edwin intended to honor the voice that had requested this of him. The voice of an entity with a drive for destruction, and the ability to bestow upon Edwin Payne more power than he could ever imagine.

The power to fix his nightmares once and for all. The power to enact revenge on the Sages who had abandoned him all those years ago. But it would require the right amount of daring, guile, and luck. He needed to make himself indispensable, trusted, and then he could look to exploit those weaknesses to enact his own great plan.

First, he could conquer the Great Library; then he would destroy the Book of Wisdom and sever their connection to Paperworld, the infernal place. He looked around at the dark skies and destruction and shook his head. If he could move the pieces to his satisfaction, he might just save his world from both the depravities of Discordia and sanctimonious meddling of the Great Library.

Edwin let his eyes drift back over to the circle of wretched, barely alive bodies as they gravitated toward one another.

It is time to go to the ritual site, he thought.

And he smiled.

CHAPTER THIRTEEN
INTO HELL

Veer stepped warily through the portal, Maïa and Paix close behind him. Their Orbs hovered along at their shoulders. None of them were sure of what awaited them.

A blighted landscape, Lynx had warned him only a few minutes ago, drawing what little information the Book of Wisdom had been able to glean about Penumbris through the portal as it opened. *Corruption*.

"Death too," Veer muttered, covering his mouth against the stench in the air as his feet crunched into what felt like rubble. Having no survey of the realm, the Sages wore sturdy boots and their travel cloaks over practical clothing. Generic and hopefully nothing that would cause culture shock. It was pitch-black, and the air was suffocating in its density. Stale. Burned. He could immediately taste ashes on his tongue and grit between his teeth. His nose wrinkled at the stink of it.

He blinked as Lynx lit up in a glow and then grunted as he realized they had appeared inside some kind of building. Crumbled bones were scattered like snow across the floor, piling up in drifts at the walls. He was standing in a pile of them. Moving his boot as the others came through, he felt the remains disintegrate in puffs of dust around his legs.

"Careful now. Go over there."

He let Maïa and Paix step past him, the two women a study in contrasts. Maïa, with her flaming red hair and tall, acrobat's physique, with the confidence and daring to go with it, as had been frequently demonstrated in perilous circumstances over the years. Paix, on the other hand, was shorter, with close-cropped hair and a burning, coiled sense of energy about her, much like the electricity she could manipulate. She was still out to prove herself in every task she was given, not because of self-doubt but rather the intense desire to be of service. They predated him as Sages, and he was aware of their accomplishments. He was in awe of them, and in that moment, he felt the weight of the mission and the responsibility of leading this group, then followed them to a clearing in the midst of the human remains.

"Grim," Paix whispered.

"You're supposed to be the Sage of Joy," Maïa said. "We're relying on you to make us see the best of everything."

The little lock of white hair that rose from Paix's closely cropped head shook from side to side. "Oh, Maïa, there can be nothing good to be found in a place like this."

As Veer's eyes adjusted, he saw they were in a small, windowless room, with a door to one side. The walls were dried, packed mud that was scorched black. They curved upward to the ceiling in a way that might once have felt as though they were embracing whoever might have used this room. To Veer, now they seemed looming, menacing. The human remains were everywhere. Too many people had died in there.

Ancient the remains might be, but it still made his stomach roil as if he were trapped within the bowels of a ship in the midst of a storm.

Paix was still looking around, growing increasingly unsettled. She wrapped her scarf around her mouth, her eyes scanning for danger, wide with concern.

"*Chilling.* I think we are underground. Are we underground?"

"We are," he said.

Maïa nudged his ribs. "She has a touch of claustrophobia about her, remember?"

"I remember, but we need to make sure it's safe to move first." Veer looked to Lynx, then stretched out his fingers, channeling his power through the Orb. Together they touched the air, connected with its essence, and Veer felt his way through the stagnant motes hanging around them.

His eyes remained open, but he wasn't seeing anything externally. The sight was inward. Almost like sonar, he had always thought. A way of exploring his immediate surrounds without moving an inch.

He sought movement. A drift of air. A current that might either indicate danger or a way out.

A tinkle in his internal senses spoke of something not too far away. A light, constant motion that suggested nothing more than a breeze.

He put his hand on Paix's shoulder and nodded toward the door at the far end of the room. "Let's not linger. We seem to be alone for now, as far as I can tell. Whatever this place is, we should try to get out and up to the surface to get our bearings."

"What do you think happened here?" Maïa said.

Veer paused in the doorway and looked back. "Nothing good. And I bet it doesn't get much better up top. Steel yourselves, my friends."

They moved quickly into the next room. This one had odd, rusted implements around the walls, like some kind of kitchen area. There were still skeletons here—a couple bent and twisted around each other in one corner, as though seeking comfort when whatever happened had happened.

Veer tried to keep Paix's eyes up and facing the front, toward the steps he could see winding up in a circular well in the wall. The tingle in his fingers grew stronger. Fresher air—if there were such a thing in this realm—lay ahead and up.

Maïa paused again, and he let out a sigh.

"What now?"

"Should we explore here, lest we miss information that might help our cause, Veer? Get a sense of where we are. Perhaps it could yield a clue as to where our quarry and that journal may be."

"I think whatever happened here was a long time ago, and it didn't end well for those who sheltered within these walls. The air here tastes old and still. It hasn't moved in some time, which means Payne hasn't been here. Only dust and death. Time itself has forgotten this place. Let's make sure it doesn't forget us along with it."

He pushed ahead. The stairs were cut into the ground. The lips were crumbling, but they held enough for the three pairs of boots to carry the Sages upward. They reached heavy metal shutters shut at an angle and locked with a thick, round padlock. From the inside. It seemed incongruous, to Veer, that here in a different realm he was looking at an object that could just as easily be from his own world.

He let his fingers work their magic. He pulled at the air, teasing and rolling it into a thin wisp, then guided it into the keyhole. Closing his eyes, he felt the mechanism inside. Not that different to anything he'd come across on his travels before, although this was the first time he'd felt wary about succeeding in picking the lock.

He cracked the lock within a few seconds though. The lock snapped open and fell away, and Veer redirected his powers to nudge one of the doors open, only for it to break from its hinges.

With a loud screech, it fell away. Toward them.

Veer cursed and manipulated the air enough to push it away. It tumbled past, inches from his face, and dropped down the stairwell with a series of horrendous smashes that echoed into the gloom.

"Not very discreet," Maïa noted, a trace of humor in her voice.

"Would you have preferred I let it hit you?"

"Wouldn't have been nearly quick enough to catch me, my dear."

She smiled and pushed past him, leaving Lynx vibrating with what seemed like laughter at his Sage.

Meanwhile, Paix was moving quickly ahead, now that she could sense escape from this tomb.

"Oh, sweet freedom," she called back, climbing up the last few steps. "Please, let's not do that again. This may be a ruined realm, but whatever is up here cannot possibly be as bad—"

As Veer climbed out after his friends and their Orbs, he felt the very tangible recoil of horror from Paix and Maïa shake the air around them. Just as powerfully as he felt the tremor within himself at the sight that greeted them.

It was like a visual shock wave. A gut punch of corruption.

They stood on the edge of a cliff. Lynx had badly undersold it. This wasn't simply blighted. This was the purest visage of despair Veer had ever witnessed. Clouded skies hung low and dark like a shroud over a desolate landscape. The surface of the pockmarked hills and valleys was rough and uneven, like torn strips of rotting skin stitched together. It was a realm so devoid of any semblance of good he felt himself grow sick at the thought of remaining here one minute longer.

The underground shelter they had arrived in was hunkered within a sharp plateau they now stood on. A rising ziggurat—one of many he could see dotted around the landscape before him—stood high among what were possibly once fields of crops, swathes of forests, and a winding system of rivers and lakes feeding it all. Lynx had mentioned something earlier: The Book had informed him this realm had likely been a paradise long ago, before its corruption by Suttaru. But in the records of the Library, they had found no references to this place, almost as if it had been closed off to their portals and the other realms. Veer could almost sense the beauty this place might have held.

But this?

He had traveled across so many realms of Paperworld and had not once expected to find anything so horrifying.

"I think I want to go back inside again," Paix said.

Veer didn't blame her.

Here and there he spotted markers of the old civilization. Gray smudges of ruined towers collapsing into one another. Strips cutting across the land that might once have been paths or roads. A giant curved rib cage stretching into the sky, the remains of long-dead land giant mammals that would have roamed the land.

Very few signs of active life, except for one or two distant flickering lights. One, to the right of the plateau, seemed larger than the others. Perhaps a collection of smaller lights. It was also the closest to them.

"Settlement?" he asked Lynx.

The Orb conferred with his companions. They formed a vertical triangle in the air, and three sets of intricate patterns danced across their surfaces as they spoke. Suddenly, the lights from the Orbs coalesced in the center of the triangle, and a directional map of the settlement formed from magical luminance showed them the way.

Yes. About a five-hour walk.

"We should try there first."

Maïa leaned into him and spoke quietly. "You think that is a good idea, Veer? Look at this place. We cannot possibly trust anybody we meet to help us. Rather, the opposite may be true. Anybody we find here could be a danger to us and a threat to the mission. To survive in a place like this would be harder than we could imagine.

"You are well-versed in tracking Payne after all these months. Can you not just find his signature in the air? Or use those tracking skills your father taught you, the ones you go on about endlessly in your foragers' classes at the Library?" She stared at Veer, straight-faced, but Veer could see the humor glinting in her marvelous eyes.

"I'll have you know, *my dear*, that the foraging teams line up for those classes." Veer managed to affect a haughty look, and his companions smiled at his attempt to lighten the mood. "This isn't exactly like tracking through the Pacific Northwest. It's going to take all my skill and Lynx's help to find what we came for. That said, when Payne attacked the Great Library with his army of Unwritten devils, I got a good sense of his pattern. It's like a fingerprint in the air, and I should be able to sense it if we get close enough to him. Even mundane prints in the earth will give me a signature to follow. And a legion of monsters such as the horde that was unleashed on the Library would likely not be able to escape the notice of any wretches who still call this place home, don't you think? Some in these settlements might have seen or at least heard whispers of his movements, or even lost loved ones to those armies."

"And if they haven't?"

"I will use my powers to try and find his trail, and the Orbs will scan. Between us, we might find a direction to head toward next. We need that journal, and I want Payne. He will pay for his transgressions, and we owe it to all of Paperworld to remove one of our own who has caused harm to so many."

Maïa drew her thick, woolen cloak around her tightly, as though for protection. "Let us be quick, please. I don't wish to stay here any longer than we must. Agreed?"

Veer and Paix nodded. "Agreed."

"What's that burning light over there?"

They had made their way down the right-hand side of the plateau, heading for the settlement the Orbs had shown them. The steps were cut into the outside of the cliff, and as they rounded the corner, Paix suddenly pointed to a thick black smoke in the distance that sat heavy over the horizon. Beneath it was a thin glow. It was far away, yet Veer could feel the heat of it smothering him.

"Fire," he said, flexing his fingers to seek more information through his power to interpret and manipulate the air and wind. The air held clues to so much nobody else noticed. It was normally difficult to distinguish details the farther away something was situated. Yet in this case, the fire was significant. "It's huge. Perhaps an entire forest. From the strength of it, I'd say it's been burning a while. We should try to avoid heading in that direction, if we can help it."

As they left the plateau and reached ground level, they found a crumbling path stretching through the wiry weeds and made their way along it as fast as they dared. Veer sensed each of them wanted to go as quickly as possible, yet they knew there was danger here—of the known and also of the unknown.

"Did you feel that?" he asked the others about an hour into the walk as he felt a rumble under his feet. "Earthquake?"

"I felt it too," Paix said.

The three Sages and their Orbs kept marching onward, heading in the direction of the settlement. Would there be some kind of clue there to Payne's whereabouts? Veer felt sure it was the best place to start looking, but in truth, he was grasping at straws a little. There hadn't been much to go on when they'd set off. The journal had alerted them to the existence of this realm, giving them a place to start. The Book of Wisdom had then been able to fill in a few more of the missing puzzle pieces. But even the Author had little to go on when it came to this place, other than whatever darkness had claimed this realm first. Veer remembered what she said.

"If it was like the other realms of Paperworld, it had likely once been teeming with life," the Author told the gathered Sages back at the Great Library, her face shimmering above the open Book of Wisdom. A moment of solemnity and majesty, and one he always looked forward to whenever the time was right to speak with the Author. Except this time the news had been unsettling. "A paradise, like the other realms, until something transformed it. A twisted force must have found its way there and ruined it."

"Survivors?" Veer had asked, knowing he was going to have to venture here even then.

"Some, I believe. But in what state they are in now, after what must be so many centuries since their world was twisted, I cannot say."

In this blackened world, Veer continued to worry about that last part. He'd seen the corruption at Bloom. The way it had taken and turned those people into . . . Well, he still wasn't sure what they were. Husks of humans. Soulless ghouls. Dark demons. Their life stories unspooled.

The Unwritten.

Now, at least, he could understand where such creatures may have evolved from. He licked his drying lips, staring around at the ruined land. It was like evil itself had gnawed away at it, like a rat at a corpse, leaving only bones as evidence of what had once been—clues to this realm's supposed glorious past.

Crumbled walls that stretched for miles indicated many more ancient townships and even cities than they'd seen from above. Beyond the boundaries of the roads, half-fallen beams and rotten frames that might once have belonged to windmills hung limp, waiting for their inevitable collapse. Strange machines with empty trailers sat like rusting carcasses in fields, wind whistling in low, mournful moans through the deteriorating metal shells. It sounded like a warning. *Run, while you can!* Perhaps the people here had been farmers, once tending to their crops. Veer rubbed the grit in the wind between his forefinger and thumb, and grimaced. He couldn't imagine anything good growing here now. Whatever happened had been all-encompassing; it was entirely barren, as far as he could see. Nothing was on the horizon for miles but ruins, rotting forests, and the gigantic bones stretching into the sky.

"I think we can agree this seems exactly like the right realm to find Payne." Veer brushed his forefinger and thumb down either side of his mustache as he walked, taking care to watch for danger as much as regard the blighted landscape into which he'd brought his team. "It's rotten to the core."

Veer's Orb glowed softly in agreement, orbiting just above them, high enough to make sure they weren't going to be surprised by anything, but low enough not to draw any further attention.

"This place stinks," Paix muttered, close to Veer's left.

Veer nodded. He himself was particularly sensitive to air wherever he went. That had been his talent, back on Earth, leading to him working with the US government on developing wind energy in the late 1950s. One of the "wind electricians," as engineers had once been called, he'd found that beyond the aeronautical design and investigations into blade materials for the turbines, he'd simply had a talent for being able to locate them to maximize their efficiency.

Yet despite his engineering accomplishments, his real passion lay in the outdoors. Always had. Being outside so much, perhaps he'd grown to understand how things worked where so many others couldn't. How air flowed across a landscape. The shifting currents within weather patterns.

Knowing where it would be strongest and, thus, where best to harness it.

Here the air was thick and clammy with threat. Sickly. A nauseating feeling seeped deeper into his skin with every breath they took, as though the atmosphere sought to taint whatever unfortunate creature moved through it.

"I might just have to hold my breath until we leave," Paix said, wrinkling her nose and wrenching her hand away from a thicket of thorns as they pushed through a narrowing stretch of the road. Maïa remained silent, but by the slight creases on her porcelain-white brow, Veer could tell she was contemplating doing the same. And given her mastery of her physical form, she might actually be able to do that.

"Let's just keep it together awhile longer, okay?" he said. "We're Sages. We can put up with a bit of a smell, I'm sure."

Paix pulled a face. "A *bit of a smell*? I'm worried if we're here too long we're going to be cast out of the Great Library when we go back. Our clothes will be held to account for crimes against humanity."

He couldn't help but laugh at that, even as the act drew in more of this rancid air than he would have liked.

"As long as we get the journal, sort out Payne, and escape here unharmed, Paix, I'll gladly take whatever criticism they want to bestow upon us."

"You really think you can track him through this place?"

"I do. But we're going to have to work for it. I can't imagine Payne or the journal will present themselves easily."

Veer almost hoped they wouldn't. He'd been working to catch the bastard ever since the attack on the Great Library, and it would be anticlimactic if he didn't have to put some work in now. Payne had succeeded in his attempt to sow destruction within the hallowed halls and had escaped capture so far.

It was a matter of pride now that Veer beat the Rogue Sage and drag him back to answer for his crimes.

He wasn't leaving this realm without him.

CHAPTER FOURTEEN
OLD FRIENDS

Nu stepped out onto the branch of the Great Tree and into a pool of afternoon sunshine filtering through the leaves above. The wind was fresh and gentle, wrapping her in its embrace as though welcoming her home. She closed her eyes briefly and breathed in, sighing contentedly at the vibrant scents that hinted it had not long rained here. It mingled, of course, with wafts of spices and sweet-smelling baked goods from the stalls wrapping around the trunk.

Even as the others stepped through the portal and landed in Silvyra beside her, she held fast to this moment. Inhaling the aromas of this magical place. Listening to the pleasant chatter from the markets and the excited chittering and occasional whistle of the flying squirrels overhead.

It seemed that wherever she traveled in Paperworld, such small, simple joys were the most pleasing. They were all that was precious about life.

"Here we are again, Antares, just like our first journey together. Let's hope this one has a bit less excitement!" Nu's Orb rotated in amusement, flashing of golden light like laughter on the Orb's surface.

It was a happy moment, but there was an element of the bittersweet to it too. This was the first time they had returned to Silvyra since being here with Helia.

How things had changed since then.

Nu gently touched her fingers to the Orb. "We need to find that fragment to make sure it stays that way. Whatever it takes. Okay?"

Agreed.

Beside her, Arturo was staring in wonder. He let out a soft, "Wow," under his breath as he looked at their surroundings with the same kind of excitement Nu must have had on her first trip here. He scratched his short black beard, grinning and whispering to himself in Spanish as he spun in a circle, taking it all in. "I had thought the Great Library was a place of much magic, but *this* is something else."

Nu smiled as Robin nudged him.

"Keep it together, man. If you wander around looking like you just arrived here from another world, it's going to make our lives harder."

"Am I allowed to take notes at least?" He patted himself down, running his hands over the local tunic they were all wearing, before sighing. "Wait. Never mind. I think I left my notepad and pen back at the Great Library."

"Probably for the best," Robin said. "Now you can live in the moment. Be present. We're going to need your eyes and ears on this journey too. Okay?"

"You can count on me," he said, nodding at the pair of them.

As they began walking, a giant bee suddenly lifted into the air before them from a hole in the branch. Its wings buzzed loudly, and it tilted its enormous round head at the visitors before soaring up into the sky. Little drops of dappled light fell from its fur as it passed overhead, showering them in Silvyran pollen.

Arturo held out his hands to catch the pollen, watching the droplets roll over his skin.

"Incredible. Just incredible."

His awe was almost tangible. He'd already lowered his voice, as Robin had asked, and she knew he could handle whatever this trip threw at him. His years of experience as a parent, and his heroics during the attack on the Great Library, made him the kind of man one knew they could trust.

"There is far more to come," Nu assured him. "Who knows where this mission is going to lead us."

Robin brushed some pollen from her sleeve, nodding. "She's right, Arturo. This realm is a wonder, truly. Simply being here on the Great Tree is often enough to melt your brain, but just wait until you see the airships drifting from the upper branches in the moonlight or look down upon the Maze as the sun sets and the shadows take hold."

"You are both very fortunate," Arturo replied, eyes still trying to take in every detail as they strode along the branch. "To travel as you do, explore new realms that exist in a way beyond my imagination, I'm sure. As Sages, the fact you get to witness such things is a true honor."

"One of the many honors of being a Sage," Robin agreed. "You would think it would be easy to take it for granted given how long some of us take on the role. But honestly, I will never get over the magic of it. Living and working among some of the most creative, inspiring minds at the Great Library. Getting to visit wondrous worlds. Being held to the standard of what a Sage needs to be—a protector, a guardian, a beacon of inspiration. Every day I wake up excited about life."

Arturo glanced over to her. "Your excitement was one of the first things that struck me about you when we met. I wish I were more like you."

"Oh, you are, Arturo dear. Deep inside, everyone has the capacity for it. Sometimes it's right there on the surface, and sometimes it's not that easy to find. You need to dig deep and find what works to bring it out."

"Well, this is working for me!"

Nu put her hand on Arturo's shoulder. "Trust me. I felt the same when I first arrived here. It's actually the same every time I visit a new realm, as it should be. The magic. The wonder. I hope we never get used to feeling it." She took in a breath, concentrating on her surroundings once more. The sounds of activity. The scents of nature. The feel of the rough bark beneath her soft-soled slippers. All of it helped to center herself. It was something she had grown used to doing these last six months. "Now, our mission is in two parts. We need to find that missing fragment of the Maksus Stone and the man who took it. To do that, we need to locate that local repository of information."

"The Rings of History," Robin said.

"Exactly. And the second part of our mission is to update the Chief Scientist at the Great Tree as to the danger that brings us here. There is a chance that both of these can be accomplished by going to meet the Chief Scientist."

Arturo was still staring at everything as if he'd just been born. "So how do we do that? Where is this scientist person?"

"Oh, well, the last time we were here we simply arrived and requested an audience." Nu looked to Antares inquiringly. "We could do the same again, I guess. But maybe it would be best to check in with my old friends first. It would be wonderful to see them again, and they *do* hold some sway here now, after they helped save the realm before. We might find our progress a little quicker that way." She glanced at Robin. "What do you think?"

Robin had become a mentor to Nu since they lost Helia, and Nu understood she was growing beyond such mentorship, but Robin was her friend, and she welcomed her advice.

Robin seemed to understand. She nodded in approval of the plan. "I think that's a good idea. Your friends might know where we can start looking for the Rings of History, or, at the very least, they should be able to guide us to where the Chief Scientist can be found."

With a subtle gesture, Robin beckoned for her quietly bobbing Orb to cloak itself, which it did. The Orb hovered over her shoulder before becoming almost invisible, just a shimmer in the air. Nu didn't even have to look at Antares before feeling her own Orb similarly hide, growing smaller and nestling snugly into the bracelet she wore around her right wrist.

She caught Arturo staring with raised eyebrows at the pair of them. "Few know who we are here. It's best we remain discreet, at least until we find my friends," she explained.

"Okay, discreet, understood. And who are your friends?"

"Two of the bravest souls I know," Nu said proudly. "Fierce and loyal and clever and capable. If anybody can help us, it'll be them."

Finding Dzin had been easier than when Nu and Helia had chased him and his brother through the Great Tree's Maze, after the attack on him and his fellow apprentice Runners, but it still took a combination of their Orbs scanning the area and some questions asked of local stallholders and passersby to locate him. Things had changed since their last visit, when the old laboratory and archives had been burned down, and the refinery destroyed. The Chief Scientist had ordered operations to be rebuilt in more protected areas, which meant everything had moved inside the central trunk of the Great Tree.

Every person they talked to was also quick to gossip of how the sickness was affecting the Tree.

"Perennia flies day and night now, watching out for us," one old lady said of the dragon. Her back was crooked, but her smile and eyes were lively. She leaned over her table of glory bakes, each one with a little cloud of sugarweave sitting astride the golden crust. Nu tried to not let herself be distracted, as the sweet smell was causing her stomach to growl. "Yet although our skies are protected once again, the same can't be said of Mother. We are told not to worry, but who knows what that means anymore. Her roots are black! Would you believe it? They say it is not rot, but then what might it be? It spreads with each passing of the moons, and although the Tree continues to bloom, the colors are muted." The old woman tilted her head at the three of them now. "As surely you must have seen on your arrival here?"

"Yes, of course," Robin said quickly and slipped some pearls onto the table before the woman could ask any more questions. "Now, we'll take up no more of your time. Three of your delicious honey-plum biscuits, please. It's been quite a climb, and we're in need of replenishment. This one here is close to fainting!"

Arturo's eyebrow lifted as she pointed at him, but Robin thrust one of the treats into his hand before he could protest. They quickly asked for directions to where the laboratory for Botanical students had moved to and then hurried off up the stairs around the trunk in the direction she indicated.

In the end, it was the smoke that gave Dzin away—a curl of gray cloud that drifted from an open porthole window in the central trunk that caught Nu's attention, alerting her to the presence of an experiment going very wrong.

She peered through the opening to see a bark-skinned young man in a tunic dancing around in a circle and bumping into to a desk full of vials of all kinds of colorful liquids. Nu grinned. A whole host of feelings flooded her—some bittersweet, others terrifying—but chief among them was the warmth of seeing an old friend again. Then she saw the panic he was in, the smudge of soot across his face, and the flames engulfing his cloak. Her smile faded, and she cried out, "Dzin!?"

He looked up in surprise from where he'd been trying to put himself out. His eyes, magnified by round glass goggles, widened as he recognized Nu, and he gave her a wave, even as he pulled his cloak clean off and started doing a jig on it to stamp out the flames.

"This is the guy who's going to help us save the universe?" Arturo asked quietly.

Nu waited as Dzin waved away the two guards standing at the mottled moss doors, striding between them to give her a huge hug. His arms wrapped around her back, squeezing tightly.

"Oh, Nu, it's so good to see you again." Then he stepped back and admired her. "You seem taller somehow. More grown." He smiled and then gestured for them to follow him along a corridor carved through the wood and into a side room, opposite to where he'd been experimenting. There was an oval table in the middle and boxes of empty Elixir of Life vials stored around the outside. "It's such a surprise to have you visit like this! Is Antares here too? Don't worry. We're safe in here, away from prying eyes and open ears." He jumped as Antares sprang to life from her hiding spot and grew to hover before Dzin, flashing her own greeting. "Oh, you *are* here! It's good to see you too, Antares. And I see you brought friends?"

Robin held out a graceful arm as Centauri similarly uncloaked above her. "The Sage of Love," she said as Dzin took her hand in greeting. "I'm Robin, and it's a pleasure to meet you, Dzin. I've heard so much from Nu about your exploits together, and I must say, you are everything I expected."

"I hope that's a good thing," he said.

Robin laughed, putting him back at ease. Nu loved that about her friend. She had a natural energy that poured from her with a look or a laugh and instantly made everyone around her feel better. Nu supposed that's what drew Centauri to her in the first place.

"It's all good, I promise, Dzin," Robin said, then turned to Arturo. It was his turn to step forward. "And this is our friend Arturo. A writer. Or scribe, as I think you know them here."

"A pleasure to meet you," Arturo said, giving the scientist a firm handshake.

Dzin stood a little taller and nodded. "Lovely to meet you, Scribe Arturo."

"Just Arturo is fin—"

The group was startled by a commotion outside the room as the main doors blew open and heavy footsteps clomped in, accompanied by a string of muttered curses in dialects Nu couldn't possibly hope to understand.

She recognized the voice though.

The towering figure of Rascal strode through the doorway, half hidden by a stack of heavy wooden crates rattling with more empty Elixir vials. Her face was covered, so she didn't see the four people already in the room.

"Blasted bangnips and sordid snafoos," she cursed as she caught her thigh on the table and almost lost the entire tower she was carrying. "I should be flying! Not being ordered about on tasks that anybody with half a mind could do. If I ever catch that dog-bastard Payne, I'll chew his face off for what he did to the fleet. Leaving me to pick up the bloody pieces."

Struggling to bend down, she dropped the crates with a crash, shoved the tower up against the others, and wiped a meaty forearm across her cheeks.

It was only when she turned around that she saw Dzin. "What are you doing here skulking around, Advisor Dzin? I thought you'd still be at your experiments when I got back! You could've warned me you were—"

Dzin coughed and inclined his head toward the other three people and two Orbs in the room, at which point Rascal's gaze found Nu, Robin, and Arturo. Her puzzled expression took them in one at a time, before she did a double take and her eyes fixed back on Nu. Her entire face lit up like sunlight breaking through a storm.

"Rot and roots! You came back to us, Nu!"

Nu barely had time to react before she was scooped up and lifted a clear foot off the ground in a hug that did its best to squeeze all the breath from her body. Her face pressed close against the thick collar of the woman's brown jacket, her mouth barely able to form words of greeting. She hadn't seen the formidable former Runner since their celebrations after defeating Suttaru at the City of Forever, and it made her heart glad to be in the brash warmth of Rascal's embrace.

Rascal finally loosened her grip and placed Nu back on the floor. Nu felt the blood rushing back into her limbs. Antares rushed around her head checking if she was okay. She waved him off.

"It's good to see you too, Rascal!"

She once again introduced Robin and Arturo and Centauri, and Rascal gave each a beaming smile.

"Well met, all of you," she said, scratching at her shoulder. One of her wings twitched beneath her jacket, as if itching to be free. "Now, as much as I love a surprise visit from an old friend, I'm guessing you Sages wouldn't have traveled here without good reason?" She looked Arturo up and down. "And certainly not accompanied with an Orb-less interloper like this good-looking specimen here. Sir, *you* are as beautiful as Bravadier Blossom and twice as delightful. And, believe me, the famed first captain of our airship fleet and the pilot of the *Wanderer*—a ship more famous than our own *Golden Oriole*—is said to have broken more hearts across these lands than there are stars above them."

Arturo's face was caught between a smile and a look of concern. He took a step closer to Robin, blushing profusely. "Um, thank you?"

"You're welcome!" She slapped him on the shoulder, a hard impact that rocked him backward. Robin put her arm around him to hold him steady as Rascal beamed around the room. "Now, let's stop nibbling at the edges of whatever this is with pleasantries. Or, as my mother used to say, 'Let the seeds tumble out and grow where they may.' What gives? Why have you returned with your friends, Nu, and how can Dzin and I help this time?"

"It's a long story," Nu said. "How about we tell you on the way?"

Rascal's smile held, even as her eyes narrowed. "On our way where?"

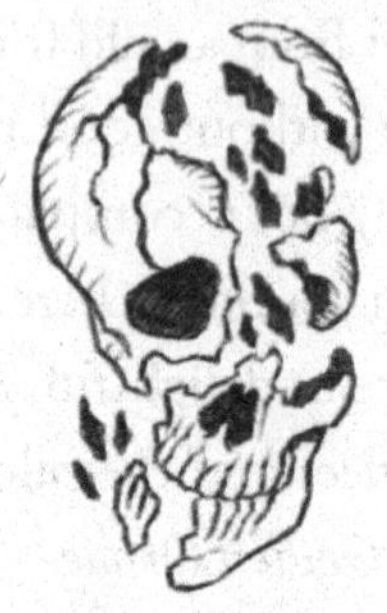

CHAPTER FIFTEEN

A HISTORY WRITTEN ON THE WALLS

Veer and his team found the first of the corrupted hounds about halfway to the settlement.

The walk until then had been uneventful, though uncomfortable, in the oppressive conditions. Even for Veer, the air was hard to push through and offered little relief from their exertions. The ground was cracked and uneven underfoot. In places, the thickets of thorns built up on both sides and encroached upon the path. Veer had to tear them apart at one point to allow them to continue without a significant detour.

Then Lynx saw something, and suddenly all three Orbs lit up in warning.

It was a beast the size of a small horse. Fallen on its side, unmoving, and entirely hairless. The closer they moved, the more detailed its scaly white skin appeared, and they could see the traces of scrawl upon it. Scars of dark words Veer was far too familiar with now.

Maïa wrinkled her nose. "And I thought the smell here couldn't get any worse."

"The Great Library was attacked by these?" Paix asked, kneeling and poking at it. The creature's throat was torn open, and the soil beneath it discolored but dry. It had clearly been dead a while. Paix looked up at Veer with something akin to admiration. "That must not have been fun."

Veer took a long look at the creature before saying, "It wasn't, but it was dealt with, in no small part thanks to Arturo and his peculiar gift. Still. The Unwritten people, the Unwritten beasts . . . It's important we find that journal and prevent it ever happening again."

"Do you think the journal can help us do that?" Maïa said.

"From what we read in the pages we have, I think it might give us a few clues, yes," Paix said, tilting her head as she stood up and regarded the creature's torn throat. "This is a large and horrifying beast. What do you think could have killed it in this way?"

"Another of its number, I'll bet. I'm guessing the Unwritten don't get along with the locals very well."

"Anything to track from here?"

Veer had been wondering the same thing, his eyes darting around the scene as they talked, taking it all in. He knew Lynx and the other two Orbs were scanning too. Looking for signs of direction of movement. Where had this thing been heading when it had been killed? How many others had there been?

Had it been accompanying Payne?

He walked a perimeter around the corpse. Paix and Maïa watched him; he could feel their gazes on his back, trying to follow what he was studying. He'd always been good at tracking as a child. Many a camping trip taken with his father had taught him so much. Mainly that he loved the thrill of the chase, following animals through the forests and across the mountains in the Pacific Northwest. Never actually hunting them, of course—animals deserved to live their lives as much as he did—but he liked solving the clues they left behind, figuring out the puzzle that marked their journey through the wilderness.

It was a tougher ask in this hellscape since the ground was too hard for tracks. Luckily, he had his Sage powers to help. Observing the way this creature lay, he could map how the air moved around it, and had it still been alive, he could have used that signature to track it. This Unwritten hound wasn't as ancient as all the other dead things they'd witnessed, but it had been killed long enough ago—perhaps a few months, judging by the state of its decomposition—for any marginal scuffs to have been blown clean. Besides, he and the other Sages who'd been tracking Payne had caught glimpses of his tracks in other realms before this could have happened, unless things decayed at an accelerated rate here. The thickets could have grown in that time, although he couldn't understand how things grew here. There *were* a couple of patches of discoloration in the broken surface of the road, heading slightly away from the road. Perhaps whatever had killed this thing had been injured itself. Veer followed the patches for a couple of yards before discovering they stopped quickly after. Possibly just a scavenger making a mess of its meal.

Lynx concurred, and they headed back to the road.

"Anything else out there?" he asked his Orb.

Very little.

"Suggestions?"

Stay the course.

Veer set his jaw and nodded to the other Sages as their Orbs relayed the same information. "We stick to the plan, then. Perhaps we'll come across something else before the settlement, but otherwise that's still our goal. All good?"

"Yes."

"Agreed."

There was a rumble beneath Veer's boots again. That distant storm hadn't abated then. He hoped it wouldn't find them. They moved on.

The settlement was close now. The ruins built up on both sides of the road as they approached. Low walls at first, barely a footprint of what had once been. But they grew higher toward the center of the town, and soon they passed buildings that were more complete, though still ruinous and on the verge of tumbling down, architectural tombstones of the ancient civilization.

But that wasn't what had Veer worried. It was the noise ahead. A cloud of it, hanging perhaps five, six hundred yards ahead. Veer hadn't enjoyed the wind whistling low through the desolate landscape so far, rustling through what passed for vegetation here. But now that he could hear the distant yells and screams, he wondered if the sounds of loss and ruin hadn't been preferable.

They slowed their movements, wary of running into people without warning. None of them wanted to linger more than they had to, but they had to be careful. So it was almost a relief when night crept from the shadows and sunk itself over the realm and Paix suggested they shelter. Maïa and Veer quickly agreed.

"There," Maïa said. Her long finger pointed to a building larger than the others, situated a little off the road and hidden behind a copse of bent, decayed trees. "A little out of the way, perhaps sturdier than the others. Should allow us to get some rest for the evening."

It was a museum, it turned out. Or at least whatever passed for a repository of historical information in this forsaken place. A circular building, two stories high, with a rock-slate roof that was only half intact. After the Orbs scanned and found them to be sturdy enough to not collapse during the night, they slunk up to the first floor to find a corner to squirrel themselves away for a few hours rest.

On the side of the building where the roof was undone, the elements rotted away whatever displays had stood here. Now there were only pedestals with nothing atop them. Yet on the other side, the Sages found not only shelter but also a gallery of inscribed paintings drawn over rolls of silver that had stood the test of time.

Veer wanted to sleep. Every fiber of his substantial frame was yearning for an hour or two of unconsciousness. Yet how could he? Upon the walls was a lost history speaking to him, the forgotten story of this realm. It was both a heartwarming bedtime tale, and the kind of horror usually reserved for telling around campfires in the woods.

"It looked very different, once upon a time," Maïa said, her voice barely a whisper as they stood together.

Lynx and Thebe were hovering above them, directing the glow to the faded stains that adorned the metal canvas. Veer said nothing, letting his eyes wander across the lush green splashes that represented hills and fields, and the blues—almost gray now—that flowed through the image as glorious rivers.

Lumbering animals, as tall as houses, with six thick legs, long, fat bodies, and necks like tree trunks, were depicted in the middle distance, one stooped to drink at a small lake.

Maïa's Orb buzzed, and she said something under her breath as she reached out and pointed a finger to the corner of the image. The stains were faded here, too, but they were distinct enough to mark them out from the rest of the landscape. A forest of white-leafed trees, like a blanket of dandelion seeds. "It's stunning. Thebe says the inscription labels this as the Forest Everlasting. Can you imagine such a sight in its prime?"

"I fear we may have seen it earlier, although it no longer looked like this."

"We did?"

"Remember the fire on the horizon? The fire in this painting is directly between these two hills, and I definitely saw those hills while we were walking. That endless, ferocious fire was exactly where this Forest Everlasting would have been. I felt the heat of it through the wind, and it has been like that for many more years than I would like to count. Perhaps ever since the destruction that rained down upon these poor beings."

"Look at this," Paix said from close by. She stood in front of another hanging on the wall, the colors of the painting rich and vibrant in the magical glow from the Orbs, despite the extreme decay around the museum. Veer imagined he might be standing in front of the scene itself.

It portrayed a huge crystal bridge spanning a great river or perhaps even an ocean. Twin cities sat on either side of the span, supporting a thriving populace, judging from the lights and structures. It looked to have been grown from pure crystal—a living work of architectural artistry, truly a wonder of any world, and an amazing feat for any realm. Veer wondered at the magic they must have wielded to achieve such wonders.

He whistled, soft and low. "Now that is a thing of beauty."

"Was," Maïa reminded him, and Veer felt a pang of sudden longing for the days when the Forest Everlasting had been in full bloom. A strange sensation, given he'd never experienced it. How could one miss something they'd never actually seen?

Yet he knew such longings existed. The feelings were real enough, and who could deny the universe was full of twisted, magical inconsistencies? He'd seen enough of them in his time, both on Earth and traveling beyond the Great Library.

"We should get some rest," he said, hiding a yawn behind the back of his hand. "The night is upon us, and we don't want to draw attention with the lights. We likely have far more land to cover tomorrow too."

Lynx spun a message in patterns of aquamarine across his surface.

We keep watch.

"That would be good. Thanks, Lynx. Not sure I could keep my eyes open much longer even if I wanted to."

Gesturing to a corner of the gallery that seemed the most sheltered, Veer led Maïa over and started sweeping the dust of the floor with the side of his boot. It didn't make much of a difference. He only realized when Maïa laughed that he wasn't thinking straight.

"Ah, of course," he said. Flexing his fingers, he pulled on the wind around them, drawing it forth through the open windows and holes in the roof nearby, until it formed a cushion of air. He nimbly tied it off, then nodded to his friend. Maïa prodded with her foot until she felt resistance, then gently eased herself down. Veer made another "bed" for Paix, then himself.

"Thanks, Veer."

He yawned again, the use of his power draining what little energy he had left. "You're welcome. Now sleep, if you can. The Orbs will alert us if there is anything to worry about."

The others might have responded, but he didn't hear them. He was already letting himself drift off, exhausted from being "on" all day, using his power constantly to scope for changes in the environment, for hints of that army. He felt not just tired but older. There were likely one or two more gray hairs in his mustache tonight, he thought. With more to come tomorrow.

Slipping onto his side, resting his head on his arm, unconsciousness quickly took him.

CHAPTER SIXTEEN
A REQUEST

Nu's group wound their way up the spiral staircase, crossed rickety bridges between branches, and did their best to avoid the general hustle and bustle of the Great Tree in midafternoon.

People were smiling, children playing, and the mood was relaxed, if a little chaotic. Rivers of shoppers streamed up and down some branches, particularly where markets were held, and stallholders' chatter filled the air in the midst of it all, trying to draw more people to their stands and provide foods and goods for as many people who could possibly fit around them.

To Nu, it seemed like everything had returned to some semblance of what she thought normal must be here. It was a blessed relief, given their efforts and the sacrifice Helia had made.

Except, Nu discovered, appearances were deceptive.

"Yes, Mother, the Great Tree, is still sick," Dzin explained in a low voice, leading them across a gently swaying log bridge on their way to find the Chief Scientist. This led through a tunnel inside a branch, beneath another market, before popping them out on the other side. He kept looking around as he spoke, trying not to let anybody overhear. "Most know there is something affecting her roots. Others have seen it spreading higher. We have attempted to quell the concerns with regular announcements about our ongoing work to find a cure, and for the most part, it's worked. There are some who spread decay where they can, insisting that this is a bigger problem than we're saying. Yet the majority of tree folk have become used to the occasional dulling of the flowers and the blackened patches, and they trust us to find a solution. They go about their business as they used to, without worry."

"But what you're saying is they *should* worry?"

Dzin bowed his head. "Yes, because so far nothing we have done has worked. The Dark Elixir repels my efforts to undo its poison. It even resisted the antidote your Sage Mwamba provided us, after he used it in your world. I can only speculate as to why. Perhaps it was an evolution of the toxin. Some twisted combination of that and some other of Payne's evil concoctions. Regardless, the roots of the Great Tree were tainted, and I cannot undo it. The poison continues to work, slowly, surely, creeping up from the soil beneath us, spreading upward."

"Is Mother dying?" Nu asked, looking around. Nothing seemed particularly obvious to her, other than the colors of the leaves were perhaps a touch muted, as if the sun had disappeared behind the clouds for a moment.

"The truth is, we don't know yet. Here, look at this." Dzin pointed to the trunk, where a small patch of yellow moss was spilling out and over the hollow of a broken branch stub. He walked over and lifted it to show the group. In the shadow beneath, the bark of the trunk was gray and rotting. He poked a finger at it, and the wood crumbled beneath his touch. "The sickness is spreading particularly fast in those areas where light is limited. At some point in the near future, this is going to become a very big problem. If it continues at this rate, we cannot see the Great Tree being able to survive. And without her, our whole realm will die. From what you have told us, this would be a disaster for us all."

Dzin let the moss slump back into place, covering the decay beneath. Nu moved around him and touched her fingers to a patch of unblemished bark, pulling energy from Antares and pushing out with her power. She closed her eyes to focus.

There was nothing at first. Then a single tendril of thought snaked through her mind. A clarion call for help.

Nu blinked her eyes open and stepped back from the bark, retracting her hand as though she'd been bitten. She felt tears welling at the horror facing them as more unfamiliar thoughts appeared, each weaving over the others, tying themselves into knots as they revealed their fears to her. She realized these were not her visions; rather, Mother was laying herself bare, letting Nu see the truth of her concern.

She saw the Great Tree withering. Her roots, stretching deep into the very fabric of life in this realm, darkened, the signs of ancient damage renewed and spreading. People pouring across Mother's branches and bridges, down the footways, spilling out among her roots. It was an exodus. The Silvyrans leaving the home they'd known for endless cycles of the two moons. An abandonment. She was to be left alone, unable to protect those she loved. The poison in her roots was already working its way beyond Silvyra.

All may die.

Nu shivered as the vision collapsed, and she drew in a breath, then another, slower this time, seeking composure.

"The problem will spread far beyond Silvyra," she said, steadying herself and turning to Dzin. "The decay here is spreading, almost like it's alive. It extends from the deepest parts of Mother's branches. This is something ancient and malevolent."

"How can you know this for sure?" Dzin asked.

"Mother showed me. Your people fleeing from a world that's dying all around them, ancient broken roots poisoning the rest. This will be an issue for everybody, everywhere, in every realm. You are one of the cleverest people I know, Dzin. I imagine you will not be too shocked to learn that Mother's roots reach so far into the soil of Silvyra they actually transcend this realm."

He nodded. "Of course. She is the Great Tree, life itself. And while we didn't have firsthand knowledge, we knew what was happening to her here must have been affecting other worlds as well. But the roots. We'd presumed the Dark Elixir had been washed away by a combination of the new formulas and Perennia's fire. We must ask the Chief Scientist for her insights. Is this why she was poisoned? To reach across all the realms? Most of our people aren't even fully aware of travel between the realms. Even our special airships' destinations are a closely guarded secret."

"Most likely that was their aim. The Dark Elixir was used at our Great Library to hurt the Book of Wisdom and make her vulnerable. That vulnerability could also spread to these other realms through our portal. Not to mention our own world."

Arturo's jaw was set hard. "But that's what we're doing here, yes? Looking for ways to defeat these monsters. If we recover what we need, our mission should help us find a way to fix what's happening across the realms."

"That's the idea," Nu said.

"Well, I'm sorry to be the bringer of bad news," Rascal said, glancing at her. "But the Rings of History are considered a myth among the people here for a reason. They might well exist; I'm not denying that. There was a saying where I was from: *The Tree remembers*. Which makes me think there was an actual archive or repository of knowledge, or whatever you called it. I wouldn't be surprised if it's here. But certainly nobody knows where it is, and even if we did, we wouldn't be able to access it. Things like that would be kept well hidden."

Dzin gave them a grim smile. "Rascal's right. I think it exists, too, but even I haven't been told anything about it as the Advisor to the Chief Scientist. So, it must be incredibly secret. We'll just have to see what the Chief Scientist herself has to say about it."

"I can't help you, I'm afraid," Lyvanda, the Chief Scientist of the Great Tree of Silvyra, said, keeping her gaze level. Her eyes were kind but firm as she looked at each of them in turn. But her words were weighted with regret.

The tall, elegant woman stood within the cool confines of her quarters in the highest bough of the Great Tree. Her long, flowing white gown made her seem more like a queen than a scientist, with flashes of her beautiful black skin shimmering with sprinkles of the golden dust Nu remembered from last time.

"So it doesn't exist?" Rascal asked.

"That's not what I'm saying, First Captain."

Nu glanced up at Rascal in surprise. "*First* Captain?"

Lyvanda smiled at Nu. "Yes, after your last adventure, Captain Finesse retired from flying. He was our most experienced officer following the losses we suffered in the explosions. I instructed Rascal to take over the helm of the *Golden Oriole* in his place. It is some time since we had need of a First Captain though. Traditionally, it is a title reserved for one who has engaged in significant acts of bravery, or during times of great peril. It seemed, in this case, we had both the need and someone who fits the description. Rascal now serves in this capacity as our Warden of the Skies, and the *Golden Oriole* is our flagship. At least until the new fleet is completed. Thankfully, she accepted the burden with good grace."

Rascal looked a little embarrassed, but Nu could see the pride in her face.

"Under duress," Rascal muttered. "I'm still not wearing that weed-poxed uniform!" Then she added a quick, "Ma'am."

"And your service to Silvyra will not be forgotten." Lyvanda gestured for them all to take a seat. This they did on the sumptuous cushions—plump and fluffy like dandelion seeds—that formed a bench of sorts at the center of her accommodation. "We've also taken aboard many new airship captains, including Dzin's soon-to-be new brother, Junic. The call to the people of Silvyra has gone out, and they have answered. It makes me so proud to lead these wonderful people." The Chief Scientist, whose shoulders had been straight and true until now, slowly leaned forward and placed her elbows on her knees. She regarded the group almost conspiratorially.

"Now, to your request. The Rings of History do indeed exist. I was one of those over the generations who heard the stories and wondered if they were just flights of fancy. In truth, such stories aid us in keeping them hidden and prevent people from looking too closely into what they are and where they might be. Burying something within a story maintains the truth of the thing, while ensuring its reality is never really taken as fact; however, my friends, I know I can trust you. The Rings of History are far more than a simple story. They have been around far longer than any of us, and their origins are more complex than you can know. The problem we have is that it is not entirely my decision to allow people to access the knowledge contained therein. The matter would have to be resolved with a third party."

Rascal began to say something again, but this time, Dzin interrupted and shook his head.

"With the greatest respect, Chief Scientist, we appreciate your trust in us. But I am a little confused about this third party you speak of. Are you not in charge of the Great Tree in its entirety? Am I not your Advisor? Who would you need to consult?"

"Authority comes in many guises, Dzin."

"Would it be possible for you to consult with the third party on our behalf, Chief Scientist?" Nu asked. "Our need is great. We are searching for a man who came here long, long ago. He took something from our world that we need returned. It is of the greatest importance to not just our realm but all of them, including yours."

"Ah, Nu, it is a shame we can never meet under more casual circumstances." Lyvanda gave Nu a sad look. "The last time we met, you were only just beginning on your journey. I'm sorry you have returned so quickly with yet more burden upon your shoulders."

"Thank you, but there is no need. It is the path we must follow, as the Great Library pledges to protect all life—all people and their stories. But we must find this man. Without him, we may not find the answers we need to fight this darkness, both abroad and in the very roots of the Great Tree herself."

"Very well. And your vision, which Dzin recounted to me as possibly from Mother herself, makes me wonder if the Rings are the very place we need to go." She looked around them, and her forearm, exposed by the high-collared sleeveless gown she wore, revealed a dragonfly tattoo, whose wings seemed to move as the dust caught the light. Dzin straightened a little, as though something of great importance was happening, and Nu could tell they were on the right path.

"As Chief Scientist, I have the honor of hosting a part of this realm's very life force. A fraction, mind you, but still one of the oldest and most honored of our people." She turned her arm toward the lights, and Nu could swear she saw the dragonfly, its fine lines impossibly detailed, ripple in place.

"Morpho here is an avatar of life, a living part of Mother whose origin story goes back to a time generations ago. To before this community was formally established under the guidance of the first Chief Scientist, Liria." She looked again at her arm, then covered up the tattoo.

"So that tattoo is . . . alive?" Nu said.

"Morpho is alive, yes. Perhaps not in as simple a way as you or me, but he lives. He is a guide in the darkest of times. A beacon to those in need and a protector when called upon. He was Liria, the first Chief Scientist's guide, and he was there when the Rings were created, in the aftermath of a battle between Mother's forebears: the Verdant and the Sere. They were, respectively, the Spirt of Life and the Spirit of Death and Decay. For a time, the Sere is said to have been bound beneath Mother, imprisoned in her roots. While they have been gone for thousands of harvests, I can't help but wonder if this is where the noxious ingredient for the Dark Elixir was born."

"I can't believe we never considered it," said Dzin. "Every child knows that history, but it's taken for granted that Mother is now our sole representative of the circles of life. The Seed of Life itself."

"How does this help us?" Nu asked.

The Chief Scientist said, "It was a time of great peril and even greater magic. We believe that the events of that time—the greatest of all Conjunctions—was when the Rings of History were created."

Nu looked at Robin excitedly, saying, "So, in our terms, that could be thousands of years ago, yes?"

"I think so, Nu," Robin replied.

"Then I think we may be in luck," Nu said.

The Chief Scientist nodded, then slowly got to her feet. The others followed.

"I cannot promise anything. But I will seek the person who carries equal responsibility for the Rings and request you be granted what you need."

"That's all we can ask for," Robin said, throwing Nu a quick smile of excitement. "When do you think you might hear something?"

"My request will be immediate, but there is no guarantee of a similarly fast response. I'm afraid you will have to wait." She gazed at Dzin. "Advisor Dzin, there are spare cubbies at the school, are there not? See to it our honored guests are given accommodation while they remain at the Great Tree. I believe your brother weds Captain Junic in a couple of days, so they will not be short of distractions! Hopefully, following that, we will have an answer for you, and we will see if we can locate your missing man."

"Thank you, Chief Scientist."

Nu's heart sunk, and she felt Antares buzz frustratedly beside her, but she bowed her head deeply as she offered her thanks. They filed out, with the Orbs following, the meeting over.

Outside, they walked along the branch before pulling up in a quiet alcove between the residences and a series of shops built into knotty hillocks in the bark. Rascal was muttering to herself.

Robin looked up at her. "Are you surprised it exists?"

"Surprised? Do flying squirrels eat gumpf stalks and then use their droppings to line their nest?"

There was a puzzled silence, broken only by Dzin chuckling under his breath. When nobody else joined in, Rascal waved her hand apologetically. "Right, of course you'd not know that. Yes, I'm surprised. And yes, they do. And they stink."

Antares pulsed at Nu with a series of triangles.

We have time.

"We have no choice but to wait," she said a little despondently. "You heard the Chief Scientist. There will be no speeding this process up; we just need to trust she will help us as soon as she can."

"Where does that leave us in the meantime?" Robin asked.

Dzin gave them all an encouraging smile. "Follow me," he said.

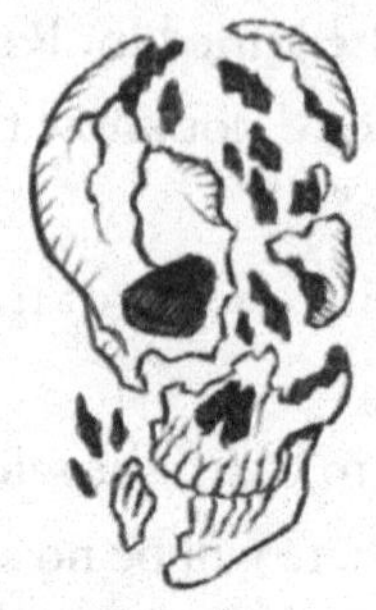

CHAPTER SEVENTEEN
THE MUSEUM

Veer lay on his back, eyes closed, listening to the low, fascinated voices of the other Sages, not far away. They were talking about dogs. Maïa kept calling them hounds. He frowned in his lazy doze, for a few blissful seconds trying to recall where he was. Then it all flooded back.

He rolled off the bed of air, snapped his fingers to allow it to dissipate, and stretched his back out with a groan.

"Morning," he said.

Nobody answered. Maïa and Paix were still deep in conversation, poring over some kind of model in a cracked glass case. Only Lynx left the other Orbs and flew over to Veer.

Veer patted his cold surface. "Anything to report?"

Nothing.

"What'd you do all night, then? Three of you sit and chat? Tell scary stories? Play cards?"

Funny.

"So?"

Studied. Learned. There is much history here.

Veer wiped the sleep out of his eyes and smoothed down his mustache. "I guess that's one of the perks of sheltering in a museum, or whatever this place is. I guess the more we know, the less likely we are to die today."

He strode over to the other Sages, who were still inspecting the model.

"Good morning, Veer," Paix said, her voice lighter than it was yesterday. Clearly, the sleep had agreed with her. "Come, look at this. It appears to be a replica of a farm or maybe even one of the first towns. And it seems to explain the origin of those cursed dog creatures we found."

She pointed to a collection of tiny model animals standing next to some humanoid figures. Veer peered through the cracked glass, moving his head to try to get a better view. What appeared at first glance to be some kind of livestock were in fact giant dogs.

Maïa added, "They appear to have been commonplace in the old world here. We've seen them in some of the other paintings and wall hangings. They worked side by side with the people once upon a time. It seems they were revered, perhaps even more than we do with our hounds on Earth."

"Okay, well, that explains them," Veer replied. "But what the hell is *that*?"

Veer had spotted something lying in one of the fields. Or rather, underneath it. There was a crack and a hint of black beneath the brown soil. Three curling strands were extended from it, across the field. He couldn't tell whether the model was broken at first, but closer inspection revealed it seemed to have been crafted that way. Around the gash, two of the hounds had been placed as though running toward it.

"That's one of the land mammals, apparently useful in creating a more fertile soil." As Veer raised an eyebrow, Paix explained, "The Orbs spent the night investigating the entire building. They found some surviving statues and other artifacts in a few of the collapsed rooms. They've been filling in some of the details of what we've seen in here. We're on the side of the realm that was predominantly agricultural. Lots of nature and a certain balance to the people's existence here. They lived underground to maximize land use and worked with the hounds on the fields. And it seems that one of the hound's jobs was to herd these underground creatures around."

"Looks like a gosh-darn octopus!"

"We're calling it the Terropus," Maïa interjected with a wry smile. "The Orbs didn't find an actual name for it written anywhere here, so that's as good as any. Intriguing, don't you think? To have something of that size navigate the soils. We were discussing how the hounds would be able to shepherd them around from the surface. Perhaps via some sort of vocal acoustic directions, which made the creatures move, or pheromonal. I suppose we may never know."

Veer frowned as he pushed his face up to the glass, trying to imagine such a sight.

"You've both been busy. How long have you been up? Did you get sleep?"

"Oh, not long, but wanted to try to see more of what we could before we had to head off," Paix said.

"Breakfast?" Veer said.

"Not yet. We were waiting for you."

His stomach grumbled. "Good. Let's eat a little and then get going. We have a long chase ahead of us."

Later that morning, the three Sages left the safety of the museum.

They pushed through a gathering of skeleton trees, their leaves withered and blackening at the tips, and the settlement they'd observed the day before came into view. A ramshackle outer wall consisting of the ruins of many buildings thrown up haphazardly, piled one on top of the other. Strange oblong doors, blackened frames, and all kinds of decaying artifacts could be seen among the stones, while miles of broken pipework poked through the wall like bones through rotting meat. It seemed quieter today—no sign of the people they'd seen yesterday.

There was another rumble of thunder, and the ground shook, closer this time. The three Sages looked at each other as they crouched in the shelter at the edge of the tree line.

"I hope that's not a portent of things to come," Paix said, looking up and studying the sky. "That disturbance seems to have been on the edge of wherever we are, the entire time we've been here."

The sound came again.

Maïa touched Veer's arm. "It's getting closer. Whatever it is."

There still wasn't any change in the sky. Was it even a storm?

Movement ahead, Lynx indicated with subdued blue flashing lights, aimed just toward the Sages. This close to a settlement, it was important to remain discrete.

As Veer pushed himself up, he finally saw some movement: the figure of a man, trancelike, walking into the open spaces beyond the settlement walls. Flexing his fingers to call upon the wind—in case they needed to disguise themselves with a dust cloud—Veer's concentration shattered as the ground broke in front of them, and the thunder noises became flesh.

Long, grimy tentacles snaked out of the soil, six or seven of them. Taller than most of the buildings around them, they whipped up into the air, reaching toward the entranced figure ahead of them. Veer's stomach roiled as the limbs curled back down toward the man on the ground. Paix gasped beside him and held out her arm instinctively, ready to use her powers to save him, but Veer knew it was too late. He put a hand on her shoulder and guided her behind him. They couldn't give themselves away for this. Not now.

The man had rediscovered himself, the trance gone, adrenaline presumably kick-starting his mind, Veer guessed, as people often did when facing their final moments. The man began struggling viciously against the binds, pulling this way and that. But his efforts were useless. His fate was inevitable now as the corrupted limbs—gray and lifeless, yet burning with a language of fire Veer had now seen all too often—wrapped around his prone body. The limbs held him against the dirt, then began pulling him down into it as the ground crumbled away and a toothy maw rose from below.

"The Terropus," Maïa whispered.

The creature they'd seen in the painting in the museum. Although it was now twisted and evil, made Unwritten by the dark forces that had claimed this realm for their own.

The man screamed. Just once. Then the creature broke his body and swallowed him and his cries whole. The ground shook as the tentacles writhed again, and the meal was consumed. The tentacles slammed against the ground with a squelch and were pulled swiftly under. The ground bucked and rippled toward the Sages as the beast departed. Veer wrapped Maïa and Paix in air and pulled them back behind the building, in case the creature turned in their direction. He needn't have worried. When he poked his head back around, the creature was gone.

Behind them, a crater remained where the victim had been.

Veer pushed his back against the building and sat for a moment. There was a plan forming.

"Lynx, what did you and the others find out about that creature we just saw?"

The Orb, still cloaked to avoid detection, shimmered in the air. *Underground mammal. Creates fertile soils. Helped farmers.*

"Yeah, but there are no more farmers. The soil is ruined. And that thing just ate someone. It's clearly not acting in the manner it once did, before things here got all kinds of screwed up. Did you see its skin? It was lifeless and covered in those markings. Just like we saw in Bloom."

Unwritten.

"Uh-huh. That's what I'm thinking. It's been corrupted. Its story undone by the same evil that helped to create Payne's army."

Maïa's eyes widened. "You think Payne . . .?"

"Yes, I think it might still be tied to the bastard somehow, because nobody who wields that kind of control over monsters will likely be too far from them. Likely it is on a magical leash of some sort. It probably returns to him when he needs it to wreak more havoc. Heck, for all we know, the guy probably sent it here for some kind of sacrificial payment from these people."

Maïa and Paix nodded in agreement.

"So, we follow it, then?" Paix said, Maïa again nodding her assent.

"I think so," Veer said. "The Terropus might lead us exactly where we need to go—or at least take us in the right direction. Hopefully, it has a master it reports to. We should follow it. Quickly."

Hurry, Lynx pulsed beside Veer's ear. *Company coming.*

Veer nudged the others back in the direction they'd come, away from the ruins of the settlement and back out into the broken pains they'd come from.

Veer spoke to Lynx. "Find out where that creature has gone. If the rumble that accompanied it is any indication, it clearly travels close enough to the surface to be felt. Chances are there will be telltale signs on the ground—cracks, discoloration, changes in the chemical makeup, whatever you can find. Locate the trail for us."

Understood.

Lynx shimmered once and then began to rise straight up to get a better view. Veer watched his little companion until he could no longer make him out against the murk of the sky.

"You think this will work?" Maïa asked quietly.

"Yes, I do," he said, hoping he was right.

CHAPTER EIGHTEEN
A HOME AMONG THE LEAVES

Nu sat next to Robin and Arturo on the curved chair against the back wall of Dzin's home. It was a cozy fit in the cubby with all of them there. Moreso with Rascal perched on a stool to the side, her metal wings folded as tightly as possible, and Antares and Centauri bobbing about just above everyone's heads. Nu didn't mind it one bit. It may have lacked the sweeping space of the Great Library, but there was a snug feel to the place that instantly felt like home, and she was wrapped up in its embrace.

She sighed contentedly and lazed back on the soft, seedling-stuffed cushions, resting her head back against the wood of the wall as Dzin's brother, Yantuz, served them tea.

"I still can't believe you're back in Silvyra!" Yantuz said, brimming with good cheer as he poured the purple, sweet-smelling liquid into each of the tiny cups laid out on the table stump in the center of the room. "And just in time to witness the Joining of me with my love, Junic. What a wonderful surprise. Did you know he's a Captain now? He's just waiting on his new airship. Please tell me you'll have time to attend the ceremony. It would mean the world to us. And don't tell me you're here to drag away my brother on another adventure. He has too much to do here helping us get ready."

"If it gets me out of helping with more planning of this Joining, then I don't care what the danger is. I'm off," Dzin said with a wry smile. "Yantuz and Junic have been talking about nothing else for the last few cycles of the moons. Honestly, if you need anybody to help you save the world, it'll be them. Their organizational skills will be a match for any foe."

The cubby filled with laughter. Nu took a sip of her drink and was pleasantly surprised by the slight fizz against her tongue and a sharp tang of summer fruits. It wasn't like any tea she'd tasted before. She felt a momentary pang; she wished she could have been sharing these new sensations with Triss.

Yantuz grinned at her through the steam rising over his own cup. His wide emerald eyes were still full of good cheer and humor, as she remembered, and his lips still had that twist to them, as if permanently on the edge of telling a joke.

The taller but younger of the two brothers, Yantuz was about as confident and positive a spirit as she had ever met. The complete opposite of the awkward and anxious man his brother had once been.

Although not as much now, it seemed.

"I don't know," Nu mused jokingly, nodding at Dzin as he cradled the cup of tea in his hands and blew it colder. "It feels like the whole adventure business worked wonders for Dzin. He's an Advisor now. A man of responsibility."

"Left a Runner and returned a hero," Rascal said, slapping him on the back just as he sipped his drink. He started choking, and she slapped him again until he stopped.

"Not . . . a . . . hero."

"What was that, Almighty Advisor? I couldn't hear you for all the power you wield."

Dzin rolled his eyes, and Nu felt sorry for him. He'd been awkward when they'd first met, and while she could see he'd grown into his new role, he was still a little unsure of himself. He cleared his throat again, his eyes watering.

"I said . . . I'm not a hero. Not even close. If anyone is, it's Nu here. She and Helia, Antares and Vega. They were the ones who defeated Suttaru. Before . . ."

His voice trailed and his eyes dropped. A lull of silence descended upon the room, until Yantuz cleared his throat.

"So how long do you intend to stay this time, Nu? The Joining is only in two moons' time, and it would be my greatest honor if you and your friends were here to witness Junic and I making our pledges to each other. I promise not to pull you into any of the organizing!"

"How come I wasn't offered that arrangement?" Dzin asked.

"Have you organized the skin painters yet, Brother?"

"Well, no. I've been busy."

"Then stop your complaining. You *have* the same deal, because you still haven't actually done anything useful."

The front door opened at that moment, and a rugged, bearded man with long, curly blond hair strode in. Rascal gave him a nod as she shifted to one side to let him through. He patted her on the wing, then passed to grab Yantuz by both shoulders and kissed him thoroughly.

Yantuz's eyes widened in surprise, before he leaned into it.

The kiss lasted a good few seconds. Nu caught a glimpse of Arturo and Robin grinning at each other. Dzin fidgeted on his stool. Nu simply waited, enjoying this little display of humanity, again wishing Triss were here to share in this moment. Finally, the men pulled apart, and Yantuz gasped a little.

"Oh. I imagine you got the outfit you wanted for me?"

"Not only that, my dear Yantuz, but the seamstresses offered to make us matching sashes. We will be the most dashing pair in the history of Joinings! Certainly better dressed than those damn . . ."

It was then he looked around the room, as if seeing the others for the first time.

"Oh. My apologies. I did not realize we had company." His gaze traveled over Nu and Robin quickly, before lingering a little on Arturo.

Yantuz coughed pointedly and took his partner's hand. "Junic, may I introduce my friend Nu who, as you know from Dzin, was instrumental in saving Perennia. And these are her friends Robin and Arturo. Of course, you know Rascal. Everyone, this is my beloved, Junic, who hails from Seven Pillars, in the West, where charm is as abundant as the kiss of the Huffbop seedlings and twice as likely to sweep a man off his feet. As it did me!"

Junic gave a very smooth and sweeping nod, letting his long hair fall across his face as he acknowledged his guests. "My friends, I am honored you have come to visit. Especially Nu, about whom I have heard many wonderful things." He nodded to her, and Nu felt her face warm as his eyes rose again to meet hers. "You will, of course, be staying for dinner. I assume Yantuz would have told you this and insisted upon it. If not, then I shall dissolve the Joining for such rudeness!" He grinned. "I joke, I joke. I would not be without him. But anyway, come to the table and sit. In a few moments, I will feed you wonderful things. Oh, I know, I will make my famous Pianna D'alatra! Salted leaf wraps with the most divine frosted center baked in Pianna nectar. It is like saving the world . . . but for your mouth!"

He grabbed Yantuz and Dzin and guided them through the doorway that led through to the eating area. Rascal shuffled awkwardly around the furniture in the front room and joined them. As Nu got up with the others and gestured to Antares and Centauri to follow, Arturo tugged on her sleeve.

"Forgive me, Nu. I don't know if perhaps I'm overstepping, but are we in a position to wait around and dine and drink as if we're on vacation? These people, this place, are amazing, but—"

"We don't seem to have a choice, Arturo," she said, dropping her voice so only he and Robin could hear. "I share your concern, but the Chief Scientist needed us to wait while she got us access to the information we needed. For now, we should rest and enjoy the company of good people. Who knows when we may have the chance again."

Robin put a supportive hand on Arturo's arm. He looked at her, and his features softened, but Nu could sense no use of Robin's powers. Interesting, she thought, as Robin dropped her arm back down.

"The Chief Scientist was graceful in her aid and honest in her responses, Arturo. That's good enough for me. The best thing we can do now is go wait for her to do what she can. And as Nu said, there's no harm in having conversations with friends. I'm excited to sit down and dig into something new, quite frankly."

Arturo looked between them and smiled. He'd seemed impatient, on edge, but was now starting to relax. Nu realized it must be very strange for him. A new world, new types of humans. It was a lot of change in what for him was a very small amount of time.

"Your role with us is important, Arturo," Nu said as reassuringly as she could.

"I get that, but I wish you could explain a little more about *how* you know that. I'd like to have more of an idea why I'm here and how I can help. I feel it—the need to be doing something. I can't explain it, but I need to *help*."

The knot in her stomach tightened as she remembered her visions. She wondered again if she could be wrong, if it could be someone else. But he was the man she saw in them—of that she had no doubt, even if the specifics were still murky.

She straightened as she formulated a reply that would satisfy him without giving too much away. "The Book of Wisdom was responsible for bringing you to the Great Library in the first place, and honestly, in the end, we all saw why you were needed. You defended the Library against the Rogue Sage in a way that nobody else could have done. Yes, when you left us, we didn't expect to see you back. But in ways we could not have predicted, you were brought back." Robin slipped her hand into his at that moment, and Nu paused, unsure of how much to divulge. Nu proceeded warily. "I believe, again, it is for good reason. I've had a vision, and I think I saw you in it, which means you are meant to be here with us."

"A vision of me? Really." It was a statement, not a question. He looked excited.

Robin seemed just as surprised as him, interrupting, "You never told me, Nu! What did you see?"

Nu sighed. "I cannot be sure," she said, finding the truth in the words while accepting they were not all the words she could have said.

If Arturo knew she was withholding information, though, he showed no sign. He seemed more content, satisfied even. *Good, he needs to be committed for what may come.*

"Do you think this Suttaru really returned? That I might be able to stop him somehow, the same way I helped stop Payne in the Library?"

A figure stood in the face of death. Light bending around him with such fury it turned him into a silhouette. Shaking, but solid. Resilient. Unmovable. Until the end.

The image flashed through her mind, and she flinched at the viciousness of it. She hoped she was wrong. That this was nothing more than an echo of the trauma she had endured in the City of Forever.

The knowing spoke of this being as real as any of her other visions of truth. Not quite a glimpse of the future but the truth of what was needed.

What *had* to happen, as the fates decreed.

"Honestly?" she said, wondering if that was entirely true. "I don't know. But I believe *help* is exactly what you will do."

To Nu's great relief, she did not have to try to explain herself further. For at that moment, Junic slipped back into the room like a breeze and put his arm around Robin and nudged Arturo good-naturedly in the ribs.

"Come, my friends! Do not linger here when conversation and fine foods await! Let me expand your minds with exquisite tastes and scents that will quiver your senses. And that's just me!"

He laughed and gestured for Nu to lead the way. She did so gratefully.

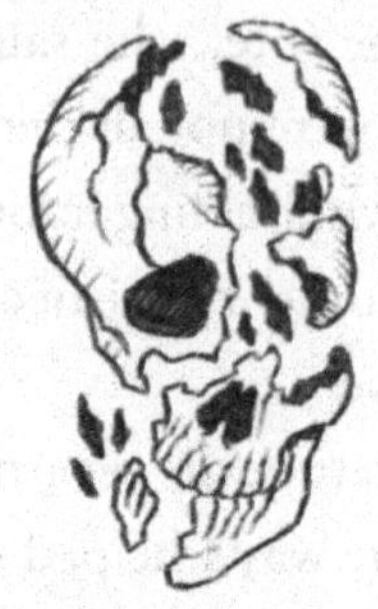

CHAPTER NINETEEN
TRAILS IN THE DIRT

"At the very least, I think we can agree this seems like the perfect place to find that bastard," Veer said, pausing at the edge of what had probably once been a farmstead.

They'd been on the trail of the Terropus for days now, and Veer was finding it difficult to keep track of time in this place. The sky seemed permanently in flux, with day and night blending into one.

The shifting earth beneath it was easy enough for a trained tracker like himself to follow, with his natural abilities enhanced by his Sage powers. His eyes saw the cracks and breaks in the ground, and if they faded, he could feel the creature disrupting the air around it while it was still nearby. Its shape was unique to them so far in this blighted landscape.

They'd walked for hours, yet he continued to hold himself straight as an arrow, ignoring the weariness he felt. He was the Sage of Strength, after all. Maïa and Paix were more than colleagues, more than peers, more than friends. They were family, and they would think no less of him, but he felt it his duty to show nothing less than a strong, resolute will in this stain of a realm. Even without looking behind to check on their progress, he could feel their presence. Maïa's graceful gait, Paix's shorter but rapid steps. But he could tell they were flagging, and he wanted to keep their morale up.

"I bet this is a lot less fun than your time back on Earth in the Winter Circus, huh, Maïa?" he said, a wry grin forming as he turned to her. "Although having daggers thrown at you night after night probably prepared you a little for what we face."

She gave him an amused look, sweeping her hair—no longer constrained with the leather cord—back behind her ears. "Sometimes *I* was the one throwing the daggers, Veer. But yes, the *Cirque d'Hiver* was a show built on danger, tension, excitement . . . and this is very different. I would definitely prefer being back in Paris right about now."

Veer and his companions finally reached the farmstead, and he took a seat on the porch, followed by Maïa, but still Paix refused to sit. Veer patted the wooden slats next to them.

"Please, let's sit and rest. This place is leeching off our souls. It's draining my spirit, and I imagine it demoralizes whoever dares to tread its corrupted surface. Let us keep our strength as well as we can, and therefore hopefully our heads. Which means resting while we can."

As Paix nodded and sat beside him and Maïa, he looked out over the blackened land and realized the exhaustion wasn't just about that for him.

All too quickly they were up and moving again, away from the farmstead, crossing yet another field. This one had stalks of charcoal-black blowing in the wind. Crops grown recently, though what food they produced Veer didn't want to imagine. He hoped the meager provisions they'd brought with them would last long enough to find the journal. He wasn't game to start eating like a local.

On the sixth day on the trail, their quarry disappeared.

Gone deeper underground, Lynx advised.

"Thoughts, anybody? I can't sense it anymore. There's not enough air moving around that far underground for me to track," Veer said.

"The direction it's followed doesn't seem to have changed, so perhaps we should just continue as we have been," Maïa said. "Unless you've picked up any trace of Payne himself?"

"Nothing yet. I've stretched my senses as far as they can reach, but he doesn't seem to be anywhere in the area. Following that creature seemed like the best chance to locate someone who may know more." Veer paused and turned to his Orb, saying, "Lynx, have you or the other Orbs sensed anything?"

Nothing, the Orb said.

"Okay, then following in the general direction the Terropus was traveling seems as reasonable a plan as any, even if it seems to have disappeared on us. You three Orbs, spread out again, go a little higher if you need to. Keep on the lookout for anything that can help us."

It was less than a minute before they found what they needed.

The crust of the soil in the next field had been churned up. There was a little of the dry, lifeless foliage still growing in patches around it, but there had clearly been a significant gathering within it in recent months. There was a lingering smell too. Faint, but identifiable. The collective scent of rotting husks. Human and hound.

"Their army, I'd bet," he said, clenching his fist with relief. "This must have been where they gathered before they attacked the Great Library, probably for a day or two. Can you imagine how bad it must have stunk here if the scent is still hanging all these months later?" He surveyed the scene, then nodded to a nearby collapsed wall. There was a charred cut straight through one of the larger rocks. "I bet that's where Payne threw up one of the portals. Look. See? The ground before it is particularly cracked and barren. There was likely a bottleneck where his minions tried to cram their way through. And there—that's another portal mark."

"And over there too," Paix said, pointing to the other side of the field. "I can see a couple of them."

"I can feel the evil linger here," Maïa noted with concern. "The taint lies heavy, like blood dried on the land or the mists of rain in the air."

"That it is," Veer said. He could smell it around them.

Fine particles of an unknown substance, Lynx noted. *I've made notes on composition.*

Veer nodded his thanks. "We can study it later. For now, we need to look around, beyond the field. We pushed them back from the Great Library when the Book shut the portals down again. There were enough of them. There must still be signs of their departure, as I'm sure they would have left together. Lynx, check over there. Thebe, go that way. Arcturus, to the other side. Orbs, what do you see?"

Within a few seconds, Thebe unleashed a series of flashes.

"She's got multiple trails," Maïa confirmed. "And they're all heading in the same direction. Can't make out distinct sets of prints, but Thebe says they're real."

Veer hurried over to study the ground.

"Any sign of the Terropus?" Paix asked, peering over Veer's shoulder as he touched the ground around the scuffs. They were shallow now, barely a graze, but they were there.

"No. But perhaps it was drawn to the lingering magic, or the scent of its master. Where it's gone after that, I don't rightly care."

"What are you saying, Veer?" Maïa had her hands on her hips, dust streaked across her porcelain brow. She looked as exhausted as he was feeling. "Give up the Terropus and follow these new tracks?"

"Yes, I think so. It's the army we're after. This is what we were looking for. I'd wager at the end of this trail we're going to find the enemy forces, and likely Payne himself. Even if Payne isn't with them, it seems our best chance of finding where he might be now."

Paix looked uncomfortable at that thought. "It's not quite as fun as finding gold at the end of a rainbow, is it? Do you think he knows we're here?"

"We've kept a low profile so far. Nobody else knows, and we've come across nothing that's seen us. The Orbs would have alerted us. I would hope we're in the clear."

Maïa blew out her cheeks. "Fine. Then we follow the tracks and hope it gets us to him, wherever in this blasted realm he is hiding. Let's drag him out and retrieve that journal and the fragment of the stone, if he has it."

"Then take him back to face judgment," Veer said. "Let's go."

"Watch your feet," he told Paix as they stepped over what looked like contaminated water. The other Sage nodded wearily and made an extra effort to leap clear of it. Her Orb bobbed along with her.

Veer saw that what liquid remained on the surface of this realm was stagnant and black, thick and viscous, like oil. He imagined it was like quicksand, dragging down any unfortunate soul who might step too close.

"Lynx?" he asked.

His Orb sampled it. *Toxic to touch. Poisonous if ingested.*

"Noted. Any other side effects?"

It seems to be alive. Feeding. Lynx went silent for a moment, still analyzing the data. *It is sapping your energy. Taking it for its own.*

"Great," Veer said, scoping the landscape ahead of them. "We'll have to try to avoid them, okay?"

"How do the inhabitants of this realm manage to survive in all this?" Paix asked, and nobody had an answer for her.

"Drinking water here is likely a precious resource, perhaps more so than food or fuel," Maïa said, echoing Veer's thoughts. "Our drinking water might make us a target."

Yet another thing to worry about, Veer thought.

The tracks of the army were gone, and he'd had to tell his companions. Their air signatures were long in the wind, and the physical signs were hopeless in such desolate terrain. It seemed the army had scattered, as best as he could tell, leaving them once again without a clear path. The others hadn't asked him about fresh trails for a day now. Maybe they assumed he was following signs that only he could see in the subtle shift of the air and wind across this cursed land.

He was now only picking up the occasional shift of familiar things as he went. Vague traces of something that could be Payne, or perhaps just a similar-size person from this world. Too much time had passed for him to be certain, but it was better than nothing. Still sticking to the trail they started on, he was hoping to pick up something more substantive when they reached drier land again. In the meantime, he kept checking in with Lynx to see if any of the Orbs had seen anything, which, of course, they hadn't, except these long-necked reptilian horrors, which Paix had unimaginatively named Longnecks, as a joke. Their efforts also allowed him to concentrate on his search for Payne, rather than permanently being on the lookout for large predators moving through the air nearby.

There was a crunching sound as one of them found its prey. A brief squeal was cut short, and the slithering head retracted from a burrow with a withered animal in its jaws, the creature's matted fur soaked through with its own blood.

A couple of crunches, and the animal disappeared down the neck of the beast. Satisfied, the three reptilians lifted from the mud again and went on their way.

Paix rolled onto her back and breathed a long sigh of relief. "I do not like those things. Snake-headed dinosaurs should not be a problem we have to cope with, even in a realm as forlorn as this one."

"Well, if our Earth truly is a reflection of Paperworld, as the Book of Wisdom theorizes, at some point we are bound to find a dinosaur planet . . ." Maïa's voice was tinged with mischief.

Paix smiled.

"At least they haven't developed a nose for us just yet," Veer said. "Okay, they've gone. We should keep moving. The sooner we get away from these poisoned rivers, the better."

"Onward?" Maïa asked, smiling weakly. "Same direction as before?"

Her gaze told him she understood what he was doing. The truth of his plan. Or lack of one.

"How long have you known?"

"For a few hours now."

"I'm sorry. I should have said something sooner. I don't know if he was ever with the army, but it seemed like the best bet. But it's just too faded to catch specific air signatures now, and the physical tracks . . . Well, you see what the terrain is like. Everything is in ruin and disrepair. It's difficult to see the passage of anomalies, when that is all you can see." Veer smiled wanly at his two companions and gently shook his head.

Paix shrugged good-naturedly. "We all understand this is the best course of action given the circumstances. My dear, I can't imagine *anybody* can track anything through this place. It would be like trying to spot trails in months-old molasses. All we can do is head onward, the direction we had already set ourselves."

"There are faint traces of movement on the winds, but nothing I or Lynx have been able to identify as an army or Payne himself," Veer replied.

"Can we send the Orbs further out to map the area, like we did before?" Paix said.

"I'm not sure that is wise," Maïa said. "We've seen there are settlements and various strange creatures. If the Orbs are seen by them—or worse, by Payne himself—we risk becoming the hunted. Better to have them scout out the immediate area only."

Veer nodded, then said, "Agreed. I think we should take our chances on this direction and save the Orbs as a last resort. If we're lucky, we'll find something in the direction the army was moving."

Lynx spoke, and Veer was momentarily captivated by the patterns of the Orb's response shimmering over his surface, as bright as the cerulean seas of the Pacific and as rhythmic as the rising and falling of the waves.

Veer?

Veer snapped back to the present.

"Sorry, bud. What were you saying?"

Lynx repeated his message, and Veer brushed down his mustache as he listened, feeling the grit embedded in it, wishing the Orb was telling him they should abandon the mission and carve a portal back home straight to the nearest shower.

We'll go looking, they said. *You make camp.*

"Okay, buddy. But like Maïa said, stay close and stay hidden."

Lynx had already spotted some relatively dry and sheltered ground within the confines of an old millhouse nearby, and after leading the Sages there, the Orbs quickly fanned out into the night.

"I guess we're on our own for a bit, then," he said, peering over the walls at the horizon.

"Anything out there?"

"Not that I can see."

"Fire, then? As a treat?"

Veer smiled and flexed his hand, reaching out to harness the wind and sweep up a few of the old, dried thickets that had once grown around the walls. He pulled them from the stone and collected them in a pile in a corner of the room. Paix unleashed a spark of electricity to set them alight, and the three of them sat cross-legged around the small but warming fire.

As the smoke began to build, Veer directed it out of the nearest window and swirled it around the outside of their shelter, hopefully obscuring the light enough so they wouldn't draw any unwanted attention.

He breathed deeply at the thought. Before his good humor faded as he almost choked on the stink of the air, and he remembered where he was. Still far from success—and trapped in this agony of a realm.

Hoping, as he did each night, this would be their last night here.

Knowing it would not be.

CHAPTER TWENTY
A PATH DOWN THE TREE

The Joining was a magnificent affair, though Nu could not help but be distracted.

As the large group of tree folk gathered at the summit of Mother, among the leaves on the tallest branch, her thoughts drifted to Triss, wondering how she was holding up back at the Great Library, missing her smile and the encouragement she always had to spare. As the sun began to dissolve across Silvyra, her emotions wavered between joy at witnessing the love on display and the horror of knowing what might lie ahead for them all.

Yet she could not do anything. Only sit and smile and be present.

Banners caught the golden light as they streamed above—the sparkling reds and browns matching Junic's uniform and Yantuz's dress suit—as they fluttered in the rising wind. Rascal had even called in a favor from another airship captain and arranged a flyby to shower petals over the crowd as the pair of lovers carved their name into a wooden plaque to solidify their promises to each other. It was a grand surprise that led to people breaking out in tears and the happy couple being bowled over by the overexuberant embrace of their celebrating friends.

Nu, Robin, and Arturo were honored guests, and for an hour or so, they were able to set aside their mission and simply enjoy the spirit of community and celebration of love. Robin especially enjoyed it. She'd been almost as excited as Yantuz was in the lead-up to the day, wedding cultures being a particular area of interest in her ongoing studies. Nu suspected the Sage of Love had been adding her own personal touches to the festivities, easing the way through any potential stresses their group's arrival might have introduced.

"This is what I live for," she'd whispered to Nu among the colorful falling petals, her smile as wide as Nu had ever seen it, yet her gaze quickly turned serious. "This is love, Nu. The importance behind so much of life. This is why we face our fears—why we've come on this journey. Our love for others is the reason we're here. And we're getting a front-row seat to the very essence of it, distilled down into the joining of two men in the eyes of their kin. May we remember this moment. May it bring us light should we ever find ourselves in the dark."

Robin then grabbed Arturo, and he'd gamely joined the others as the dancing began in earnest and carried on long into the night. It had been a spectacular night, even dispelling Nu's thoughts about the upcoming mission.

Nu joined in for a time, first dancing with Yantuz, then with the slightly less elegant Dzin. After which she'd taken a seat by the side, letting her gaze drift from the merriment, out beyond the leaves, past the Maze, into the night. Knowing that their time here was almost at an end.

The call from the Chief Scientist came at dawn the next morning.

"I am aggrieved," Rascal remarked again as the group gathered outside the main doors where they'd been staying. "It's too early for this. Did she not know we had a Joining last night?"

Overhead, silhouettes cut through the first rays of sunshine as the flying squirrels started about their business. The soft *whoosh* of their leaps through the air made for a nice accompaniment to the rumbling carts and shouted greetings of the market holders on one of the lower limbs.

"I love getting a good start on the day," Nu replied happily, breathing in delicious gulps of fragrant air. It smelled like pine and honey, with a dash of citrus. Refreshing. Exciting. "If you get up when it's relatively quiet, there is a certain calm in the air. The promise of so many possibilities that lie ahead. The day is yours, and you can do whatever you want with it! That anticipation . . . It's the best time for me."

"Agreed," Robin said, looking not quite as bright, thanks to her late-night dancing, yet still smiling at everyone. Between them, their two Orbs spun little flashes across their surfaces like petals blown on the wind. Then Centauri made a quip with a bold burst of zigzagging patterns and nudged Arturo's shoulder. Robin laughed as he quickly brushed the Orb off. "Although I don't think everyone here agrees with us, Nu."

Arturo looked a little disheveled, his hair more ruffled than usual and his short beard perhaps in need of a trim. "I think I'm on Rascal's side here. I could have used a few more hours of sleep." He looked over at the First Captain and grinned before continuing. "The sun is barely up. But I confess: I'm eager to finally see these Rings of History." He looked around. "And where are the happy couple? Are they not accompanying us?"

Dzin was busy locking the door behind them. His eyes were pinched as though trying to shut out the light, while still trying to navigate the keys into the locks.

"They are both still sound asleep," he said, with a very clear undercurrent of wry bitterness. "The benefits of being newly joined and not directly involved in matters of state." He tested the handle, and satisfied it was secure, he turned back to the others with a sigh. "I should *not* have had that third nectar brandy."

"You had four," Arturo said, clapping him on the shoulder. "Same as me. And let me tell you—it is far smoother and stronger here than it ever was back on Earth. Potent." He smiled wide again, the evening's entertainment giving him a boyish aspect that belied his approaching middle age.

"Pair of seedlings, the both of you," Rascal said. "I had ten. As for what you drink back home, Arturo, I'd wager our distillation process here is beyond reproach. We've spent generations honing the practice."

"I can feel the truth of that statement," Arturo said with a smile, though his face was still pale. He made a gentlemanly pretense of offering his arm to Robin, when it was clear he was the one who needed support. Robin took it anyway. Arturo nodded to Dzin. "Lead on, friend. History awaits."

It was true: They'd been up far too late the night before, but Nu didn't regret a thing. This entire stay had been wonderful. The dinners at Dzin's had been divine. Junic was not only an excellent cook but a talkative host, and the group had enjoyed many hours sitting around the table over the last few days, feasting on the mouthwatering snacks and drinking concoctions of sap mead and nectar shots while listening to him tell stories. Then there had been the Joining celebrations to cap it all off.

Unlike the others, Nu hadn't really partaken in the nectar drinks. She'd found warmth instead in watching this found family of whom she had accidentally become a part. A group of like-minded people from different realms, who'd found solace and friendship with each other.

Brought together to stand against a common enemy.

The cold sinking in her stomach made her stumble. Dzin reached out quickly to stop her falling.

"You suffering too? I didn't see you drink much!"

She tried to wave off his concern with a smile. "I just wasn't paying attention. That's all."

You're worried, Antares said, drawing a little ahead of her.

Nu gave a subtle nod but didn't say anything. Despite the distraction of the last few days, the concern she carried for the safety of everyone remained constant, heavy, and uncomfortable, like rocks jostling in the pit of her stomach. And every step they took toward their goal brought worry that it would be the one where the ground collapsed beneath them, and they were lost forever.

She took a moment to breathe, and she let her fingers flex and weave their magic.

In her mind, the truth was still laid bare. A figure stood against fire.

Nu tried to focus, to bring herself closer to the vision and see what it might be. She had to know for sure.

"Nu? Are you okay?"

Reluctantly, she snapped back to the moment. Dzin had stopped and was waiting for her at the entrance to a rickety log bridge. It dipped out of sight and then rose some distance away, connecting with the main network of pathways winding around the trunk of the Great Tree.

"We're about to take a shortcut, but this bridge is a bit older than the rest, and it's only wide enough for us to travel single file. It's not quite Clockwork Mountain levels of danger"—his lips curved upward at the corners, both a smile and a grimace—"but it's best to keep your eyes open, as there's still a way to fall. We don't want to lose our fearless leader just before we get to the good bit."

Nu chuckled and let slip the vision she found herself still holding on to. She would just have to trust that her instincts had placed her on the right path.

She glanced over her shoulder to the others. Looking at Robin, she wondered if she should confide in her friend. Then she wondered if she should tell Arturo about what she thought lay ahead.

In the end, the moment passed. She quietly followed Dzin across the bridge.

It took the better part of the morning to get to where they needed to be. Traveling the height of the Great Tree was no mean feat in any state, but the weariness of the group meant Dzin took it perhaps a little slower than he might otherwise. Besides, as Arturo's head cleared in the fresh dawn air, his enthusiasm for the strange and wondrous sights around him grew tenfold. He soon began stopping to peer in awe and ask questions about whatever they were passing.

Nu hadn't realized how enormous the main trunk of the Great Tree was until they got up close and Dzin led them into a borehole. After a hundred yards of wandering through the wood-cut tunnel, they emerged into a magnificent hollow with lush, vibrant gardens sprawling across the wall and purple vines twisting up and over the ceiling. From these, other golden-leafed plants and candle-shaped sapphire flowers dangled like chandeliers, while birds and insects and other creatures Nu couldn't name swooped around, feasting on the bounty.

"Oh my," Arturo gasped, pausing and staring up and around him. Robin had to tug his arm and get him to move again.

He led them through a well-worn path in the spongy moss, toward a pool of beautiful amber from where a gushing could be heard. As they got closer, Nu could see that the nectar gathering in the pool was falling into a hole, creating a circular waterfall around a spiral staircase.

"This is the Heartwood," Dzin said, striding across the small walkway to the stairs and gesturing proudly to the stunning view around them. Nu followed carefully, trying to take it all in while not falling into the pool of nectar. "It's the core of the Great Tree—the living, breathing heart of Mother. It's a collection of every floral species the Runners have come across. They say there is one of every plant in Silvyra in here, but of course, we know there are always more to be discovered. Isn't that right, Rascal?"

"Aye," Rascal's reply came from the back of the group.

Robin looked around, confused. "How is that possible? There must be species in Silvyra that thrive best out in the sun? Or that may need to be underwater? Or bloom only under a moon's light? They all require different environments to grow, do they not?"

"They do," Dzin said.

"And then there are the natural relationships and rivalries between them. Some plants rely on devouring others to grow; others need the nourishment provided by particular flowers. There are so many variables to take into account. How do you maintain them all in this single space and keep them all alive?"

Dzin and Rascal laughed in unison.

"Nature is a puzzle," the winged woman said. "And we Runners have spent many ages solving it."

"My winged friend is correct," Dzin added, "but there is a little more to it than that. Put simply, we coexist with nature. We have maintained a balance, which has enabled us to better study the right time and place for everything to flourish and live its best life. It certainly wasn't easy bringing the Heartwood into fruition, and maintaining it with every discovery and addition is tricky, but we have managed it. They are all puzzle pieces, and we have fit them together to ensure they thrive."

"It's like paradise," Arturo said.

Dzin took the first step onto the steep staircase, his knuckles whitening as he gripped the guide rope that spiraled down along with it. Nu found herself doing the same, feeling the coarse fibers itch against her skin. She realized very quickly as they spiraled down within the nectar waterfall—by the distant sound of the splashing below—that there was a hell of a drop. It would not do to lose herself in such a fashion.

The nectar fell like a curtain around them, so smooth it almost seemed stationary. A fine mist of droplets trickled against her face, cool and refreshing. She licked her lips and savored the sweetness on her tongue.

All too soon they reached the bottom, underneath the falling golden liquid—sheltered by an arch—and strode out of another tunnel through the trunk, onto a lower limb.

Here they were accosted by a market in full voice and swagger. Traders had set up their stalls all down the branch on each side, and the crowds were already bartering for the unusual and incredible items being sold. The group pushed their way through, trying not to lose Arturo as he kept stopping and picking things up to wave at Dzin and Rascal and ask what they were. Eventually, Robin had to have a word with him and hurry him on, as some of the stallholders and those shopping were giving him strange looks.

"We're supposed to be blending in," she reminded him.

"Yes, but look at all these wonderful things, Robin! I've never seen such sights before."

Nu could understand his excitement. She breathed in the marvelous experience as they continued through the market. The woodsy waft of freshly baked pollen pies and swirls of stacked nut buns. The sweet, exciting tang of floral spices punctuating the air of one merchant's stall and the smoky, musky, but not unpleasant cloud hanging around a cook's grill, from which strips of delicious-looking dried fruit and plants were hanging, waiting to be cooked and devoured by some hungry shopper.

"It's so noisy," Arturo continued, a little louder for them all to hear. And it was. The noise was overwhelming, with shouts and cries from the traders like rocks breaking up the constant swell of chatter of the tree folk ebbing and flowing across the branch. Meanwhile, there were giant bees and flying squirrels and tree stags and all manner of smaller, stranger creatures flying, running, or slithering around them. "It's like the city where I live. Full of life. Perhaps not quite as wild as here, but still."

He laughed, but as they moved on, something caught his eye. The good humor faded across the group as he hesitated, and the rest saw what he was looking at.

"The poison," Robin said, staring at a clutch of blackening stems and wilting petals to the side of the branch they were on. She gestured then to where the bark between them was drying and peeling away from the main tree. "Is it getting worse?"

Dzin cleared his throat, as though uncomfortable about answering that question truthfully. Nu could see the concern in his eyes though.

"It's difficult to tell if it's getting worse, but the signs of its effects on the Great Tree are definitely spreading higher, seemingly reaching further each day. Mother is sick—of that there is no doubt."

"Which is why we should step up our pace and help our friends," Rascal said. "Perhaps that way we might more quickly find a way to help cure her."

Dzin nodded. "Point taken. Quickly now."

He continued hurrying them down a wooden ramp that was slippery underfoot. This far down the Great Tree, the light didn't stretch as far. It was a little murkier. Like the constant twilight of a forest, broken only by fleeting fingers of sunshine. He took a turn through a tunnel in another knot of wood. It was tall and had windows in it, but gray moss was crawling up the outer walls, and to Nu, it looked like whomever had lived here had abandoned it.

"Dzin, do you have any idea who Lyvanda might need to speak with about the Rings?" Nu asked him as they neared the roots. "She said she wasn't solely in charge, but who else could she need to consult. You're the second-in-command here, are you not?"

"Well, I'm an Advisor, which comes with a lot of responsibility, but I wouldn't say I was second-in-command; however, I do not have the faintest wisp of a cuckoo's clue as to who the Chief Scientist needs to check with. There is nobody at the Great Tree that . . ."

His voice trailed off, and he walked a few more steps without speaking.

"Dzin?" Nu said.

"Oh, sorry, yes. I was saying, there is nobody at the Great Tree *that I know of* who she'd need to consult with. But she does receive a visitor I don't know on occasions. A small woman, wearing glasses the color of crimson blossoms, her hair long and twisted in knots around her neck. I've never seen her or anyone like her elsewhere, but she has now visited twice during my time as Advisor, and each time, Lyvanda greets her with the use of a strange word, and she responds in kind. I always thought she was some kind of ambassador. Perhaps from the lands beyond the Rose Garden or on the coasts of the Unknown Sea. But now I'm not so sure."

"What's the word they speak?"

He stopped, thoughtfully. "I can't quite recall. I do remember being intrigued enough to study the word and couldn't find it in any known dialect of Silvyra. I assumed it was some kind of greeting. Yet perhaps it pertains to the Rings? On both occasions that I'm aware of, the visitor was met in the Chief Scientist's study, but shortly after, the two women would leave and venture somewhere for a few hours. They would be gone long enough to head all the way down to the bottom of the Great Tree, where we're heading now. And the Chief Scientist would return alone."

Rascal leaned down. "Why in the two moons did you not mention any of this sooner? We could have gone straight there!"

"There is a process to be adhered to," Dzin said, looking aghast at the tall woman. "Even if I had been sure of the Rings existence and where they might lay, we always needed to consult with Chief Scientist Lyvanda. There is a method to what we do, Rascal. You know that. And it is now more important than ever to follow the rules as we rebuild in the wake of all that destruction with the refinery and the airships. The Chief Scientist deserved to know what the Sages were requesting, and she needed to be the one to make the decision. Which she has done now."

"Then let's not keep her waiting," Nu said, nodding for Dzin to hurry onward.

CHAPTER TWENTY-ONE
THE RINGS OF HISTORY

Nu and the others reached the meeting point as the sun rose directly over the Great Tree, but they were so far down, nearly hidden among the roots and mulch, that she felt little of the warmth or light. It was a perpetual twilight.

The perfect place to hide a mystical repository of Silvyran knowledge, she decided.

Lyvanda was waiting for them, sitting quietly on a particularly mossy knot of wood. Her eyes closed. A picture of serenity. Nu felt a stab of envy, given she was starting to feel the weight of the mission upon her again. Perhaps, when all this was done, she would return here. Silvyra was her favorite of all the realms she'd visited so far, and she wished she could spend some time in this magical place when time and evildoers weren't against her.

The Chief Scientist opened her eyes and rose as they drew near.

"We hope you haven't been waiting too long," Dzin said.

She stretched in a way that was still somehow regal and smiled at the group. "Not too long that it was a problem, Dzin. Long enough that I was able to meditate and strengthen my connection with Mother. I find it's easier down here, where it's quiet and I'm among her roots.

There is a certain calm that cannot be found among the bustle of activity in the higher limbs."

"I will have to try it sometime. Are you alone? I wondered if you would bring whoever it was whose counsel you needed to seek."

"They will be along presently. But I have been given leave to take you inside to see if Mother will allow you access."

Nu's heart sank. "What do you mean? I thought access was dependent on you and this other person?"

"It is, young Sage, but the ultimate consent must be given by Mother. Because, of course, this is her history. Even I do not enter the Rings of History unless she deems the need worthy. That is the way of things and has been so for the longest time; however, I can see the concern in your eyes, and you have no need for it. If your need is true, she will grant you access. And as the Sage of Truth, I cannot foresee your need being anything but!" She jumped down from the knot and gestured with a sweep of an arm to a half-hidden path that ran between two root curls. "Now, come, let us go forth and see what Mother has to tell us. It's only a little way from here, past the cells."

As they moved, Lyvanda in the lead and Dzin encouraging the others to follow swiftly after, Arturo spoke. "If you do not mind me saying so, this does not seem a society where there is much need for locking people up. Especially not somewhere that takes such a long time to travel down to. Why have these cells here?"

"You are too kind, but I can imagine anywhere you have people, you have the need of a place to separate them from the rest and allow them some time to think upon what they have done. It might only be that they've enjoyed themselves a little too much in the pollen taverns and have acted in a manner not becoming of the Great Tree. They still benefit from that time and space for reflection. As for why we have them down here, it's worth the trip. As I find my connection best served close to Mother's roots, so do they. The connection to her is strongest here, and it does not take long before you remember how we are all united and must respect one another for us to succeed in life."

They passed a few windows cut into the roots, beyond which little rooms lay. Each was empty, but Nu noticed Rascal eyeing them with a wary familiarity.

"I've been down here before, so I can vouch for that," Rascal said. "But, Chief Scientist, I have never seen or heard of anything else around here. Are the Rings of History truly down here? Why hide such an important place so close to where the ne'er-do-wells frequent?"

The Chief Scientist gave a light shrug. "Mother decided it was the last place anybody would go looking for it, I suppose."

Crunching across the fallen leaves, she drifted into the shadows, following the line of one tall root and then ducking under it as it looped overhead. On the other side, she followed it back again until she paused in front of the very faint outline of a circular door carved into the wood.

There was no handle, no window. Only etchings making up a vague impression of entry, with no discernible way of making that happen.

Lyvanda reached out and pressed her long fingers and palm against the door. Within moments, little green shoots appeared and grew quickly into vine tendrils. They wrapped over her hand and up her arm, slithering into the sleeve of her robe.

She closed her eyes and exhaled. Then spoke a single word.

"Vernassia."

As they watched, the door immediately grew more distinct in form, and then with a satisfying click, it broke open, revealing light from within.

The vines withered, and Lyvanda brushed them from her skin, then pushed the door open for the others to enter.

They went down within the roots at first. While there had been a few gigantic, thick snakes of them on the surface, there was an entire mass of them below ground—a labyrinth of roots that made up the strangest network of rooms and tunnels Nu would have been hard-pressed to imagine in her dreams. A few steps in any direction and the outlook changed drastically, which meant she felt lost within a few steps and hurried after the Chief Scientist to make sure she wasn't left behind.

"This place is confusing," she heard Arturo say to Robin as they did the same.

"I imagine that's deliberate," Robin replied. "A way to keep it safe. Now, please keep up the pace, or you're going to be a permanent resident!"

Nu wondered if she should offer Arturo the chance to stay here or return to the Library. She had sensed that his presence was necessary, but the details were still murky to her. And he had a daughter to think of. But no, she knew they needed him on this mission.

Lyvanda suddenly paused at a junction between two separate root systems, with vines dangling overhead and flowers winding their way up the walls. She looked from one path to the other, chewing on her lip thoughtfully.

"Now . . . where is it today?"

"You don't know where it is?" Dzin said a little too loudly. He blushed and bowed his head. "I apologize, Chief Scientist. I just thought you'd been here before."

"I have, Dzin, or else me leading you to the Rings would be a fruitless task. But one of Mother's tricks to ensure only the worthy find it is to change the path every now and then. I do not have need to come down here all that often, so invariably, when I do, it's a matter of discovering the route all over again. Ah-ha! It's okay. I see the sign now."

Whatever sign it was that she'd seen, Nu couldn't tell. But they were already off again, taking a few more twists and turns ahead, followed by a climb up some steps carved into the shape of mushrooms. Soon they came across another door much like the first. Solid, no handle or window. Barely imperceptible.

This time the Chief Scientist gestured for Nu to take the lead.

"You must be the one to request this of Mother. It is your need that brings us here."

"You want *me* to talk to Mother?"

"I do . . . and so does she. Only those who seek her help can ask, so that she may feel and understand your intentions."

Nu hesitated, then stepped forward and placed herself in front of the door as she had seen Lyvanda do earlier. "I'm afraid I don't know how. Should I just put my hand on the wood as you did?"

The Chief Scientist inclined her head. "That's exactly right. Mother will be the one to take control. She will reach out to you to converse in a way that will instantly feel natural to you. Her code is written in nature itself, and as you Sages have informed me before, her roots stretch past Silvyra into the metaphysical of the beyond. The other realms, as you say."

Nu did as she was instructed. With a buzz of encouragement from Antares, she stretched her arm out, touched the wood, and pressed her palm against it.

Warmth. That was the first sensation. A delicious warmth that spread deep into her skin and through her bones, rushing in waves out from her hand, up her arm, and into the rest of her. She had been greeted. The tendrils of green sprouted and grew, writhing around her fingers and wrist, binding her to the bark of the door, and the Great Tree welcomed her as an honored guest.

She was unable to resist smiling, such was the force of the majesty pouring into her. A language she could not hope to decipher, yet one that was instinctively understandable to her.

Mother was here, in the bark she was holding her palm against, in the room around them, in the roots they had wandered and the trunk they had climbed down. She was everything and everywhere.

And she wanted to know how she could help.

We need to learn the location of a man from our world, Nu thought. *A man who came into these realms long ago, carrying an artifact of great importance. We need it returned if we are to help stop the same people who have poisoned you. With its return, we hope to prevent any further destruction and maybe, hopefully, it will help us save you too.*

She tried her best to keep the words distinct in her mind, in case it was hard for her—as a visitor to Silvyra—to be understood. As she thought this, Mother let out a mighty laugh that reverberated through Nu's entire body, causing her knees to buckle. Mother explained she had been around long enough to have seen and heard many others from the Great Library.

Then you will help us? Nu asked.

As if in answer, the door became distinct and solid, the bark rough against Nu's palm. And it opened for her and the others to go through.

They climbed another staircase away from the roots, up into the trunk of the Great Tree herself. Nu was still awash with adrenaline after talking with Mother herself, humbled to have been given such an opportunity and found worthy enough to pass.

"Look, there's light ahead," Rascal said. "Is that it?"

At the top of the steps was a curtain of vines. Stepping through, they found themselves in a large circular hollow within the center of the trunk. There were seats of a sort, carved into the floor around them, each one like a wooden wave frozen in time, its crest tipped back just enough to allow any visitors to rest and recline.

Then Nu looked up and understood why.

The ceiling above them was awash with the glow of a thousand colors. This was the true heart of Mother, a stunning series of concentric rings that spoke of thousands of cycles of life here at the Great Tree. Each one distinct in its thickness and vibrancy of color, rings upon rings, glowing with energy, weaving around each other, laid bare the past of Silvyra.

A vast galaxy of history.

"Oh my," Nu gasped. "It's simply beautiful."

Antares seemed lost for any kind of response. Nu watched her Orb as it rose reverently to inspect the Rings. Centauri quickly joined her. They hovered like moons, occasionally pulsing a pattern to one another.

Incredible, Antares said.

She couldn't help but agree. It was as magnificent a sight as she'd seen in all her travels. Yet it was more than just a visual spectacle. There was a very tangible feeling of history within the hollow, as though it seeped from the wood and imbued the air with the past. She felt as though if she reached up and let her fingers dance in the light, she could actually touch the centuries gone by.

"It's actually *real*," Rascal said again, taking a seat to breathe it all in. Her usually sardonic expression gone for the moment as she witnessed this myth come to life. "I can hardly believe I am witnessing this sight with my own eyes. And there I was, thinking I knew all there was to know about the Great Tree."

Dzin's eyes were still locked on the glowing rings above them, mesmerized. "This honestly surpasses anything I could have dreamed. That we are here now, on the cusp of actually using the Rings. I am rendered a little speechless."

Robin had taken a seat. Still remaining close, taking comfort in her company, Arturo sat beside her. From the air, Centauri noted his proximity with a blink of two circles that moved closer to each other across his surface. Nu grinned as Robin rolled her eyes and ignored him.

"Why do you hide this from those who live here?" Arturo asked Lyvanda, ignorant of the Orb's quip, too busy staring around him in awe. "This is a wondrous thing you have. It deserves to be seen, don't you think?"

The Chief Scientist shrugged lightly, her gown billowing as she did so. "It does. But there is more to this place than a visual feast, Arturo. This is history. A lot of it." She pointed up, letting her finger drift in circles. "There are thousands of rings here. Think of the information stored within them. The entire lifetime of Mother is stored in here. That deserves a little protection from those who might have used such information unwisely."

Nu met her eyes, and both were thinking the same thing.

Thank goodness Payne didn't find it.

"So how do we read it?" Robin asked.

Her question hung in the air without an immediate response from any of the group. Even the Orbs seemed to hang there, unsure of what the answer might be. Only the Chief Scientist stood there, smiling knowingly.

Then the room suddenly pulsed with light. Nu thought it had initially come from the Orbs, but she caught the flicker of an emerald glow within the smooth wood of the walls. It fizzled and disappeared, like lightning after a strike.

"Ah, they are here. Excuse me for a moment while I speak with them, ahead of your meeting."

Lyvanda drifted across the floor of the hollow and back through the door they had come through, leaving the group to ponder Robin's question. And who the mysterious "they" were. How *did* they read these rings? There were no control panels around the smooth, grainy wood around the hollowed-out chamber that she could see. No patterns or hints of places to put your hand to commune with Mother. Nothing that might indicate a way for the Great Tree to offer up knowledge.

"The Chief Scientist will know," Nu said, looking around. "I wondered if it was just like with the doors. I heard Mother within me when I touched the wood, and she spoke to me. Yet I can't see anywhere to place my hands, and there *are* all these seats, so maybe it's more metaphysical than physical in here. Perhaps we simply sit back and stare at the Rings, and the Great Tree will show us what we need to know."

To test it, she sat in a spare seat and leaned against the curves. The others quickly did the same, Arturo letting Robin take his and moving to a different one, while Dzin and Rascal did the same. All of them stared at the ceiling for a moment, letting the gentle, natural shades of reflected light wash over them.

"Anything?" Rascal asked.

"Nothing," Dzin said. Robin shook her head. Arturo too.

Nu frowned, but before she could say anything, she watched Antares begin to do something strange. Her Orb and Centauri had gone to hover in the very center of the Rings, before starting to spin.

"Antares?"

The Orb didn't respond, too busy concentrating. Nu watched as soft swirls of light blew across her surface. Centauri's too. Then they stopped spinning and began to move in small circles. Very small movements at first, as though caught in a whirlpool in the air. Yet slowly it became clear they were moving outward in concentric circles, patterns rushing across their silver surfaces.

Arturo chuckled disbelievingly. "Are they trying to read it? Like needles on a vinyl record player?"

Robin tilted her head as she stared up. "I think they are!"

As the Orbs continued their dance above, a quiet, smooth voice, like icing pouring over cake, spoke from the doorway.

"They won't find much that way, I'm afraid."

CHAPTER TWENTY-TWO

STORIES OF THE FOUNDER

Nu saw that the owner of the voice stood no taller than a child. But their presence spilled through the doorway and filled the chamber.

They had a face that seemed on the verge of adulthood, but with wizened creases at the eyes and closely cropped gray hair that spoke of great age. They stood straight and true, in a shimmering viridescent robe that dropped to their feet, with darker sashes at the wrists and waist.

The Chief Scientist stepped into view beside them.

"May I present the Chronologist, the keeper of the Rings of History and the interpreter of all the knowledge of Silvyra contained within."

"It is my great honor to meet you all," the Chronologist said, offering an enigmatic smile that bordered on that of a patient teacher. The Orbs had stopped trying to read the Rings and were slowly sinking from the ceiling as though caught doing something they shouldn't. The Chronologist laughed. "Yes, even you small things! I had half a mind to stand here and watch you attempt to do what I have been learning to do since birth. Had you succeeded, of course, I may well have taken that as my leave to retire."

Lyvanda guided them both into the room. Nu could see she still held the power here, even though her light touch on the Chronologist's arm was full of reverence.

"We could not possibly do without you, as you well know. The Great Tree chose you to be its keeper of secrets, and there is no one else who could do it as well, or with as much enthusiasm." She glanced at the Orbs. "No offense, little ones."

"They were just a little curious," Nu said. "I hope you don't mind."

The Chronologist walked into the room to join the others. They waved their hands as they talked, as though conducting the words drifting from their lips. "Of course not, my girl. One cannot help but admire their desire to lean into that curiosity and learn what they could. Such is the true nature of life. If only we were all as curious."

"It's as I told you," Lyvanda said as she followed her companion into the room. "Their need was great. When Sages travel all the way here from the Great Library to seek Mother's help, we know it must be of great importance."

"Ah, indeed! I have met one or two of your number in the past, long ago, and it will give me just as much pleasure to help you now as it was for me then." They walked in slow, deliberate steps toward the center of the room and took the seat directly under the wide expanse of Rings above them. The colors ebbed and flowed, bathing the short-statured Chronologist in a variety of hues. "So, my friends, tell me: What is it you seek?"

Nu strode over to take the chair opposite the Chronologist.

"We are looking for a man who ventured beyond our Great Library many generations ago, around the same time as travel between our realms became possible. His name was Haruto, a scholar, and he brought with him an artifact of great importance to us."

"Many generations? Then he would be long dead! How do you suppose you will find a dead man?"

"If we could just find a clue to where he landed or settled, it might help us track his journey onward. Following that could then lead us to the artifact he took. It is a long shot, but it is believed we need it back if we are to stop the evil that threatens us all."

"Ah. Yes, I know of what you speak."

"So you'll help us?"

In response, the Chronologist reclined in the seat and lifted their hands to the ceiling. The anticipation built within Nu, and she leaned back in her own chair with a growing excitement.

Then it began.

Nu gasped as shards of green and gold suddenly wove into bright cyclones of light and spun down to meet the Chronologist's hands still waving in the air.

They talked as they worked. "I am but one of a long and prestigious line of keepers of the Rings of History. We are skilled in communicating with nature, witnessing its history, and interpreting it for ourselves. There were many of us, a while ago, yet times change and interests wane. Not everyone is as focused on the knowledge the natural world can give us as they used to be, which I find to be a shame. Anyway, the mantle fell to me alone many moons ago, and it shall be passed from me to the next many moons in the future. Interestingly, perhaps to you, it was a stranger from your world who first worked with Mother to create this room you find yourself in now."

"One of us?" Robin exclaimed. "But who?"

"Ah, that is a story for another time. Now . . ." They closed their eyes, and their arms locked into place. The colors began to spin faster around them. ". . . here we go."

Nu shuddered against an explosion of emotions. They burst out from the colorful whirlwinds wrapping around the Chronologist, rippling across the room in visible streaks of berry reds and sunset purples and nectar oranges, before passing *through* each of them. Nu's spirit was suddenly filled with the most glorious sensation, like falling upward through afternoon sunlight. She was everyone and everything at once. Every emotion one could feel, all vying for attention within her. Excitement, love, despair, fear, joy—an incredible moment of being life itself. She suddenly tasted a lifetime of flavors. Breathed in all her favorite scents, her nose tingling, her eyes watering with the sheer intensity of it all.

Even as the impact faded, the sensation held. Everyone present at that moment within the Rings of History had become a living part of history now.

The Chronologist spoke.

"Can you feel it, seekers? There is much here to be found. A world of memories. A vast universe of them, in fact. The roots of Mother run deep and wide, beyond Silvyra, stretching to every corner of the known and unknown, and she will find the man you are looking for. Even now . . . Yes, the Rings are opening up. They are showing me . . . a stranger arriving from beyond these borders. Not to Silvyra, no. Another realm. One with a sky full of islands."

"You can see all this?" Nu asked, trying to hold herself together as the oceans of lived lives flowed through her.

"Yes, my girl. Every significant act or event is imprinted on the Rings of History. It's all here in some form. In each realm beyond this one, you will find a nexus of nature. And Mother is curious. Her roots stretch to them all, like children, and between them they share love and understanding across the divides. Information flows easily this way. It may not provide the details you might expect, but rather feelings and vibrations. Everything from the breath of a bug to events that have shaken entire worlds."

They paused and frowned in concentration, their arms still conducting the cyclones of color. Nu saw flashes of green pulsing through the veins in their hands. They were in sync with the Rings now, moving faster, learning more.

"This man you seek, his arrival caused a ripple that made the Great Tree take note. Even now, there are others taking note of him too—a pair, siblings I think, whose own paths orbit his. They watch him. Guarding him."

Nu tried to center herself as the sensation began to grow again, the room pulsating with energy. Something the Chronologist had said was niggling at her. What was it?

Then.

"Wait," she said. "You are speaking in the present tense?"

"I am."

"Are you saying he's still alive!?"

The Chronologist paused, as if seeking confirmation. Then they nodded. "Yes, it is true. That is what I am seeing here. And the Rings do not lie. This person is older than he should be. Some have whispered that he is immortal. That . . . Yes, his name is Haruto. They say Haruto is immortal. He lives still, in the realm of the sky."

With that, the electric tension in the Rings of History began to subside. As the Chronologist began to slow their working, Robin walked over and sat beside Nu.

"You realize what this means? If he's still alive, he's either still got that fragment, or he's hidden it somewhere because he knows how important it is. We'll actually get to meet one of the first scholars of the Great Library and ask him directly for his help! Maybe we can even convince him to come back with us. He could prove an advantage against Suttaru, knowing him as he used to."

"Either way, we found what we came for," Nu said, feeling the weight on her shoulders dissipate, knowing they'd located this mysterious man they had come to find. That he was still alive was a welcome surprise too.

Perhaps this would go more smoothly than she had bargained for.

"Adscendo!" Rascal said suddenly.

Arturo almost fell off his chair with surprise. He looked around the gathered faces as if wondering what was going on.

Rascal gave him a strange look, then turned to the Chronologist.

"A sky realm full of islands. It must be Adscendo. I traveled there once before, with Captain Finesse, on a delivery run for the Elixir of Life. There can't be that many sky realms out there, surely?"

"The name rings true," the Chronologist confirmed.

Nu couldn't help the grin creeping across her face.

"Would you know where in the realm we could find him, Chronologist? This is the last we'll ask of you and the Rings, I promise."

Her question, however, was met with a sigh.

"Alas, Sage, I cannot. There is nothing solid here. It is as though he has become a blur. I'm afraid you will have to go and seek him directly if you are to find him."

"But if it's a realm full of flying islands, he could be on any one of them," Dzin argued.

"And yet it was said he was being watched over by siblings," Arturo said, frowning in concentration. He looked around the group. "That they were spying on him, yes? Maybe if we find *them*, we can find him. At the very least, it gives us three grains of sand to search for instead of one."

He smiled at the joke, as did the Chronologist.

"You are correct. And of them I know a little more. They are performers. Acrobats of great skill. Their performances create big ripples in that realm. In many realms, apparently. Mmmm . . ."

Their voice drifted as their hands continued to seek knowledge, pulling at the swirling colors of the Rings above them, twisting and mixing them.

"And where can we find *them*?" Nu asked.

"There is only one place they can be, only one island in Adscendo that can hold their talents. Seek them in the hive of excitement."

Rascal smiled, and her wing tips twitched as though eager to leave immediately.

"Oh yes! I know exactly where that is. Good, then we have what we came for. Shall we get going?"

The Chronologist shifted in their seat and let their arms drop wearily by their sides. The cyclones awash with a vast array of colors, powerful and majestic, now shrunk back to the ceiling, where they continued spinning and pulsing around the rings of the Great Tree.

The reading was at an end.

"I hope I have been of some help," the Chronologist said.

Nu stood, then held out her hand to help them up. As their fingers touched, Nu was filled with a blast of residual energy. She froze in place, her mind reeling, unable to utter anything other than a loud gasp.

The evil is coming.

It was Mother. She was speaking to her through the Rings. Through the Chronologist. As her words rang in Nu's ears, her sight was suddenly lost in a flash of white fire, and in her mind's eye, she saw him. Suttaru.

He's coming.

Hurry.

Then the energy dissipated. Nu shook herself free, her pulse racing, pricks of quickening fear stabbing through her.

"Are you okay, my dear?"

She blinked and stared at the Chronologist.

"I'm . . . I'm not sure what happened there," she lied. They needed to be on their way, and fast. Time was running out. "You have helped a great deal, Chronologist. Thank you for your counsel and reading the Rings for us. And to you, Chief Scientist, for your generosity and guidance. We will need to make our way back to the Great Library now, ready to travel to Adscendo."

"Wait, Nu," Rascal said. "The properties of Adscendo would make arriving by portal there particularly dangerous. It's a sky realm, with hundreds of floating islands and continents. The landmasses are ever moving and at the whim of wind currents and storms. There is no way to determine their locations at any single point."

"Oh, well, the Book of Wisdom would be able to get us there, I'm sure."

Antares and Centauri buzzed in disagreement.

We can't portal.

"We can't portal?" Nu repeated. "Why not?"

Glitches, remember?

She and Robin sighed in unison. Of course. The portal might get them to a fixed landmass safely, but to take the chance it might glitch and miss a moving island in the sky? They were just as likely to step out into thin air and drop to their deaths as find their feet on dry land.

They couldn't risk it.

"What do we do, then?" Robin asked.

The Chief Scientist smiled, a glint in her eyes. "I believe we can help. We have ways to allow you to reach your destination safely, as well as venture between these floating islands with little fuss. It is one I know Nu herself is already familiar with. Isn't that right, Rascal?"

"I believe it is, Chief Scientist," Rascal replied with a grin. "Come on, then, let's be going, you lot. We've got another adventure to be on."

But as they said their goodbyes to the Chronologist, Nu heard Dzin hang back just long enough to ask, "When this is done, can I come back? I have some particularly pertinent questions about the voyages of one Bravadier Blossom . . ."

CHAPTER TWENTY-THREE
THE POWER OF A SILVER COIN

The Burning Forest, a simple but accurate name, spread out before Payne in all directions. The soles of his polished military-style boots were covered in the centuries of ash and charcoal that littered the nearby landscape, a testament to the suffering this place had endured since centuries—perhaps even longer—before he'd been born. But now he stood on its edges, the wailing, living fire of millions of trees, tormented in flame for an eternity because of what it represented.

The Tree of Eternal Flame, a once sacred part of this land, had resisted the forces of Discordia when the world fell. It had towered above its smaller cousins, reflecting the light of the dual stars and dancing in a flames of reddish-orange sunlight. The remaining stories of this world—those that had been written down and not yet found and burned—spoke of its wonder and life-giving properties. People would travel from far and wide to bask in its flames and come away refreshed. Its resistance had been strong, but ultimately foolish. As Suttaru told it, the tree, bereft of one star's light, had faltered when the darkness arrived.

It shone no more, as Discordia's darkness enveloped this world. But its resistance was noted, and a suitable punishment was created. Payne had listened on, attention rapt as his master told the tale.

You see, Vassal, these world trees are the symbol of life on their respective realms, a living network, like weeds, spreading everywhere, and there was an opportunity to control this light. To make it Discordia's. It took the forest first, then the tree itself. Oh, how it screamed. The spirit of the tree was torn from its natural body and forced to burn. And burn and burn, until it lost its sanity. Once broken, aflame, Discordia returned it to its empty husk, where the old tree burned, and so did its forest.

Discordia used the tree to Unwrite this world and its people. The strength of its power over the natural life story was such that we still reap the benefits of its crimson fire. Its ash forms my cloak, its twisted script the manifestation of our power to Unwrite the weaker realms to our will. Discordia has sufficient strength now to exert its will upon the realms, to start to Unwrite this whole reality, but the lessons of the tree remain.

Come, my Dark Sage, and I will teach you its secrets, and you, too, shall have the power to Unwrite the living memories of our enemies and transform the world around you.

The power he'd experienced that day had been his last test and his initiation into Suttaru's army. The Tree of the Unwritten, as they now called it—or simply, the Burning Tree—would once again be his to command.

He looked at the trailing misfits and outcasts following him. They were what was left of this realm's citizens. Broken, Unwritten, and little more than useless on a normal day. But with Suttaru's journal, and what he had found bound beneath its cover, he was sure he could use them to bring back his master. He looked toward the burning forest, the heat enough to drive any sane person away, and strode toward it.

The fire grew intense, but Payne ignored it. His affinity to the darkness afforded him the protection of this realm, and while he could feel the heat beating at his military-style woollen greatcoat and gaberdine pants, it never threatened to burn him.

The trees he passed were sorry things, twisted in the endless fire until their branches were broken and deformed. They looked to Payne like dryads from some dark poem, perverted from nature into something wicked and malevolent. The forest closed in around him, his attendants left behind the wall of fire for now, until he reached the burning one. He heard the snapping of branches and the popping of pine cones. He passed a fallen creature, melted into the side of a small stone outcropping, its face an agony of tortured existence. He paused near it, freeing his army saber from its fine leather sheath, and poked the wickedly sharp tip into what might have once been the face of a kind of bear, or other large, furry creature. Half of its body was melted into the stone, which bubbled in a semiliquid state. As the sword's point pierced its skin, the creature moved, howling through burning lungs. Payne smiled. It was fascinating to him, this entire place trapped in an endless nightmare. He turned away, leaving the wretched creature to its fate. It wasn't for him to intercede. No, his plan was altogether grander.

He walked for hours, until a natural clearing started to open up before him, marked by the sacrifices of past ages, both human and animal. Eternally dying offerings, crimson text written across their hides, mindless in their agony. Finally, he stood in front of this realms Mother Tree.

It was largely unchanged. Its flames had been treasured in the days before Discordia, and they still burned brightly, but these leaves and branches gave off a sense of menace that even he felt disquiet being so close to. He approached its blackened trunk, as large as his home country's largest oak, yet veined and almost delicate. Fleshy, perhaps, before its transformation.

He removed his deerskin leather gloves and offered his hand to its burning flesh.

Before Edwin Payne had set his plan into motion, there had been time for study, time to divert the foolish Sages on a chase across the realms to keep them from his true objective: away from Penumbris. Edwin had placed the tattered journal onto his lap and cast his eyes over the putrid, pulsing circle. Did it look right? Whole? Was it in line with the theory Adi had postulated after his tests had hinted at what could be achieved?

As Adi the scholar had written:

I have tried to focus on my work. Testing the metal scrapings, exploring the reactions of the energy levels in the presence of inanimate objects and varying degrees of distance from the Maksus Stone.

The results were . . . well, the word remarkable *is what scientists use, but it is too weak a word for this.* Incredible? Unbelievable? Unprecedented?

I made a silver coin spin on its axis and leap into the air.

How? The inner spirit of the metal. The base energy infused in it, the source of which is the Maksus Stone. I conducted an energy transfusion of sorts, soldering the molten metal onto the coin. In doing so, it brought with it the Zen energy previously noted. With some prodding via heated elements, the coin moved, danced, and jumped. And then was still.

Haruto was rendered speechless, as was I. Fairen believes more than ever there is an element of magic to this. Energy. Magic. Perhaps they are two sides of the same equation, viewed through different lenses.

She warns me to be careful. It is one of the few times of late she has bestowed any kind of worry for me, so consumed she has been by other activities. We rarely spend time together now. Not that I have much of it to spare. Regardless, she was not wrong to show concern. There appeared a streak of gray in my hair following this experiment, and I wonder if some of my own life force—being the closest to the coin—was harnessed in the creation of life, if only for a moment.

It could be that a sacrifice of life is needed to create life. I have not informed the others, but I will retest with a protective shield of other creatures, to protect myself from any draining . . .

The silver coin had been the only experiment Adi would run in the end, at least for this reason. He soon became distracted by the revelation of the realms accessible through the portal and Fairen's attempt to control it. He had become distracted by Fairen herself.

It was weakness, plain and simple. One that made Edwin uncomfortable to read about. He had always been unflinching in his pursuit of whatever goals had been set and laid out before him. If Adi had only continued his research with full focus, he would have discovered the potential Edwin felt he was about to realize.

The energy of the Maksus Stone was powerful and could animate small objects for a time with careful manipulation and a sacrifice of the fuel of life. Now Edwin was taking the experiment to its natural next step. Some might say its destined conclusion.

Reaching into his pocket, he pulled out Suttaru's fragment of the Maksus Stone. The one he had always carried around his neck, on a chain made of the molten metal infused with the same energy. Edwin held them up to what little light the constant twilight of this realm afforded. He saw the ribbons of fire running through the fragment. He reached into another pocket and removed the coin he'd found bound into the journal's back cover.

Adi had once brought this silver coin to life. It was a foolish thing, the act of an idiot. Payne had sensed its presence almost as soon as he'd touched the journal for the first time, but he hadn't yet had time to identify what it was. A wrongness, a sliver of something out of place and possibly insane. What had possessed Suttaru's former self to animate an inanimate object was beyond him, but he supposed the young scholar had thought he was doing nothing wrong. But, in fact, what he had done was create something so very wrong that it might now hold the secrets of how to bring his master back.

Now Payne's hands burned, held to the trunk of this magnificent atrocity. He felt the tree's spirit awaken and saw it slowly manifest through the charred wood of its own. It had taken on the appearance of a woman, in the most basic of forms. Her face was cruel—scornful, even—but when she saw his face, Myrtilus the Orb gleaming from his empty eye socket, she looked almost mournful.

"What would you have me do now, Sage-That-Was?"

"I would have you obey me, Spirit, as you were instructed to do by our master."

She snarled, and he wondered if it were possible she still held some shred of herself back from the darkness, as he well knew was possible. After all, his own plans were at odds with Suttaru's designs on the Library.

"Our Lord Suttaru must be brought back if we are to defeat the Great Library and their pious Sages. They interfere in our plans at every turn. We must have him back."

"How, Edwin Payne, would you have me do this thing? I can Unwrite the living using the fire of my body, and that of what was once the Forest Everlasting, and I've taught you how to channel that yourself. What more would you expect me to do?" She seemed petulant now, and he felt his anger, and some uncertainty, grow.

"I have discovered the origins of Suttaru's talisman," he said, holding the necklace aloft, the shard of the Maksus Stone dangling free. He'd retrieved it from the ashes of Suttaru's remains at the City of Forever before the moronic Sages had even thought to examine his remains and kept it on him ever since. The tree spirit looked momentarily hungry. "You know it, Spirit?"

"I know it. I know it was built to raise us high, but it became our downfall. But what use is this paltry fragment if you had the whole . . ." She looked hungry again, perhaps even desperate.

"I have the ashes of his body, or at least some of them, bound to you through his cloak and your forest, taken from the site of his death at the City of Forever. And I have this!" He held the living coin aloft, the flames reflecting in its shining silver surface. "An artifact crafted by our lord before the stone was shattered."

"A twisted relic now, Dark Sage. Twisted and pitiful in such a stunted and mundane form."

"Agreed, but perhaps we can change that. I have studied our lord's calculations, and I believe if we combine the shard, the coin, and your ability to Unwrite the living, we can bring him back."

"It will take more life magic than that trinket to even attempt such a thing."

"I agree, but we have a whole world of subjects to use for our cause. They are pitiful creatures, for sure, but their Unwritten flesh could perhaps be transformed into that of our master."

"As you say, it might be possible. But it will require a sacrifice the likes of which we haven't seen since the great burning. And even then, their waning life force might not be enough to do what you ask. It may not be possible."

"Then, Spirit, we will try until it does. Our enemies are on the move. They are following trails I'd not considered, and we will need our master to stop them. Unless you'd rather explain to Discordia itself how you have failed it?"

The spirit shivered and shrank back into itself. "Bring your sacrifices, Dark One. And I shall conjure a flame that can perhaps Unwrite the dead back to life."

The circle of bodies grew larger as Payne's adjuncts, those with enough intelligence left to follow orders and mimic free will, brought their brethren to be sacrificed. They sometimes came one by one, sometimes in packs, returning from journeys Edwin Payne cared little about, only that the weak-minded fools had returned with more fuel for the great fire.

The fuel was those foolish enough to have been caught. It was that simple. Edwin did not want to decimate his army, for they would be needed soon, but a few among them were needed for this ritual, this grand experiment. So he let them select those unworthy of continuing along their path.

There was no need to ensure the bodies were a certain type. Man, woman, or child, they would all provide the essence needed.

He looked up from the journal, studying yet again younger Suttaru's notes, watching the captured bodies continue to writhe, moan, fight against their bonds, unknowing of the part they would play in history. Not understanding what their sacrifice here meant. The burning forest had opened itself to Payne's charnel house. A vast path cut through the forest now to the Burning Tree, a nightmare circle of living dead creatures forming an arena of sorts. The wails of the captives were second only to the tortured souls of the forest itself. Payne had considered sacrificing them, but he needed the tree at its most powerful, and the suffering of those who had once been a part of its closest circle, animal and plant alike, fueled its dark magic already.

He flicked his tongue out, licking them, savoring the delicious sting and metallic taste of bloody ash as they bled and strained against their bonds.

These wretched creatures served a purpose; they were a means to an end. They might have longed to rest. To sleep. To die mortal deaths on their own terms. And die they would . . . but on his terms and according to his plans.

He would make it so.

He thought back to that fateful time, Myrtilus and himself cut off from the magic of the Great Library, his body physically aging once more and in the grip of dark forces he still hadn't understood. He had changed enough for the Book of Wisdom and her Sages to no longer recognize him, and soon the ability to truly change his appearance, to shift his form, had come to him. His missing eye the only constant, until recently, when disguises like those he'd been obligated to wear at Silvyra were no longer needed. A reckoning with his former colleagues would come if Edwin was successful here. Because it would mean a second chance to take the Library. All had seemed lost in the wake of Suttaru's death. And as he looked over at the intricate array of human fuel being arranged around the Burning Tree, he felt his time was coming. His master would reward him—perhaps with the lives of the Sages, or perhaps with the Library itself. Once the Great Library of Tomorrow was his, he could sever its link to Paperworld, destroy the portals, and cut Earth off from the realms of Paperworld. Until that time, he would play his part, no matter what that required of him.

Edwin Payne was going to bring Suttaru back. And the fires of damnation themselves would help him.

CHAPTER TWENTY-FOUR
THE SKY REALM

"The *Golden Oriole* has become the flagship of the Silvyran fleet," Arturo heard the Chief Scientist say as they neared the docks at the top of the Great Tree. "Ever since we lost most of our other airships, she has led the charge to get the Elixir of Life back into the hands of those who need it. I would normally be remiss to let Rascal's ship leave when there is still a weight of responsibility here."

"And yet you understand our need is potentially greater, don't you?" Nu said, walking beside her.

"I do, Sage. You must find the man the Chronologist spoke of and the artifact you seek, for the benefit of all." Arturo saw a hint of humor pulling at the corners of Lyvanda's lips. "Besides, if you are to travel to this realm of sky islands, you must not fall to your deaths upon arrival. It would not do."

It soon became clear that while Rascal was going to fly them to Adscendo, Dzin was going to stay behind. Arturo grabbed the younger man into a fierce bear hug and lifted him off the ground, leaving the smaller man smiling and happy. Yet as they said their goodbyes and climbed on board, Arturo saw the young man grow more somber, and he seemed to catch that mood. His natural enthusiasm at yet another new experience dampened a little by the realization they were heading away from relative safety and into the unknown.

Arturo had peered through the porthole and waved to these new friends, who had given him the gift of their hospitality, friendship, and even family. As the *Golden Oriole* shut its door and lifted from the landing pad, he paused and took it all in once more, this magical world, so different, and yet, at its heart, not so very different from the community he'd grown up in. Meanwhile, the Chief Scientist held more of a solemn look as befitting the role of a leader in this realm. She didn't wave, merely nodded, hands behind her back, as they rose.

As she stood on the landing platform, disappearing below them, Arturo, Robin, and Nu strapped themselves into their seats and watched Rascal at the controls. Switches were flicked. Levers were pulled and pushed. Then a piece of wood shaped like a medallion was pulled from a compartment. Rascal waved it in the air as she glanced back at her passengers.

"We all ready?"

"Ready!" Robin said, positively beaming with excitement.

"Ready," Arturo echoed.

Rascal glanced over her shoulder. "Oh, I really don't think you are," she said, chuckling under her breath as she took the wooden medallion and placed it into the console.

About five seconds later, the *Golden Oriole* had catapulted them away from the Great Tree and then, abruptly, from the realm of Silvyra with a thunderous blaze of nausea-inducing transition.

Arturo's heart tore inside his chest with exhilaration as the *Golden Oriole* buckled and shuddered. It swung one way, then another, then dropped as though caught in some mystical thermals out in whatever was out there.

The ether. The eternal void. A space of nothingness and everything, caught between collections of stories that formed worlds. A place of lights and darkness that exploded into being again and again beyond the glass of the porthole window, beside the narrow seat Nu had ensured he was strapped into, whose curled golden armrest he was currently gripping so tightly his knuckles were white.

He wanted to scream with the thrill of it.

"Are you okay?" Nu shouted from across the aisle.

"Never better!" he replied. Beside him, Robin was grinning widely, similarly enjoying the ride.

His mind raced, thinking of his daughter and what she would have made of this airship ride. He wished he could have brought her along. Perhaps he'd try to get her to come with him next time.

Robin leaned over and reached for his left hand and gave it a little squeeze. He felt the warmth of her skin, noted the darker hue of her fingers intertwined with his, and grinned back.

"If it feels like you're about to die, I just want you to know that's totally normal," she said cheerfully. "Crossing the threshold between realms like this is the equivalent of threading our way through the roots of a complex, living metaphysical system. It's a little harder on the nerves than using the Library's portal!"

"It's like a roller coaster," he said, gripping the sides of his chair. "I don't know whether to laugh or scream!"

"Hold on. We're nearly through," Rascal yelled back. They held each other's gaze as Arturo felt his fingers digging even further into the armrests until he didn't think he could hold on any tighter. The temptation to just let go and raise his hands into the air in celebration was strong, but he wisely kept them at his side.

The light outside the airship grew even more intense. It poured through the main windshield and streamed through the porthole windows. He squeezed his eyes shut as the cabin became a swirling mass of color, driving its way through until he started to see a map of light lines, green and gold once more, like in the Rings, and carrying him with it. It was so strong it filled his mind, his thoughts. The airship shuddered once, twice. Rascal cursed and slammed some switches on the dashboard. Nu was whispering something to herself. He could barely hear her beneath the roar of the airship, and then they must have been approaching the wall of the new realm, as the patterns of light grew denser, as though it resisted their attempts to penetrate it.

Rascal started counting down.

"Five . . ."

"Four . . ."

"Here we go!" someone yelled, and he braced, feeling a brief moment of connectedness with those around him, those they'd left behind on Silvyra, and even—he imagined to himself—this new world.

And then they were through.

It was like pushing oneself headfirst through a powerful waterfall. An instant of noise and pressure, and then nothing. Just a little ringing in the ears and slightly aching eyes.

Arturo opened his eyes.

And took in a brand-new world.

He had heard this was a sky realm. He had pictured it in his mind and even let himself consider what it might be like to witness such a thing.

He'd been on long-distant flights back on Earth. Watched through the gently fogging window as clouds raced past below. Yet there wasn't much else to marvel at, except the deepening blues of the sky as it rose toward space.

Here?

This was a painting on a canvas of reality. An entire world of blue skies, awash with floating lands of all shapes and sizes. His jaw dropped at the sheer scale of the view, while his heart raced with the sight. It was quite frankly astonishing. Incredible. Unbelievable. Like a collage of fantastical places the universe's greatest artists might conjure up in their wildest dreams. An improbable plane of existence, as if the world below had shattered and all the jigsaw pieces of the landscape had floated up to drift upon the clouds.

He felt the magic then. There was no way to explain it, but there was a feeling, a tangible energy in the air here. It vibrated against his skin and seeped into his bloodstream. It filled him with an excitement he imagined birds must feel when they swooped and glided through the sky. His hair stood on end, and he felt the goose bumps across his skin.

The floating islands were all so beautifully different too. Some were like blank canvases of nature, nothing but fertile fields, rolling hills, and rivers that cascaded over the ragged edges and disappeared into the mist far below; while others were sprawling urban masses, with bridges slung between spiraling towers, walled castles, and endless city streets. It made him feel like a child playing in his parents' yard, having once more escaped reality to lose himself in an imaginary world of fantasy. Except this was real; he could feel the arms of the chair beneath his fingers, the bump of turbulence as the *Golden Oriole* shook. He badly wanted them to stop and land somewhere just so he could get out and explore.

There were small islands, barely a windmill, and a house on a hill. There were bigger lands with meadows and towns. But it was the others Arturo could see that held his attention and made him draw in his breath suddenly—gigantic shadows of what looked like entire countries, whose masses were filled with smudges of forests and outlines of mountains, and the sporadic glows of beautiful cities bustling with activity.

"It's . . . amazing. Like I just fell into a dreamscape," he said.

"Welcome to Adscendo," Rascal announced from the pilot's seat.

Arturo pressed his face to the window but quickly grew frustrated that it wasn't nearly big enough to take in the view properly. He unbuckled himself and apologetically climbed over Robin to get a better look through the cockpit window.

"I can't believe we're really here," he said to nobody in particular. "Truly. It's like I've stepped into a movie back home, but beyond anything they could have imagined."

"Quite something, isn't it?" As she talked, Rascal tugged gently at the hourglass-shaped steering control and pulled the airship around port side. There was a rumble through the cabin; they must have caught a current. The *Golden Oriole* suddenly picked up speed, and they coasted along through the spectacular skies, with Arturo relishing every moment of it. At first he thought this must be commonplace to the others, but he saw both Nu and Robin gazing out of the window in a similar state of dazed awe. To Rascal, captain of the ship and clearly experienced in this kind of jumping between worlds, it was perhaps another day aboard the ship. But even for the Sages, who he presumed had visited many of the realms of Paperworld, it seemed like this world was something special.

"Have you never been anywhere like this?" he said.

"Yes, several times. It is a very singular world, from our records, and I longed to see it," said Robin, coming to stand beside him. "Ages ago, they suffered an environmental event that meant living on the surface of their world was becoming impracticable. This was before the Library's time, you understand, but from our subsequent investigations, it seems there is a natural magic here—in the clouds and the birds—that they were able to harness and use to transform their world." She looked at Arturo now, not the endless vista beyond the ship. "And they became one with their world in a way we could only dream of back on Earth."

"And you've never been here?" he said.

"Not I, nor Nu. She is very new to our ranks, you'll recall, and while she has been into Paperworld many times, often with me, we haven't as yet had a need to go here. Others of our order have been, I imagine. It is a unique place, after all."

"I'm glad we will experience it together, then," he said, reaching out to brush a stray hair from her face, holding back at the last moment. She held still and took his hand, and he felt the soft skin of hers, a moment of intimacy he felt he'd cherish more than the view outside.

It was like they'd entered a painting. A stunning piece of art pulled from the minds of people with far more imagination than he. Everywhere he looked, there was movement. They stayed still, making a connection as real as anything he'd ever encountered. Even as the airship sped through this world, the lands floating seemed to have some semblance of motion across the sky as they stood still, until finally he noticed other kinds of craft, and the spell was broken. They turned to the ship's small window. They were not quite airships like the one he was standing in, but various styles of flying machines. Some buzzing like insects with beating wings, others gliding like birds between destinations.

Then he noticed the birds.

They flocked mainly around the islands, concentrating in stunning murmuration as they moved as one, swirling and dancing through the skies as if of a single mind, but there were others too. Smaller groups of *much* larger birds, each easily the size of a small plane—their beaks curved like hunters, their black-and-white plumage glossy and magnificent, sparkling under the sunlight—were soaring on the wild currents out in the open.

Fingers found his shoulder as Robin leaned in, her breath a whisper beside his ear.

"I have traveled to many realms in Paperworld, Arturo. Seen a lot of different ways of life unfolding. But even I wasn't prepared for this." She turned to Rascal, who had approached silently as they were talking. "You've been here before, then?" Robin asked.

"Aye, I have, just twice. Both brief visits, and they were a long time ago. But such a place leaves a mark on the mind."

"I'll say," Arturo said.

Nu had joined them at the cockpit window, putting her hand on Rascal's chair to steady herself as the airship rocked and bobbed again, this time to avoid another flock of brightly colored birds. The creatures doubled back as if to stare through the window back at those watching them, then they soared up and disappeared from view. Nu seemed torn between fascination and impatience.

"Alas, Rascal, I think our entertainment will have to wait until we get the chance to visit on a more leisurely schedule. We've spent enough time waiting to locate where Haruto might be, and now we know he's here, under the watchful eye of these mysterious siblings, we need to work fast. Do you know where we need to go? You suggested you might know where the siblings can be found."

"You're right. I did say that, didn't I?"

Nu's lips thinned. "There's a *but* coming, isn't there?"

"Well . . ."

"Rascal?"

"Okay, yes, I have a fair idea of where we can find them. Like I said, I've only been here a couple of times in the past while on trips with Captain Finesse to distribute the Elixir of Life. Finesse was strict about timekeeping, and we didn't get to spend much time to ourselves. But he *did* allow us to unwind in one of the most exciting places in the realm. And if we are looking for performers, then I reckon that's where they'll be performing. It's a place of entertainment and thrills and fun, designed for those who like to take a few risks and those who like to watch them. I know that's where they'll be."

"But?"

Rascal kept her eyes on the horizon. "But I don't know how to get there. Captain Finesse brought us last time. I didn't navigate. So how he found that settlement, I don't rightly know. These islands are constantly moving, shifting in relation to one another. It's an ever-changing realm, and trying to locate any one place is fraught with navigational challenges. Some use birds as navigators, but we don't have any to hand, I'm afraid."

"Okay," Nu said. She looked to Antares. The Orb pulsed a series of patterns at her. Arturo couldn't tell what they were saying, and Nu didn't elaborate. She simply nodded and returned to staring through the window thoughtfully.

Quiet descended on the cabin as they left the shadow of the smaller island passing overhead, a new landmass hovering into view in the distance. A vast mountain citadel rose in the center of a walled city, which reminded Arturo of the famous Mont-Saint-Michel, only bigger, much bigger, with willowy towers twisting up into the heavens. Beyond this, atop a hill, a glint of sunlight flashed off what looked like a huge glass dome. One that either sat on the hill or perhaps even floated above. It was difficult to tell at this distance.

"The city of Arcadiana," Rascal said wistfully. "The jewel in the crown of Adscendo. That's where I sneaked back on my second trip and managed to pay someone to give me my wings, despite only being a visitor, technically guildless, and certainly not a windrider." Her folded wing tips quivered above her shoulders. "It was worth it though. Flying here is revered, as you can imagine. The birds are held in the highest regard. They don't just coexist alongside the people who live here; they all work together for the greater good. It's been like this for as far back as the scribed records go. The birds can be messengers or even navigators, helping to ensure safe passage through the skies for the multitude of islands and the craft that fly between them."

"And there are so many of them!" Robin said. "Look at that!"

Her face lit up as a flock of bright green-and-yellow birds with crimson tail plumes formed a circle around the *Golden Oriole*, before darting off again in a trail of color. Then she gasped in amazement as a flock of much larger birds soaring in the wilderness between the islands suddenly shifted course as if to meet the *Golden Oriole* and grew larger and larger in view until Arturo was sure they would surely hit the airship and send them all plummeting to their deaths.

At the last minute, the flock swerved, and only one bird grew closer, swooping by the window as if to give those inside a show. It was a beautiful sight, with plumage that glistened in a range of blues, from eggshell to turquoise to the blue of a midnight sky. Its bright eyes glowed a spectacular amber, and its body was interspersed with streaks of golden feathers that had a metallic sheen to their coating.

"What was *that* one?" Robin asked. There was wonder in her voice, and Arturo smiled, appreciating her great affinity for all living creatures. He supposed that the Sage of Love quite rightly understood that animals' capacity for such emotions was far greater than most humans gave them credit for. He'd observed her wondering at the local wildlife at the Great Tree and thought wistfully about how much Rosa would have loved to be there with them. Although he wasn't sure the people of the Tree were ready for a twelve-year-old Earth girl. That might be a culture shock of a different kind!

"Those birds are the Golden Aurics, I believe. Children of Amare herself."

"Amare?"

"She is the queen of all birds. A magical being unlike any other. She saved Helia from the Rose Garden and watches out for all who need her."

"Ah yes. I remember some talk of it when I first arrived at the Library. Although, so far, I feel like I'm constantly playing catch-up!"

"Can *they* help us find the city we need?" Nu said, bringing the conversation back to the immediate a little forcefully.

Rascal chuckled, though it was laced with a touch of awkwardness Arturo hadn't heard from the woman so far. If he didn't know better, he could have sworn her cheeks were reddening with something akin to embarrassment. "I'm afraid not, Nu. Or if they can, I wouldn't know how to ask them."

Nu straightened, looking again to Antares. "Then I will guide us."

"You can do that?"

"Antares seems to think it's worth a shot, and we have no other choice. Now, tell me more about this place of entertainment, where you think the performers will be found. You've been there before, yes?"

"I have."

"Then what exactly are we looking for? Where is this city?"

"It's in a volcano."

"A *volcano*?" Arturo said. "But surely . . ." He gestured around the sky, as if pointing out the obvious difficulty in finding one nearby.

"Yes, a volcano," Rascal repeated, "but you don't need to worry! It's perfectly normal and perfectly safe. As you can imagine, floating in the skies are all manner of landmasses. The volcano is long inactive. Any power it had drained away long ago."

"Fascinating."

"You look excited."

"Well, it's becoming my new normal," he said.

Arturo stood taller and straightened his tunic, realizing they were still dressed as Silvyrans. Apparently, the Great Library's magic didn't allow for outfit changes on the fly.

"You've flown me through some kind of interdimensional space, to a world of floating islands, there's a volcano in the sky, and you want us to fly inside and find some possible spies. What isn't there to be excited about?" He attempted to look nonchalant, knowing he was fooling no one. "Ah, if my mother could see me now. She always said I'd find my way eventually. I'm not sure she quite meant *here* though."

He felt Robin's fingers caress his shoulder reassuringly, while on the other side of Rascal, Nu sat herself into the copilot's seat.

"Are you ready, Rascal?"

"That depends on what you're about to do."

Nu broke a smile at that, but her response was silent. She closed her eyes and reached out with both her hands toward the windshield. Her Orb, Antares, hovered closer to her shoulder, her surface an unblemished silver, no flashes or patterns.

The Sage and her Orb were deep in concentration.

Then, ahead . . .

"Great leaping squirrels!" Rascal exclaimed.

The sky in front of the *Golden Oriole* was split with a bright amber light. As it dulled, Arturo could see it was like someone had thrown an overlay over the blues and whites and greens of the world. And while they could still see the sky and islands through it, something else had become visible too. A little distance away. Like the frayed end of a crimson thread. It led away, spinning and shining, weaving through the heavens.

"Follow that path," Nu said, eyes still closed. Her breathing was slow and deep. Her hands unwavering. "I will reveal it as long as I can, but be quick, if you please."

Rascal licked her lips and gripped the controls more firmly. "You got it. The rest of you, take your seats, buckle up, and let me concentrate. This could start getting a little bumpy."

"Start?" Arturo said, letting Robin lead them back to their seats.

He strapped himself in not a moment too soon, as Rascal swung the airship directly toward a long cluster of isles drifting across the sky like dandelion seeds. The engines of the *Golden Oriole* dipped in pitch, then whined as she pulled them straight up in between two of the islands, almost clipping the ship on the starboard side.

"We have the whole sky open to us," he muttered to himself. "You couldn't have gone around them?"

"Unless you're going to let me in on a secret you've been withholding, Arturo, I believe I'm the only pilot here. We might have the whole sky, but everything is in motion all the time. The entire context of this realm is in a constant state of flux. Nu said to follow the thread. It's not my fault the thread weaved so close to the islands!"

"It's not an exact science," Nu said, still focusing. "My powers can only reveal the truth of the way there. You're going to have to improvise as best you can."

"As I will," Rascal said. "Now hold on. I've spotted an air current that should take us alongside. Let's dive in . . ."

Which she did. Dramatically.

The *Golden Oriole* went into a sheer vertical dive. Arturo would have cried out, except the force of the descent squeezed all the air out of him and left him breathless for the few seconds they were in free fall.

Until.

"Gotcha," Rascal yelled, her thick arms straining against the controls as she wrestled the airship back to being level again, just as they reached what Arturo could see were quickly moving wisps of clouds. The *Golden Oriole* crested the tops of them and suddenly they were flung forward, as if suddenly caught in a raging river.

Which Arturo supposed they were. A sky river.

Rascal leaned back in her seat but kept her fingers gripped to the controls. She made minor adjustments to their course, keeping the thread in sight as they followed it through the sky, bucking and weaving, rising and diving.

For the second time while on the airship, Arturo felt the rush of excitement flow through him. A feeling he allowed himself to sink into for at least the next hour as the *Golden Oriole* hurtled through the afternoon. Unable to help his grin, he thought again of Rosa and wished she was there with him.

And then a voice cut through his reverie.

Rascal pointed to one side. “We’re on our way! Look!”

And he twisted to see an entire floating continent emerging through the swirling cloud.

CHAPTER TWENTY-FIVE

TRAPPED IN THE WARREN OF SPOIL

Bad, Lynx conveyed to Veer, hovering above the lip of the crevice they had found themselves trapped in. *Big trouble coming.*

The Sage of Strength murmured to himself, pushing himself into the rock as far as his big frame allowed. They'd actually thought themselves lucky, when one of the roving bands of desperate locals attacked them a few nights ago. They'd been in no real danger, but the desperation of those poor wretches had made Veer sick. They'd treated the poor, desperate souls with kindness, dazzled them with a little magic, and managed to get information on Payne that led them to this awful place.

In this perpetual twilight, it was just dark enough for them to go unnoticed by the gangs that had chased them through the streets of what the locals had called the Warren of Spoil. It wasn't a name that inspired confidence, and unfortunately, given what he'd seen of this corrupted realm, luck was thin on the ground that it might improve.

"Lynx is suggesting we head farther into the city to escape," he said to the others as his Orb continued to speak. "He thinks it might be dense enough that we can hide out until these gangs either give up on finding us or resolve their business with each other."

"Just our luck to wander into the midst of a breaking fight," Maïa whispered from her position on the other side of the small trench.

"I imagine fights here are a common occurrence. What else do they have to do other than hunt for food and try to survive? We need to get out of their way and let them forget about us."

"Whatever we decide, we need to move quickly, Veer." Maïa's own Orb was farther along from their hiding place, but came floating back to the Sage of Integrity now, before flashing a message in dazzling white flurries of snow across her surface. The Sage inclined her head, letting her curls of long red hair fall around her face. "There are twenty of them ahead. Ten to the side. All approaching fast."

"Any Unwritten?" They had seen a few of the tainted, dead-eyed people wandering the wasteland already. Hanging around on the fringes, like viruses ready to attach themselves to a host. But they had been loners, lost from the herd, certainly not a gathering of them like the one the Sages had been following to try and find Payne.

"Thebe doesn't think so. Simply more poor wretches who were born into this hell and are trying to survive."

Suddenly, there was a scuffle behind them, sneakers kicking up puffs of dust, as the slight and slender Paix slid back from her scouting, accompanied by Arcturus. Veer raised an eyebrow as the Sage of Joy offered a smile. Weary, but still a glimpse of life and light.

She ran a hand over her closely cropped hair as if to keep it tidy and said, "Hate to bring more bad news, but there is another gang approaching from the opposite side. Intentional or not, we're caught in the center of this convergence. I don't think we can avoid the fight, try as we have." She stretched out her arm and allowed trickles of electricity to dance over her skin. Where there should have been crackling, Veer could hear the barest hint of electrical hum as each shock of energy bent and twisted. "Should I give them a bit of a shock? See if it can buy us time to escape? It worked well on those bandits."

"There are probably too many, and I don't want you to wear yourself out completely. We still have a fight ahead of us." He gestured further into the city, where they could just about see an unkempt sprawl of buildings, like a garbage pile on the horizon. "Let's go that way. Keep low. Keep ready to defend ourselves, if need be."

"After you," Maïa said.

He nodded. "Lynx, you good?"

The Orb flashed a low light beside him. *Ready.*

With that, they left. Sneaking out in the one place Veer had guessed they could squeeze through the converging groups. Holding fast to spoil heaps, ducking behind broken walls, and climbing into more ditches to avoid the gangs as they pressed forward looking for trouble.

"Warren of Spoil is an apt name for this place," Veer whispered to Lynx as they pushed onward. It was a confusing snarl of a settlement, with buildings pushed up against each other as though jostling for space, while hills of rubbish and rotting foods were piled high throughout—some tumbling into little landslides as the Sages moved past. They were nothing more than hints of what had once been. Faded markings of ancient roadways dividing the town. Badly worn columns implied magnificent architecture, once upon a time. Fountains had run dry, likely for centuries, Veer suspected, their basins now stained with black sludge and other things Veer didn't even want to guess at.

Same here as elsewhere, Lynx said with faded light, so as not to draw attention. *Drained of life. Ruined by darkness.*

"Whatever happened here must have been cataclysmic," Maïa said, hurrying alongside them. "Can you imagine how terrifying it must have been for those here? The fear that swept through the population as it occurred? And then, later, the survivors would have emerged like worms in the rain to find chaos in their once pristine world."

Veer grimaced. "Chaos is definitely what they seem to have embraced ever since. I see no collaboration here, no attempt to rectify what evil they'd suffered. Where's the rebuilding of society or even the buildings themselves?"

And then there are the gangs, Lynx added.

"That presumes they have a choice in the matter, Veer. If Suttaru has been their overlord since this world fell, what makes you think they would be allowed free will?" Maïa said.

"You're right, Maïa, of course. But no resistance at all? It must be much worse than we realized. How could Suttaru do all of this, even with Payne's help? Can this Discordia he follows truly be so powerful?" Veer said.

"Hopefully, these are answers Payne can provide, when we find him," Paix said.

"Indeed," Veer replied.

The Sages had soon discovered distrust reigned supreme in this city, and the survivors weren't looking out for each other; they were in competition. Gangs formed through necessity, through power in numbers, to stay alive. Roaming the sprawl looking for food, water . . . and a fight.

It wasn't long before they got to witness another brawl. "Hide quickly," Maïa said, having seen it coming, and pulling Veer and Paix into a roofless stone hut. And all three ducked, their Orbs hiding, too, as a roar of aggression spilled over the ruins when one gang ran into another.

Veer listened, knowing he'd never heard anything like the ferocity or volume of the hatred exploding just beyond the stones. Not even in the fight for Bloom. The Unwritten were mindless drones, he figured, driven by someone else's hate. This noise though? This was the essence of man's inhumanity to man throughout history, distilled into a sound that would give anybody nightmares. It was violent and fierce, full of anger.

Afterward, the Sages emerged to find a bloodbath. Bodies laid in the rubble, with limbs twisted at unnatural angles, skulls shattered, some with the blood-splattered weapons still embedded.

"We should go. We don't want to be seen by anybody who can do this," Paix said quietly, her positive demeanor muted. "This is barbaric."

"You're damn right it is," he said. He tried to pick up the pace and hurry his friends through the rest of the battlefield. "I never thought I'd say it, but I fear there's a chance these people are beyond saving.

Whatever corruption rained down upon their homeland has filtered into their very essence. It could have been going on for generations."

There is always hope, Lynx reminded him, and Veer wanted so badly to believe. But the hopelessness of their situation in this realm seemed insurmountable right now. Was it possible they had become evil because of it?

A scream shattered their chance of a quiet escape. One of the injured, begging for help as he spotted them. Paix wanted to offer them help, to get them on their way to somewhere safe, but it was already too late. The noise had aroused unwanted attention.

The victorious gang howled and turned back, knowing there were others to attack.

"Run!" Veer urged, and the Sages and their Orbs broke away at speed through the labyrinth of what passed for streets, ducking through long-abandoned cottages and over walls.

Until they reached a dead end.

"Lynx, any chance you've seen a way out of here?" Veer asked, curling his fingers and coaxing the wind back under his control again. The power flowed from his Orb into him, through the sinew of his skin, vibrating in his bones, pulling at his fingertips. He could feel the strength around him building, despite his exhaustion. He'd never had to call on his powers so extensively for days at a time.

Thankfully, Paix's Orb gave them a far better option than standing and fighting. After a quick message to the Sage in the form of symbols that fluttered like pink rose petals caught in a breeze, Paix took off through a small gap underneath a half-collapsed wall, calling back, "There's an underground passage not far east, Arcturus says. Fifty yards, perhaps. It might give us a chance to catch our breath."

They hurried, hearing the stampede of hatred bring up their rear. Roars of anguish sounded as the chasing gang bottlenecked at the collapsed wall and tried to push through. There was scrambling and yelling as one of them caught sight of scuffed footprints. Paix continued leading the way with Arcturus, until finally they dove between a couple of spoil heaps and drew up against a rusty gate built into a leaning rock face.

There were steps beyond, leading down into an unwelcome darkness.

"In *there*?" Paix said to her Orb. Veer looked at Maïa. They knew their friend enjoyed the open air and got a little claustrophobic in tight spaces. And from what they could all see down below, there was little space to be found ahead.

But Arcturus was insistent, and Lynx and Thebe both confirmed this was the only way now.

Caves, Lynx said to Veer.

"Looks more like dungeons," Veer said.

When his Orb didn't correct him, Veer sighed inwardly. They were heading into danger, but it seemed there was little choice of avoiding that now. At least down there they had a chance to avoid hurting those who were chasing them.

Using his power to pull a tepid, rank puff of air, he quickly pushed it into the lock and broke the mechanism, then flung the gate open.

Maïa grabbed Paix by the hand and stepped through. The Orbs began to glow softly, leading the way.

Veer followed behind, pulling the gate closed and binding it with what little breeze remained under his control.

Then they descended into the dark.

Veer crept along in the dank cave system, feeling his way around as much as following the soft glow of the Orbs. He'd taken it upon himself to take the lead, making sure he was the first to any danger.

What had been natural now became unnatural. The twisting and turning caves and hollows that riddled the ground beneath Penumbris grew thick with death. It was the walls pushing inward, constricting the already narrow spaces. Faces appeared in them, as though trapped and trying to force their way out.

Except they weren't faces.

"They're skulls, Veer," Maïa said loudly, having to lean into him to be heard over the screaming. "They've been crushed into the sides and the roof of this tunnel."

"And even in the floor," Paix added with a grimace as one shattered beneath her shoes.

Veer looked around to see that they were surrounded, and there were countless numbers lining the way ahead too.

What's worse . . . they had all started screaming.

Paix's jaw was fixed, her face grim. She tried to turn around, already sweating profusely, but Maïa and Veer gently ushered her forward—even though Veer knew they were both only moments away from turning tail and running too.

"They brought the dead down here," he shouted into the maelstrom of wails and cries for help, for someone to end their torment. He knew his words were a statement of the bloody obvious, but sometimes in the midst of a nightmare, you needed a real thing, tangible and honest, to cling to. "They must have buried them after the sun blasted the surface. God damn, must have taken a while!"

"I don't think this is a burial, Veer," Maïa called back, her face grim in the light. He watched her point out markings on the skulls, deliberate etchings. Then she indicated up the walls. "There are patterns here. The skulls are marked and have been intentionally placed in positions that don't make sense if people were just trying to bury their dead."

He paused, unsure. Maïa had always seen the world for how it was. As long as he'd known her, she had been open about the balance she saw between light and dark. She had long been fascinated with witches and the occult and had studied them widely before first arriving in the Great Library.

"Then what?" he asked. "Sacrifices? Surely not."

Maïa shook her head. "I fear so."

"Then let us get out of this cursed place," Paix said, gesturing for them to hurry along.

"The light," Veer said. "It's not coming from the Orbs anymore. There's a new source."

Paix looked around with horror etched across her face. "Why is it red? It's like the air itself is bleeding."

Veer glanced to the walls and saw that along with the gaping jaws unleashing a torrent of wailing, the empty eye sockets were now emitting a powerful glow.

"We need to go. Now," Paix said again.

She's right.

"Yeah, I don't really want to hang around here either."

Good, the Orb replied. Then, abruptly: *There is movement.*

"Where?"

Ahead.

"Screw it, let's go." He pushed the others ahead as a cold fear rose across his back. "Whatever is moving ahead of us, we'll deal with it when we see it. It can't be worse than staying here."

Moving quickly, they burst from the narrow vent into a larger chamber. The screams continued, unabated, unleashed from so many gaping jaws in the walls. The red glow was thicker, and motes of dust swirled in the air, not falling, just held in the air, as though they were all floating underwater.

Yet that wasn't what held Veer's attention as he drew up alongside the other Sages and regarded their surroundings.

Dungeons, Lynx noted with muted light.

In between the thick mass of bones all around them were doorways. Thin, arched, coffin-shaped holes in the wall with gates affixed to each one. Veer felt his stomach tighten as he noticed arms and legs sticking through in various states of decay.

The screaming continued around them as the Sages walked, warily looking into vertical graves. Each provided little room for any occupant to move around in. Just enough to stand and turn a little, like sow stalls back on Earth, the kind Veer remembered seeing pictures of once in those horrendous factory farms.

He felt the connection with Lynx, the slight surge in readiness of his power seeping into his fingers and causing tingles in his palm, before the Orb even blinked the message to him.

Apparently, not everybody down here was dead.

Veer tugged on Maïa's arm to warn her. He wasn't going to try yelling over the screams that still roared around them, lest he give away their presence to whatever lay ahead. Instead, he pointed to himself and then the path of bones ahead of her.

Let me, he mouthed.

She shook her head and made to move again, until he tapped her arm again.

Please, wait.

Why?

He held up his hand, then glanced to Lynx, clenched his fingers, and allowed a small burst of power to pass between them.

It was enough to alert the Orb to what he wanted to do. Lynx immediately conveyed that to Thebe, who flashed the message to Maïa.

The woman tilted her head in consideration, or perhaps wariness that what he was about to try wouldn't work, but then she nodded.

Stepping past her, he faced ahead. The corridor of skulls and cells stretched out some fifty yards, before ducking through a smaller door and seeming to continue beyond that. His hands lifted before him, palms open, before his fingers flexed and balled into a fist.

There was little subtlety to it, as right now he was channeling as best he could with death surrounding him and his friends, and the fate of everything resting on their shoulders.

He reached out, pushing tendrils of movement through the currents. Feeling his way through the corridor to find the source of the movement, expecting anything. A creature. A monster. One of the corrupted. Perhaps even the Rogue Sage himself. It seemed a fitting place for a devil such as he to hide.

Then he felt a ripple through the air. A small one, but enough to allow him to feel through the power to find the source.

Which he did, only to recoil in horror.

There was a child down here.

Veer bent the dank air to his will, curling his fingers, tugging on the strands of power he felt, and teasing them through his being until they did just what he wanted. He tried first to pick the lock with it, but there was decay in there—rust, most likely—and he reckoned even the key wouldn't work. So he went to plan B: He pulled more of the power from Lynx, letting the Orb boost him, until finally he yanked the door clean off its hinges and sent it crashing across the room.

The child prisoner spilled into his waiting arms.

He was a waif of a boy, barely eight or nine, although in his condition, it was hard to tell. His skin was pale and grubby beneath the clothes that hung off him, and his eyes were watery and red.

Veer looked at Paix and raised his eyebrow. The Sage of Joy was needed here, and given the horrendous noise around them, filling their ears, pressing in on them, he knew she could do with the distraction. She stepped forward, focusing on the boy, giving him a smile that instantly calmed him before making a drinking motion with her hands. He nodded lightly, and she slipped her flask from her hip belt and put the water to his lips.

The waif drank as though he hadn't touched a drop in days. Torn fingernails dug into the metal of the container, pressing it to his lips as though it might be snatched away at any moment. Paix let him for as long as she could, before she had to put a hand on his chest and gently push him back, ensuring he didn't throw it all up again. His body wasn't used to getting so much water.

Maïa stood guard behind them both, keeping watch. She kept looking at the youngster they'd rescued, her face grim. Veer understood her reaction. This was no place for anyone, especially a child.

Go, he mouthed to her.

She barely nodded before she moved away, scouting ahead with Thebe bobbing alongside her. Veer picked the boy up in his arms, aghast at how light he was. He paused only to let Paix slip a morsel of Chef Tahini's famous sugar bread between the boy's lips, something to give him a shot of sustenance, before they moved off after the Sage of Integrity.

The journey through the dungeons got worse before it got better. There was nobody else alive along the path they were on, only corpses of poor souls in various states of decay. Veer saw that some of them had been tortured before death. Some perhaps even *to* death.

Veer swallowed and kept moving, ensuring the boy's face was turned away from the sight as he continued to drift in and out of consciousness. The skull-lined, screaming labyrinth continued to twist and turn, and Veer pictured huge, mutated worms or rock snakes squirming beneath the surface of the planet, creating an elaborate system of caves, caverns, and tunnels that had been co-opted by the survivors of this heinous realm and used for evil.

All three Orbs flashed at the same time when more movement was detected. More prisoners?

Maïa threw Veer a pensive look as she held at the turn of a tunnel. "What do we do?"

The movement is distant, not on this level, Lynx informed him. *It's below us.*

"Anything else?" Veer asked.

It is not one entity. There are others.

He set his jaw. How far did this cursed place go? How many people were being kept here?

Veer noted Paix's face, still strained, behind the smile she gave the boy whenever his eyes flickered open. She patted his head, sweeping his locks of hair out of his face. Veer saw her hands were shaking. She was struggling too. The fact she'd made it this far at all was incredible, considering her claustrophobia.

Ahead, Maïa waited for him to make a decision. He knew what she was thinking. She wanted to go and see if there were other people who needed saving.

But Veer shook his head.

"We can't!" he said. "We have to stick to the mission." His voice was quiet, but the tone was urgent. He looked away, knowing his eyes would betray his lack of desire to help. As the Sage of Strength, he should have been able to rescue whoever else might be held here.

His two companions nodded their agreement. None of them spoke, but Paix touched both briefly on their arms, offering comfort as only the Sage of Joy could. They all knew that finding the journal and stopping the evil that had done all this was the best way they could help these poor wretches.

They moved on as quickly as they could, until the caverns grew small again. Constricted. The ancient bodies pressed closer to them. Pushing. Reaching.

Weaving through the holes, pushing themselves forward, Veer noticed an excited flash of light ahead, burning through the red gloom, as Thebe must have sensed they were close to an escape. The screaming seemed quieter now, not as intense. Although Veer could still hear it in his mind. He wondered if he'd always be able to hear it.

Finally, they rounded a corner and fed the boy through a particularly tight gap. The walls of bones ended. The bloody air grew thin and normal. There was light ahead. And they burst into the night, stumbling into the blessed twilight world.

In a copse of rotting trees, they threw themselves to the ground, gasping for breath as though they had been holding it all this time.

Perhaps we have, Veer thought as he looked to where the boy was pulling himself into a sitting position and staring at the three of them with relief, gratitude, and more than a touch of madness in his eyes.

CHAPTER TWENTY-SIX
ATMOSPHERE

Arturo felt himself fill with excitement as the airship crested a wave of air, before dropping again and hurtling faster along the sky river as it weaved among the clouds.

The landscape below them was vast. A gigantic stretch of land that contained multiple cities, fields and hills, rivers and lakes. Yet as Arturo looked down, he realized there was a patchwork feel to it all. One set of lush, green crops ended abruptly as a jagged scar tore through the ground, across which multiple bridges had been thrown together like stitches over a wound. The land swept up immediately into desert dunes on the other side, before the airship lifted and rose up as another tear in the land signaled a change to snow-covered mountains littered with thousands of buildings, each twinkling with firelight.

"It's a monster of an island, this one," Rascal commented, noting Arturo's fascination. "Centonis. A place thrown together over the generations, sometimes gaining new sections and alliances, sometimes losing them after political disagreements saw divides grow too big for any bridge to span. There are some who suggest it's made up of over a thousand separate lands. Yet somehow it all works. The people who are here choose to be here. They work with their neighbors, no matter where they may have originally hailed from. The separate forces make the whole stronger."

"It's incredible," Arturo said. "So huge I can't even see where it begins or ends. It's almost like my home city."

"Aye, it's the biggest of the islands, so they say. Although there are plenty who also say that not all the lands in the sky have been mapped as yet. Even now, hundreds of cycles after they left their fixings far below, there are probably plenty out there drifting beyond the horizon, waiting to be discovered."

Robin was peering out of one of the porthole windows. "And you think this particular island is where we'll find the people who can help us?"

"That's what I believe to be true, yes."

"Based on?" Nu asked.

Rascal grinned. "You've become a real leader since I last saw you, Nu. Confident and straight to the point. I like it."

Arturo glanced back to see Nu trying to hold back a smile. She nodded in thanks. "I'm just aware we spent more time in Silvyra than we wanted to. The sooner we find Haruto, the safer I'll feel."

"I understand completely. Well, to answer your question, while these siblings we're after may well be guardians of our friend Haruto, if they are performers, people who live and breathe to entertain, I am willing to bet this airship and all of you on board that there is only one place we can find them in Adscendo. A place half hidden here on Centonis."

Arturo leaned forward expectantly. "Which is where?"

Rascal's grin widened. "You'll see."

Arturo's eyes roved the desert and the mountains, over a town made of sparkling blue glass and another buried in the ground. Only its hillock rooftops could be seen as the *Golden Oriole* finally approached a ferocious-looking city.

"Is that—" he began to ask.

"We're here," Nu said suddenly.

Rascal glanced over her shoulder and nodded in approval. "That we are, Nu. This is the city we've traveled to find. Where we'll hopefully find some answers. It's known as Jaele's Mount."

Arturo looked down at the city, and his breath caught in his throat. It was a ringed city full of undulating towers, bridges, and canals. A surrounding wall looked like it held an entire city of its own, circling everything else. And it all lay on the slopes of a jagged mountain rising from its center, a peak that would have rivaled any on Earth, such was its scope. It dwarfed everything around it, and even from up here, Arturo could tell that many of those tall towers within the city were the equivalent of skyscrapers, rising above the population. Around the city and mountain, he could see small airships and balloons milling about, with small specks moving between them, light glinting off what he thought might be wings similar to those worn by Rascal. People, he realized, flying about the mountaintop.

He felt the hairs on his arms stand on end.

"This is the volcano you were talking about, Rascal? I think you undersold it. That is an *immense* sight."

"You like it?"

"I think *like* barely covers it."

He was excited, yes. It was impossible not to be out here in this dreamlike world, flying in an airship, witnessing sights like this.

"So . . . why did they raise up a volcano from the surface?" he asked.

"I've no idea, although presumably there was already a large settlement on it."

"Where are we landing?"

"Pretty close!"

"We're not going to land somewhere on the outside and walk into it?"

She pushed the craft faster over the city, toward the peak. "Where's the fun in that? This is a special place, Arturo. It's the biggest entertainment center on this or any other world I've been to. A hive of singing, dancing, and performing, where only the most talented or the biggest daredevils hang out and perform. And we don't have time to burn." She gripped the controls and gave him a look of warning. "I suggest you hold on. This might get a little bumpy."

Arturo laughed and checked his seat buckle. "You should carve that as a warning into the doorway of this airship."

The *Golden Oriole* lifted suddenly in a climb. The engines groaned, and the cabin creaked under the pressure. Arturo was pressed back into his seat and grabbed his armrests. As the ship reached the end of its climb and leveled out, there was a moment of calm.

They stopped and began to drift.

A rope appeared from nowhere, shooting past the window from below. Then another appeared. Arturo saw barbs at the end of each, aiming to catch the webbing holding the balloon above them. He expected to hear the balloon burst at any moment, but it never came. Whoever was shooting was clearly accurate enough for the barbs to find only the nets.

The airship began to be pulled downward.

Rascal leaned back in her chair with a satisfied grin. "Okay, so it's not as dramatic as I suggested it might be, but it saves me trying to negotiate the drop. Better them take control and pull us in. Finds us an empty place to stow our fine airship, and I get to just sit here and enjoy the ride."

Arturo unclipped himself and tried to get a better look out of the window.

Rascal spread her hands wide. "Welcome to Atmosphere, the finest, edgiest city you'll ever visit."

Arturo didn't try to explain the realities of Mexico City to her, let alone LA, Paris, or New York. But as soon as he saw the sprawling, towering volcano-perched settlement, he had to confess that the city lived up to the name and then some.

"Well, whatever happens in Atmosphere, stays in Atmosphere." Robin stifled a chuckle, but Rascal frowned.

"We need to find information here. What good would—"

"Ignore him, Rascal. It's a joke from our world." Robin gave Arturo an amused glance, then continued, "Don't tease her, Arturo," she said in mock admonishment. He grinned and nodded, then stooped to get a proper look outside the window.

But Arturo realized that despite Robin's joke having made him chuckle, this place was starkly different from anything he'd seen or heard about on Earth. The inside of this giant inactive volcano was a hive of activity, almost literally, he considered. They descended into its depths, and he witnessed life buzzing everywhere he looked.

Small airships and balloons were piloted with an ease that verged on nonchalance, with no visible system of air traffic control, but there was a ballet-like grace and efficiency of movement that was at once as captivating as it was confounding. Their balloons were works of art—tapestries of multicolored wonder that put the *Oriole*'s, if not to shame, then certainly in a less flamboyant class.

"Look!" said Robin, lightly touching Arturo's arm to steer his view to her line of focus. "Those smaller shapes. They're people!" Her voice was keen with excitement, and he could feel the warmth of her hand through his sleeve.

"You're right!" he said, hearing the excitement in his own voice matching hers.

While the airships and balloons moved above the settlements, people were *flying* between them and the settlements below. Small figures, jumping off moving aircraft and taller buildings, using equipment that seemed to match Rascal's wings.

"Rascal, why don't you join them?" he said. It was a jest, but her answering look was one of longing, and she shook her head.

"Not today, Arturo. Perhaps when this is all over I can come back and soar like these fine folks." She grinned and added, "Perhaps teach them a few tricks!"

He nodded, smiling back at her, then turned his attention back to this impossible city they were approaching.

Inexplicably, the settlement clung to the slopes of the volcano like a mass of wood and stone honeycomb, circling the inside with curved buildings, pagodas, and courtyards, with rope bridges and walkways slung between them. On the outside of the volcano, there was a more permanent feel, with stone walls and wider open courtyards, even circular canals at regular intervals. There were huge waterspouts in the shape of elegant birds, their heads and beaks gushing water down vertically from the canals in great streams. Arturo could see people splashing in the water—children, most likely—or perhaps just people relaxing.

People were everywhere, wearing all manner of light, flowing clothes, ribbon belts, and sandals that wrapped around their calves. As they grew closer, he saw that the wings on some made Rascal's look primitive, and he regretted his earlier quip. She was likely realizing the limitations of her own rig in the face of the airborne people of this land. Yet the familiar vibe of people out enjoying themselves, and each other, was evident. There was almost a carnival feel as they streamed around the district like rivers, up the outside of the mountain by foot, flight, and what he realized must be quite advanced funicular transports—the carriages being pulled up on cables that were being regulated by the water from the waterspouts. Then, as they passed onto the inner side of the volcano, the people wound around the inside of the empty mountain.

"More airships," he said to Robin, and she beamed another smile in his direction. Arturo took careful note of the other craft—some docked, others lifting off to pass the *Golden Oriole* on their way out—although none of them looked like their own airship. In fact, there were no other balloon craft at all. It was a varied mix of flying machines that all looked very much like something a futurist Leonardo da Vinci might have designed—mechanical skeletons and multiple birdlike wings that beat up and down. Not for the first time, he wished he had his notebook so he could record this and perhaps sketch it for later contemplation. Instead, he worked to commit every last detail to his memory.

There was vehicle that had a tail swishing back and forth like a serpent, presumably for propelling the craft forward. And adjacent to one of the larger wooden platforms was a long train with at least five or six carriages behind it, each one carried beneath a couple of grass-blade rotors.

"What a place!" Robin said in delight and slapped him on the arm once more. "It is truly breathtaking. I can *feel* the excitement from up here." Arturo wondered if she meant that literally. Love may well have been in the air, if this were a party time. He found himself relaxing against his better judgment.

Nu was scanning the crowds, as though willing the people they had come to find to step into view and save them from sifting through this city in search of them.

"Rascal, there's too much going on here to navigate our way quickly. How sure are you that we'll find who we need here, in all this?"

"Trust me, Nu. From what we learned of the ones we're trying to find, I think there's really only one place we'll need to look for them." She looked up to the rim of the volcano. "But we're going to have to go up there." The *Golden Oriole* slowed to a crawl and was now pulled sideways toward a spare platform, with sparse wooden railings and a couple of engineers operating the docking system. The two women looked a little curious about the airship, one of them pointing and the other nodding as they finally popped down onto the dock.

"Fair warning—I don't think we're exactly inconspicuous here," Rascal noted as she hit the button for the exit and then directed everyone out. "This airship is likely a bit of a relic in Adscendo. A curiosity, as we ourselves might well be. But there are enough rapscallions coming and going from this district that if we act like we belong, we'll probably be fine. We won't be the only unusual sights about today."

Rascal was the last out of the craft and placed her hand on the locking pad before following the Sages and Arturo. Once they were on the platform, she gave the engineers a nod, as though there was nothing out of the ordinary here whatsoever, then led them from the dock down some stairs and onto a walkway.

Arturo found himself once again next to Robin. He couldn't help but look both up and down, amazed at how the city spiraled around the inside of this volcano from the rim all the way down to . . . well, he couldn't see the base at all. It disappeared into craggy rock. There was a strong breeze blowing up from below, suggesting maybe it wasn't entirely solid down there. There were rows and rows of lanterns, not yet lit, all brightly colored and presumably there to safely light the way when darkness came.

"That's where the magma would have been," Robin said. "Although it would have all drained out when the island ascended." She sighed happily and pulled him along after the others. "Nothing beats traveling, seeing new sights, and having new experiences. And this place in particular seems to have a musical life to it, don't you think?"

"Indeed! And just think—come nightfall, these lanterns will make the volcano seem alive."

He grinned as he realized he could hear the music she was talking about. A rhythmic cacophony of noises swirled around the air, bouncing from the walls, driven through the beams of wood. The footsteps of the people reverberated in time with the caws and squeals of the birds circled in the air at the center of the shaft. The shouts of market traders somewhere, combined with the delighted laughs of an audience who then burst into applause. Even the gusts of wind fell into the beat. It was an orchestra of movement and sound, and somehow it all held together. The air itself was music.

"Quite something, isn't it?" Rascal said as she kept walking. "Although I've no idea how or why it's happening."

Robin looked at the shimmer in the air leading the way. Centauri was cloaked, but as the air grew brighter, Arturo realized the Orb was speaking to her.

"Centauri says it's the way this city was built," Robin said. "The design of the buildings and the reverberation provided by the circular walls all play their part in crafting the music you're hearing. It's part of the reason they decided to build this district in the volcano. Not only does it give the place a certain unique ambience and edge, but the acoustics are better than you'll find anywhere else in this realm . . . or the next."

Rascal stopped, impressed. "How'd you know all this?"

"Ah, I don't. Centauri is pulling the information from the collected texts at the Great Library. We Sages travel widely and gather as much information about the realms as we can. Clearly, other Sages have visited Adscendo in the past. And unless things have changed since their visit, we should expect for this very human music to last from dusk until dawn."

"Now that is certainly true. I can tell you from experience," Rascal said.

Arturo looked around again. There were people everywhere, eating, drinking, and partying. Some were heading to large decks with finely embroidered gazebos, similar in style to the intricate-patterned tapestries of the airship balloons. From some, the sound of laughter flowed out, then cheers, others music, and Arturo could almost feel the heat of too many bodies, lost in dance as he had once been in his student days. The buildings here were less permanent, it seemed, than on the outside. No stone, but rather complex wooden structures that seemed designed to be moved and adapted. They were a variety of colors, with balloons, pennants, and striking paintings colored everything. People were serving food on the decks, while others were playing what seemed to be a version of football, but wearing wings similar to Rascal's, and goals spread across the higher stories and low. It looked frenetic and probably deadly, if you misjudged your path, but the crows of happy spectators reminded him of matches with his father, the old man cheering for the home team while enjoying a cold beer on a hot day. It made Arturo feel a little homesick.

"It's a wondrous place, for sure. I wish I'd come here sooner, and we had more time to explore." Robin sighed, and Arturo caught Nu giving her the nod. "But we are racing the clock here, so to speak. Let's stick to our goal. Rascal, where do you think we will find these performers? The entire city is bustling with entertainment. I can see street performers. Bars with posters for all kinds of acts. Where will our particular pair of siblings be, do you think?"

They reached a tall wooden post that had at least twenty signs haphazardly nailed to it, each pointing in different directions and likely ever changing in this moving jamboree of music, dance, and revelry. Rascal paused for a moment, looking for something, then nodded and strode past it to a set of rickety steps.

"You can bet your behinds all the good stuff happens in the heart of the city, Robin. So steady your nerves, try not to look over the edge, and let's head down."

With that, she led the way, and the others followed. Arturo tried not to miss a step as he looked around while heading toward the bottom of the volcano, wishing for a moment he, too, had a set of wings so he could soar below with those barreling about the sky.

Ah, Rosa, he thought to himself. *Perhaps one day I can bring you here.*

Arturo didn't know how long they had walked. He was used to wearing a watch, but of course he hadn't been able to bring his with him, as Earth technology wouldn't pass through the portal. Not that it would have made any sense here, in a world of flying cities that bore no relation to the spinning of his own world. But that didn't stop him from unconsciously looking at his wrist. He was too busy staring with wonder at everything to be keeping track of time. From street performers playing in little courtyards and upon pedestals at the edge of balconies to scores of pamphleteers vying for the ever-moving crowd's attention. He grabbed one of the offered sheets of paper but could make nothing of the writing. The illustration—of a woman dressed as a bird, standing on the shoulders of a similarly attired man—suggested an act of some kind. He was about to tuck it inside his tunic, when Robin took it out of his hand.

"No time for souvenirs, my dear. We try to take nothing back through the portals, if at all possible." The last was punctuated by her scrunching the pamphlet into a ball and effortlessly punting it into a nearby bin. At least, he thought, they might recycle here . . .

"It sounds like everyone is having fun," he said, peering into a glassless window from which blazing light poured, along with a few laughed curses and the sound of calls for an encore. He gazed longingly at a series of nearby market stalls offering food and drink, but Rascal led them ever onward.

Rascal shrugged an apology. "I certainly had a good time last I was in town. This is a place of entertainment and fun. Magic and mystery. Where those of open mind reside and those seeking thrills and adventure come to visit. My crew and I enjoyed our brief visit the last time we ventured to Adscendo. Although Earnest, the first mate, was always a little wary—especially after he lost his shirt and one of his gold-leaf rings in one of the many card games you'll find in the more shadowy parts of town."

Rascal took a shortcut through a giant bathhouse, where the ceiling was filled with hanging flowers of all colors, a veritable rainbow of foliage, and water poured from the garden into the circular pool below. Several bathers were enjoying themselves in their tight-fitting bathing clothes, and Arturo raised an eyebrow as they walked past a couple of women who both gave him a sly smile.

Robin nudged him in the ribs a little harder than may have been needed.

As they were led out of the bathhouse and along another bridge, Arturo let his arm brush against Robin's. Not very subtle, he thought, but he felt like this was perhaps his only opportunity to show her he was taking notice of her voice, her laugh, the scent of her near him. He realized he was becoming powerfully drawn to her, although he wondered if she just generally had that effect on people. *What it must be like*, he thought, *being the Sage of Love*. Neither of them said anything. They didn't need to. Arturo had lived long enough to know that sometimes it was best not to burden such moments with words. Better to just feel when it was right to act and to live in the moment.

Nu walked ahead of them, although to Arturo it seemed as though she was holding herself back, rather than charging forward. He could hardly believe her progress since he first met her. The young woman in the bookshop had tuned into a woman with the cares of the world on her shoulders. He didn't envy her or Robin the job of leader, but the two women seemed naturals.

On one balcony they passed, a sign pointed down a precarious-looking spiral staircase. Arturo made the mistake of looking over the edge, and his vision spun momentarily as he saw a very thin-looking platform below, filled with a circle of people watching a magician touch each one of them in turn and make them disappear, before bringing them back to cheers of applause.

Nu didn't let them slow, however. They followed Rascal down, past the magician and his audience, then farther down still. The gusts of wind were growing wild as the air forced its way up past the walkways and buildings, shaking the brightly colored signs above the various stage areas and causing the group to have to raise their voices to be heard now.

"Where are you taking us?" Nu asked, holding on to the railing as a strong breeze tried to carry them back up the inside of the volcano.

Rascal's wings shuddered, but she didn't bother holding on to anything. Arturo figured she could probably just fly back up on the current, if she wanted. She walked a little farther and then turned and walked underneath a wooden awning that led into the side of the crater.

"Little place I remember staying in last time. It's small and rough around the edges, but one of the more permanent structures on this side of the mountain, and it's cheap, so it'll be a good place to set up camp." She tapped the sign above her head as she walked underneath it. It was old and cracked, but Arturo could just about make out the words: *Bore Hole*. It seemed apt for a place this far into a volcano.

"That will do. Rascal, after we're settled, we will go hunting for information on these performers. If we're lucky, they'll be around; if not, someone will know where they are. Will that work?"

"That should be fine," Rascal said, and the rest just nodded their agreement.

After Rascal requested and paid for rooms for each of them, a pale man in a faded blue uniform quietly led them through the network of tunnels and chambers. Arturo could hardly believe he was staying at a hotel in an otherworldly party town. He ran his fingers over the rough, rocky walls as the guide explained in a dull, monotone voice how this place had been formed through the passage of lava. Robin and Nu made noises of acknowledgment as he droned on, until they arrived at the first room.

Rascal, gesturing toward him, said, "Right. Arturo, this will be yours. Seeing as you're just an ordinary, normal man, and not like a Sage or anything, I'm guessing you probably want to rest up. Nu or I will let you know what's happening later. If you don't hear from us, we'll regroup at the front entrance tomorrow at daybreak."

Arturo paused at the small wooden door the guide had opened, letting him look through to the incredibly dark chamber beyond.

As the others moved off, Robin lingered, then gave him a grin and a cheery, "See you in the morning!" But as he watched her leave, she turned back and met his eyes. He shut the door behind him and followed her around the corner, seeing her pass through her own door. She didn't close the door. Arturo knocked once, gently, and it drifted open a little more. There was little space, and there she was, standing by a small window looking out into the noisy evening. There was a coziness to the room he liked, and he moved over to stand behind her. She turned around, and he saw her eyes sparkle with mirth.

"Was it that obvious?" she said.

"I'd never presume. But ever since you came back into my life, it's felt like we had more than a simple connection." He reached out and took her hands in his.

"Well," she said, "I *am* the Sage of Love. Connection is sort of my thing."

He started to pull back, but she held his hands and pulled him toward her. "But no, you weren't wrong." Her eyes lit up again, and she dropped one of his hands and touched his face. "Now, be a good man and close the door before one of the others wanders by."

"Yes, ma'am," he said, and closed the door from the inside.

CHAPTER TWENTY-SEVEN

SEARCH FOR THE SIBLINGS

Nu had wanted a short nap, but try as she might, sleep had not taken her. Even Antares had been unable to keep still, such was her anticipation finding the siblings. The Orb bounced around the little cavern, floating from wall to wall, until Rascal finally knocked on the door.

They were both quick to react.

"I'm here," Nu said, flinging the door open and bounding out. Antares whizzed past. "Let's get on with things, shall we?"

"I guessed you would be eager," Rascal said, ducking to let the Orb pass. Nu saw a proud, almost big-sisterly look in her eyes as she regarded the pair and placed a hand on Nu's shoulder. "Come on, then."

As Antares cloaked herself to stay hidden, they left the way they'd come in, back onto the walkways of the hidden city that clung to the inside of the volcano. The circle of sky above was weak with light as the afternoon waned and twilight seemed on the cusp of arriving. Nu decided that probably didn't matter here in Atmosphere though. It felt very much like a place that came alive at night.

Wandering up stairs and ramps, the pair wound around the crater from building to building, across bridges between them, the brightly colored lanterns, a mixture of red and orange, with flashes of purple and silver, lighting their way, occasionally stopping for Rascal to make inquiries, all to no avail.

"This is a city of entertainers and performers; we can't possibly know everyone," a stall operator told them as he tended his increasingly numerous clientele. Rascal slipped him a pearl for his trouble anyway and nodded for Nu to leave, just as a small band of musicians broke into a very loud tune in the corner.

"You sure you can't do that thing with your power to find them?" Rascal asked again. She waved in the general direction of where Antares floated, seemingly getting used to locating the shimmer in the air. "It would be great not to have to wander the entire circumference of Atmosphere."

Nu shook her head once more. "It doesn't work like that. There are thousands of people here, so thousands of paths would present themselves. I don't know enough about the two people we're looking for to be able to see their distinct paths clearly."

"And finding the city of Atmosphere was different?"

"I know it's hard to understand, but yes, it was, in a way. As you described it, this city was unique. A city within a volcano. The truth presented itself without obfuscation. I'm sorry, Rascal. We'll just have to keep walking, asking, and looking."

At one point they paused for a snack on a balcony overlooking the drop of the crater, a large, ornate fountain with another magnificent bird in its center. This one was regal, and even though carved in stone, seemed to glint of golden feathers.

"A Golden Auric," Rascal said as they sat on the edge of the fountain's rippling pool of water, nodding politely to others taking their ease around the feature.

"I wonder how they got this thing here," Nu said softly to herself, thinking of the incongruity of the impermanence of the wooden structures all around and the all-to solid stone of the very thing she was sitting on.

"Balloons, no doubt," Rascal said, startling Nu, who was momentarily lost in her own thoughts.

"Ah yes," she replied, her thoughts interrupted, and then sent Antares off on her own little scouting party. "You're not going to find the people themselves, but perhaps there's a clue to them somewhere. Two brothers or two sisters or a brother-and-sister act that stands out."

I'll do my best, Antares shimmered back to her.

"You always do," Nu replied, before the Orb floated off with purpose.

"I'm going to find something for us to eat," Rascal said, and Nu nodded her thanks.

Her attention was drawn to a large structure built out into the empty space below, where the most curious melody sounded from. She had noticed the vibrations in the area around her, but she hadn't connected it with the sounds coming from the enclosure. Still waiting for Rascal, Nu moved toward the sound, the steady pummeling of the ground and air becoming more pronounced with each step she took.

There was a large, ornate archway leading into the space—hand-carved images of birds, a myriad of species large and small, intertwined with one another. People were coming and going, and Nu moved inward. It was a large tent, held aloft by means she couldn't quite see, with a flock of birds moving gracefully above, a woman dressed in white standing at the center with her hands aloft.

Their eyes locked for moment, a chance mutual greeting, and Nu could *see* the magic coming from the woman's hands, moving in intricate webs toward the birds, who were singing in unison, the birdsong accompanied by the flapping of wings and somehow reverberated by the dense fabric of the tent, which Nu now realized depicted the same Golden Auric as she'd seen at the fountain. It was a tapestry of celebration, and she knew the truth of it. Islands rising into the sky, a young woman standing with the Aurics and her people, united in celebration. She was in the presence of a birdsinger, one of those gifted with an affinity for the native wildlife and the magical essence that kept their world safe in the skies. The other woman nodded to her once, an acknowledgment from one magic user to another, and then went back to her song. *Their* song, Nu realized. She could see the connection everywhere now, the people dancing and celebrating, their friends their family, their loved ones. Their realm.

Nu's clarity was so piercing that she saw Triss for a moment, back at the Library, standing with Mwamba, and for a moment, she thought her lover could see her back, but they were deep in conversation. She saw her compatriots, Arturo and Robin, back at the hotel, and she reflexively blushed. Nu saw Rascal making her way back to the fountain, and she snapped herself out of her trance, realizing she had been dancing with the people around her, unconsciously moving to the melody the birdsinger had gifted them. Her heart leaped for a while, and she realized that for the first time in a long time, she had let herself be free from her worries, her obligations.

Her guilt at not telling Arturo she'd seen a future where he might fall to darkness sprang up, threatening to shatter the joy of the last movement, but she saw the magic in this place, connecting everyone, and understood her place in things.

Truth, she thought, *is a terrible burden to bear.* But she knew she must. Nu moved away from the crowds, back to the fountain, her spirits lightened despite the renewed sense of responsibility. For a little while, she had experienced the connection of these people, and it was just the inspiration she'd needed to find her feet.

Meanwhile, Rascal returned with small savory cakes and what she described as "volcanic glaze," which to Nu seemed very much like a cross between a cocktail and a science experiment. It was a long, thin tubular glass filled with a bright pink liquid that looked like it was *moving* to the beat from the music. She had no idea what to do with it.

Rascal, grinning like a lunatic, lifted her own tube and poured it all over her own head. The effect was immediate—her hair turned the color of the liquid, and her face, where it ran down her head, looked like hot lava for a moment, then soaked into her skin to leave an amazing pulsing glow. Rascal shivered, then howled with delight.

Nu looked at hers, shrugged, and followed suit. It was like caffeine and sherbet were soaking into her head and down her face. She immediately felt alert, like she'd been on a coffee drip, then it faded quickly to a low buzz.

Rascal grinned again. "Don't worry. The lava effect washes off. But in the moonlight, we'll be hard to miss!"

Nu laughed and put her hand gratefully on Rascal's arm, and the pair sat staring across the divide to where the buildings curled around the other side of the crater.

"So," Rascal said, "you look happier than when I left you. Even before the glaze. Have you finally realized what we all knew back in the City of Forever? That you did, and are still doing, everything you can to sort this mess out?"

Nu smiled at Rascal. Of all the people on this mission, only Rascal understood what she had gone through the last time they had been thrown together on an adventure. She had witnessed Nu graduate from tagalong to Sage before her eyes.

And now she was back, this time as the one to lead her friends on a quest.

"That means a lot, Rascal. Thank you."

"So, how are you doing? After all we went through with . . . you know. And then you went back to the Great Library straight into this new role of yours, I assume. Can't have been easy."

Nu took a bite, giving a little shrug. "Honestly? It's been wonderful, Rascal. It was something I'd dreamed about but never thought possible. How does anybody react to becoming that which they aspired to be? No matter the challenges we faced or the difficulties that have presented themselves, I couldn't be happier or more honored to be a Sage." Her smile grew. "And I've been so lucky in having Robin show me how things work, traveling with me across the realms. Being a guide when it was needed and a friend the rest of the time. I consider her a sister now."

Rascal made a noise of acknowledgment as she devoured the rest of her snack in one go, stick and all. Nu stared at hers in surprise, realizing it was all edible. She nibbled at it and added, "Being given the chance to lead this mission is a privilege. The other Sages have placed their faith in me, and I will ensure I repay them. A lot depends on us finding Haruto and that artifact of his. I refuse to return to the Great Library until it's done."

Nu stood as she finished her snack. Yet as Rascal joined her and the pair were about to move off again, the air shimmered ahead of her.

"Well?" she asked the returning Antares.

I've found something, the Orb said.

Nu woke the next day in the cavern at the Bore Hole ready for what lay ahead.

The clue Antares had found the evening before had been another pamphlet. It was crumpled and stained, but it clearly depicted a man and a woman who looked very similar, flying hand in hand. She had a sudden moment of clarity and remembered Arturo clutching one of them the previous day. She sighed, *knowing* his would have been of the same duo. Still, they were acrobats, and they had a show every morning in the lower levels of the crater city, so they had missed yesterday's performance. She realized that her group would be better rested, and they'd lost no time. A good result.

"Best shot we've got right now," Rascal said before ushering Nu to a nearby bar to have a drink to celebrate and then escorting her back to get a good night's sleep.

Now the group had gathered again and were making their way down through the murkier sections of Atmosphere, away from the dawn light above, feeling colder with every level they descended. Finally, Rascal grunted in satisfaction and pointed a meaty finger at a painting that adorned a nearby wall; this one looked a little older and more established than the poster Nu had seen yesterday, but it was basically the same image.

Embrace the Vortex! the title declared proudly. Below it, the image featured two olive-hued people, a man and a woman, both with their arms outstretched as they seemed to fall. In the center, a giant green four-winged bird with silver streaks and jeweled claws hung in the air between them, its dual wing tips touching each of their hands.

Nu noticed that Arturo and Robin were walking close together this morning, more so than usual. And Robin's fingers held on to his, though perhaps out of necessity as the group walked along the narrow channel cut into the outside of the volcano. A small, fairly insignificant railing had been put up to give the impression of safety, but Nu didn't think any one of them wanted to test it.

It was dimly lit down here. Sunlight was in short supply, so all that was left was more of those crystals in the rock around them. Still, it gave the otherwise hard, unforgiving place a soft, glowing aura that wouldn't have been out of place in a circus tent in the middle of the day, and she enjoyed that. It felt apt for what they were about to experience.

The wind poured upward now, likely channeled through the empty magma tunnels below. Nu imagined this was the Vortex mentioned in the painting. A place to witness . . . well, witness *what*, she had no idea. But she could see there were more audience channels cut into the wall of the rock below, and even from here, she could tell they were deeper cuts, filling with people.

"We've made great time," Rascal yelled over her shoulder as they took rock-cut steps up to the next level. "The fates are on our side this morning. Looks like the show will soon be starting!"

As they arrived at the seating galleries, Nu watched Arturo gawping at the sight of hundreds of people taking their seats. Rascal quickly pulled up at a set of steps that were currently unoccupied and gestured for them all to take a seat. Arturo and Robin went together. Nu leaned over the railing to take a good look down, marveling at the endless drop. She felt a powerful thrill at doing so, although she knew some of it was the anticipation of nearing their goal.

"This is it," she said to herself.

She hoped it was true.

Arturo was trying to push himself as far back into his seat as the rock allowed and did his best to avoid asking Nu to sit back down because she was making him nervous.

Robin squeezed his hand. "You okay?"

"Sure, never been better!"

He realized immediately she saw through his lies, because of course she did. There then followed a warmth flowing through her fingers into his skin—a warmth that relaxed every part of him within seconds, allowing the constriction in his chest to ease and for him to breath and let the excitement back in.

"And now?"

Her face tilted ever so slightly. Her deep brown eyes fixed on his. Her lips curled up at the corners, on the edge of another one of her dazzling smiles that he found intoxicating. Her nose wrinkled a little in that way it did when she was teasing him. In a way he had come to find delightful.

He grinned, this time without holding back.

"Okay, *now* I've never been better."

He kept his hand in hers as they both waited for the show.

They didn't have to wait long for Vortex to give up her secrets. As the seats became filled to bursting—Arturo wondered if these people lived here or were visitors like them—a hush descended upon the arena, and even he felt himself leaning forward in his seat expectantly.

It started with a *bang*. Or, rather, with a *swoosh*.

A wave of wings that descended from above as a phalanx of large four-winged birds dove straight down into the cavernous colosseum, before the singular crash of their beating wings, delivered in unison, created a roar of noise. The act held them momentarily in the air, before they split off and swooped around in a stunning display of aerial acrobatics that kept in time with the social music of the city hanging above them. Music Arturo could still feel in his bones, even if he could no longer hear it over the wind and the crashing of wings here.

It was an incredible blend of bass and whistles, crashes of wings and calls of the birds. A symphony that accompanied the visual feast unfolding.

Arturo recognized the birds as the same type painted in the advertisement for the show. The multiple wings. The claws glittering like jewels. And their size. They weren't close to the size of the Golden Aurics, but they were certainly larger than any birds he'd ever seen on Earth, with a dual wingspan double the height of most people.

The way they whipped around the space, filling it with their strange, otherworldly music, was incredible. There shouldn't have been enough room for them in there, not with so many of them and their size. Yet they dipped and swooped as if a singular mind, their wings stretching and folding when needed, weaving around each other without touching. Each a breath of air on the wind. A gasp of melody. Beautiful. Magnificent. A dance worthy of the heavens.

If this had been the entire show, Arturo would have been ecstatic. But soon enough, the two people from the poster with the birds appeared.

Falling from the sky.

Everyone gasped. There were some muffled screams, too, as the two figures dropped straight down in free fall, through the chaos, the speed of their descent creating an anxiety-causing crescendo of whistling that brought everyone's hearts into their mouths. The birds instantly changed course and became one again, swooping around the walls of the arena in unison, a tornado of feathers, their own version of the vortex. Arturo leaned forward, expecting to see the pair drop right through the center. He wondered if this was the show where these people, whoever they were, made a mistake and paid the price. Lost to oblivion. His fingers constricted around Robin's. His breath caught once more.

At the last second, the woman's descent was suddenly halted, and she swung in an arc. The man dropped past her, before his hand caught her ankle as she swung upward. It was a rope swing, Arturo realized. Or something much finer than rope, barely noticeable in the soft light of the shaft as it hung from the claws of a bird.

In perfect harmony, the pair leaped at the zenith of the arc, somersaulted, and each grabbed another nigh-on invisible swing from different birds. They were carried behind the creatures, seeming to glide as they spun in concentric circles around the shaft, amid the other birds rising higher and higher, until they reached the audience.

Both leaped onto the backs of a single bird, which hovered easily on its four wings long enough for the pair to wave. The audience erupted in cheers.

"Incredible!" Robin said, her face lit up with wonder. Arturo could only nod in agreement, even as his eyes remained fixed on the dazzling show that was unfolding before them.

The aerial dance—that was the only way Arturo could describe it in his mind—continued for the longest time. It might have been hours, days even, such was the trance it put him and the others in. Occasionally, his glance would slip, drawn by a nearby gasp or a delighted chuckle, and he'd catch sight of Rascal and Nu watching the performance, rapt in innocent, childlike awe and excitement.

Leaping, twirling, gliding, and falling, the man and the woman were in sync with the birds and the birds with them. It was a display of the utmost dexterity and superhuman skills, but also one of unity. Of collaboration and an unspoken bond between creature and human. Perhaps even telepathy. That was the only reason Arturo could come up with to explain the timing and luck of the performers and their companions.

He realized he would never see another sight like this in his life. And to be perfectly honest, he was fine with that. Surely there could be nothing better than this.

Suddenly, the light darkened.

Clouds appeared overhead, and such was the force of the Vortex that the cloud was pulled down into the arena, a swirling mass of mist that descended upon the birds and the humans alike. Someone in the audience half stood, thinking this wasn't part of the act. The birds within the cloud seemed to move slower, as though trying to fly through molasses. There was a screech, the first time any of the birds had made a sound. It echoed around the cavern. A cry of shock. A warning.

Then there was the very distinct sight of a silhouette as one of the figures tumbled from the back of a bird.

The man. He cried out.

And fell.

The birds exploded into action, but it wasn't controlled like before. It was a burst of movement in every direction, seemingly mindless and panicked, like one might see in a park or a plaza when a toddler runs toward a flock of pigeons.

It didn't seem right for birds of this elegance and intelligence. There had been purpose in their movement, but now it was chaotic. Everyone watching knew this was wrong. It wasn't part of the act. It led to several of them, Arturo included, instinctively getting to their feet. It didn't matter that none of them could do a damn thing. It was human nature to help, always.

The figure continued to fall.

The feathers continued to fly.

The woman? She was nowhere to be seen now. The cloud swung around, twisting like a tornado within the arena. Had she fallen too? Arturo couldn't see her. He felt Robin let go of his hand and begin to reach out. He caught the glow of Centauri from where he hovered, almost invisible.

Only Nu had the presence of mind to touch her arm and draw her attention away. A quick shake of the head. A mouthed, "Wait."

Robin frowned, clearly torn between helping the falling people if she could and not wanting to give away who they were. Arturo didn't know what to think. But as he turned in the other direction, he saw that beyond Nu, Rascal was still sitting, looking on calmly.

She gave him a smile.

And that's when the birds stopped panicking. As one murmuration, they turned, spun around the walls as they had before, in a direction counter to that of the swirling cloud. Faster and faster they flew, building their melody of beating wings, until the cloud slowed.

Then slowly it began to thin. The birds stopped flapping and soared across the still-churning currents, seemingly held suspended in the air.

And in the center of them, the man and the woman hung with their arms linked, holding on to the invisible rope swings slung between two birds, their feet dangling above the bottomless chasm.

The crowd erupted as once again the birds rose and brought the couple in front of the audience. They let go of each other, allowing themselves to swing up and over onto their respective rides, where they paused for effect and gave elaborate, sweeping bows.

Arturo, Robin, and the others were clapping loudly. Even Nu seemed to have put aside her focus for a moment and was enjoying the moment of exhilaration.

It was only then that Rascal stood. She had been applauding but took this moment to rise head and shoulders above the gathering. Standing out just enough to catch the woman acrobat's eye, before nodding very deliberately.

The woman stared for a moment longer than necessary at their group. She kept smiling throughout, so it was unlikely anybody else would have noticed had they not been paying attention. Then she casually slipped back into waving and soaking up the applause.

"Do you know her?" Arturo asked Rascal, leaning up on tiptoes to give her a better chance of hearing him.

"Not yet," Rascal said. "But I figure if she's a good enough guardian, she'll now be pretty damn curious." She turned to leave and beckoned for the others to follow. "Come on, let's go find ourselves a table at a nearby bar, grab some drinks, and wait. I'm betting we won't be there long before they seek us out."

CHAPTER TWENTY-EIGHT
THE DARKNESS BEYOND

Ready, Myrtilus the Orb said, with a cold, wintry swirl of symbols.

Payne nodded. "Finally."

The words were spoken with his usual solemnity, but as he turned to view his masterpiece, he did not feel the excitement he thought he might while standing on the precipice of his goal. In the back of his mind, the last entries he had read in the journal continued to rankle him, prompting him to confront what had been a growing concern.

The existence of Suttaru's humanity.

His Orb readied himself, hovering just above where the fragment of Maksus Stone had been placed on a chained Unwritten and the writhing chest of his most-trusted lieutenant. He'd trusted him enough to sacrifice him as Suttaru's new form, in the center of the ring of horrors that looked like the imaginings of Dante's Nine Circles of Hell.

The rings were hundreds of victims, bound into intricate patterns that Payne hoped echoed the symbols Suttaru used in his own experiments. The Burning Tree, fully committed now to their grisly task, had advised on the most practical aspects of their locations, each group of unfortunates near to one of her primary roots or nearest surrogates.

Their cries had grown weak now, the intense heat keeping them docile, but if they didn't act soon, that alone would kill them, and they would have to start all over again.

"You understand what you need to do, Myrtilus," Edwin said.

I'm the fuse, the Orb said.

"Yes, you are. And our connection is the spark. Our innate power, amplified by Discordia's sway in this realm, will flow through you to connect the fragment and the coin to the glorious fire all around us. At that point the Spirit will begin her magic and try to bring him back."

Are you sure this will even work?

Edwin bristled, irritated that Myrtilus should be questioning his strategy or expertise.

And yet . . . the doubt was valid. To his knowledge, nothing remotely like this had never been done before. Not like this.

"Admittedly, the experiment in the journal was on a much smaller scale," he replied carefully. "But I have followed the process and pulled apart the theory. There is nothing to suggest this won't work. We have Suttaru's ashes, the fragment, and its chain, as well as the living coin. Its molten metal will play the crucial part, binding his essence to the life force of the fragment, at which point the spirit will Unwrite our *volunteer* into a new body for the Master. Once ignited, the energy will draw on the spirit still left in these diseased bodies, and it will all pour into the center, into his new body, bringing him back."

Edwin should have been celebrating at the thought. Yet even as he described to Myrtilus what was to happen, his thoughts were elsewhere—back in the journal, where the segments had been increasingly paranoid, and less about Suttaru's experiments than they had been about his worries over a woman. It was unnerving to think of his master as a mundane, powerless human, pining over the attention of a woman.

Edwin didn't like the idea one bit. It had even made him wonder if he had made a mistake bringing him back the first time.

Suttaru had been trapped in a prison of the Book of Wisdom's making—a veil drawn across Paperworld that held back the evils of Discordia in all its forms. Edwin had long known the stories of this "Ash Man"—a nickname spoken in hushed whispers in the halls of the Library—and had been pleased to find, upon releasing him, that the figure that lay behind the myth had been every bit as fearful and uncompromising a champion of destruction as he had hoped.

Suttaru would be such a leader, Edwin hoped. Or at least he had. Now there was concern where there had not been any before. Because this journal was giving him deeper and deeper insights he did not wish to have. Suttaru had bade him to steal it back to ensure the Sages did not have access to the workings within it—and the way to stop the greater threat—which had perhaps been a mistake on his part. He had obviously not expected Edwin to read it in its entirety. Its original discovery had initially been the signpost Edwin had needed to find Suttaru, but he had only translated and read a few pages before knowing that his salvation lay in finding this alleged villain. After that, he had needed to know nothing further.

Once again his mind went to the nightmares of his war years and his frustrations with the lack of power or inclination of the Library and the Sages to fix him as he needed.

"Memories are who you are. They are not to be wiped clean," the Author had told him, after he had gone to her for help. "It is a dangerous path to seek to eliminate your past, to forget, no matter how painful they might seem now. Let us help you to accept them. To grow from them and flourish. That is how we can help you, Sage of Creativity. To free you from their chains and allow you to become a better Sage because of it."

They'd done nothing to help him.

It is lucky you found the journal, Myrtilus said, breaking the silence and bringing Edwin back from his reverie. *It helped you free Suttaru the first time. It will bring him back now.*

"Yes, lucky," Edwin replied, thinking back to that first time. How he'd been so pleased to find a way through the barrier to Discordia to reach the infamous figure. That he'd been so sure he'd be rewarded with help to rid himself of the nightmares that plagued him.

But now wasn't a time for doubts; it was a time for action.

This time he would help himself. Then, together, he and Myrtilus would end the Sages, their Library, and free his world from Paperworld and Discordia.

Edwin waited silently as Myrtilus lowered enough to touch the Maksus Stone fragment. It rocked slightly at the pressure, the red fire within the material gleaming brighter at the touch. Then it connected to the coin, and the bodies in the circle around them began to squirm harder, perhaps knowing what was coming.

"Do it," Edwin said.

Those in the Great Library liked to remind people that everyone was made of magic.

Edwin knew those who became Sages had found a way to tap into that magic more than any others. They were evolved. Special. Greater than the rest. And once bonded with their Orbs, they were then able to build upon that magic with power drawn from the same fire that lay within the original Maksus Stone. Here was an example of just what could be achieved with the appropriate determination.

The fires around the great forest intensified, and the screams of the still-living humans could be heard once more. Near death already, this new torture made them wail anew as a surge of immense power and intensity ignited the Maksus Stone fragment and brought the ritual circle to life.

"Now, Spirit!" Payne called out to the Burning Tree, and she responded.

Her fury poured back into those surrounding her, rocking and shaking them to their cores. The heat and pain throbbed through Edwin's skin and roared in his ears. It was if he'd fallen into the middle of the ocean during a storm.

Waves of fire crashed around them. Fireballs struck overhead, and the surrounding trunks all exploded with the intensity of the power and heat. Payne could do nothing but drift within it, protected by his and Myrtilus's magic, both a part of and a spectator to the burning chaos.

The tree let out a fresh scream of fire, and the pulsating, writhing letters began to form on her trunk, cascading through her roots and into the bundles of human flesh spread around her. These Unwritten, already remade in a parody of true life, convulsed and began to smolder, the fiery writing singeing their flesh until the clearing reeked of burning meat. They were like burning batteries, Payne thought, overcharging with the raw power of perverted nature.

Suddenly, the energy found an outlet. Payne gasped as the burning letters flowed together in a seething mass, moving at first in an uncoordinated surge, narrowly missing him, despite the wards he'd placed around himself. Such was its ferocity that he considered retreat, but now it shot out, surged into the central ring of bodies he had created to feed the last stage of the ritual. The Unwritten strained within their bonds and perished quickly; he heard their spines snap as they arched in incomprehensible agony, their bones breaking as they spasmed and tried to free themselves from the heat. There was a chorus of screams as the magic was ripped from their bodies and the surge grew in strength and moved toward its final destination: the last body in the very middle.

The forest screamed again, and again the ball of pitch-fueled fire wrote its way across the center, seeking its final destination.

"Hold," Edwin said through gritted teeth, watching his Orb shaking against the torrent of power flooding through the clearing. "We . . . must . . . *hold*."

The forest's screams reached a crescendo as the burning letters engulfed the final sacrifice. What few motes of energy that still clung to the disintegrating remains of the other people was now being drawn out. Their physical presence was no longer enough, so their ethereal selves, the very magical essence of their being, was sucked dry. Their personalities. The memories of loved ones they'd once had. Lives they'd once lived. All of it torn from the circle of life, a whirlwind of human agony and death spilling into the air as the bodies were drained of every last ounce of magic they'd contained.

As the circle grew ever hotter, burning with a fury of a thousand suns, the process Edwin had carefully set into motion took a different turn. The central body suddenly shattered outward, breaking the circle. Payne, the red fire dancing all around him, until all he could see was an undulating mass of words, undoing the very fabric of the man it used to be.

The man's scream was agony itself as his entire body lit up. Then even his cry was engulfed as the fire surged out through his mouth, and he was consumed alive by the power.

Payne could barely hold his eye open against the light and the heat, yet he was not going to let this moment of supreme pride escape him. He saw with delight that the power had taken on a life of its own, directed by the Burning Tree and combined with the power of the stone and even Suttaru's original experimental coin. He was witnessing the Unwriting of one life-form and the resurrection of another.

He was bringing Suttaru back from the dead.

In the center of the ever-expanding circle of life-consuming white fire, the remains of the body, now Suttaru, which until now had been still, limp, and lifeless, began to stir.

Close, Myrtilus said.

Payne screamed as the expanding fire reached him. It had only been a matter of time, yet his wards held, and the flame simply coiled around him, the Unwritten sacrifices long spent and no new fuel for the flames. The fire needed yet more.

He felt his own magic, channeled through Myrtilus, pour into his spine, into his skull, down through each and every bone in his body. It ignited every fiber of his being and pulled the life from it, all at the same time. His skin began to wither. His hands, held out in front of him, directed at his Orb, became ashen. This wasn't what he'd expected, but it was necessary. Life without success here was meaningless.

How long can I last? he thought.

And then every trace of the fire was pulled instantly away. It ran like a spiderweb between bodies and fled from Edwin's soul itself. With a crack of thunder, it caved in on itself and surged into Suttaru's body.

Myrtilus shot up into the air—half in escape, half blown backward by the force of the magic.

For a moment Edwin thought he'd done this wrong, that somehow the fire would consume his liege as well. But the silhouette in the light jolted, his back arching, and through the flames that continued to consume him, Suttaru's ragged outline grew more and more solid. Until finally the fire dissipated. The bodies of the Unwritten fell into dust and ash around them. Edwin sagged to the floor, drained but still alive.

In the midst of the smoky haze, Suttaru pulled himself upright, lifted his featureless face to the heavens, and raged.

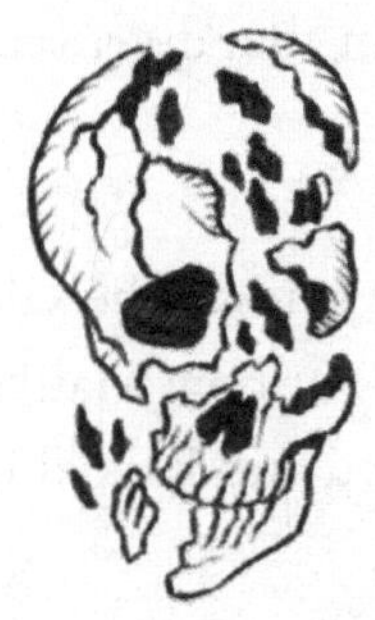

CHAPTER TWENTY-NINE

MATILAUX

The rescued boy's name was Matilaux.

His face was blank as they spoke to him, eyes barely seeing them, responding only to questions when asked, usually in dribs and drabs of one or two words, softly spoken, as though only just trying out his voice for the first time.

"Lynx, are you able to translate? Can he understand us?" Veer said.

Yes, the museum texts gave us enough to communicate, at least on a basic level. The more he speaks, the more fluent we will become.

They didn't speak of the dungeon. Not yet. It seemed too soon to ask the "what" and "why" of it all. Instead, they fed him and gave him water. Ensured he knew he was safe. Tried to allow his mind the space to recover from his ordeal.

Paix took the lead. She held the boy's delicate hands in hers as they walked and talked gently. There was no expectation of a response, only a need to fill the empty air with simple, positive words. A kind of walking therapy.

It seemed to work. With exercise and words as a distraction, it gave Matilaux time to find his thoughts. Slowly, he reconnected with whatever emotions were rising back to the surface within him. His eyes flickered with more life than they'd yet seen, and there was fear there as well as hope now.

He finally spoke.

"They take them to the bridge," he said, straight out of nowhere, interrupting Paix talking about how Matilaux might like Maïa's cat, if she were present. He stopped and looked up at her. "They took those who didn't die to the bridge."

It would have meant nothing to them if they hadn't seen the picture at the museum. But the flash of anger in the boy's eyes when he spoke gave away its importance to all three Sages. *Those who didn't die.* He'd seen it all down there—family and friends taken or killed. And somehow he'd retained enough of what he might have heard to provide the clue they were looking for.

Paix nodded encouragingly and ruffled Matilaux's hair. Veer and Maïa looked at each other and dropped back as soon as the other two started walking away.

"This bridge sounds like a good place to start," Veer said, but Maïa looked troubled. "Okay, out with it, Maïa. Why do I have a feeling you're about to tell me something to rain on the parade?"

"It was a little easy, do you not think?" she said.

He sighed and pulled at the ends of his mustache, twisting them into points. "Perhaps. But perhaps we were also due a stroke of luck. If this is some sort of base of operations, then Payne might be there. And we need that journal."

"I am just not convinced this is all it seems."

"I know, Maïa, but I don't see us having much of a choice. The boy has given us a destination that might bear some fruit. We have to try. I think it's that or we admit defeat and go back. We have no trail, no other hints at where he might be, and we can't just wander around this godforsaken realm forever, can we?" He was tired, and he knew his words were terse, but it felt like this was their last lead.

"And if it's a trap?" Maïa said.

He frowned. "I can't say for sure it isn't. But what are the odds?"

"We need to go," Matilaux said. "Please?"

"Sure thing, kid," Veer replied. He gestured for Maïa to hurry, and they set off. As they pulled alongside Paix and the boy, he asked, "Any particular reason?"

"It will follow."

The Sages all looked at each other.

"What's *it*, exactly?" Paix asked.

"A Ravager. It finds you inside your head. Nobody gets away. Not ever. Please, let's hurry."

"What's a Ravager?" Veer asked. The boy didn't answer, so he asked his Orb, "Lynx, is that a name or a thing?"

Not enough data for a comparative analysis as a noun or a proper noun.

"That's not superhelpful, buddy."

"Okay, let's do what he says." Veer gestured for them to hustle. "Which way, Matilaux?"

"Follow me," the boy replied.

They traveled for several hours across the blighted landscape, Matilaux guiding them with more confidence than Veer felt rational, but the dangers didn't register with the boy. They went from fields to forests to settlements, and everything they passed was in ruin, despite what was likely centuries since the damage had initially been wrought across the realm.

The boy warned them to look out for what he called the mindless, which, it turned out, were what the Sages had come to know as the Unwritten. Those who had fallen under the control of Suttaru. Of the mysterious Ravager, there was no sign yet. Veer took that to be a rare bit of good luck.

"How did this happen to you, young man? And to these mindless?" Veer asked as they took a stop to rest. The boy just looked at him, and for a moment, Veer wondered if the Orbs translation abilities had still failed to adjust to this cursed place.

"Steady, Veer," Maïa said, pushing him away from the boy. She knelt beside him and tried to comfort the lad.

"Come, little one, tell us what happened to you. You needn't be frightened of us. We mean you no harm. Here"—Maïa gestured to a water bottle, near the last of their supply—"drink something."

The boy darted forward and took a long, almost desperate swallow from the bottle, draining the last few drops.

Then he spoke: "They're bad folk, miss. They ain't got no stories. Not of their own. He takes them, then they work for the Master, do his bidding. Not like us young'uns. The Master likes us to have something to lose, you see, when he takes us. Even a little tale like mine might keep him entertained for a moment. I don't want no part of that. I run, and hide, but sometimes they find you anyway. He always wants more bodies, see."

Matilaux looked earnest, and while he hadn't been too heavy on the details, his face crinkled up.

Stories. Veer didn't know exactly what that meant, but he had a theory. It made sense. Their run-ins with the Unwritten had made the enemy seem almost mindless, like automatons. If Suttaru and Payne were absorbing these poor wretches' memories, feeding on them, that might be a source of their power. Was it memories, perhaps? Personality? Whatever the case, these beings had been flayed alive, stripped of their identities and left as mindless vessels of hate.

Matilaux spoke again, slowly. "Those in the dungeon were the ones who wouldn't give themselves over to the smoking man. The one with the burning cloak, like embers. They put us down there to soften us up, and then they take us . . ." The boy trailed off, and Maïa patted him on the arm again, trying to calm him.

"Go on little one. That man can't hurt you anymore. Tell us," Maïa said.

He looked up at her and continued. "They hurt some of us to convince the others. Others just gave up, like there was no point in goin' on. I heard from another prisoner, a woman, that those who had been taken to be corrupted were taken to the old crystal bridge. At least, it did back in the old times. I think that's where those evil men live. The one with the burning cloak and his one-eyed friend."

"You know this for sure?" Veer said, his intensity startling the boy. Paix and Maïa both gave him matching looks and shook their heads. He was in danger of blowing it. But the boy rallied.

"I ain't seen them myself, but everyone knows about them. You run if they're near, if you can. Sometimes you get away. Sometimes . . ." He paused again, then continued. "Sometimes they catch you. Or their creatures do. But we all know about the bridge. We shouldn't go there, but because I owe you, I'll get you close."

The boy hadn't said how he himself had survived where so many had not. Veer wanted to ask, but Maïa and Paix wouldn't hear of it.

The shortcut to the bridge turned out to be a transport system. It was a relief to know they wouldn't have to walk, however far it was, and soon they descended some stone steps into what looked like a gaping mouth in the ground, all overgrown with sickly vines and half hidden from the surrounding area.

So down they went, the Orbs lighting the way. When they reached the bottom and stepped out onto a cracked, grass-covered platform, they got to witness one such sight.

The transport they were to take was like one of those fanciful European steam trains Veer had always wanted to try out, elegant and stretching into the distance. Except there were no carriages to speak of; it was one long vehicle of concertinaed metal that was pinched and bunched along its length where it had been clearly forced to twist and turn around the half-pipe track that lay ahead of it.

All along it were opaque patches that seemed to be windows, while arched doorways were just about visible every twenty yards or so—one or two of them off the hinges. Inside was darkness. Nothing seemed to be working.

"Do you think I need to charge anything?" Paix asked, holding out her arm and letting ribbons of electricity dance across her skin, before forming a ball in her hand. She looked around, clearly seeking anything that might look like a battery.

Matilaux shook his head and simply stepped forward. As soon as his foot passed beyond a faded blue line that ran the length of the platform, an ancient sensor must have been triggered. The transport groaned as it leaped up off the track, clearly not having done this for a while.

With a few feet of clearance, it stopped and hovered.

"Interesting," Veer muttered to Lynx. "Magnetic?"

The Orb swirled an affirmative symbol in a sharp sea blue before bobbing backward in surprise.

The roof of the transport unfolded. And several gigantic, iridescent sails—each one in the shape of a leaf—blew upward, towering above the vehicle.

"Looks like it's your kind of transport, Veer," Maïa said. "A wind-powered train, and it looks like everything is still working. Care to get up there and get us to our destination a little faster?"

The three Sages followed Matilaux along the platform. There was a statue a little further along, a monument of some kind with an arc of stone bending upward to two globes. Or at least that's what they probably had been. One had been half destroyed, and the pieces were scattered on the floor, growing weeds on the floor behind.

"The Twin Suns," Matilaux explained. "This was once a beautiful place when they were in the sky, so the stories go. I think that's what that says, though I can't read."

He pointed to writing etched into a rusting plaque at the foot of the monument. Veer didn't need to ask Lynx to study it for him. The Orb floated lower, scanning it, then began to let his patterns reveal the text. Veer relayed it to the others.

"It's an ancient memorial to a place called Old Solernia. I imagine that's what this realm used to be called. Looks like the survivors of whatever happened here erected this in the aftermath, so they wouldn't forget what had come before, in the hope they could find it again in the future. They placed it here, next to one of their greatest achievements. They called it a windcatcher."

"Is that the transport?" Paix asked.

"I guess so."

Maïa looked around her warily and kicked a chunk of rubble along the ground. "We should get a move on."

They moved toward one of the windcatcher doors. It slid down into the floor, allowing them across the threshold to where they could see rows of tattered, deteriorating seats inside.

"Not exactly first-class," Paix said.

"I've been in worse," Veer said, only half joking. "At least it still seems to be operational."

Matilaux smiled along with them, even though he unlikely understood any of what they were saying. But before he could step onto the windcatcher, a gust of something blew down the platform and over them all. A scent of death, far worse than anything in this rotten realm so far.

Veer looked down at his clothes to see them damp with something.

Something red.

He glanced up as footsteps echoed on the stairs behind them, building to a thunderous crescendo as though a bull was charging them.

"What's *that*?" Paix gasped as a shape materialized at the end of the platform.

It was made entirely of red mist. A humanoid figure but with arms that were far too long, ending in clawed fingers that were as long as swords. And from the head, antlers jutted out like upside-down lightning strikes.

"Ravager," the boy gasped.

"I thought you said it was in our heads," Veer said.

"It is. In all our heads. And it will ravage our minds until we are no more." Matilaux made a low moan of horror. He grabbed Veer's arm, pulling him onto the transport. "We go. We go *now*!"

Veer looked back, then followed the boy aboard the windcatcher.

The sails flying high above the windcatcher train carried Veer and his group along the fields and valleys of Penumbris. It moved through mountains and under what he figured must once have been vast lakes. It bent and curved around the track, snaking through the low light of the realm, beneath ever-ominous storm clouds that hung overhead. It likely hadn't traveled in centuries. Veer felt the thing groan as it moved slowly through the landscape, like a snake with a full belly.

And still, the Ravager came for them.

The creature was like metallic smoke and surged after them, but the ancients who'd built this thing had known their business, and Veer was a master of the air.

Arms outstretched on either side of him, Veer drew on the air, pulling the wind around him and lifting him up off the floor of the transport. With a flick of his wrist, he latched on to a minuscule imperfection in the ceiling above him and pushed it open. It exploded outward, and he rose up through the hole.

Landing softly on the roof, he felt the air buffet him as the windcatcher pushed along the track. They were now moving across some plains crisscrossed with rivers of that black oily liquid. Each time they passed over one, the train slowed for a moment, as though it was being drained. Veer almost lost his balance once or twice and had to hang on to Lynx, who was hovering by his side.

"You ready to do this, Lynx?"

Ready.

Veer reached out, flexed his fingers, and pulled on every tiny whisper of air he could. It was like trying to create a rope from the tiniest strands, yet he kept pulling, wrapping it around and around him, feeling the strength of it grow stronger.

"More!" he yelled to Lynx as the roar of the air contained within his grasp thundered in his ears.

Trying.

"Try harder!"

The Orb didn't respond, focusing all his concentration on doing as he was asked, helping Veer to channel his need as powerfully as he could, and drawing the air to such an extent Veer half worried they'd create a vacuum around themselves.

Finally, it was enough. Pushing his hands upward, he let the strength flow through him and let it pour upward, outward, and against the sails flying above them.

The windcatcher lurched forward, and the Ravager disappeared behind them.

His arms ached. His bones burned. Every muscle in his body strained.

The Orb stuck beside him as the landscape shot past them on either side. The sails were bulging now, and the sight gave them both encouragement.

"We . . . might . . . just . . . do . . . this!" Veer gasped.

Lynx might have said something. If he did, it was lost to the buffeting as the windcatcher shook, and they shook with it.

Then everything fell.

CHAPTER THIRTY
THE SIBLING SPIES

Nu sat in the back room of a large multichambered gazebo, part bistro, part gambling den, and what was clearly a magician's act in the back, where the crowd went from deathly silent to rapturous applause in quick succession, followed by the occasional bouts of smoke and flashes with a smell like an unholy blend of sulfur and jasmine. She was still coming down from the high of watching the aerial acrobatics. The adrenaline of the performance was still warm in her veins, her pulse continuing to race.

Although now the feeling was mixed with nerves.

They had found their way here straight afterward, and Nu had paid the large gazebo owner extra for the privacy. She had a feeling Rascal's actions had been enough to draw the attention of the performers, and they wouldn't be long in waiting until they turned up. If they were half as alert as they were good at acrobatics, they would be here soon. Better to be prepared to talk in private now rather than later.

"Do you want us to stay?" Rascal asked. "Or would you rather Arturo and I hang around elsewhere when they show?"

Nu and Robin shared a look.

"It might be best if we talk with them alone," Robin said. "They might be more open if it's just us."

Rascal's wings twitched with mirth as she lifted her own mug and downed half of the green fizzing liquid in one go. "Then we will retire to the main lounge when needed. Sound good, Arturo?"

"Understood," he said, swirling his own golden bubbling drink and staring at it with a curious mix of interest and hesitation.

Nu smiled graciously, appreciative of Rascal's good sense. There was no room for mistakes here. They had come a long way to find Haruto, and these were the people they needed to locate him. It would be best for the Sages to talk to them alone.

Antares glowed reassuringly from her bracelet, sensing her nerves.

Faith, she said.

Then the thick, woven curtain to the private room opened, and the performers walked through.

"Ah-ha!" Rascal said, placing her drink on the low table and wiping the back of her forearm over her mouth. "They found us, and quicker than I thought. Time for us to leave, Arturo. Come on."

The visitors stood aside as Rascal and Arturo strode past, nodded their goodbyes, and headed out to the main communal area. The pair turned to Nu and Robin, still seated on soft velvet cushions.

The woman's waves of blond hair framed a dusky face, with two bright blue eyes glimmering like oases. She still wore her outfit from the performance, although she was now wrapped in a finely woven red-and-gold robe over the top. The man, all strong jaw and easy smile, wore the same robe, with a touch of extra silver embroidery at the hem.

Fancy, Antares buzzed. Nu patted her to be quiet.

Nu stood and gestured to the two empty cushions at the table.

"Thank you for heeding our admittedly vague request to join us," Nu said, trying to find a good way into this conversation. "Please, sit and drink. We would appreciate a conversation with two wondrous performers such as yourselves."

The pair didn't look at each other, but Nu could tell they were each weighing up the danger of the situation. It was almost a slight on the Sages that the performers very quickly took their seats.

"Something tells me we're not here to meet with fans," the woman said, lazing back in her chair and crossing her arms over one corner of the back of the seat. A waiter appeared just long enough to drop two swirling blue-and-red glasses before them, then left again. The performer stirred it, then took a sip. "So, who are you two, and what do you want with us?"

"We're seeking your help," Nu said. "I'm Nu, and this is Robin."

The man beamed again. "Well then, it's good to meet you two. I'm Wilx, and this is my sister, Zavia. And I suppose we don't need to introduce ourselves as the aerial acrobats of the Vortex and the finest trapeze act around."

He said it with the confidence of a man who had been told as much in the past and the dry self-deprecation of someone who knew it sounded egotistical.

Robin raised her glass. "No, you don't. That was quite the performance. Breathtaking, in fact."

Zavia lifted her glass in return. "Very kind of you. And please forgive my brother for his ego. For better or worse, he has come to believe his own hype over the years." She took another sip of her drink, then looked between Nu and Robin, her gaze settling on Nu and her eyes narrowing. "Now, this is obviously not why you're here. You didn't seek us out for help simply because of our aerial dexterity, did you?"

Nu held her tongue for a moment, wondering how much she could give away. She held Zavia's gaze, and just as the woman had sized them up upon arrival, she now did the same in return. Nu didn't need her power for this. She already had an inkling about what the woman was going to reveal.

"You'd be correct," Nu said. "I can tell there is more to you both than may appear at first glance. And we certainly wouldn't be seeking you out for any old reason."

"Then let us cut to the quick. Name your reason, Nu."

Wilx let out a theatrical yawn and waved his drink in the air. "Oh, come now, Zavia. Let's dispense with the games. They have surely guessed by now we're of the Amicorum Spectaculum!"

Nu's heart skipped a beat at the mention of the name. She held her face straight, trying to maintain a calm exterior, but on the inside, she was chaos. It was a feeling mirrored by the reaction of Robin as she sat bolt upright in her chair.

"The Amicorum Spectaculum?" Robin said, looking between the pair. "Well, that explains why you're so good!"

Zavia nodded her thanks, while Wilx gave a wide, toothy grin. Likely he was used to such reactions, while Zavia was probably the more wary of the two. Not quite cagey, but certainly a little more discerning about revealing all to complete strangers.

Nu appreciated that. She held her palms outward to try to convey that she and Robin could be trusted. "It is our great honor to meet with two members of such a prestigious and famous group of performers. Are you here in Atmosphere to hone your skills?"

"Not that the blade of our skills needs much whetting," Wilx said with a lazy drawl that suggested he was enjoying the attention but trying not to show it too much. "But yes, this is what we do in those long periods between being called upon for the big events. Because we need to be ready at a moment's notice."

Nu smiled and nodded. It was quite something to meet performers from the Amicorum Spectaculum in person, and on any other day, she would have loved to talk to them about it more. She'd grown up on stories of their shows. They were legendary performers throughout Paperworld, yet there was a mission to adhere to, and she needed to press on. There was much at stake, and that sense of time ticking away was stronger by the moment.

"Zavia, Wilx . . . we've been told that performing is not all you get up to in your time here. Is that right?"

"People say lots of things about us," Zavia said. "Some good, some not so good. What exactly have you heard?"

"That you use the cover of being performers to undertake other, less . . . traditional . . . roles."

The siblings laughed. "And who told you that?"

Nu took a chance. "The Great Tree in Silvyra."

Had they not been who they claimed, the very mention of Silvyra should have left them with blank looks. Yet Nu understood those in the Amicorum not only knew of the existence of other realms, but they had to travel to perform in them when called upon.

The siblings gave little away, but there was the faintest glimmer of recognition at the name in both. So they were who they said they were. Good.

"I see you know the place of which I speak," she said. "So, is what we were told true? Do you have other—how should I put it?—obligations?"

Wilx's eyes met hers as he held his drink to his lips and took a sip.

"Ah, but you see, Nu, the truth is a complex and difficult bird to catch at the best of times. She can soar through the heavens as easily as she can skim the ground. Some say her wings lift her up, carry her weight, but others say it's the air that carries the bird. Or perhaps it's a combination of the two." He was curious now, leaning forward with his elbows on the table, making a point of taking in her outfit. "Tell me: What island could you have possibly come from that dresses in a way reminiscent of the clothing they wear in Silvyra? I know of no such island here. Which makes me wonder who exactly *you* are?"

"A pertinent question, Brother," Zavia said, watching Nu carefully. "How do they know the existence of such a place?"

"Because we just traveled from there."

The Amicorum looked at each other, then both set aside their drinks and leaned in.

"Okay, now you have our attention," Zavia said.

Nu looked to the door and drew on a little of her power to make sure nobody was standing behind it. Then she let a half smile creep onto her lips. "I can't imagine *our* reputation has preceded us, so we should speak plainly, without the need to cloak our words . . . or ourselves." She nodded to Antares to show herself, which the Orb promptly did, appearing just above the center of the table. Centauri quickly followed suit. The Amicorum siblings came about as close to gasping at the Orbs as Nu figured was possible for a pair used to secrets being revealed. "These fine pair are Antares and Centauri. They are Orbs of the Great Library of Tomorrow."

"*Catch me and never let me fall*," Wilx whispered to himself. "The Great Library? Orbs?" He paused and frowned. "Wait . . . But if they are Orbs, who are you?"

"We are Sages," Robin said.

If they knew the title, they didn't show it. Wilx simply finished his drink and placed it back on the table with a flourish.

"Then well met, Sages! It was an honor to have performed for you earlier. Now, perhaps we should move to the business at hand, for I am nothing if not professional." Zavia laughed. He shot her a look. "All I am saying is that I am intrigued by the reason for you being here and seeking us out. What could have brought you from the Great Library to meet with me and my troublesome sister?"

"We require information," Nu said, glad they could finally get to the point. "We were told you two would be the ones to have it. Being as you are . . . *more* than just two talented acrobats, but dealers in secrets."

Wilx laughed lightly. "When the Amicorum was formed, it became clear that we could be useful in many ways. Dealers of secrets is one way to put it. Couriers of important information, operating in plain view, is another. We were encouraged to help individuals in need, as and when we could. Be it gathering knowledge for them, carrying messages, or going on missions for whatever reason was required. Usually in places where darker stories had taken root in realms where they should not have been."

"Which," Zavia added, "we hear has become commonplace of late. There is more evil penetrating these worlds than ever before. Monsters from the darkest depths of imagination walk the lands. Creatures that should not exist run rampant in previously peaceful realms. It has been an escalation of darkness. When we heard trouble had come to Silvyra, then the City of Forever, we knew that things were coming to an end, one way or another." Nu and Robin shared a glance, remembering they'd been at the center of that trouble. Zavia continued. "And so, we return to the crux of our meeting. You seek our help, and it will be our honor to serve you in whatever way we can. But our insight only goes so far, for we are not mentalists and cannot read your minds. Tell us, Sages, how may we be of service to you, in these ends of times?"

"I do not believe these to be the ends of times just yet, Zavia," Nu said firmly, trying not to let the mood slip too far. "We are looking to instill some hope back in the realms. To do this, we seek a man who came to Adscendo from our Great Library long ago. His name was Haruto."

Zavia and Wilx didn't react. Didn't move, didn't blink, just kept looking at Nu as she spoke. To anybody else, it might have suggested the pair didn't know a thing.

But Nu had drawn on a little of her power again, not willing to waste time trying to read tells as if she were playing a card game. Now that she knew they were Amicorum, she understood they could be well practiced in hiding what they knew, and she couldn't take the chance of missing anything. The air before the pair shimmered, and she saw the truth of their reactions, as the knowing in her gut confirmed it.

If that wasn't enough, Antares's glow lit up the room.

They know him.

Nu cleared her throat. "Let us not skirt around it, Zavia, Wilx. You know the man of whom I speak." She kept the inflection in her voice straight. Not a question but a statement. Acknowledgment of the truth of the matter. "You know Haruto, and that means he's still alive. Which is good and confirms what we had been told. Now all we need to do is find him and talk to him. He has something we need, and if he's still alive, there is a chance he'll still have it."

Wilx glanced at his sister. Zavia, though, kept staring at Nu, warier now of the shifting balance of power. She crossed her arms and leaned back in her seat. Nu could tell she was itching to react in some way, to glance at her brother and ask him what they should do. But she held firm, maintaining some semblance of control over her emotions.

"We know the man you seek. And yes, he is still alive. A miracle, so they say, but perhaps a curse too. We could locate him for you, if it came to that. But how do we know your intentions with him are honest? Haruto left the Great Library long ago, and there are certain people who might seek to find him again who we would not wish to do so."

Robin leaned forward. "Yes, and they are likely the same people we are trying to defend the realms against. Our need is great, Zavia."

The woman's eyes narrowed. "That may be so, but if you know what he runs from, then you surely understand why it might not be in our best interests to help you. We gave our word to our predecessors to protect that man at all costs. It has been a task handed down through many generations. The key directive of any of us within the show. We could not possibly give it up that easily, even during these increasingly worrying times. If he was found by certain . . . foes, it would mean his death."

"We understand," Nu continued. "Yet if we don't locate him and retrieve what we came for, it could mean the deaths of so many more. Perhaps all those who exist, everywhere."

"There has been trouble in the realm, sure, but I was joking when I said it was the end times!"

Nu didn't respond. Instead, she held up her hands wide across the table and closed her eyes. Drawing on the power, with Antares's help, she sought to show them, this brother and sister, the truth of what they faced.

This time, there were actual gasps.

In her mind, she saw it. The devastation in the plaza. Her and Helia fighting to bring Perennia back to life. The Unwritten masses swarming the city, while Rascal, Dzin, and Yantuz fought them.

And then the horror of Suttaru.

Nu couldn't bear to bring forth any more of this particular memory. She knew what came next. She would never forget it.

She let slip the power, and calm fell over the air once more.

For the longest time, nobody said anything. Zavia and Wilx simply stared into the vision that had been.

Then Zavia nodded slowly. "What is it you plan to retrieve from

Haruto, Nu? I thought you wanted to talk to the man, not take his possessions."

"I'm afraid we need to do both. He deserves to know what's happening and how he might help. But the artifact we need is something he took from the Great Library once upon a time. We were hoping he might be convinced to part with it."

Wilx and Zavia looked at each other. There was something else they weren't saying. Nu reached out with her power again, concentrating on the knowing deep inside her, felt at the fringes of the two people at the table with them, seeking any evidence of what it might be. She felt . . . surprise. That was quite strong between them. But there was also an epiphany. The siblings had just realized something that had bothered them about Haruto, and Nu could only guess that it concerned the artifact. They clearly had no idea about it, and yet knowing of its existence, that he had brought something here with him, had solved some puzzle in their minds.

Nu felt a little thrill that she had been able to surprise these spies with information they had not already possessed. But now she was worried that it would only serve to stoke their wariness. To make them shut the doors to their secrets and keep the Sages at bay.

So she placed her hands on the table, palms up. Focused on the power and used it on herself this time. Brought it out in a controlled flow, letting it spread up and outward just far enough above the table to allow Wilx and Zavia to see her.

She had no idea what it was they might see, only that it would be the truth of who Nu was and what she was saying. The essence of her spirit, perhaps. Of her soul.

Her truth.

Laying herself vulnerable in this moment, she could only hope they would understand the purity of the words that would follow.

"I give you my word: We don't want to harm him. We're Sages. Like you, we are tasked with helping people, individuals, lands, entire realms. But Haruto possesses something we need. It's of the utmost importance to not only this realm but every realm, everywhere. You know the evil out there exists, and it is growing stronger, and we must stand together if we are to defeat it." She stopped and let out a long, controlled breath, letting the power dissipate above her hands until normality had fallen back over the table. Reaching for her glass, she lifted it to her lips, ready to take a sip. "Now. Please. Will you help us?"

CHAPTER THIRTY-ONE
HOLD ON

It was like the world had suddenly stopped, and they had kept going, as if they had flown off the very edge of the known physical plane, into the great unknown.

"What's happening!?" he yelled to his Orb.

Lynx didn't know either.

The windcatcher shuddered and dropped faster. The bond with Lynx was growing weaker by the second. The tracks had simply disappeared, their absence obscured by dark clouds rolling across the landscape. Their speed and momentum, guided by Veer, was stopping them from plummeting like a rock, but it wouldn't last.

"Hold on, buddy."

To what?

Maïa cried out, holding on to the nearest solid object for dear life. "What's happening?!"

"Hold on," he urged the others as he collapsed to the floor, diverting all his energy into maintaining the connection with Lynx, trying to continue drawing on his power to keep the transport flying. "We are not done yet!"

Veer was trying to fly a train like an airship, with no navigation, steering and holding its weight with only the air around him. Was he doing it? He couldn't tell. He feared he could still feel them falling. He was drawing strength from anywhere he could—his Orb, his own body, even the other people in the carriage. Something he'd never done before, but the other Sages sensed his need and let him in, enhanced by their Orbs.

And yet the wind was refusing to help him. The foulness of it strained against him, years of corruption fighting his every whim, mocking his attempts to cajole it to grow more than it already was, to find strength where it declared it had none. It was going to bring them all down in a mess of twisted wreckage.

Veer pushed the wind anyway. Argued with it. Riled the wind into anger and then used that anger. Channeled it how he needed.

Rage against us, you bastard. Come on!

Suddenly, it whipped into such a frenzy that it billowed out the sails of the windcatcher. The entire transport immediately groaned and wrenched upward again, caught on the current.

"Just a little more," Veer said through gritted teeth.

"Take what you need, Veer!" Maïa said, her voice muted by the wind, but determined. Sages united at times of great need, sharing their powers, and when all ten aligned, they could work miracles, or so the histories told them. It hadn't been done in Veer's lifetime, outside of their ceremonial duties, and certainly not while plummeting to their likely deaths in a wind-power train, whose tracks were lost to time.

He could feel the ground beckoning him. The power he was exerting was unbearable.

"Just . . . a little . . . more . . ."

"The bridge!" Maïa exclaimed.

Veer opened his eyes just in time to see a hell of a sight through the opaque transport windows: a vast bridge, stretching out across a deep gulf that was entirely desert. Perhaps that was once the huge body of water that split the realm. It had to be. And the bridge seemed grown over it. Like it was formed of organic crystalline material, with giant buttresses and arches, stretching from landmass to landmass.

This was their destination.

They were almost—

The windcatcher suddenly steadied, and the resistance he'd been fighting surged once more and then disappeared. Just ahead, the vanished track was back in view, its missing section perhaps having been annihilated an age ago, but now Veer fought again, descending this time, too fast, too fast, but coming close, until—

"Brace for impact!" Veer yelled, almost hysterical now, until, with a deafening crunch, they were on the ground once more, leaving the windcatcher careening far too fast along the track as the strength of Veer's power, combined with Lynx, pushed the sails to the limits of their control.

Everything shook violently as a couple of sails broke free and spun away past the windows.

The transport tilted and didn't stop.

Then it was only noise and movement.

When Veer woke, a figure was standing over him.

The Sage was lying with his cheek pressed against the brittle ground. His entire body ached, and he couldn't move his legs. For a moment he wondered if he still had them, then he looked down and saw that he was buried underneath part of the windcatcher. He clenched his fist, drawing the wind to him, lifting the metal off him and shimmying out from underneath. Then the metal dropped, the last of his power spent.

"I'm sorry," Matilaux said.

Veer looked up, blinking the sweat and what felt like blood from his eyes. "Are you hurt?"

"No."

"Okay, that's good. Can you help me up?"

"No," the boy said.

It was then that Veer realized Matilaux wasn't alone. None of them were. For there was movement on all sides—quiet, still figures surrounding them all.

The Unwritten.

Veer looked up again and realized he'd made a terrible mistake as the boy moved his head slightly more into the light and revealed the grin on his face.

CHAPTER THIRTY-TWO
THE CHASE BEGINS

"So why couldn't we take the *Golden Oriole* again?"

Nu watched Arturo looking around him with a mixture of wariness and astonishment as they sat strapped into their seats on the small deck of the flying ship. It was Adscendo's pride and joy, Wilx had repeatedly said, while failing to hide it was also his ship.

It *was* quite something though—a small, sleek vessel that looked like a hummingbird in shape and style, although it had four wings and a long, pointed nose, within which she could see a cluster of wisps fluttering about. These turned out to be small birds, the size of butterflies and almost transparent. They pulsed and shimmered within the nose cone of the ship as it sped through the pink-hued skies.

"Your friend Rascal's antique contraption would have drawn too much attention," Wilx explained from the pilot's seat, coaxing more speed from his craft. They leaped up on a current and skimmed a cloud, then twisted around a low-flying mountain. "It wouldn't have caught up with Haruto's ship either. Or been able to dock without shattering itself. No, this was the only choice." He gave Arturo a wry smile. "Why do you ask? Is the decor not to your liking?"

The decor was gold trim and dazzling cyan paneling. It was a master class of artistic creativity, and Nu got the sense Wilx, at least, was used to traveling in style like this. Perhaps being part of the famous Amicorum Spectaculum had its benefits. She fidgeted in her seat, gripping the armrests as the ship somehow got even faster.

"Oh no, it's magnificent," Arturo replied. "I was just curious as to why we needed to split up, that's all."

"He's toying with you," Zavia said from where she sat in the copilot's seat flicking levers and adjusting a series of dials on the dashboard that seemed made of stardust. The center ring sparkled as she spun it one way, then adjusted the outer one a touch in the opposite direction. Ahead, the butterfly birds shimmered and changed direction. The ship turned on its axis and followed suit. "Don't worry. We'll rendezvous with Rascal at the Shimmering Tree. But we needed our ship to reach Haruto. Normally, we use our birds as messengers to get word to him and hear back. But if you want to see him face-to-face, this is the only way. Navigating in Adscendo is difficult at the best of times, and these are complicated calculations, far beyond any other in the realm."

"How so?"

"Everything in this world is found using the Shimmering Tree as a focal point, Arturo. It's all interrelated through the magic that lifted it to these heights in the first place. But Haruto's ship stands apart. If you think navigating between the various islands is tricky, try locating the one object in this realm that follows its own path!"

"The Shimmering Tree is supposed to be a sight to behold," Robin said, nudging Arturo with excitement. Nu could see her enthusiasm spread to him. "There are books within the Great Library that talk of how we're all connected . . . on Earth . . . in the Great Library . . . and beyond. Nature connects us all, and in each realm, there is a concentration of natural power. Coral. Flowers. Trees. The Shimmering Tree is the heart of this realm. And the books say it's one of the most unique and spectacular of them all."

"It is truly amazing," Wilx said, allowing himself a wistful sigh. "But right now we need to concentrate on the one thing in this realm that resists its pull. Haruto's craft was purpose-built to break convention. It was designed centuries ago to do what no other islands or aircraft in this realm can do—to stay in constant sunlight. It maintains a heading that keeps it beneath the glorious sun and avoids ever being swallowed up by night. Everything else in Adscendo is unified and part of a seamless, natural whole, working in unison. Haruto's ship is the exception, which makes it harder to find than a blade of grass in a Kestrine's nest. How are we doing with the final coordinates, Sister?"

"I'm working on it."

"Can you work faster, perhaps?"

"Bite your words, Wilx, or I'll fashion them into a blade and cut you with them."

Wilx laughed and danced the ship around another island.

"So this was the one realm Haruto could be safe in?" Arturo said thoughtfully, connecting the pieces of the story together. Nu could tell his mind was always working, collecting information, trying to make sense of the world he saw. "This being a place he's not really tied to land, he can be in perpetual motion and avoid the darkness. Where I presume he fears being discovered by the darkness he thinks will find him?"

"Or more likely the artifact," Robin said.

Nu nodded in agreement. "That's what I was thinking. Haruto thinks the evil will be able to sense *that* if it falls into darkness."

"What is this artifact you have come all this way to collect?" Wilx asked, picking some dirt from his chair and flicking it onto the floor. His gaze fell upon Robin, then shifted to Nu. Perhaps sensing if he was going to get the truth of anything, it would be from her.

Nu wasn't ready to divulge that information yet though. They'd only just met this pair, and although she knew of the Amicorum and what they stood for, could she trust them enough to ensure this mission was successful?

"Oh, we weren't told exactly," Arturo said, perhaps sensing it was more likely he could get away with pretending to be naive to deflect the question. "We only know that it's important and Haruto has it. So, I guess we'll all find out when we get there."

Wilx gave a curt nod and didn't pursue it. Arturo glanced over at Nu and winked, to which she smiled her thanks. With that, the cabin grew silent for a little longer, until Zavia gave a "ah-ha!" of triumph and twisted her dial once more, before hammering her palm onto the button at its center.

"We're locked in," Zavia said. "Now the ship will do her thing."

Wilx eased off the controls and grabbed a snack from a compartment in the side of his chair. He threw one to Zavia and then offered the strange-looking biscuits—crooked and salty-looking—to the others. Arturo took one, while Robin and Nu politely declined.

They all sat in relative silence, broken only by Arturo's curious noises of enjoyment of the snack, as the ship was thrown into a complex path that saw her bounce from island to island for the next few hours.

With her face pressed against her window, contemplating what lay ahead, Nu soon began to doze. It had been an exhausting few days of travel, in addition to feeling the constant weight of responsibility for her friends and the retrieval of the artifact. It was all catching up with her. The vibration of the ship wasn't helping, trying to lull her into a cozy sleep. So, as they joined a cloud river, a raging torrent of air currents and water vapor that sent splashes against the windows of the craft, she began to drift off. Dreaming of flying like the magnificent birds here. Swooping and soaring. Skimming the orange-tinted clouds and over a rolling plain of wild grass that was filled with nothing but empty doorframes.

Until suddenly her wings grew tired and limp, and she saw with horror a darkness forming beneath her, spilling through one of the doors, reaching upward. A maw of utter despair, its breath foul, its pull unimaginable.

It wanted to devour her. To swallow her whole. To eat away the light inside her and erase her life from existence.

She started to fall.

A cry woke her up. She sat up, rubbing her eyes, still a little shaken. Zavia was pointing through the side window to a luminous presence in the distance.

"Look, the Shimmering Tree!"

Even from here, with it being a speck barely over the horizon, it was clear how gigantic the focal point of Adscendo was.

Nu gasped, letting the light of it burn away the nightmare she'd just had. "It's like a sun in itself. It's incredible!"

"Those are the leaves, capturing and enhancing the sunlight. The entire place is where the magic is strongest in the realm, creating a gravity that binds all to it. A feat celebrated on rare occasions with a gathering of all the main islands back together, much like a migration back home. They return to its magic, dock with the tree, and celebrate the union of Adscendo among its branches."

Nu saw Robin tug Arturo's tunic back as he leaned over the seat in front to get a better view, cutting her off from the Amicorum performers.

"I've heard amazing things about the bridges that allow incoming ships to land," Robin said. "We'll get to see that later when we catch up with Rascal, won't we?"

"We will," Wilx said. "But right now we've got a date with Haruto to keep, and our timeframe is tight. We have one shot to intercept him and board before he breezes past, and we don't see him for another cycle. You Sages need this to happen fast, yes?"

"We do," Nu said.

"What's the plan, then, Zavia?" Wilx asked his sister. "The same approach we took with that building that fell off the Isle of Ulma when we were kids?"

She smiled grimly and quickly explained to the others what he was talking about. As she did so, Nu found her nerves returning.

It was a plan that spoke of desperation, less like intercepting Haruto's craft and more like crashing into it.

Arturo didn't look convinced. "You're going to harpoon his flying ship? We can't just dock with it?"

"I promise you, it's far more like docking than it sounds," Zavia said with a laugh, flicking some levers on the dashboard and above her head. A panel opened up in front of her, and a targeting wheel unfolded itself. She grabbed on tight, as a heads-up display appeared on the cockpit window. "Okay, maybe there's a little thrill of the hunt to it, but it's fine. I promise. No need to panic."

"I wasn't panicking," Arturo said quickly.

Nu watched the Amicorum closely now, reaching into herself to find the knowing and pushing it out just enough to feel at the fringes of the woman's energy. There was truth there. Zavia was being honest. Or at least she thought she was.

"Okay, let's do it," Nu said, then glanced at Robin and Arturo. They had placed their trust in the Amicorum by boarding the ship. Now it was time to have faith it was the right decision. She nodded to her friends. "If this is the only way, it's what needs to be done."

Arturo frowned. "Given the nature of how we're about to try to meet with him, he's not going to take it badly and fight us off, is he?"

"Hopefully not," Wilx replied.

"*Hopefully*?"

"He knows us," Zavia continued. "That we're out here in this realm, keeping watch for him. But we've only been in touch with him by bird, through the Kestrines. We've never had reason to board his ship before, and I don't think our predecessors ever needed to either. This will be a first for all of us."

Nu looked back to Arturo with a wry smile. "Okay, *now* you can panic."

The airship's engines whined as they fought the air currents outside, trying to maintain a stationary location within the web of lands drifting around them.

"Any sign of his craft?" Arturo asked as he stared out of his porthole window.

"Nothing I can see," Wilx said, drumming his fingers on the dashboard and staring through the starboard side of the windshield. "Although we're almost at the heart of this realm with that Shimmering Tree nearby, eye of the storm. Which means there are plenty of islands out there right now, all moving around us. If there's a small ship heading here through them at speed, we might not see it until it's upon us."

"What if it's not a small ship?"

The writer tapped on the glass, pointing to something only he could see. Nu peered through her window, scrubbing it of dust mites to try and get a better look.

A speck in the distance. A glint of light, getting larger by the second.

The knowing pulsed inside her gut.

"I see it," she said. "Wilx? Are we in position?"

"Yes, we are, Sister. Good to go."

"You got the harpoon ready?" Wilx asked, peering back to the horizon in the direction of the incoming craft. "If he's seen us, he's showing no sign of slowing down, and his craft is a lot bigger than I'd predicted. If that hits us . . ."

"Don't fail me now, Wilx. I'm ready to go. Just keep us above him and align our heading with his. As soon as he's within two jumps, push the ship as fast as she'll go, and I'll do the rest."

Nu was staring out of her window toward Haruto's ship speeding toward them, except she could see now it wasn't just a ship. Maybe that's how it had started out, but it looked far bigger than any craft they'd seen here. It was almost an island in itself. In fact, there were actually small islands attached to it by the looks of things. And at the sides flew several long, rippling streamers of light, like wings.

Solar sails. They were glowing with heat, enabling the craft to speed along at a breakneck pace.

"Fixing the heading," Wilx said under his breath.

The airship immediately shifted in the air, pulling to the port side, twisting until they could no longer see Haruto's flying island. They could only hear the distinct and distant whistle of something moving at high speed through the heavens, moving closer.

"Ready," Zavia said. "Come on now, Haruto. Keep it steady. Don't move, and we'll get this done as smoothly as possible."

An alarm sounded on the dashboard, and Wilx threw the ship into motion. It leaped forward just as the whistle became a roar issuing from behind and below them that definitely wasn't just their own engines. For a moment Nu wondered if she'd made a mistake trusting this pair. This wasn't any kind of midair boarding she'd envisaged undertaking when she'd agreed to this plan. She half expected the solar ship to crash through them, smashing them into little pieces and scattering them to the winds.

Except it didn't. The Amicorum's ship was sleek and nimble. It pounced from above and gave chase as Haruto's island flew straight underneath them.

"Great skies, he's fast," Wilx said, struggling with the controls.

"Hold her steady, Brother!"

"What do you think I'm doing?"

"That's it, good, good. Just like reeling in a Nifdarl on the last day of the skimming season. Now, just bring her down a little."

The ship's nose dipped. The tiny birds in the cone were all straining in the direction of the island, as though by sheer force of will they could pull the Amicorum's ship fast enough to catch up to it.

But even from the passenger seat behind the crew, Nu could see they were falling behind the mishmash of technology and islands that made up Haruto's craft.

Then Zavia gave a whoop and the harpoons flew. They landed directly in the soft verges of grassland behind what seemed to be some kind of ancient sailing barge more suited to the sea than clouds. The golden ropes went taut, glinting in the afternoon sunlight. And then, as they were dragged through the skies behind the behemoth, Wilx pulled a lever, and they slowly began to reel their craft in.

He leaned back from the controls, looking a little relieved. Meanwhile, Zavia flicked another switch and turned to the passengers.

"And that's how it's done," she said, getting up out of her seat and walking down the aisle. "Come on, ye of absolutely no faith. Let's go get your artifact."

Ahead, through the window, Nu could see them approaching Haruto's ship, the rope shortening as it was wound back in, pulling them closer by the minute. She watched as the gigantic Frankenstein's monster of a ship grew larger in their windshield, wondering if in fact they were still going to crash into it.

Until, finally, a soft bump told her their craft had come to land safely aboard.

She let out a sigh, blinked away the sweat that had collected across her eyelids, and followed the others out of the cabin.

CHAPTER THIRTY-THREE
THE MAN BEHIND THE CURTAIN

Suttaru's rampage lasted hours.

Edwin realized the man was still reeling from the battle at the City of Forever as he woke from death. For him, time had ceased to be while he'd been lifeless, only restarting again after his own journaled experiment had been used to bring him back.

Edwin watched from behind the ruined towers of the bridge city as the Unwritten, those who had born witness to his dark miracle of resurrection—the first in the history of this realm—were dispatched in various horrifying ways in Suttaru's rampage.

Fodder for the cannon, Myrtilus noted, in much the same way that Edwin's old comrades would have said back on Earth.

"A necessary evil," Edwin agreed, keeping his voice low. "Better they are chewed up in the fury of his awakening than us."

He'd known there was a chance of this happening, so he made sure there were plenty of Unwritten around. He'd beckoned them from their lurking around the city, across the bridge spanning the divide of this realm, and lured them into these ruins.

We have enough of them, at least.

The Orb was right. The army was plentiful in number, even after so many had been decimated with Suttaru. Hundreds of thousands remained on Penumbris, and there was no need to lose sleep over a few more lost now. Suttaru needed to burn his anger away. He would be easier to deal with afterward.

"I brought him back, but I am not so stupid I would count on his mercy upon his awakening," he muttered to himself.

Mercy was a disease. A crutch for the weak and foolish. Edwin had long dispensed with it, knowing it had no place on the battlefields he commanded nor within the ranks of the men he ordered to fight. You could not face your opponent and win if you had let mercy crawl into your mind. It would eat you alive, gnaw at you and make you hesitate when you needed it least and give your opponent the upper hand. He had seen it often enough, in men, women, and children who inevitably ended up at his feet, skewered and bleeding out. They had sought mercy in his humanity and regretted it. He would not make the same mistake.

And yet . . .

He looked around the sunblasted plinth of a female carved in stone, lifting a shield to the heavens, and watched Suttaru place his palms against an Unwritten man and burn holes right through him. Despite the brutal act of violence, Edwin's thoughts returned to the journal and its revelations. Revelations that painted a picture of Suttaru as one who had been very different long ago.

He wondered how much of that remained now.

Edwin returned to his hiding place, back to the stone, and sunk down onto his haunches to think. He had initially known very little about the background of the infamous Ash Man. Even in the Library, those who had known his story refused to say more, and when they died, their knowledge became rumor. Over the passing of generations, rumors became campfire tales, stories to tell the young as a bit of fun. Edwin had only bought into it when he'd learned of the journal's existence, and one night he had managed to sneak a look at it, before the irksome Mwamba had caught him and locked it away again.

That had been enough though. A glimpse at the power of the man behind the ash. And Edwin had badly needed that kind of power to fix his addled mind and exorcise himself once and for all these unjustified nightmares that plagued him.

You are impatient for him to fix you, Myrtilus said.

"You speak the obvious," Edwin bit back, irritated that the Orb was right. That he had been made to wait until he had aided Suttaru had initially been acceptable. The figure had revenge to enact. So Edwin had allowed himself to be kept on a tight leash. One did not rise through the ranks of the British army and command men into battle without understanding the need to control and be controlled. Discipline and patience were everything.

Yet he was still waiting. And reading this journal once again was giving him an increasingly troubling insight into the man Suttaru had once been. A scholar who had loved and worried and feared. All cracks of weakness that could be exploited, rendering him far more fragile than perhaps even the greater darkness knew.

Could he still be reached by those he once loved? What if he read the words in his journal that were once his, only to be reminded of his own humanity?

Edwin's lips thinned behind the plinth, hearing another mindless Unwritten being torn asunder by Suttaru's rage.

"There must be no weakness in our ranks," he said, thinking aloud. "I've witnessed the decimation of entire battalions owing to a single weakness, a crack that was exploited by the enemy. We cannot afford such a thing here."

You worry he is weak. From what you read.

Edwin didn't respond to that. He and his Orb had forged a bond, a connection, beyond any other. Yet he was not a trusting man. He could not admit his concerns about Suttaru out loud.

"I want to see the Sages, the Library, and that damned Book burn in hell," he said instead. "They claim to represent the best of humanity, but they did not help me. I could have led them to greatness, as I had others. Yet they were fools. Shortsighted. Too eager to collaborate and meander. They did not show me the respect I deserved. They left me to suffer, Myrtilus, as you know. I want to fix myself, yes. But I also want to make them pay."

Unfortunately, Suttaru was still integral to that. The darkness of Discordia had been there when the Sages hadn't. It had wrapped itself around the nightmares in his head, understanding his anger, acknowledging the injustice of it all. Willing him to release Suttaru from this prison of a realm in order to gain the help he needed to cure his nightmares.

The darkness itself had earned Edwin's allegiance. The entity understood Edwin's capabilities and had trusted him with this mission, and Edwin would see it through until the Library was ashes and the light and beauty of Paperworld was consumed by darkness.

And Earth?

You think you'll be granted power when this is over?

Edwin smiled. Myrtilus knew him well, for that had indeed been a pleasant little thought lingering at the periphery of Edwin's actions this entire time. That perhaps he might be rewarded with a position of power, one where he could run things as he saw fit. Where people would finally appreciate what he could do for them. He would be admired and respected and finally allowed to create order out of chaos. To build a new kingdom upon Earth, one far beyond the reaches of anything the British Empire attempted.

A true world order.

Buoyed by the thought, he finally got to his feet and stood with his back to the cold stone of the column. Myrtilus hovered before him, silently appraising his companion as if wondering if he were up to the task ahead. Beyond the Orb, the perpetual stormy twilight of Penumbris stretched beyond the bridge and out to the horizon in all directions. The ravaged land lit only by the single sun that struggled to shine through the swirling, viscous clouds that shrouded the sky.

Edwin pondered for a moment the mutinous thoughts in his head and the opportunity for power that lay within his grasp.

"Suttaru has returned. He will yet help me clear my mind of nightmares."

And after that? Myrtilus asked.

"We will do what we must," Edwin replied.

There could be no weakness in their ranks as they sought to take down the Library. He would make sure of it. Suttaru had instructed him to retrieve the journal, and rightly so. Not only because it had helped Edwin resurrect his liege and master, but because it clearly contained information that could help the Sages understand how the darkness came to be and what could be done to stop it.

And yet now he understood that the words in it were also potentially dangerous to their own cause too. If Suttaru saw in them a version of himself he'd forgotten, his humanity might bubble to the surface through the cracks. Widening them. Impeding his judgment as they sought to destroy those he loved and all that he used to represent.

Edwin could not let that happen. Not now. Not after all he'd done and with all that potential power within his reach.

Thankfully, he knew Suttaru wouldn't bother questioning Edwin on how he'd resurrected him. It could have been a gift of the darkness. Or some hidden dark magic Edwin had learned along the way. The reason would not matter to Suttaru, only that his faithful servant had done as he would have expected.

So, for now, Edwin decided to withhold the journal.

He needed to know more before he made his move.

CHAPTER THIRTY-FOUR
AN UNWELCOME CHOICE

Haruto, the man they'd traveled across two realms to find, was a small, stoic figure, with smooth brown skin and black hair, who held himself with pride.

For all intents and purposes, Haruto still seemed young. No more than twenty-five. That would have been Nu's guess, anyway, had she not already known. And had it not been for his old, tired eyes the color of dust, belying his true age.

He had met them in the courtyard of his home, a small, quirky building a little like a lighthouse that sat as the centerpiece of this bizarre island ship. Nu had never seen anything like it.

His craft was a mishmash of everything they'd seen so far in the realm and a lot of things they hadn't. Haruto's home was clearly the original ship, perhaps the very first he'd commandeered upon arriving, but it was now a drop in the ocean of the various landscapes that had been tied to it.

To the right of the lighthouse were rolling plains, green and lush. Flocks of small red-and-blue birds gathered among the wild grass, cooing and cawing. Yet to the left were rock pools held within a granitelike plateau. Steam was rising from the pools, giving the impression of a natural thermal sauna. Meanwhile, they'd just walked across several smaller islands that had been held together with thick, translucent chains. Some held small crop gardens, and one was simply a gathering of trees resplendent with small green fruits among their branches.

Haruto had made himself his own little paradise of sorts. One that contained everything he needed, including the ability to speed through the unending skies.

Nu regarded the small man stood before them and was both impressed and a little curious as to how he'd done all this himself.

"Ah," he said, after his little formal bow, addressing Wilx and Zavia. "I thought it must be you two when I saw the Kestrines. My own grew excitable to see its kin. Welcome!"

He gestured to the Kestrine that had flown to meet them as it circled above with the acrobats' birds.

Zavia bowed herself and nudged Wilx to do the same. "Haruto, it is good to finally meet you in person. I feel as if we are old friends, such has been the length of our correspondence through our birds all this time."

Haruto smiled politely, his teeth small and yellowing, as befitting someone who had lived for so long. Kindly eyes took each one of them in, resting in particular on the Orbs with a puzzled expression. Then he gestured in the direction of their ship. "That you have traveled here yourselves, and brought such strange company, says much. Let us retire to my home, and I will make us tea while you explain."

Nu held up a hand as the others began to move. She was trying hard not to worry, but they had taken so long to reach this man that she couldn't possibly extend the anticipation any longer.

"Haruto," she said. "Sir. It is an honor to meet you, and we have traveled far for the privilege. But time is against us, and we must not delay a moment longer. We are in need of your help."

He paused, confused. "Help? From me? But I do not know you! What could I possibly help you with? I am merely a tired old man who lives a very simple life, though at speed. From where did you say you had traveled?"

"The Great Library of Tomorrow," Nu said.

The spark of recognition was not long in coming. Haruto's eyes grew wide. He turned back to her, all thoughts of tea gone. His lips formed a silent word, though Nu couldn't tell exactly what it was.

"The Great Library?" When it came, his response was thin, like a weak breeze. His voice wistful and sad. "Oh. My old home. I think of it every day, yet I have not heard those three words uttered aloud in a long time. I sometimes wonder if it was all a dream."

"I can assure you it is still very real. Although I imagine a lot has changed since you left."

"Yes, I would think it must have."

He gestured for the group to follow him further into the garden, toward his home. Nu bit her tongue and decided there was nothing for it but to let the man do what he must. She couldn't hurry this; she had to do it right. Still, she felt her fingers fidgeting with the hem of her tunic, and she had to stop herself lest she seem impatient.

They soon found themselves on the deck of his lighthouse craft and realized it had once been some kind of ancient wooden sailing vessel, more suited to the sea than the skies.

"You see this ship? I've had her since the beginning. When I knew I had to outrun the night—outrun *him*—I found the fastest ship I could upon landing here, and I am sorry to say I stole it, but I had no choice." His words grew stronger as his memories were given life. He rushed on, trying to paint the picture for them all. "I have added to that first ship with the Atelier Guild, using their skills and smarts, until I have what you see before you. A home that gives me everything I need to live. One that keeps me safe. My island paradise. My world of sunlight and movement. I live here with my sanity and my birds." He laughed, a brittle but not unpleasant sound, like the rattling of teacups. "Although only the birds are still here!"

He waved his hand to more of the red-and-blue birds that lined the railing of the cabin ahead and then pointed to a circular bench that sat in the courtyard near it. There they sat in the sunshine in silence for a moment, enjoying the warmth and the roar of the wind in the distance, where the edges of Haruto's craft cut through the sky.

"So," he said eventually. "You have come for my help. You are from the Great Library, so I would not refuse. But how is it I can assist you?"

Nu took a breath. "I'm afraid it is a matter of the utmost importance."

"That much I can deduce. Nobody comes to visit me on this island . . . well, very few, at least. Not even this pair have visited in all the time we've been corresponding. As for the Great Library, I've had no word from that place since I left it all those lifetimes ago, and I expected never to hear anything again. Fairen and Adi . . . well, they were a complicated pair. I suppose you know about them. I can only imagine what resulted from that situation later, after my leaving. But still, I failed Fairen, and I betrayed Adi, in a way. Both my only friends. So, for you to be here now, to have searched for and found me, someone there must be desperate for my assistance. Fairen cannot be alive, bless her soul. But perhaps someone connected with her had left word to seek me out?"

He lifted his chin and straightened, preparing himself. Calm. Ready to do what he must. "What do you need? My counsel? Information on the man my old friend has become? I am not sure how I can be of help to you, emissaries of the Great Library. I know a little of how the Great Library has changed in the generations that have passed since I left. I know of the Sages of which I am sure you are one, but knowledge of all that means nothing. Speak of what is now. Let it out, so that we may pick apart the pieces and put the whole together."

"Well then, I will do just that," Nu said. "We're here for the fragment of Maksus Stone you brought with you when you left the Great Library."

Her words brought silence to the land, broken only by the cries of the birds nearby.

Haruto's expression veered from weary to worried in the blink of an eye.

"Oh."

"Do you still have it?" Robin asked.

There was a very audible sigh, and his hand went to his chest as though he was in some discomfort.

"My girl, yes, I do, but the situation with that artifact is far more complex than you can imagine. I don't know where to begin or how much exactly you would understand."

Nu saw Arturo sit taller on the fringes of the conversation, ready to talk and stand up for his friends again. The man had taken this all in his stride; Nu couldn't help but admire his courage to accompany them on this journey into the unknown.

Haruto looked at Arturo and tilted his head curiously. Nu wondered what he had seen in the other man's face, but her powers were telling her nothing.

"And you, sir, do not have the look of the Library about you." Haruto held Arturo's gaze, and Nu held her breath.

"No, sir, I'm not. An interloper, you might say. I'm just a writer far from home, trying to help."

"Ah! A writer! I knew a writer once too. One of my close friends. Perhaps my closest."

"Fairen?"

To everyone's surprise, he shook his head. "No. I'm talking about my friend Adi. At least, that was his name then. He is known in a vastly different way now and has been for a long time. Almost since I left the Library that final time. He became something else entirely. A demon. A vessel of evil. You know him as Suttaru."

Nu shifted uncomfortably.

Haruto sighed. "And he is the reason I created this island, this craft of such speed. It has powered through the skies of Adscendo for centuries, always ahead of the darkness, keeping me hidden. For should I fall into darkness, he will know. He will sense it and discover me, and the evil that corrupted him will finally have what it wants. I cannot let that happen. So long ago I held myself, to do what must be done for the good of everyone. I have kept myself away from people, unable to live a normal life, both saved by motion and trapped within it. Yet

I do it because it is right and just to do so. I will not allow him to find me."

Zavia looked confused. "I thought it was the stone he was after."

"That's right."

"But you just said he will find *you* if you slip into darkness and out of the light. Which is it?"

Haruto slowly undid the top two buttons of his robe and pulled back the collar. As they all leaned forward to look, Nu saw in horror that near his heart a rounded piece of metal was still buried into his skin. Wedged. Immovable.

Her stomach sank.

"You still carry it in you?" she said. "I had thought—"

"You had thought I might have pulled it out myself? Seen a healer to extract it?" Haruto shook his head sadly. "These were all things I considered, believe me. Yet it was not to be. When I left the Library, I carried this fragment of the Maksus Stone with me. Although it was through no fault of my own. It was part of me, as a result of my own incompetence as I sought to stop Adi's experiments; it exploded and led to me and the fragment becoming one. Perhaps that was what did it?" The birds nearby cawed mournfully, a troubling sound. "I was the one ultimately responsible for his loss to the evil. Maybe if I hadn't been convinced by Fairen to stop him, we would all have been okay in the end."

He let the robe fall back over his chest.

Nu could only stare at the man, feeling guilt on so many levels, not least for the thoughts now running rampant through her mind.

The fragment they needed was still in Haruto.

Could they even remove it?

"You can't take it," he added sadly, as if preempting the inevitable question. "I tried many times, but very quickly the tendrils of it grew within me, like crystal, and fused directly to my heart. To remove it would likely mean my death. What's more, the stone is the reason I have survived all this time. For I am not a special man, only one who was beset by extraordinary circumstances. The stone is a part of me now, and I cannot part with it, even if I wanted to. And there are times I long to be free of it." He raised an eyebrow. "I do not believe you have come to take my life, have you?"

"Of course not," Nu said, her voice wavering. Unsure now if she meant it. Could she take a life to save countless others? Could she condemn this man to death to ensure she fulfilled the Great Library's needs? Even for the greater good, she did not think so.

"That is good to know; however, there is a far more important reason why I wish for it to remain with me."

"Why?"

"Because, my girl, I know Adi . . . Suttaru . . . wants it. And I have kept it safe all this time. Despite my predicament, I have been able to hide it from those who would use it for torment. And to remove it from me means placing it at risk of falling out of the light, into darkness, where *they* can sense it. They will come after me, rip it from my body, and use it for their own nefarious ends."

"How do you know for sure?" Robin asked.

"Because this is not my first hiding place. I believe the connection the fragments share can traverse the metaverse, and as soon as I come into darkness, he will know it, just as I have been warned of his proximity to me in the past. He will just . . . *know* where I am. And then he will come for the fragment." He stopped, staring at them with an intensity born of a singular mission.

Haruto continued. "You confirmed its importance the moment you arrived here from the Great Library of Tomorrow." When Robin looked confused, he elaborated, "That you need it, for whatever end, and have come all this way searching for it, means it is of great importance. You would not have sought me otherwise. Am I not wrong?"

Nu shook her head. "You are not wrong, Haruto. We need the piece to stop the very people who will come looking for it. For they have begun along a path of war with us and threaten all that is good. We believe the fragment can help us prevent that."

Haruto gave a brief nod as though he had guessed as much.

"Then we are in quite the predicament."

Nu looked to her friends, to the watching Amicorum performers, and then inside herself. There had to be an answer here; there just had to be. She had been tasked with a mission. She could not lead them to the brink and then fall short. She *would* not. Everyone was counting on them to succeed in returning the Maksus Stone to the Great Library. There was no way she was simply going to give up now.

"Haruto," she said. "We did not come to harm you, and we will not now. But we must have the fragment. Is there any chance we can persuade you to come with us? We have a craft waiting at the Shimmering Tree. We can take you back home to the Great Library, where you will be safe, at least for a time. There are great minds there who will help us figure out another way to shield the fragment from those seeking it, and it should buy us time to figure out how to extract it without hurting you. I firmly believe there is always hope of a solution, even when the problem seems to present none."

She looked to the skies and noticed pink hues at the cloud edges around them. The sun was waning. There wasn't much time to do this if they were going to do it. They had to act now.

"Haruto?"

He was looking through her, deep in thought. She sensed a struggle in him. A need to do right, versus what he knew to be a risk. Yet as they sat there—a group silent among the wind and birdcall, the wildflowers of the plains rippling, steam continuing to rise over the thermal pools—Nu realized she hadn't done enough to convince him. He was going to stay. She could feel it in his energy.

As he opened his mouth, she held out her hands in front of her. And like she had done in Atmosphere, she brought to life the truth of what they faced.

She showed him his old friend and the destruction he had already wrought. The chaos and fire she had witnessed in the City of Forever. The remnants of the Rose Garden. The death rippling through the streets of Bloom.

She watched him through the vision, saw the heartbreak and fear in his eyes. Witnessed the strength threaten to leave him. His knees buckled, and only Zavia reaching out to grab his arm prevented him from collapsing to the deck.

Nu let go the power and simply waited. The guilt for what she'd just done to cause him hurt was overwhelming, but she pushed it back down, containing it like a cork in a bottle. There was no time for it here and now. She had a job to do.

Looking to Robin, she gestured to the weakened man before them. Her friend didn't need to be asked. She was already weaving her own power, letting little ribbons of light and love wind their way around him. It was just enough to keep him upright and give him the strength to push his shoulders back and regain his stoicism. Then she let go, unwilling to coerce him into anything, just wanting to allow him to be himself again.

"Haruto?" Nu asked again as gently as she could.

This time, he met her eyes. And despite whatever reservation he held on to, he lifted his chin and held himself as tall as he could.

"I understand," he said.

CHAPTER THIRTY-FIVE
DISTRUST

Edwin closed the journal and sat for a moment on the edge of the ledge looking to the burned side of the realm. The distant dunes gave the horizon the look of a desert ocean, rolling waves going nowhere, a vastness of death and destruction. While above, the shadow of the dead star that had brought ruin to this landscape continued its silent passage across the sky.

Myrtilus hung like a storm cloud before him. A flash of patterns, a wintry shroud, passed over the Orb's surface. A question.

Edwin ignored his companion. He had no answers right now. Concern continued to niggle at him, the last few scribbled words in the journal squirming like maggots in his mind. Eating away at the last vestiges of respect and confidence he once had for the figure of infamy.

It hadn't been like the first time he'd read the entries. Something had splintered in his mind, but he'd dismissed it. Now he'd read it again, it grew worse. Laying bare the hypocrisy at play.

Before he had become Suttaru, the scholar known as Adi had been in love and was prepared to sacrifice everything, himself included, to stop the greater evil.

That was quite the revelation. Not entirely surprising given the previous few entries Edwin had read in the journal, yet still, to see it so plainly written in the man's own hand was troubling.

Did Discordia know?

Edwin sniffed and dismissed the thought out of hand. Of course the entity would have known. It was a sentient being of intelligence far greater than any in the known universes. One strong enough to burst free from Discordia and taint the River of Letters itself with its evil. An entity that had devoured this very realm, in the aftermath of its inhabitants' foolish exploration of their star.

The evil had known. Which then begged the question: Why had it allowed Adi to live?

The answer to that, too, was obvious the more Edwin thought about it.

Adi had been betrayed by his lover and his friend. Disrespected. Sabotaged.

Anger was a powerful emotion, but the desire for revenge could be even more powerful. What better ally than one who had been closest to your enemies, only to be hurt by them?

But the journal had stopped before all this was clear. Well, aside from the last four pages that had been ripped out back in the Library. They had contained the final entries, detailing what Adi was thinking in those last few moments of his time there. But Edwin had long known that part of the story from what he'd pieced together on his research through the ancient tomes and from the stories rife through those who had a predilection for such things. He'd even manage to worm some secrets from Mwamba, under the guise of late-night drinks in the Sage's reading room.

Adi had indeed ventured through the portal, Mwamba had told him. The darkness had lured him, and he had been of a mind to answer, stepping through to face it.

"For how else could one of us—a scholar no less, friend of the Founder himself—have been twisted against us so quickly and easily? How could intelligent, compassionate Adi have been turned into the fearsome Suttaru, a

power so destructive that when he returned, he almost destroyed the entire Library all by himself, and would have done so had Fairen not joined with the Book of Wisdom and stopped him? He has become the devil here, Sage Edwin, his name spoken only in whispers for fear of calling him back. How else could this have happened, unless he gazed into the abyss and experienced the darkest evil of all?"

Mwamba's words had struck home with Edwin at the time, but not for the reasons the foolish Sage might have thought. It was the moment Edwin realized there was another power in existence beyond the Book of Wisdom. One that might offer him a quick and easy salvation where those in the Library had always resisted, trying in their own damned way to manage him as they saw fit. It was the moment Edwin realized there was still hope of finding a way to rid himself of the hauntings in his mind.

If the Sages and the Book would not help him directly douse the flames, he would fight fire with fire.

And that's what he had set out to do. Centuries after Adi had become Suttaru and had been banished by the Book of Wisdom, Edwin Payne had left the Library to find him and release him from his prison.

He had done that and more. But their subsequent plans to enact revenge had not gone smoothly. They had killed Perennia only for the Sage of Hope and the young girl who had tagged along with her to find and resurrect the dragon again—and she had gone on to kill Suttaru. Meanwhile, at the Library, the damned Sage of Love and that bumbling writer had somehow stopped Edwin from undertaking his part of the mission.

Or, at least, most of it.

He stared at the journal in his hands, turning it over in the dim light. Noting once again the ragged edges where the pages had been torn out in his escape. His finger traced the line, drawing blood. Edwin stared at the trickle of crimson seeping out of him dispassionately.

No choice, Myrtilus's patterns told him. The Orb kept its lights low so they would remain unseen for now. But Edwin could sense his companion's impatience as the patterns and symbols flashed across its surface. Edwin put his finger to his lips and relished the bitter metallic taste of his own life force.

"I know," he said.

Tell him. Now.

Myrtilus was right. Edwin couldn't hope to explain how he had brought back Suttaru without the journal. It was the man's own research. He would know that Edwin had recovered it from the Library, as he had been instructed.

He stood, swung his legs back to the bridge side of the ledge, and stretched before treading softly through the debris that littered the crystal city streets.

Suttaru waited for him beneath the single arch left of what had perhaps been a place of ritual and reverence. The cloud of ash that accompanied the figure was growing strong again, and the flakes whipped against Edwin's cheeks as he strode through and knelt before his liege.

You brought me back.

The words crawled through Edwin's mind like spiders looking for food. He fought a shiver, but only because he detected something hidden beneath them. A hint of regret, perhaps. Puzzlement maybe. Certainly, there was no thanks.

"I did," Edwin said, keeping his eyes on the floor lest his concern be noted. "It was the will of the darkness that we finish what was started. There is work still to be done to bring down the Sages and their Library. To enact our revenge, while making Paperworld vulnerable to the hunger of the one we serve. Not even death was meant to stop us."

Silence followed. Edwin waited as the moment stretched out and threatened to snap with every passing second. Was Suttaru angry about being brought back? Or that it had taken a lesser being, such as Edwin, to save him once again?

Finally, he could stand it no longer. He looked up at the featureless face.

Suttaru's head was inclined just enough for Edwin to know he was being watched. Studied. Inspected. As one might a cornered animal, before its throat was slit.

You found my journal. That is good.

Edwin held in the sigh of relief he felt and nodded.

"I recovered it from where it had been kept in the Library. After learning of your fate in the battle with the dragon, I had no choice but to remain here. I was willed to open its pages to learn what I could, and it was there I discovered your research, creating life from where there was none, using the stone."

The Maksus Stone is truly of a magic that can undo death. Suttaru went to study the fragment hanging upon his chest.

Edwin held out the journal.

That Suttaru had not already asked for it back spoke of the fact he had clearly stabilized himself after his initial rampage. And that had served Edwin well, as it had given him time to secretly finish reading the rest of the account.

It had been a risk, holding on to it. But regardless of what happened now, he was glad he had. Because it told him that he must be wary, and that Suttaru was not all he had hoped.

His hand wavered as the figure seemed to regard the book without bothering to reach out and take it. The swirls of ash grew thicker, as though drawn in by the tension hanging between them.

Finally, the Ash Man reclaimed that which had once been his, many centuries ago. He lifted the journal from Edwin's grasp and held it up before his face, as though the eyes he did not possess could look it over.

"You should destroy it," Edwin said suddenly. He hadn't meant to, unwilling to risk the wrath of Suttaru for pointing out the obvious. Yet the thought had been buzzing around his head ever since he had started reading it, knowing what it contained. Understanding that if the Sages ever got hold of the journal, they would realize how the darkness could be defeated. It was too dangerous to keep.

Suttaru knew that. The darkness did too.

The book, though, remained intact.

No.

"My liege?"

This is what will draw the Sages to us. Even now, they are here in this land, searching for it—and you. I will not destroy one or the other, not yet, until they are within our grasp. He paused. *The missing pages?*

Edwin tried to hide his irritation. "They took what I wanted them to take, as they were meant. I had little time to act, but I pulled out some pages that appeared to give them something, without giving them anything. Just enough to nudge them into venturing here after me."

Where their fate will be sealed, Suttaru's voice replied in Edwin's mind. He sounded eager. That was something. *We will take the Sages and make them open the portal into the Great Library. And then, at last, I will burn it all to the ground and have my revenge.*

The words were everything Edwin wanted to hear, but even as they echoed through his mind, he realized he wasn't entirely sure he trusted them.

"Of course," Edwin replied.

Thankfully, his rising ire went unnoticed by Suttaru, as a young boy with blood smeared down his face approached from the shadows, eyes lowered in reverence. The life in his eyes, frightened but authentic, marked him out as human, not one of the Unwritten. Not yet, at least.

He was one of the traps Edwin had laid in his wake for the Sages to fall into.

"I've brought them," the boy said.

CHAPTER THIRTY-SIX

OFF THE RADAR

Mwamba listened to his Orb with growing consternation.

"And you're sure?"

Disappeared. No signal.

Canopus was as close to concerned as Mwamba had ever seen his Orb. Orbs were grown through magic in the Great Library, yet they still remained technological creations, lacking human emotions. "They exist without fear," so the Author said. But he wondered if that was entirely true. Perhaps they'd evolved over time, little by little, without anybody noticing. Because he'd never witnessed any Orb, let alone his close and dear companion, be this worried.

"What's wrong?" Triss signed.

His assistant sat at a nearby table, resting with a book and drinking bluefruit tea when Canopus had started flashing urgently. Mwamba appreciated that his assistant had sat patiently, waiting for a break in the conversation, before asking anything. He just wished he had more positive information to pass on.

"Temporary loss of communications with the Orbs in Penumbris," he signed back.

He held up his hand and gently touched his Orb, patting the cold surface. The patterns gathered around his fingers in response.

"Anything to worry about?" Triss persisted.

"Not yet." His hands dropped into his lap as he stared at the fire some more. It was his favorite place, this reading room. The best place for thinking and for wisdom to find him. And goodness knows they had needed it lately. This development had him on edge, and it was only a moment before he changed his mind, got straight to his feet, and made for the exit.

Both Triss and Canopus followed quickly.

"The Orrery?" Triss asked.

One of the reasons she had become such an invaluable assistant was because she paid attention and had a logical mind. She would probably have considered it as a way of tracking down the missing Orbs almost as fast as Mwamba had.

"Yes," he replied as they walked from the room.

Had it only been six months since he'd needed to journey along this route with Helia and an inexperienced Nu? It seemed no time at all since the start of all this. Time was a fickle and funny thing. It played tricks with your mind and left you wondering about so much.

On his way, he saw the usual scholars milling about. They also bumped into Arturo's daughter, too, accompanied by Sage Eldra and Hocus the cat. They were wandering the halls, eating handfuls of some delicious treats from the kitchen. Eldra waved as they approached, and Triss signed a greeting back.

"Hello, Rosa," Mwamba said, mustering a sense of calm authority as they met in the corridor. "How are you finding our wonderful home?"

"Oh, it's lovely, thank you," Rosa replied. "Sage Eldra has been showing me the kitchens. We're off to ride on the streetcar now!" Then she turned to Triss and held up her hands, signing slowly. "Hello!"

Triss grinned. "Hello, Rosa!"

Rosa smiled back, then shoved another handful of tiny green snacks in her mouth. She looked up to Mwamba. "Has my papa been in touch? Is he okay?"

"I'm sure he's fine, Rosa. We haven't heard anything in the last day, but I know they will be busy. Don't worry. He'll be back soon."

With that, he nodded for Eldra to continue the tour. They said their goodbyes, and Hocus the cat dutifully followed the Sage and Arturo's daughter down the corridor.

Mwamba and Triss hurried in the other direction.

The reddish-brown lettering above the double doors they eventually reached announced the room's purpose with grandeur. *The Hall of Finding.* Mwamba pushed through and entered the cavernous room with his assistant, ignoring the walls of metaphysical maps and scrolls and constellations and intricate contraptions with varied incredible uses. He headed straight to the great machine rising before him, with its brass, steel, and crystal assemblage and so many concentric rings.

"Like galaxies within a universe," was how he'd heard Nu describe it to someone once, and he liked that way of thinking. It truly felt like he was able to gaze over the vast realms of Paperworld and know things.

He hoped that would remain true today.

With Canopus's help, he began the task of locating the Sages. The machine's dials whirred, and its levers clicked into place as his fingers moved across the controls like an accomplished pianist, while his Orb engaged with the Orrery, complimenting his Sage's actions.

Triss stood a little further back, watching with interest.

Lights lit up the map above him. The sparkling crystals scattered across the machine grew in color and life, and then . . .

Nothing. There were no other lights. No markers to show the Orbs' positions. He'd concentrated the Orrery's powers of discovery on the location the Book had sent Veer, Maïa, and Paix—a realm no Sage had previously ventured to—yet according to the map, the Orbs were no longer there. There had been no alert to signal they were leaving. They were simply gone.

Canopus let loose a single dull glow.

See?

Mwamba rested his hands on the machine and hung his head, thinking.

The last time Canopus had heard from Lynx, Veer's group had picked up a survivor and were heading to a transport. They were being chased by something, but Mwamba had the utmost faith in the ability of those three Sages to be able to protect themselves. Whatever it was, it couldn't stand against Veer's strength, Maïa's deftness and skill with a blade, or even Paix's joy. That one was able to calm even the most heated arguments with a little discreet shower of musical sparks.

No. Something had gone badly wrong.

But was it the signal between the Orbs, preventing both Canopus and the Orrery from locating the three travelers?

Or was it something else?

"Canopus, let the other Sages know what's happened. Tell them to be on their guard. And Triss, please go and ready the Volare for surveillance on the Great Library. Let me know if they find anything unusual. Best to be safe, yes?"

Yes, Canopus and Triss replied together.

Then she signed "Worried?"

"Not yet," Mwamba said with a deep sigh, though he was beginning to feel the time for that might soon be approaching.

CHAPTER THIRTY-SEVEN
THE SHIMMERING TREE

The performers' ship raced back through the skies of Adscendo toward the Shimmering Tree; every pink- and orange-tinged cloud they skimmed past indicated that time was running out.

Nu admired the way Haruto had remained calm on the journey back to the ship and committed to the decision he'd made. Whether or not it would involve a physical sacrifice, he didn't know. But he had already given up the safety of the home he'd known longer than the rise and fall of most civilizations, and that was something.

Zavia and Wilx had said very little, although Nu was sure they were unhappy Haruto was being removed from their care. They had been responsible for his safety all this time, as had generations of guardians preceding them.

"Do you promise he will be safe at the Great Library?" Zavia asked again from the seat beside her. "I think I would be happier if you were telling me he was going to be placed in the Great Fortress. Since when does a library hold significant protection against anything other than loud talking?"

"It is more than a library," Nu said, wishing she didn't think Zavia had a point. Yet what choice was there? "I promise we will take care of him as you have, but you have seen what I showed you before. The devastation that has already come to pass and that which may yet happen if we don't do this. We have to stop the darkness, and this is the way to do it."

Wilx looked back from the pilot's seat. "What was that thing that you did before, Robin? With the light and Haruto? I've never witnessed anything that beautiful in my life."

Robin allowed herself a small smile, her cheeks blushing ever so slightly. "Thank you. That's very kind of you to say. The light was love and compassion. It was something to help take the edge off his shock and fear, to allow him to regain himself without being held hostage to it. Nothing more than that. He had to make the decision to come with us by himself or else this would be tantamount to kidnapping." The smile widened mischievously. "Although both Nu and I did consider it for a moment."

Nu didn't react. Her friend had been joking, but there was an element of truth to Robin's words that brought a level of uncomfortable guilt. She cleared her throat and loudly asked, "Wilx, how are we doing? Will we make the Shimmering Tree before the sun sets? We need to reach Rascal and get on the *Golden Oriole* as soon as we can."

"Of course. Should be easy enough."

Nu looked around the cabin. Arturo sat by himself next to a window, still gazing with wonder at the realm they'd found themselves in. His eyes were glazed, almost dreamy. He seemed tired, but no less excited by everything they were seeing.

On the other side of her, Robin sat next to Haruto, and Zavia next to Nu.

"How do you cope with carrying the knowledge of what you've shown us?" Zavia leaned in and whispered. "The destruction. The agony and the fear. Do you keep all of it inside you like a memory of some sort?"

Nu chewed her lip, frowning. "I've never thought of it in that way, but I guess there is a sense of everything flowing through me when I call on my power to show such things. What I showed you actually happened. I was there. So, in that case, it was a true memory."

"You witnessed it?"

"I did. That and so much more. I'm sorry that I had to share it with you and Haruto, I truly am. But you deserved to know the truth of the matter, of what faces us and everyone, everywhere."

Zavia sat back in her seat. "And I'm sorry we put you through that. I wish there had been no need to convince us. But I know you understand why there was."

"Of course. This is all for the greater good, and that requires each of us to make sacrifices big and small. We rise with courage. We fall with inaction."

Zavia nodded and went back to staring out of the window. Nu looked past her and noted with concern the waning light in the sky.

Must hurry, Antares flashed beside her.

"Wilx, what's our estimated time to the tree?" she asked.

"Not long."

His cheerful tone was at odds with the gnawing inside her now. Anticipation? Or dread? It was like a storm was approaching.

"Rest, Antares. We'll be there soon enough," she said, hoping she was speaking the truth.

The rest of the journey was undertaken in almost near silence, until Robin slipped into the seat beside Arturo, and they began to talk.

Nu caught snippets of the conversation every now and then. She heard the low laughter they made at a shared joke or something the other had said. She had known for a while there was more to their relationship than appeared on the surface. Nu didn't need her power to tell her that. The looks they both gave the other when they weren't looking were almost comical in their cliché.

But at the heart of it, there was friendship. A solid and true connection between two people that transcended anything else and was as pure and sweet as any Nu had known.

As they continued bantering, and Robin feigned irritation at something Arturo said, poking him in the ribs, Nu sat back and smiled to herself, glad to witness some semblance of happiness in all the worry and pressure they were under. She thought again of Triss, as she did in these moments when there was time to think. She pictured her face, the last time they had been together, the touch of her hand and the smell of her hair, and Nu took comfort in remembering what it was they were all trying to protect.

Each other.

She let the thought warm her as she drifted into a dreamless sleep.

"We're here!"

Nu woke with a jolt, feeling far groggier than she would have liked, as Wilx announced their arrival. Yet as her body remembered where it was, the nervous excitement grew within her, and she leaned out of her seat to get a good look.

"Oh my," she muttered, rubbing the sleep out of her eyes as she stared in awe at the sight engulfing the windshield of the craft. The light was almost too bright, and she had to partially shield her eyes. "The Shimmering Tree!"

It was a sight for which none of them were prepared.

Whatever it had once been—and according to Zavia, it had been much smaller, emerging first above a cave on one of the floating islands—it had obviously overgrown and overwhelmed its home, and had kept growing. Because it was now a vast sphere of twisting, flowing branches filled with leaves of bright white and gold that were held in the skies as if nature had created its own sun and thrown it up to light up the entire realm.

Soon the magnificent sight swallowed the horizon ahead of the ship and filled the entirety of its windshield. Little reflections of light found their way into the cabin and sparkled on the walls and ceiling and each other. For a moment nobody said a thing, content to simply breathe in this wondrous and magical sight before them.

Nu couldn't quite believe the beauty of the thing. And the size too.

It hung here, like the central point of a galaxy, and she could almost feel the gravity of it. An undefinable pull. A power over everything around it that drew lands and people and gazes toward it.

It was stunning.

It was also starting to move.

"Bridge ho," Wilx yelled as he eased the craft down to a crawl ahead of where the leaves of the tree were fluttering faster and faster, as though something was swimming beneath the surface of a shimmering sea.

A spray of fine mist swept over the ship as thousands of invisible creatures were stirred from where they had been resting, lifted from the leaves, and took flight. All Nu could see was the ripple of the leaves they left behind, until they found the light. Then she could see the outlines of a flock of translucent waterbirds, each just a sheen of movement as they beat their wings and took to the skies, spraying water droplets like pollen over the ship.

As they gave way, the white-and-gold leaves they'd left behind parted, and Nu leaned forward with delight to watch a knotted, gnarled root unfurl itself and stretch out, winding like a snake across the sky toward them.

It stopped short of the vessel, but even from here she could see it was easily as thick as the deck of their ship and had a flat surface across the top of the bark, allowing access into the tree itself.

Robin gasped beside her. "Look! There are more ships here!"

She was right. As Nu followed the point of her finger, she saw they were not alone in docking with the Shimmering Tree. High above them were small specks that she could just about tell were other flying craft, bound to the tree by the root docks.

"The One World Bridges," Zavia said, appearing relaxed as her brother brought them into dock. "That's what these are. We use them to dock with the tree itself, but they also act as bridges from our ships and lands to this special place. They are living creations, as you can see. Just wait until we start walking along them. You'll see they are filled with stories and messages of unity and love, words that have been spoken into the bark and now appear as writing in it."

"Where did they come from?" Arturo asked, looking up to the curved wall of shimmering gold and white rising above and the thick brown root that was reaching out toward them. They watched as it drew alongside, almost caressing the side of the ship, before wrapping around to hold it fast. They drew still. Peaceful. At rest.

Wilx cut the engines as his sister continued.

"The Shimmering Tree fulfils one of the instincts of nature: Unification. Some in the Amicorum say it's the guidance of Mother herself, wanting to find a way to unite the various islands and guilds of this realm. To bring the families back to the place where the focus of magic was strongest and allow them to come together as one. To heal rifts and prevent division. The roots create bridges and docks that allow that to happen. It's nature's magic."

"That's a lovely thought," Nu said, eyes drifting beyond the performer, to the darkening hues of the sky. "Let us hope this magic speeds us on our way, then."

CHAPTER THIRTY-EIGHT
TRAPPED

Veer couldn't believe it. The boy they'd rescued . . . tried to protect . . .

Beside him, more movement—Maïa pushing herself up on her elbows, inching herself from a pile of broken seats. Veer had never been so glad to see her. Yet the knowledge that she was there, too, was a discomforting one—that was two of them in this predicament.

From beneath her bloodied hair, her eyes found Veer's. She didn't seem surprised in the least.

"Matilaux knew who we were," she whispered. "Back on the transport, he called us 'Sages.' Yet we'd never said the word . . ."

A man stepped from the crowd and stood near the boy.

"Yes, he did well, didn't he?" a voice said in a clear, clipped English accent. It seemed both entirely out of place in this realm of evil and perfectly at home. The Rogue Sage inclined his head to Veer, in a gesture of mocking respect. "Exactly as we'd asked!"

Matilaux's eyes twinkled at the compliment, his face flush with something resembling pride. Just then there was an explosion in the wreckage behind them. They all turned as the Ravager burst upward and roared as it saw a prone Paix lying nearby.

Paix cried out weakly as it strode toward her, flinging aside twisted and smoking machinery. Veer tried to move, to help, but he couldn't. He was spent.

Lynx? Where was Lynx?

A glance back at the Rogue Sage revealed the answer to that. Three Orbs—colorless, lifeless—were held by one of the corrupted in a metallic rope sack.

Veer slumped against the ground, only able to lie there, listening to Paix's exclamation and watching as the boy standing above him grinned hungrily as he watched the monster approach Paix.

It was the last thing Matilaux did.

Ash began to fall around them, a thick cloud of it, and as Veer tried to understand what was happening, he saw a featureless face appear through the gloom. His insides constricted as he realized that this—*this*—was someone who should not be here. Someone he had been told had died.

Suttaru stepped up beside Matilaux and placed a white hand on the boy's shoulder. The kid screamed in agony as his skin glowed with bright red heat, blistering and charring in an instant beneath Suttaru's touch. His face contorted as it quickly spread up his neck, across his cheeks, and down the left side of his body. The red mist quickly dissipating, shrouding Paix in blood just as it reached her.

Veer couldn't move. Couldn't think. Could only watch as Suttaru stepped back and Payne took his place, grinning widely as he crouched beside the Sage.

"We all carry monsters inside of us, it seems," Payne said. "Especially the young. To think, if only you had thought beyond your Library-driven positivity, you might have seen the shadow in your midst. Too late now, though, I'm afraid. For the young man. And for you."

He stretched and stood, his silver eye glinting beneath his cropped gray hair. Then he nodded to the Unwritten masses around them.

"Bind them and bring them with us. They are about to help us get into the Library."

Veer was yanked to his feet, his hands and legs bound with rope, and his fingers splayed open with the binds across his palms to prevent him using his power. He looked to Maïa and Paix and saw the defeat in their eyes. They felt the same languishing within him, drawing away the last of his strength.

They had failed in their mission.

And if what they'd just heard was true, even worse was to come.

Veer sat silently within the tent, barely breathing.

Outside the leaves rustled around their campfire. It was undercut with the guttural laughing of two men and the cry of a third.

How had this happened? Where was he? He couldn't think. They'd been camping. As night fell, there'd been movement. Slow, deliberate movement accompanied by the stink of beer and hate. His father had bundled him in here. But why? What was happening out there? *Not now. No time to figure it out.* All Veer could do was wrap his arms around his knees and squeeze his eyes shut and wish with all his might that the men would leave his dad alone.

There was the scuff of what sounded like a boot kicking something. A whimper and a scream.

Shit, shit, shit.

"You wanna say something, huh?" someone drawled.

A can crumpled. Another laugh. "He ain't going to be saying anything for a good long while. You kicked those teeth right outta his head!"

"He's got more of 'em. I'm gonna keep kicking."

Veer tried to hold in the cry of fear that badly wanted to escape him. He was expecting to feel warmth in his pants, torn between the need to pee and the sheer *want* to run out there and attack the bastards killing his father. And they *were* bastards. That was the word you used for people like this. Bullies. Hateful and violent and everywhere. The spawn of the worst of humanity, casual evil made flesh.

"Oh Godddddddd," came the muffled groan of his father again as Veer heard the flick and switch of a knife being unfolded. Something moist was cut, sliced open, and his father screamed. "Runnnn! *Runnnnn*!"

Veer knew it was for him.

Could he though?

Could he run and leave his father to die?

He blinked the sweat from his eyes. Or was it blood? He suddenly couldn't tell. Then, in an instant, the tent around him was gone, and he was shivering, huddled, clutching himself, tucked away in damp darkness. A cave? He was wedged into a fold of the rocks, the uncompromising stone tearing at his skin, only the light of the entrance to keep him company.

He could see a figure lying prone at the entrance, sprawled across the dirt. His father?

Where had the men gone?

"Hey," he whispered, trying to keep his voice low. "Dad?"

The echoes were slight at first, enough to reach the man, who still didn't move. Yet the noise continued, his words growing in power. More insistent. More insidious. So much so that it wrapped around his head like barbed wire, pulling taut, biting into his scalp. His voice but also not. Something more, twisted by the darkness in here and turned against him. *Shit.* His head wanted to explode with the pressure of it ringing around him, taunting him, mocking him.

He put his hands up to his ears and found them sticky and wet with his blood. He tried to pull his top over his head and bury himself in his clothes, but then realized he wasn't wearing any.

The rock cut his skin again as he shifted and tried to get out. It scraped him more and more as he moved, further draining him of life. The cold bit his wounds.

Movement behind him, in the dark. He couldn't see it, but he knew what was coming for him. Who was coming for him.

The men.

He whimpered, only for his plea to be lost in the maelstrom of his own echoes.

He was just a boy of ten. How did he get here? Where was his father?

Runnnnnnn!

But Veer couldn't move. He was frozen, knees up to his chest, naked and wedged into the rock. Bleeding everywhere, the cold, rough stone on his back. His cuts oozed with every breath. The cave seemed to grow around him, pulling him into itself.

He was being consumed. Eaten alive.

Move now!

Somewhere his father screamed again, and the sound became muffled as Veer's face was finally pulled under the rock, like it was consuming him. He breathed it in, gravel tumbling down his throat, pouring into his lungs. He convulsed against it, his body straining, limbs pushing in all directions without going anywhere. He was drowning in stone, unable to move, unable to even blink.

If hell existed, he had found it. An unbearable agony of helplessness. Until once more the world changed. He exploded outward, launched free of the rock, light enveloping him. He sucked in a lungful of dank air and felt his sleeping bag around him. He pushed it away, realizing he was back in the tent.

"What the hell was that?" a slurred voice said.

Veer didn't know what was going on, but he knew he needed to run. Run as fast and as far away from whatever was happening as he could. He shifted to all fours and inched toward the tent opening.

The edge of the clearing was only feet away. Beyond the trees was darkness. Safety? He didn't know. It was where all manner of critters lived and hunted and tore strips from each other. He remembered having nightmares about such things, about being lost in these woods. Yet this was nature. The animals feasted for survival, not fun. There was no torment out there.

Veer didn't fear the forest, just the *something* that lay beyond it. A creeping sense of doom. Of death. Of evil.

Footsteps kicked up dirt against the canvas of the tent.

"Well, well, what have we—"

Veer lunged forward, slipped on the sleeping bag, and for a moment, he thought he'd fall flat on his face, but his fingers found purchase in the dirt. Mud oozed between them, but they pulled him onward and out of the tent.

Straight into the grasp of a giant's hand.

Thick gray fingers formed a cage around Veer, squeezing as he was lifted high into the air, level with the canopy. He was pulled toward the face of the towering monstrosity that held him, except it had no face. It had nothing. Its face was a blank canvas, a hole in the universe. The hand pulled Veer closer to it, wanting to eat his being, to erase him from existence.

He kicked and fought, then looked down to see his father's twisted, bloody, and broken body below him. Surely it couldn't be real, but all he knew was that it *was* happening.

Tears welled in Veer's eyes and fury burst forth from within him. He struggled and fought and bit. Somehow he was able to wriggle out of the grip, but only to fall the huge distance to the forest floor. His ankle snapped as he landed, but he didn't care. Through the white-hot pain, he stumbled and crawled away, falling beyond the clearing edge, bouncing off a tree, and into the darkness of the forest.

Nature would help him, keep him safe. The giant's roar behind him splintered and became very human shouts. Threats of violence. Laughter. Then there was the crack of a gunshot, the ringing lasting long in his ears. Veer heard his own heart thumping, the blood loud in his mind.

Another crack. A tree stump exploded to his left.

Then he tripped. Fell into the mulch. Scratched his face all up on twigs and dried leaves from the summer heat.

Crying now, tears mingled with dirt down his cheeks, and he tried to crawl onward.

Help, he called in his mind, unable to voice it. Not brave enough. Not nearly strong enough.

Help me.

A hand burst from the earth and grabbed his shirt, pulling him face-first into the earth . . .

Veer shook free and stumbled backward.

Suttaru lowered his arm, then beckoned two of his army to drag Veer. To one side of him, Payne sneered with glee.

You cannot hope to survive this, Sage, Suttaru said, leaning down and pushing his graying, sunken face into Veer's. "We can do this for as long as needed. Either we will break you or we will break your friends. One way or another, you will open a portal to the Great Library."

"Wha . . . what are you doing to me?"

Veer looked down at his hands, noting they were big and strong, like an adult's. He wasn't camping. He wasn't trapped in a cave or facing a giant.

He was back in this tainted realm and captured.

The memories of his experiences here on Penumbris came flooding back again, and he groaned with despair. How many times had they done this to him, sending him back to his dark memories? Five? Six?

Payne said, "We can twist your darkest fears and make you relive them over and over until you give us what we want."

Veer shook the man off. He stared down at the dirt beneath him, trying to remember.

He and his dad had once encountered a couple of drunken huntsmen on one of their camping expeditions, hadn't they? They were on their way back to the tent when he'd been pulled aside by his dad, hidden in the mouth of a cave Veer still had nightmares about, and made to wait not even a hundred yards from the clearing where they'd chosen to camp.

No words had passed between them. The concern on his dad's face had been enough to convey the importance of staying still and quiet.

But the men hadn't seen them. Instead, father and son had watched for a good half hour as the bastards had wrecked their home for the week, looting what provisions they could and stealing whatever else they wanted. He still remembered the tears in his eyes and the sense of injustice and helplessness in his heart.

"They're not real," he said to himself.

"Not yet," Payne replied, standing and walking around him. "But the more we corrupt what's inside your head, the more real it will become."

The Rogue Sage's face remained impassive as he talked—the epitome of the stiff-upper-lipped soldier, with a calm facade and polite, clipped tone to his voice. Up close like this, Veer hated to admit he could understand how this psychotic murderer might have escaped for so long at the Great Library without being flagged as a danger, and how he was even picked in the first place by an Orb. There was something authentic about him. Twisted and wrong, but also grand and ingenious. Perhaps his Orb had sensed that. Perhaps thought he could have done magnificent things for the Great Library of Tomorrow. And the other Sages, over time, had simply put his demeanor down to eccentricity, even when this former Sage of Creativity had clearly been losing his way.

Even so, Veer had never wanted to punch a man more.

"I don't believe you," he said, spitting in the dirt.

"It doesn't matter whether you do or don't. It's happening. We will take what you had and give you something altogether more horrifying to accompany you in the remaining time you have left."

Veer swung his groggy head to the side to see Maïa and Paix. Both looked as bad as he felt. Paix was weeping silently, shaking her head. Maïa's eyes were wild, almost verging on madness, and he imagined his own looked the same.

Veer turned back to Suttaru to find him waiting patiently, perhaps enjoying the show. It was hard to tell. Veer wasn't sure he wanted to truly know what the monster was thinking.

He struggled pointlessly against his captors and tried to channel his power, but he was too weak. He'd spent everything he had on the trip on the windcatcher. Looking down at his hands again, he noticed they were older than he remembered. Was that a trick of his mind, too, or had such use of his power drained him of life?

Lynx! Where is Lynx?

There was a weak, barely imperceptible glow beyond Suttaru. There, still held within a bag of blackened weave, were the Orbs. They were unable to help, trapped within the binds of dark magic.

Veer was all alone.

"If it helps, Sage, please understand that you have had no chance in any of this," Payne said. His arms were folded across his chest. "You've not realized it, but we've been following your Orbs all this time. Tracking you Sages wherever you've ventured."

Veer frowned and shook his head. *What? How is that even possible?*

"Oh dear, did you not realize? How else did you think we were able to eliminate your new Sage of Hope? We followed you Sages to that beach."

"But . . . how? You cut yourself off from the Book?"

"Because, you senseless fool, the magic in the metal encasing the Maksus Stone was used in the creation of the Orbs. Had you bothered to apply your knowledge of the Library—that is, if it is within your capacity—you would have understood that the same method the Orrery uses to locate the Orbs could be replicated by myself! The chain my lord uses to secure his fragment of the stone around his neck is the same exotic metal that once surrounded the Maksus Stone, and it is part of the Orbs. That, plus the power of the stone fragment, was all we needed to devise our own method of tracking your Orbs!

"The Maksus Stone created the doorways between realms in the first place: a result of the curiosity of the people of this realm—of Solernia—gone wrong. The stone stole the fire of one of the stars. It created the portal, gave the scholars and Sage access to a universe of possibilities, yet here in the realm of its creation it left only a single sun. It allowed the magnificent darkness within Discordia to escape. And now it will Unwrite *everything* that has been written." He scratched around his eye socket and sneered. "Both the stone and the chain that holds it around

Suttaru's neck carried the same energy—an energy that can also be tapped into, harnessed, read, as the Book of Wisdom was designed to do. We simply did what she did! I've been able to track all your movements through the portal and around the realms. I used it to lead you here. I set a trap, and you walked into it with all the bravado and confidence and foolishness I expected. How does that feel?"

Veer barely had the energy to keep his head upright now. That was almost too much to take in. They'd been tracking them? No wonder they had been able to intercept Helia and Nu so often during their search for the dragon.

He had to get back. Warn the others.

Yet as he struggled against his bonds, he realized he wasn't going anywhere.

He heard footsteps and looked up to see Suttaru walking calmly to Maïa.

"Hey! You're not done with me yet," he said, trying to keep the villain's attention on him.

Suttaru ignored him and reached out with his hand toward Maïa.

Maïa locked eyes with Veer, on the edge of defeat. Then they rolled back in her head, and she was sent somewhere else, into the depths of her mind. Where whatever she was being shown made her cry out in terror.

Then a shadow fell in front of Veer as Payne knelt before him, blocking his view. A jagged grin, horrifying and unstoppable, crept across his face like an earthquake.

Veer woke in confusion. He didn't know where he was.

In Penumbris?

In the woods?

There was a moan to his left, and he recognized it faintly as Maïa. As disheartening as it was, it helped wrench him back to the present, from the nightmare that was slowly becoming his reality.

I can't take much more of this.

He looked to Maïa and saw her curled up, face between her knees.

None of us can.

It was like he was straddling multiple realities now, and it was a dice roll as to which one he would fall into forever.

In front of him, Suttaru stepped back. There were footsteps as another approached. Veer didn't know who it could be, but as he tried to focus, a man—possibly another hoodwinked minion, like Matilaux—stumbled into the arena to whisper something to Payne.

Payne then looked at Suttaru.

And to Veer's surprise, both drifted away from their prisoners.

Veer flagged, his head dropping, trying to hold himself together. What was happening? Where had they gone? What had they just learned?

Oh, please don't them have captured Nu's team.

He shifted his gaze to the surrounding ruins. Slowly, the circle of Unwritten people around them began to disperse. It was almost as if without their leaders here to direct them, they'd already forgotten about the prisoners in the midst. Veer felt something akin to hope . . . then it slipped through his fingers.

There was no way out of this. Suttaru and Payne would probably be gone only temporarily until they were ready to inflict more psychological damage. The Sages were seen as such little threat now, bound and damaged as they were, and they didn't consider them worthy of guarding properly.

Escape, Lynx flashed from where he was still trapped in a sack left against a pillar.

Veer tried his hands again. No use. He was bound tightly, and he couldn't access his power.

"Can't," he mouthed back. "Stuck."

But then his Orb did something peculiar; it burst into such fierce light that Veer had to look away. He was sure it would draw attention, and someone would come back to them. But then the light disappeared, and there was still nobody guarding them. A few Unwritten were milling about among the ruins a little distance away, but they hadn't seen anything. Perhaps the Unwritten couldn't even see light.

It didn't matter. What *did* matter was that when Veer looked back to Lynx, the Orb was floating out of a hole he'd burned in the sack and was now hovering over to his Sage.

"I don't know how you did that, but help me out. Fast."

The Orb sped across the gravel and forced his way into Veer's open hands. There was a sharp bite as Lynx unleashed patterns of heat across his surface, but it did the trick. The dark-magic ropes binding Veer's fingers were burned just enough for him to pull at them and tear free.

There was no time to celebrate. The corrupted would surely spot them soon and raise the alarm. Veer scrambled over to Maïa and gave her a hug to let her know she was safe. Her Orb, Thebe, burned away the ropes holding her.

Finally, it was Paix's turn, although she was now unconscious. It was probably a mercy to leave her that way.

"You okay?" Maïa asked weakly, staring at Veer as though either of them might crumble at any moment.

"Maybe if we can get out of here before they come back."

He felt a little guilt looking in the direction of Payne and the journal they had come to get. The fragment of stone was still around Suttaru's neck too.

Yet there was no chance of retrieving either now, and it wasn't worth his friends' sanity to try. All Veer could do was get them back to the Great Library alive. That was as much of a success as he could manage.

Given what they had been through, it would have to be enough.

CHAPTER THIRTY-NINE
THE ONE WORLD BRIDGE

The Shimmering Tree was magnificent. Not only visually beautiful, but there was a sense of home to it that swept through Arturo as soon as he placed a boot upon the root bridge. He smiled briefly, enjoying what felt very much like an embrace, as if nature itself was wrapping its limbs around him and guiding him to the comfort of its shade.

He didn't have time to enjoy it though. "We have to find the *Golden Oriole*," Nu said, gently nudging him along the One World Bridge in search of the airship home.

As they walked, Arturo noticed the writing in the bark. There was so much of it in so many different scrawls, conveying so many feelings. He wanted to stop and read them all, to learn what the people of Adscendo and visitors to the Shimmering Tree had to say to each other and to anyone who might follow them, but he barely had the chance.

"Keep your head and the sky of storms will pass," said one written into a sliver of root that ran along the route like a railing. Arturo's fingers brushed the raised strokes of the words in the wood as he passed.

Then a simple, "You'll always be with me," caught his eye.

There were more like that and then others that seemed more personal, maybe written to long-lost friends, lovers, or family. To those living and dead. All messages of love, connection, and unity, spoken into the tree to allow the magic to bring them to life.

As the group picked up their pace and moved into the canopy of leaves, away from the sun, it grew suddenly colder and darker.

Zavia grew jittery, her fingers twitching as she walked ahead of them. Her head turned this way and that, staring about the tree—and beyond it—as though any moment the night would descend all at once, and Suttaru himself would crawl from the shadows.

Arturo saw Nu lean into the woman and quietly say, "Maybe the light from the leaves of the tree will keep Haruto hidden. They are dazzling, a little like the sun. Perhaps they will act as a shield of light."

Wilx overheard. "And if not, what will we do? After what you showed us, I don't think we have the power to stand against him. We are brave and daring, but we know enough to avoid risks we cannot hope to overcome. And night is drawing in."

"Much faster than I care for," Zavia said under her breath.

Haruto looked at the pair. To Arturo, he still seemed calm on the surface, but there was a nervousness to the way he smoothed down his clothes repeatedly as he talked.

"Please, let us find your transport with speed. The birds can help. They are fast and nimble and have a better view than us way down here."

"Excellent idea," Zavia said. She put her fingers in her mouth and whistled. To Arturo's surprise, two of the Kestrines appeared from nowhere with huge wings beating a downdraft as they circled overhead. With her fingers dancing, Zavia communicated something to them, and they flew off quickly in between the branches.

"Were they here this whole time?" he asked.

"They go where we go. And now they've gone to locate your airship so we can get there as fast as possible. Hustle, please. Onward we go."

It was only a few minutes later when both the birds returned and called to them.

"They've found it," Wilx said. "Should I go ahead and get Rascal to warm the engines?"

Zavia nodded. "Go."

The birds above them split up, and while one stayed behind to guide Zavia, her brother loped off after the other. Arturo watched him jump across to another branch, then swing across the back of one of the Kestrines onto a higher platform. Soon the acrobat was gone from view.

"What now?" Nu asked.

"We follow as fast as we can." Zavia gazed back to where the opening of leaves that had allowed them entry were starting to draw in around the bridge to the ships. Both birds were little more than silhouettes now against the backdrop of the setting sun far in the distance. "And hope you were right that the brightness of the leaves does a job at hiding our friend here."

Haruto was still looking to the air at the departing birds. "The consideration of my safety is noted and welcomed. It has been a while since I have felt anything like kinship."

"I can't imagine you saw many people on your island?" Robin asked as they hurried after Wilx. "Hiding in perpetual motion probably doesn't lend itself to social interactions. How did you live like that for so long?"

"The birds were good companions. They are wise and watchful, full of life, and in some cases, magic. They are the jewel of this realm and have been my savior. Loneliness is a difficult obstacle to face, whatever your situation. They made it less so."

Robin put her arm around his little shoulders and gave him a squeeze. Arturo walked on the other side, noting the man's warm glow, even as his eyes darted with concern toward the darkening skies.

They simply had to make it back to the Great Library before nightfall. They could not let this kind, stoic man down. If they were caught here, Arturo didn't think they could remove the fragment they needed, not without killing the man. Haruto looked young, but he had the air of age about him. He warned them he wouldn't survive such an operation, and Arturo was inclined to believe him.

As Robin let Haruto walk after Zavia, she dropped back with Arturo. Perhaps she could sense his mind was spinning with questions. After a moment, she glanced at him.

"What's on your mind, Arturo? I can see you're mulling something over inside that handsome head of yours. Out with it."

Arturo dropped his voice. "What if we have no choice but to operate on Haruto to remove the fragment?" he asked. "What if our time runs out, and it's up to us to take it out?"

It was a difficult question to answer, yet Robin showed no sign of being surprised by it. She'd been wondering the same.

"It won't come to that," she said.

"But what if it does? We'll need to do it, yes?"

"It's easy to be so confident about such things when it's not your life on the line," Robin said, clearly unwilling to concede the point.

"And yet when there is *more* than just your life on the line, surely the decision is an easy one to make! Haruto himself must realize he'd have to make the sacrifice. He'll have to let us do it."

"The fate of the people we love, the worlds we care about, are all on the line," he continued. "Who wouldn't risk their own safety for that?"

"Not everyone is like you, Arturo."

He could tell she meant it as a compliment, an acknowledgment she saw the kind of person he was, one who would stand up to be counted when needed. Yet it stirred an element of frustration in him too.

"Let us hope he is," Arturo said quietly.

CHAPTER FORTY
THE SICKNESS SPREADS

Nu rallied the others to push through the Shimmering Tree as fast as they could. They scrambled up branches, leaped across some, and fought their way up and across to the other side of the tree while always keeping Zavia's bird in view.

"The light's almost gone," she said to Arturo.

"Then we move faster," he replied, his jaw set, determination etched in the lines at the corners of his eyes. Despite the danger here, he was calmer than she expected. Resolute.

They followed Robin, Haruto, and Zavia. Fingers of sunlight still stretched through the canopy toward them now, but what had been bright rays only moments ago were now barely visible.

It gave her some confidence that with the fading sun, the leaves of the tree came alive. They'd been storing the sun's heat, and now they grew bright, bathing the interlopers with a warm glow.

Nu tried to embrace the thrill of finding herself in yet another magical realm. Channel some good to push away the concern and offer a distraction to them both. "I wonder what this tree looks like from afar," she said. "I bet it makes quite the sight over the skies when darkness falls."

Arturo gestured for her to skirt around a knot in the branch ahead of him. "I imagine it would be quite beautiful. A moon of leaves hanging in the endless night. I have hope that one day, after all this, we can return and see it."

"I like that idea, Arturo. We should do that."

The idea of there being an end to this—an *afterward*—filled her with the same hope he spoke of. It kept her moving even as she felt her legs ache and stiffen as they passed by the trunk at the center of the Shimmering Tree and saw the little isle at its base.

"The High Eyrie," Zavia explained, pointing down. "It was known as the highest of the soaring isles. And the Shimmering Tree grew from it. Once it was just a part of this isle, and now the isle is a part of the tree. Such is the way of life." She skipped on ahead. "Come. No time for sightseeing."

They kept climbing up the network of branches. The brightness of the leaves lit the creeping shadows, aided by Centauri and Antares offering little immediate glows to highlight dangerous notches that might catch a foot or holes straight through the bark.

Nu kept glancing over to Arturo. The vision of what came next tugged at the corners of her focus. She bade it away.

"I'm glad you're here," she said. And she meant it. Not just because she thought she'd seen the need for him on this journey in her mind's eye. But because his presence was calming. His years of experience—perhaps not of *this*, but of life and difficulty and everything that came with being a parent—provided a rock for them all in the swirling ocean of the unknown. "Nobody except the Sages travels the realms. That you have taken it all in your stride is inspiring. We owe you a debt of gratitude."

"No thank-you is necessary, Nu. It was my honor to be asked to help. For the greater good, right?"

She nodded. "For the greater good."

A few moments later, they paused to let Haruto catch his breath. Zavia was almost bouncing on the spot impatiently, wanting them to move onward. Nu half expected her to pick the man up and sling him over her shoulder, carrying him the rest of the way.

It was Arturo who stepped up and put a hand on her shoulder. "This isn't perhaps the performance you're used to, but you're doing a fine job," he said, and Zavia laughed. The restless energy immediately dissipated a little.

"Take your time," she said to Haruto.

But he knew that was the one thing they couldn't do, and after five deep breaths, he waved her on. As they set off again, Nu slipped her arm through his.

"I don't believe this is how you imagined your day going," she said.

"It isn't," he replied with a smile. He gave her a sidelong glance and added, "You bear a lot of responsibility here."

"I do?"

"Yes, just as I have felt it myself all these passing orbits, I sense it in you. I know you feel a duty to your friends, to the Great Library. You try to carry it all within you."

"I am a Sage, Haruto. That is my role, no matter how hard or what struggles come my way."

He bowed his little head. "I have come to know that sometimes life is not fair when dispensing such heavy burdens upon us. It should not fall to the young to save the old. There should be a balance to life in these ways, where we can unite and work together as one. The energy of youth, the experience of age. Yet it is what it must be. All we can do is carry these burdens as best we can."

Nu carried on in silence for a moment, trying not to glance back at Arturo. The guilt curdled within her, a feeling mixed with the knowing they were fast approaching whatever he had been brought for.

"I hope you are not offended by my words?" Haruto asked, gazing over as she helped him up a particularly steep part of the branch. "I simply wanted you to know that you are seen."

"Thank you," Nu said, bowing her head as he had done before. "And I see you too. What we have come to ask of you is . . . a lot."

"It is. Yet I am glad you asked. It is a privilege to assist you."

Antares dropped down to hover beside Nu.

The light is fading fast.

"I think we're almost there."

We are. A pause. *Are you okay?*

How to answer that one? There was so much going through her mind.

"I'm tired," she said, settling for the answer she could at least place her finger on.

One last push, Antares said.

Nu felt an overwhelming burst of emotion as Antares gently nudged her shoulder. There was a ripple of patterns across her surface with the contact, and she wondered if the Orb felt something too. They were bonded, after all. Companions forever. There was a lot in Nu's head right now, but it gave her a burst of warm comfort to know she had Antares. She hoped the Orb knew.

The group continued ahead in near silence now, listening to the tree come to life around them. There was an undercurrent of noise, like an orchestra warming up, before little breaks of music erupted as various birds called out and their cries were reciprocated from elsewhere.

"Woah," she cried out as Antares stopped dead in the air in front of her.

She flashed urgently.

The sickness! It's spread.

Nu stopped and looked around, confused. "What sickness?"

The Shimmering Tree.

And then Nu looked around and saw. The branches of the Shimmering Tree here were not as bright as the rest.

Zavia saw it, too, her mouth opening in horror.

"The leaves are darkening. Do you see? They're not shining as they should . . . And look at the branch beneath them. It's turning black!"

Nu, Robin, and Arturo looked at one another.

"Just like at the Great Tree," Robin said. "It looks like the poison has spread from Mother, through her roots, and beyond Silvyra. Centauri, can you confirm?"

Her Orb flashed a single circle in the affirmative, and Nu's stomach tightened.

The Shimmering Tree was the light at the heart of Adscendo. Nature was the strength of each realm. The life of it. If this tree, too, was failing, how many others were suffering right now? How much of Paperworld was being laid vulnerable to the darkness?

And now there was a bigger problem.

Haruto's face suddenly twisted in pain. His breath grew into a moan, and he clutched at the fragment in his shoulder. Simultaneously, Antares and Centauri both lit up in furious glowing lightning bolts that flashed across their surfaces.

Nu stared at the messages they were relaying, the blood draining from her face.

Something in the skies beyond the Shimmering Tree stirred.

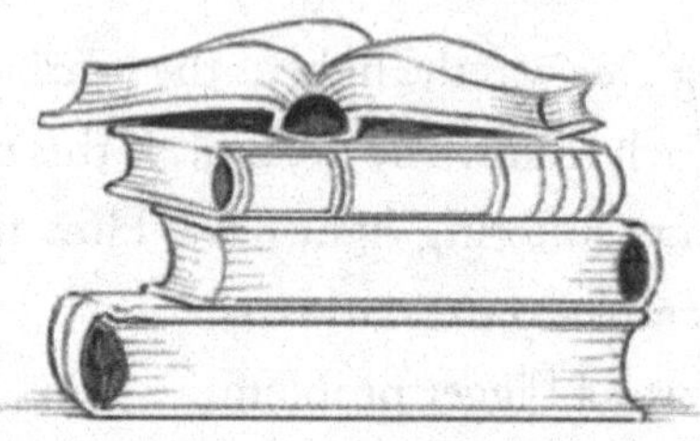

CHAPTER FORTY-ONE
MEMORIES OF AN OLD FRIEND

Maïa led the way across the bridge, with Veer following close behind. They moved from cover to cover, with Veer carrying Paix slung over his shoulder in a fireman's lift. And although his body ached like there was fire through his bones, the thought they might yet escape this nightmare spurred him on.

That and Lynx.

Move. Faster.

Veer grimaced as he almost lost his footing. Maïa flung him a *be quiet* look, then continued leading them away from danger, toward hope.

At least, that was the plan.

Thankfully, the three of them didn't need to get back to the place they'd entered this foul realm. Yet the Orbs couldn't simply conjure up portals back to the Great Library from just anywhere. There were special locations in every realm that were particularly aligned with the pathways through Paperworld, and despite being consumed by evil long ago, this realm was no different. If they were to get off this bridge city with their lives, they needed to seek such a place. And fast.

Lynx had once mentioned having to "tune into" something. Since then, that's how Veer had thought of it. The Orbs needed to find the right frequency before they could tune back into the Great Library and create a doorway back.

Maïa looked back and gestured to her Orb.

"Thebe says we're close," she mouthed.

Where?

Maïa pointed ahead, toward a three-pronged tower.

Veer paused for a moment to flex his fingers, then shifted Paix into a slightly less painful position in his arms and continued. The Sage of Strength he might be, but he'd just had his brain nearly broken by Suttaru, carried the windcatcher across the realm, and spent days traipsing through this nightmare world. He was beyond exhausted.

They scampered toward the three towers, slipped around one side, through an overgrown garden, and found themselves in a courtyard. There was a statue in the center of it, must have once represented someone important as it towered into the skies. It was now a leg broken off at the knee and a giant head smashed into the ground, whose features were smooth and worn from the ravages of the weather and time.

Lynx bumped him. *Here.*

Thebe had paused to the side of the yard. She was quickly joined by the other two Orbs, and the three conversed briefly in their colorful way. Veer drew up next to Maïa, who gave him a once-over, touching the strands of hair at his temple.

"You've aged," she said with a frown.

He pulled his best *I'm fine* face and said, "I defy anyone not to have gone a little more gray here."

She rolled her eyes and gestured to let her help him. He relented. Gently lifting Paix off his shoulder, he let Maïa take her.

"Open the portal, Lynx," he said.

The three Orbs did just that, vibrating between them as they tuned in to the Book of Wisdom and began to pull at the seams of this realm's reality. The air moved, shimmered, then split right down the center and pulled apart to reveal a sight that had Veer almost crying with relief.

The Haven.

Nothing more needed to be said. They had come here for the journal and the stone, only to leave empty-handed. He knew that was potentially bad for the Great Library. But he hadn't bargained on Suttaru being here in person, alive, and so damn powerful. Nor had he expected Payne to have orchestrated this whole thing to lead them into a trap.

Who even knew if those artifacts were of any use to them anyway? Perhaps it had all been misdirection from the start.

Veer guided Maïa to the portal first and then let her carry Paix through. Then, with the two Sages and their Orbs through, Lynx and Veer followed them.

The familiar sound of his boots echoing on the rock floor of the Great Library caused a swell of relief within him. They'd done it, gotten back alive. Yes, they'd returned without what they'd been searching for, but they had each other and even had invaluable information about Payne and the fact Suttaru had returned from the dead. That wasn't nothing. As far as he was concerned, the mission had found some success.

As Lynx let go of his hold on the portal, Veer turned to watch the hellscape disappear. He desperately wanted to make sure it was gone for good, never to be seen again. The people left behind—well, there wasn't much he could do for them right now. Perhaps later, when this was won. But in the meantime, he wanted nothing of that world connected to this one. It was rightfully going to be shut away for good.

Except . . . the portal didn't close.

"Lynx?" Veer said urgently.

The Orb began spinning his patterns in a panic.

Stuck, he said, then repeated it over and over. *Stuck. Stuck!*

Veer looked back to where Maïa was still leading Paix away to get help. He must have made a noise of concern himself, because she took a moment to glance his way and saw the portal was still open.

"Veer . . .?"

He couldn't move. Couldn't breathe. He was stuck fast in this nightmare. The portal was stuck.

Why? Why isn't it closing?

And then Veer saw two figures step from the shadows of the three-towered building into the courtyard under a cloud of ash.

A cloud that began to pulse and grow above them, before billowing fast toward the portal.

Veer held the thick, swirling ash cloud back from the portal, pushing with all his might, using all the wind in the Great Library he had to muster. Whatever it was, it was *strong*. He didn't know how long he could hold it. He could feel his skin puckering and drying, while the hairs on the backs of his hands started turning white.

He had been so drained already. This was probably going to kill him.

Despite his efforts, despite throwing everything he could back at the maelstrom, Veer knew it was not going to be enough.

Suttaru's magic on the other side was still holding the portal open. And slowly, surely, the cloud swelled inevitably toward it.

Veer had no idea what it was or what it might do if it got in here, and he didn't want to find out. He also knew that Suttaru's army of Unwritten souls was probably lurking behind it, waiting for their chance to run rampant in these hallowed halls after failing at their last attempt.

And then there was Payne. Veer could almost see the Rogue Sage in his mind, that shit-eating grin splitting his face in two as he must have sensed victory.

He groaned at Lynx, feeling his power begin to weaken. "I gave them exactly what they wanted. They didn't even need to ask for it."

Not your fault.

That didn't matter. It was clear to Veer now their escape had been but a ruse. An illusion granted in order that they lead Suttaru directly to where he wanted to go.

The bags that carried the Orbs had not been designed to shield their power or hold them hostage. At least, not for long. Lynx had been able to burn his way through eventually, and in his eagerness to escape, Veer had not questioned the ease with which it had been allowed. It seemed so blindingly obvious now, but they had set him up.

"It is my fault. I've done this."

Focus, Veer.

Veer gritted his teeth, even as he felt on the edge of passing out. "I'm trying. But they're . . . too strong. Whatever that cloud is . . . it's coming . . . through."

And then it did. Small motes of ash at first, drifts of it across the marble floor. Gently landing on Veer's cheeks. An acrid burning smell followed. It reminded him of that wildfire he'd seen in the distance once as a child. The one that had burned for days, wiping out miles of forest. His first taste of destruction.

Now it was heading his way again.

As the billows of darkness pushed through the portal, Veer weakened further. Through the haze, he saw the two figures approaching.

"Go to hell, Payne!" Veer snarled as best he could.

"I have been there often, Sage!" the taller of the figures called back. "Now I invite the Library to experience the same!"

Payne turned to Suttaru, perhaps seeking permission to finish Veer once and for all. Whatever he was looking for, though, he did not find it. As the darkness poured all around Veer now, and Suttaru stood on the periphery of victory, Veer could tell the monster wasn't paying attention. His featureless face was lifted, as though listening for something.

Then, suddenly.

Laughter.

It came from everywhere and nowhere at once. A deep, victorious vibration that was both silent and reverberated through the very power Veer wielded, into the Great Library itself. Veer looked around for the source, only to realize with a sickening horror that the laughter was *inside* him.

Suttaru.

The figure's roar of pleasure rattled Veer's bones and curdled the contents of his stomach. Worse still, it wasn't just in him anymore. The laughter was now rippling out from Penumbris, across the army of Unwritten that waited on the other side, through the suffocating cloud that was filling the Haven.

Veer flinched as a voice spoke from within the cacophony. Again, within him. A sickly voice that crept through him and filled his entire being with the fears and nightmares of the darkest stories ever written.

Haruto, you fool. You finally broke. I can feel it. After all this time, I can feel it!

Then.

I am coming for you!

Suttaru raised his hands to the skies, his silent laughter continuing to tear through the souls of all those present. Shadows seeped from his fingers as he drew them across the air, creating a jagged tear in reality.

Light poured through from another realm. Veer caught a glimpse of sunset clouds, and a cold fear struck deep within him. Nu's team. Something had gone wrong and drawn attention to the fragment of the Maksus Stone they'd gone to find.

"Lynx," he said, his voice barely a whisper in the wind now.

He looked around to find his companion still desperately trying to both shut the portal and channel more energy into Veer's powers.

"Warn them," he mouthed.

A brief flash from his Orb told him the message had already been conveyed.

All he could do now was hope. Except hope was the one thing Paperworld was running short on, without Helia and with nobody to replace her. Perhaps that had been Suttaru's plan all along.

The villain pulled back the edges of the tear to the other realm. More light shone through, but it was muted now as the darkness of his ash cloud pulled around him tighter, in protection. Veer could also see the cloud that was pouring into the Great Library now move the other way too. Suttaru stood on the precipice of stepping through.

"My liege?" Payne was seemingly confused by what was happening and had taken his eyes off Veer. "Where are you going? This is what we have worked toward. We finally have the Library within our reach!"

And yet, Suttaru's voice vibrated inside them all, *it appears a long-lost friend has just made himself known.* The dark lord of Penumbris put his hand to the fragment around his neck, and had Veer been able to see the monster's face, he thought it would be grinning.

I will not pass up this opportunity to retrieve what he once stole from me. Suttaru hadn't bothered to turn away from the view. His face was tilted back as though breathing in the victory he clearly saw ahead of him. Veer could almost feel the sense of satisfaction oozing from him and slipping over everyone watching. *Suffocate the Library with the Limniss Smoke, then let slip our forces and hold the Sages there. Do not kill them unless you are forced.*

"Don't kill them?" Payne repeated.

They will be useful in controlling the Author if she proves . . . difficult. Can you do that for me, Payne? Can I trust you with this?

The Rogue Sage bowed his head, though Veer could sense some reluctance in his movements.

Do not fail me.

Suttaru made one more gesture toward Veer's portal, and Veer felt his magic begin to crack for good. Then the evil figure stepped through into the other realm and was gone.

Can't close the portal, Lynx flashed in warning. *Save the Book!*

Veer refused to panic, despite the fact the Library was in crisis, the Sages unable to unite in its defense and the people who called it home not trained for battle. Oh, how he wished the writer, Arturo, had not gone with Nu. His wonderful, mysterious talents had turned the tide with the pure magic of imagination. Veer kept up the wind shield, but the Limniss Smoke was still coming, and Payne was coming with it, his army at his back. He twisted just enough toward the Book of Wisdom. Wisps of the Cloud had almost reached it. Lynx was flashing wildly now.

Veer didn't know what to do. Should he try to run and grab it? Where could he even run to keep it safe? His legs were beginning to shake. His knees threatened to twist and drop him to the floor. He was so damn tired. Lynx, too, was on the verge of depletion.

Then a voice spoke through his Orb. The patterns were different, enough for Veer to realize it wasn't Lynx speaking.

It was the Author.

Stay strong, Veer. Our story is not over yet.

"Author?" he whispered.

Suddenly, a cage sprang out of the floor and clasped around the lectern holding the Book of Wisdom. It shone like crystal, and the tendrils of Limniss Smoke writhed upon touching it. As it did so, the wail of alarms—crafted after the last incursion—rang out around the Haven and, Veer guessed, throughout the Great Library.

He'd never heard them before. It sent a chill through him to hear such things in his home.

"Lynx, let the others know what's happening. If they hear the alarms, they might come running and end up like me. They cannot fight this. Tell them to run."

The shield began to give.

"You need to go too, little buddy."

Lynx hesitated. Yet as he did so, the power briefly stopped flowing, and Veer's own energy gave out. He collapsed to his hands and knees, head bowed, sweat dripping off him and pooling on the rock.

His face then followed, his cheeks landing on the cold stone, pressing against it.

The Smoke swirled over him, stinking of death and burning, smothering him. He felt fingers within it pulling at his clothes and his skin.

Somewhere a roar issued. Probably the Unwritten, sensing victory. There was other shouting, too, from within the Great Library. Then the screams began.

The Great Library of Tomorrow was falling. And he, the Sage of Strength, was unable to do anything other than lie there and listen in abject horror.

He heard the footsteps approaching. Wondered if he was back in that nightmare again, half hoping this time it would finish him off.

Payne crouched next to him.

"Ready, Sage?" Up close, Veer could see the empty socket of the Rogue Sage's eye. Blackened and cold, just like the man himself. His Orb hovered behind him. "Are you ready for the undoing of everything you and your foolish friends have strived for these last few centuries? It is the coming undone of your collective arrogance. You believed so fiercely that you were the chosen ones, that you could keep the world safe, make it a better place. Except you only ever saw the bigger picture. So many horrors escaped your notice. Too small to care about."

Veer's head lolled. He blinked to keep himself conscious, though the smoke burned his eyes.

"What did we . . . ever do to you?"

"You failed to see people's pain," Edwin spat. "You spoke of doing the right thing, the best thing, for everyone. You didn't stop to think it might not always be the best way. When I came calling for help, I was turned away. Ignored. Forced to help myself." His face crinkled as though tasting something bitter. His eyes suddenly distant, remembering. "And so I did. I went looking for my own answers, away from this wretched place. And in the end, the answers found me. They led me to the journal, to Suttaru, to this moment of triumph. I was guided by forces beyond your comprehension, and look where I am now. I have returned, and this Library is now mine!"

With that, the smoke swept over and smothered Veer.

Everything went dark.

CHAPTER FORTY-TWO

A SKY OF STORMS

He's here!

Antares was spinning wildly in the increasing gloom, flashing the warning at Nu. Not that she needed it. She felt the truth of what was happening.

Found us. Coming now.

Further up the branch, Centauri was doing the same with Robin as more warnings came through.

Library under attack. No return, no return!

Robin glanced at Nu in horror. Nu could only shake her head, unable to articulate what her knowing was telling her.

"He's here," she said to Antares, as much confirming it to herself as asking her Orb to confirm it for her. "Suttaru is here."

Yes.

"And the Great Library is being attacked?" Nu asked.

Yes! Both!

Nu could feel it, sense the horror of what was happening elsewhere. Yet having the Orbs specify what exactly was happening only served to compound the knot of fear trying to form in her gut. She immediately shut it away, focusing on the moment. There was nothing to be gained from being distracted by feelings. She knew what had to be done.

Robin swept her dark hair from her face. "We shored up the defenses after the last attack, and the Book of Wisdom is back to good health. How has anybody from the outside opened up the portals to attack the Great Library again?"

Nu had no answers. All she knew was that she had to leave the worry about their home to the Sages left behind. Their own situation had just become as dire as it could possibly be.

"Suttaru's here," she said. "He's alive, and he's come for Haruto. We need to focus if we're going to get out of here. Are you with me?"

Robin straightened. "I'm here. What's the plan?"

Nu looked to Zavia, who was peering up through the Shimmering Tree in the direction her brother had gone. She wore a grimace of desperation. "I'm sorry, Haruto. I've failed you."

"It is not your fault," Haruto said with a strange calmness. He seemed to have accepted his fate. "The responsibility lies with me and what I did, long ago. I have been a fool all these years, trying to run and hide from him."

"We shouldn't stay here," Arturo said, looking around with fierce determination. "How close are we, Zavia? Do you think we can still make it to the *Golden Oriole*?"

There was a rustle through the leaves to the west. The branches shook and blew apart as the wind rose toward them. Except now the air had been tainted. It was foul, dank, and smelled of death. In the distance, Nu could see the fading light of the sunset blotted out by a small island shrouded in thick gray smoke. It was growing closer, a smudge of horror in the twilight. She could feel its evil pouring forth, corrupting the air around it, leaving a trail of ash and darkness in its wake.

The Maksus Stone in Haruto had slipped from the light of the sun, and the darkness had sensed it. *He* had sensed it. And he was there to claim it and anybody who stood in his way.

Had she seen this in her vision? She might have. Everything she had feared was on the cusp of becoming reality.

"We can still make it," she said firmly. "We can still get to the ship and get out of here. I refuse to sit here and wait. If he wants the stone, he's going to have to work for it."

Zavia had spotted other frightened folk on the tree. They were watching the sight unfold with confusion. "Perhaps there is another ship we can reach," she said. "One that has enough speed to get us someone else. Maybe Arcadiana? Plenty have sheltered within her walls in the past."

Nu shook her head, grabbed Haruto's arm, and kept moving.

"There's nowhere in Adscendo that's safe now. I'm so sorry. He will burn it all. Unless we leave on the *Golden Oriole*, we won't leave at all."

They kept climbing. Nu hoped they still had time to reach the ship before Suttaru reached them. As another gust of evil breeze blew aside the leaves above, Antares flashed another warning, and she looked up to witness shadows flying their way.

Their Kestrine guide called loudly. Nu hoped it was for reinforcements.

She stumbled as there was a sharp burst of light in her head. Haruto held her up as she pressed her fingers into her temple, squeezing her eyes shut.

The vision again. A man standing against the darkness.

It was more powerful than before. The darkness was distinct, billowing. A cloud of ash.

And the man standing against Suttaru, facing the evil.

Oh no.

Nu saw him in her mind now, as clear as anything. The thick wavy black hair, the broad shoulders, the tunic he was currently wearing.

It *was* Arturo.

"Nu? What is it?"

Zavia had returned to her, her brow crinkled like the bark of the tree. Antares was floating with worry behind her. Nu tried to explain she was fine, but her voice refused to cooperate. Perhaps she couldn't speak such a blatant lie.

The performer slipped her arm through Nu's and helped her to keep standing, then pulled both her and Haruto along. Nu reluctantly allowed her feet to move toward the inevitable.

The Shimmering Tree was alive with panicked movement. Flocks of birds exploded around them, flying from their nests and out through the leaves in all directions. The waterbirds spread a shower of dew as they made their escape. There were trails of figures rushing up and down limbs, climbing knotted ladders, running across bridges, as everyone scurried to get back to their docked craft. Nu found herself trapped in the moment of chaos, feeling it slow around her.

So many people.

All going to die.

She stumbled on, knowing nowhere was far enough away to be out of danger here. The corruption spreading through Paperworld would reach everyone eventually.

Hope, she chastised herself. *Don't lose hope.*

Yet the stench on the breeze was growing fouler with each passing moment. Through the leaves, Nu could see the billowing cloud getting closer, accompanied by waves of those shadows.

Flights of corrupted birds, descending on the Shimmering Tree.

"Robin?" Nu called.

"I see them," Robin called back.

Antares floated alongside Nu's head.

Are you ready?

"As ready as I can be," she said, not feeling the truth of her words. "We faced him before, and we survived. We can do it again . . . can't we?"

That's the spirit.

There was more commotion up ahead. A figure was leaping from branch to branch toward them. Nu held up her hands, ready to wield her power in any way she could to slow any potential attacker. Adrenaline rushed through her. She felt wired, focused, and hyperaware of everything around her in that moment.

Then she saw the Kestrine swooping before the man. It was Wilx.

"Brother!" Zavia called. The relief in her cry was plain.

Then there was another cry. A howl that spoke of terror and loathing, of hate and anger and all the terrible emotions that had ever existed.

It raced across the entire realm, filling the skies with despair.

It came from Suttaru. It must have. His primal evil was back and seemingly stronger than before. An evil that had collected in some dank, foul place and poured into him to somehow return him to Paperworld.

Nu's senses went into overdrive, even as her Orb blasted out flashes of warning around them. She saw the bursts of slight grow slower. The sounds of panic around them became one long noise. The world slowing as another vision shook her.

This time it was felt rather than seen.

A vast stretch of cosmic dust flowed before her, streaming through eternity, but not dust in any sense she knew. It felt like more than that. Grander. It glimmered and sparkled and shone, and soon she saw the bursts of light were words.

No, not just words. They were entire stories.

There were so many trails of them, stretching across time itself, that she wondered if they could be all the stories that ever existed. She could feel them as they passed above and around and through her, so many magnificent, wondrous stories tumbling through the emptiness, before splitting off into tributaries that wound away from the main stream and pooled into entire realms.

She gasped at the beauty of it, breathing in the endless magic of what she saw and now knew to be true.

The entirety of existence, laid bare in the vastness of her soul.

All too quickly, the awe transformed into horror. She tasted shadows muddying the flow. Darker words and stories ebbed and flowed with the others, before being drawn elsewhere. Into a hidden stream. One that pooled into a place that was not like the others. A rancid swamp of evil. It formed a realm of dark stories, nightmares, horrors. And as it grew, it threatened to burst its banks and sweep back into the main flow. Either by force of will or the kind of subconscious programming inherent in all life, the main stream of stories dammed it up. Two bright suns held it back, held the darkness captive, separate and secret from the rest.

It was here the nightmares swirled and came to sentience.

The largest force of evil in existence. Ancient enough to have taken on sentience and hunger. Driving it to devour.

Now it was released, back into the river, and it had poured its evil into Suttaru. Driving him to madness. To destroy and corrupt all the realms . . .

Nu was knocked back to life as Zavia let go of her and ran to her brother.

"Zavia!" Wilx called as he saw her. His skin was ashen, his eyes wild. "He's coming! Please, hurry!"

There was a flash of blackened, charred wings, and one of the shadows reached him before Zavia could. It was a huge bird, one whose feathers were rotting and whose skin was bloodied and oozing.

Its filthy claws reached out for the performer. He ducked instinctively, and it was just enough for him to avoid being impaled.

Zavia wasn't as quick.

She'd paused in horror, arms outstretched, reaching for her brother. As the Unwritten bird missed him, it twisted in midair, and Zavia's body convulsed with contact of a much different kind.

The talons ripped into her face, tearing strips of skin away. Her scream was muffled as blood gushed from the wounds. Her limbs flailed, then went rigid through shock as the claws dug into her head and lifted her up.

The Kestrines went wild, wailing and flying at the Unwritten beast.

But it was already over.

Zavia's body dangled lifelessly as she was carried away.

"*No*!" Wilx cried from where he'd been knocked over. He looked as though he might give chase, but more shadows were approaching, the gold and silver of the leaves growing muddy with the onrush of furious death.

"Everyone, move!" Nu yelled, running to grab Wilx. "Where's our airship? Did you find it?"

He was too shocked to do anything but lead them stumbling onward, back the way he'd come. She let Robin and Haruto go next, with Arturo close behind.

Nu felt sick at the way he was still looking to protect the person he clearly loved, even in this incredible danger.

The anguish of that thought stuck fast in her mind, knowing what must lay ahead.

As another shadowy bird burst through the leaves and swooped through the branches, diving for them, Robin pushed Haruto aside to fling up a barrier of pure love energy up in front of the group, just enough to shield them.

The shadow fell apart as it reached it. Not quite bouncing off but disintegrating a little as it spun away.

Nu felt Antares buzzing beside her, chastising her to stop waiting. She nodded and pulled her power to her fingertips, ready to use her truth to shatter the lies of these nightmares as she ran after the others.

CHAPTER FORTY-THREE
THE FACE OF EVIL

Nu hurried through the branches, the hissing caws of the shadow birds above and around them.

It soon became clear the path back to the *Golden Oriole* would not be an easy one. Wilx moved along in a daze as he guided them, trying to duck and dodge the flocking creatures out for blood. His gait was precise, the muscle memory from his years of performing with Zavia still clear. But grief was a powerful shroud, and there was no visibility of the confidence and bravado Nu had seen from him earlier. He was reeling.

They loped across a rope bridge and ran up another branch, watching as a smaller, but no less terrifying, shadow scuttled along the path they'd just left. Nu recognized it as some kind of tree scarab. Suttaru's evil was already corrupting the creatures native to this place.

This was all on her now. As the leader of the group, she had no choice but to steel herself and get them out.

"Blast and blood, there's the bridge, but I don't think we can reach it," Wilx muttered, pulling to a stop behind a knot of wood that stood as tall as him.

Peering through the leaves, Nu could see wisps of Unwritten birds weaving in spirals around the One World Bridge they were heading toward.

"What do we do?" Arturo asked.

"What *can* we do?" Haruto said. He looked to Nu. "I should step from this branch and fall. It may lead him away from everyone here as he tries to follow me. There is a chance it will give you the time to get away, perhaps even to live a few more orbits in peace. Although eventually he will retrieve my body from whatever land remains below and use the fragment to his own ends. It would be a delay of the inevitable, nothing more."

Wilx scowled.

"You cannot do that, Haruto. Zavia and I have watched over you for too long to give up. No, I will go and get Rascal to bring the *Golden Oriole* to you. I can move quietly by myself. If she's detached already—which she might have, in order to stay clear of the beasts up there—then I'll swing across on my birds and get her to move down here." He pointed to a branch a little further down from them. "Go and wait down there. The tree will see the airship coming and stretch a bridge out for you to run along it. You won't have long, but it could catch them by surprise enough to give you the time to make it."

"That will work?" Nu asked.

"I will make sure you can escape. I promise."

With that, he loped up the branch.

Nu led the others carefully back the way they had come, until they met the intersection with the lower branch. They maneuvered across carefully, Nu trying not to think of the endless fall that awaited any who slipped.

The branch here grew thinner than the others, while the canopy seemed thicker. They'd be better hidden, but after a moment, they had to move from walking to crawling along it.

Nu clasped the rough bark under her fingers, warm to her touch. The air was growing clammy too. She felt the sweat dripping down her neck, sticking her tunic to her back.

Finally, they could go no further. They pressed up against the underside of the giant leaves, trying to remain hidden.

"How long do you think they'll be?" Arturo asked.

"Hopefully not long," Robin replied, letting out a sigh as she clasped her hands around her knees and leaned against him. "Why, are you not enjoying yourself?"

He laughed quietly. "How about next time I take you to a nice restaurant? A bar. The theater. All good places where we're not likely to face certain death at the hands of a fire-wielding madman."

As the pair grinned at each other, Nu was blinded again by the vision.

Arturo. Standing alone, facing the evil.

She clenched her eyes shut, willing it away. She didn't care if that was the truth of what must happen. She would not let it come to pass.

The branch shook. The leaves ahead parted. Everyone looked up, expecting the *Golden Oriole* to be floating into view.

It wasn't that.

Nu recoiled as the small dark isle shrouded in darkness bore down upon the Shimmering Tree. Suddenly, ash was falling thickly around them. The already dimming leaves dulled almost completely, as if life was being choked out of them. And then there *he* was. Through the choking smoke, a figure in black robes, with a garishly pale head, striding across the plateau of his dark platform toward them.

The ash was smothering the tree now. The birds still hiding there, somehow remaining free from being Unwritten, now escaped and flocked in huge numbers across the skies. Thousands upon thousands of them, panicking and lifting from their perches, flying in all directions.

For one of the Golden Aurics, it was the last thing it would ever do.

Nu watched in horror as Suttaru reached out a hand and a blast of flames erupted across the sky, not enough to make contact, but to split the bird off from its companions. Lost and alone in the cloud, the smoke creatures retreated from the tree and swept around it, coiling like a snake, pulling it to the man below.

The beautiful creature began to thrash against its bonds as it reached him. Then its feathers began to darken, as though they were burning from the inside out. Slivers of light were slowly stripped away, its life being extracted. There were now patches of crimson, burning like hot coals.

"What's he doing to it?" Robin whispered, the agony of the sickening act audible in her voice. She turned to Nu, clearly wanting to do something to stop it.

Nu could only look at Antares, who was flitting mournful shapes across her surface. They both knew there was no rescue to be had here. Suttaru was Unwriting the bird, like all the others. Flaying it alive, in a way, extracting its stories and carving darker ones into its skin. Bringing it under his control.

Soon it was over. The bird, or whatever it was now, was his. The creature bowed its head and let him climb on. Then the bird lifted into the deepening purple hues of the heavens of Adscendo to seek their prey.

Haruto, Suttaru called, his voice echoing through their bones, perhaps the bones of every living thing in this realm. It was a call of mocking, one that was eager and dripping with excitement. *Haruto. I'm coming for you.*

Nu saw Haruto's visible reaction ahead of her. The whites of his eyes grew as the fear of recognition rushed through him. Robin immediately sent ribbons of light wrapping around his body, letting him know he wasn't alone, giving him strength to face his terror.

The corrupted Auric flew above them. They couldn't see it now, but Nu could feel the ferocious beat of the bird's wings as it scoured the Shimmering Tree, looking for the man who carried the fragment of the Maksus Stone within him. She gritted her teeth, unwilling to give in. Not after they'd come so far.

The tree began to shake again. The branch beneath them groaned and moved, stretching, reshaping itself. Nu shifted her knees as the wood expanded outward. She witnessed words spring to life beneath her feet and her hands.

The One World Bridge was forming again, right underneath them.

It was reaching out of the Shimmering Tree toward a craft.

"The *Golden Oriole*!" Arturo shouted and pointed as the gold-painted bow of the grand airship appeared ahead, the leaves parting to let the bridge connect to it.

Through the windshield, Wilx and Rascal waved them across in urgent sweeps of their hands.

The branch had grown enough that there was now enough room to stand without fear of falling. The group got to their feet and began to hurry, just as Nu felt the waft of a breeze across her scalp.

Air, beating downward.

Found you!

The thump of wings accompanied the voice inside her. Nu fell to the side, and only the outstretched arm of Arturo stopped her from sliding off the edge of the branch. Above them, Suttaru descended on his nightmare steed. In the corner of her eye, she also saw Unwritten insects swarming toward her companions.

Robin was still leading the way, her hand on Haruto's back, guiding him along. Arturo hurried just behind, while keeping one eye on Nu. He hadn't seen the beasts ahead.

Watch out! Antares flashed.

Arturo yanked on Robin to pull her out of the way of a scarab pincer that sliced across the air where her leg had just been. As more creatures streamed up the branch, Nu realized they were surrounded. Centauri started trying to knock them off the branch, and Arturo kicked alongside them. Between the pair, they were able to continue, but slowly.

Then there was a horrifying screech as a great bird, flaming Unwritten text curving around its form, folded its giant wings and dropped from above. *A Golden Auric*, Nu thought.

Nu had only a momentary glance at Antares to understand what they needed to do. She lifted her head toward the incoming Suttaru and reached up toward him.

Suddenly, she was back in the City of Forever. Helia at her side, wielding her powers to grow Perennia back to life. Nu held back the rushing tide of evil that Suttaru, the Ash Man himself, had tried to unleash upon them all.

It had been the first time she'd unleashed her powers deliberately. At the time, she'd had no idea how she'd done it. Other than it had been a moment when she'd needed to reach within herself to believe.

To hope.

Helia had taught her that much, and in the woman's absence since, Nu had taught herself the rest.

Now it was all intent and power.

The connection formed between her and Antares. A warmth spreading from her soul. Power. Magic. Pouring through her, through her Orb, connecting them to the Book of Wisdom and the world around them. Perhaps all realms everywhere. It was an incredible feeling of unity. Of being a part of something far bigger than any one person could ever imagine.

Of power.

She screamed as a blast of truth rippled outward from her hands, curving up like a shield over the branch, giving them just enough protection as a rain of fire fell upon them. Her power shattered the illusion of the fire, disintegrating the dark magic that had brought it to life. Magic that she would likely never have come to wield if Adi had never been turned to darkness. Xavier would still be alive, and she would still be the old Nu, welcoming visitors to the Great Library and content with her life.

The man himself must have felt what she was doing. He yanked hard on the bird's feathers and pulled back, trying to avoid falling into the shield of truth he knew would lay him bare once more, as it had done in the City of Forever, showing the man behind the myth, the man known as Adi. It had been enough then to hold him off briefly. It would do the same here.

Nu pushed harder and sent the shield out further.

The Unwritten bird bore the brunt of the power. The truth showed the bird exactly as it had been only moments ago, a child of Amare, with gold-tipped feathers, full of goodness and light.

With the shackles of corruption temporarily thrown off, the bird bucked its rider, twisted and swooped upward to escape him. There was a flash of light, and suddenly the bird unleashed a terrifying and agonized screech as Suttaru burned away its skin. He pulled the feathers once more, steering it to the nearest branch, before it disintegrated completely beneath him, and he fell to the wood, landing in a crouch.

Nu let go of her shield and ran after the others. But not before a glance back revealed him stepping onto the bridge in pursuit.

CHAPTER FORTY-FOUR
THE STORYTELLER

Arturo leaped over the knots and twists in the wood beneath him, urging the others up the limb that stretched toward the *Golden Oriole.* It felt like the world was ending around them. All was chaos and noise. There were shouts throughout the tree, screams cut short, and the constant, high-pitched clicking of those horrific scarabs.

"She could have parked closer!" he yelled, jumping over a scorch mark on the bridge. His lungs burned, and he'd nearly rolled his ankle several times. He wasn't as nimble as he would have liked, though men his age rarely were.

"No time. Run!" Robin said.

Somehow she and Haruto were pulling away. Arturo eyed the small, ancient man with envy.

The world was ending, but it wasn't his world. It was a distinction that helped keep him going. If only for the knowledge that if they failed to get Haruto out of there, he imagined from all he'd been told, it wouldn't be long before the ash-covered suffering wrought by Suttaru found its way to the Great Library and then to Earth.

To his daughter.

"Come *on*, Arturo!"

Robin was still guiding Haruto, using more of her power to keep him from freaking out. Arturo half wished he could tap into some of that.

"I'm right behind you!" he yelled. "Just w—"

The chittering came from over his right shoulder. There was a breeze, and he smelled charred skin for an instant, before a leathery wing flashed out and claws raked at his face. White-hot pain shot across his cheek as he was caught, and he yelled out as the gray blur landed right in front of him, pinning itself to the bark.

What had once been a bat now twisted its pointed, unblinking face toward him, baring its teeth. Arturo pulled a face at the sight of it. Its fur was burned away, its raw skin blazing with dark words and furious intent.

It scrabbled toward him, and he danced backward out of its reach.

"Watch yourself," Nu said, coming up behind. The air rippled ahead of them. Whatever the bat saw confused the thing enough to hesitate. Arturo took the moment to kick the beast off the branch. It spun with broken wings into the clouds.

"Thanks," he said to Nu, touching his cheek. His fingers came away slick with blood.

"No time for thanks. We'll fix you up on the airship. Let's move, or we aren't going to make it."

"Understood," Arturo said, gritting his teeth as they started running again.

Nu continued using her power to shield them from behind as Suttaru continued in their wake, directing attacks from his Unwritten hordes. Aside from the scarabs and bats, more ash-covered birds with feathers askew were sent streaking across the twilight sky to dive-bomb them. One skimmed the edge of Nu's barrier and narrowly swooped past Arturo's other cheek. As its razor-sharp beak snapped at him, he threw out an arm and knocked it away.

Ahead, the *Golden Oriole* shone like a jewel through the smoky haze.

Nearly there!

Through the windshield, he could make out Rascal at the controls. She was waving them to hurry.

"We're nearly . . . there," Robin called back, echoing his own thoughts. Arturo had time to admire her as she leaped over a tree scarab as it scuttled up the side of the root and snapped its pincers. Whatever else was happening, he was glad they'd been able to find time to be with one another. There had been too many wasted opportunities in his life, and he was determined to make what was left count. While the creature was still focused on Robin, Arturo let fly another kick, and his boot splattered through the belly of the small creature.

He pulled his foot out again from the sloppy mass of guts.

"Faster!" Nu insisted again, pulling up beside him. Yet as he heard another two scarabs crawling up the other side, he pushed her onward without him.

"I've got this."

The look on her face, frozen in that moment, caught him by surprise. There was heartache in her eyes. She was gazing through him at something unseen. A realization. An understanding.

A hesitation. Understanding came over him. He smiled back, then thrust his head forward in mute acceptance.

"Arturo—"

"Go, Nu. I *understand*. I've got this."

There was no time to argue, though, as Antares was flashing wildly above her in warning. Arturo slowed and watched her, and beyond her, Robin, as more scarabs crawled around the bridge and poised to leap at them.

"Just *go*!"

He put his back to them, breathing easier now that he wasn't running for his life, ready to defend their escape as the creatures came again. His feet danced and found their targets as he fell into a zone. The kind of trance he used to enjoy when playing football with his friends at school, where the sights of the players, the smell of the sunburnt grass, the calls for passes and shots. It was all drip-fed through his brain like the filter on the most intense cup of morning coffee.

He relished the excited burn of adrenaline in his chest as his leg stretched out, and there was the satisfyingly crisp connection of his boots, feeling the slick of sweat across his face and a grim smile touch his lips.

As the scarabs were fired into the air in slow motion, Arturo's memories hurtled forward to fatherhood. He remembered playing with his daughter on that very same school field he'd made his own.

Rosa. His reason for being here. He had to keep her safe. Everything he'd done since she'd been born had been in pursuit of that goal, and this mission was no different. In the thick of this chaos and danger and insect guts, it was the one thing he knew for certain. Even as death approached on all sides, protecting Rosa was the only thing on his mind. This was all for her. He flashed back to the Library and the anger he'd felt at this maniac and his thugs coming for his little girl. A righteous anger, rising up to fill his tired body, giving him the energy of youth, the fortitude of parental love, fear, and hope.

Someone shouted behind him. Robin? The words carried through the heat of the air, but he didn't hear them. They were lost in the roar of engines as the *Golden Oriole* burst to life.

He risked a glance back and saw Robin had made it to the gleaming brass prow of the airship. She was helping Haruto over to Wilx, who grabbed the old man in a bear hug and carried him back into the cabin.

Robin sagged against the railing for a moment, waiting for Nu and looking for Arturo. She saw him and looked alarmed, shouting at him again. Once more, he couldn't hear her. His ears were ringing from the noise around him. The air was simmering with heat, and the stench of burning was getting stronger. He looked at her once more, imagining what their lives could have been, telling himself a story with a happy ending; then he sighed and let her go.

He glanced back to see the Shimmering Tree was on fire.

The black smoke spiraled up from the leaves, bruising the evening before his eyes. The sky, already thick with soot, was now filling with the dank, sticky taste of despair and death. The cloud of ash swirling around Suttaru was growing closer too.

Arturo could barely breathe; the air was filling with ash. He gagged, and then he slipped.

There was still some tree scarab shell on his boot and guts splayed across the bark. It sent his boot one way as he moved the other. He collapsed hard to his knees, sending jolts of pain up both his thighs.

"Shit!"

He looked up to see Nu reach the airship now. She glanced back once, and he could have sworn she seemed on the edge of running back to him, before Robin grabbed her shoulders and heaved her over the railing. They were nearly safe.

Flocks of Unwritten birds who had been swirling above them now dove and swooped against the airship, trying to burst the balloon and sever the ropes that held it to the cabin. The two Sages threw their power into defending their way home.

Arturo climbed back to his feet. Suddenly, there was a crack, and flames licked his face as Suttaru sent a fireball careening past him directly into the wood of the bridge between him and the *Golden Oriole*. He threw himself sideways, behind another sturdy knot of the branch.

With his back to the branch, he watched the root wither ahead, slowly withdrawing from the airship as it tried to protect them from the fire now burning through its defenses.

As the ship drifted free of the dock, Arturo caught Robin's eye over the flames.

She was yelling now, her words lost in the storm all around them, crying out and struggling to get to the railing as Nu realized what she was doing and tried to hold her back.

Arturo simply sat there, a slow creep of knowing what this meant setting his skin on edge.

There was no way back to Rosa for him. Nu had seen it and hadn't been able to tell him. He felt bad for her. She was the Sage of Truth, but she was still young and hadn't been able to see the truth right in front of her. A father's willingness to sacrifice for his daughter. The anger came back, but not at her. At Suttaru. He was a living nightmare, but he wasn't a father. He only understood fear and hate, not love.

He was cut off from his friends. From Robin. From the only way out of this realm back to his daughter.

Another fireball hit nearby, exploding shards of bark across him. He barely felt the scuffs and scorches as he saw the two Sages staring at him through the shimmering heat.

Nu with a strange look on her face, almost apologetic. Robin still screaming, trying to force her words to him through the chaos.

Arturo took a breath. Shook his head.

There was nothing to fear now. The weight of trying to survive had been released from him. All he had left was to make this twist of fate count.

He raised his hand toward the airship and gestured for them to leave. He saluted Rascal, who looked aghast back at him through the cabin window. He smiled at Robin and touched his heart with his right hand.

Then he stood and turned to face the hurricane of evil accompanying Suttaru as he strode toward him over the bridge.

This would probably be quick, at least. He was alone and had no weapons with which to fight back in any useful manner. Fists and feet were not going to last long against a villain with such dark magic at his disposal.

If only he had his notebook with him. He might stand a chance of writing his way out of thi—

Arturo stopped.

Looked down.

There they were. Words carved into the bark beneath his feet. Words brought to life by this majestic and magical bridge to inspire people and change worlds. Words that could make a difference.

He stared, even as the heat before him became unbearable and another fireball flashed past him.

Close, but not enough to kill.

Suttaru was toying with him now.

Arturo stared at the words on the bridge, knowing this was the moment he'd waited for his whole life without understanding exactly what it was he was waiting for. He'd always wanted to do something of use. To make a difference. He'd been Rosa's father, and that had been everything, but now he had a chance to protect her and so many others like her across so many different realms.

He wasn't just a tired marketing guy writing endless copy anymore. He wasn't even just a desperate father. Somehow, in a way he still didn't understand, he was more than that. He felt it rising up in him.

Magic.

"This will be something new," he said, starting to walk forward. "I'll delay him. Distract him, at least, long enough for the others to get away. This world's words will be my weapon, and I'll cut him with them like a knife!"

He almost laughed at the thought of it. He'd seen what Suttaru had done to this world in just moments. Even now, the figure was larger than life, a vision of terror stalking toward him, cloaked in ash and smoke with fire at his fingertips. But Arturo knew he could do this. He did not have his trusty notebook. No pencil or pen to write with. But the One World Bridge was full of writing, grown all over its bark. There were stories here. Stories that had been *spoken* into the wood, whose words were then brought to life through the magic.

This was his element. Where his power might actually come into its own.

If he was going to make a stand, there was no better place for it.

Ahead, he saw Suttaru hesitate. The sight caused him to laugh again, louder this time.

He has no idea what I'm doing, he thought. *He sees me as something to play with, a hindrance, soon to be crushed beneath his power. Suttaru doesn't understand sacrifice.*

Arturo knew now it had been inevitable. Nu had known, or at least suspected. Someone *had* to stay. To make a stand. To offer a distraction. The birds were still ripping into the *Golden Oriole*, and even if his friends managed to escape them, Suttaru would simply send more fireballs to reach and consume the airship in fury and flames. All this would have been for nothing. They would fall from the skies of Adscendo, and everything and everyone across the realms would fall along with them.

Had he not slipped, he would have doubtless found himself making the stand anyway. The Sages were powerful, though just two against this monster wouldn't have worked. It needed someone else who could rewrite reality to his own wishes. He wondered for a moment at the similarities in their powers, then the thought left him.

It didn't matter now. Fate had placed him here regardless, and he intended to do it justice.

As Suttaru tried to understand what Arturo was doing, the creatures doing his bidding had no such pause for thought. Another wave of scarabs scuttled toward him, and more bats and birds dropped form the skies to pin themselves to the bark ahead.

Only now did Arturo find cover again, pulling behind a large outcrop of root. He had no idea how this would work, but there was nothing to lose now. This was his chance.

He ran his fingers over the bark, the rough fingerprint of the outer shell, and parts where the smooth, pure wood underneath shone through. As he did so, he began to recount aloud what he wanted to happen. It felt silly—crazy perhaps—but he spoke with confidence, thinking all the while of Rosa and his friends on the airship. He felt the power rise in him again, like it had done in the Library. It was frightening. Exhilarating. Freeing.

"And then flights of birds swept up from nowhere. They fell upon the scarabs and carried the disgusting insects away, protecting the writer in their midst . . ."

The marvelous thing was that, as he spoke, he expected something to happen. After everything he'd seen, he knew it was possible. *Magic* was possible.

The wood moved beneath his hand. There was a very tangible

vibration, before his very own words burst into life under his fingers. He read them back and marveled.

"*See*? It worked!"

Except it hadn't yet. The words were there, but would the magic in them appear as it had when he'd written back at the Great Library?

He looked around the knot of wood as the bugs closed in. For the longest moment, nothing happened. The creatures clambered over each other to reach him, their pincers snapping away. The larger bats leaped alongside them, their pointed teeth bared, their claws slicing through the air with each landing. Overhead, tattered, scarred birds swarmed, ready to dive.

There were so many of them, all converging.

They were going to consume him alive.

Come on . . . come onnnn . . .

Then it happened.

A brown beast of a bird, as large as an eagle, flew up from beneath the bridge. It came from nowhere, a blur of sight and noise, swerving around the knot of wood and grabbing a bunch of scarabs in its talons. Arturo gawped as it lifted it away, before a rain of entrails spilled over him.

He wiped a sleeve across his mouth, trying not to taste anything of the decay he could smell, unable to help the grin that lit up his blood-splattered face.

As the other creatures reached him, more birds appeared to help. Screeches filled the air as claws met talons. The bats panicked and scattered, sending a pungent breeze across the bridge. The scarabs hesitated, too, before scoops of them were grabbed as Arturo's winged saviors carried them off—just as his story in the wood had said they would be.

As his birds continued protecting him, he glanced back to the airship. The other Unwritten birds were still all over it. From this distance, they looked like a cloud of gnats, tearing at the balloon, throwing themselves at the cabin below.

He spoke again into the wood, pressing himself against the knot and closing his eyes.

"It was then that the bridge grew once more. It set aside its agony from the Suttaru's fire and stretched out as it had done before. It curled toward the airship, batting away the foul creatures attacking it . . ."

The bridge shook beneath him again, and he blew out his cheeks as he saw it moving the other way now. Behind him, the curled end of the root shot out toward the escaping craft and lazily swung from side to side across its top, before swinging around its front. Even from here, Arturo could hear Suttaru's Unwritten nightmares caw in fury, before there were sickening popping sounds as the root smashed through them. They quickly swarmed to attack the root, pecking and tearing at it, leaving the *Golden Oriole* alone.

I did it.

Arturo blew out his cheeks as it limped away. He saw Robin, still leaning over the railing, her hands outstretched toward him, Centauri flashing beside her.

It was then he realized the warmth, the energy flowing through him.

He was feeling her power, like a waterfall of the purest love rushing through him, sweeping around him, giving him a heightened sense of everything positive and beautiful about the moment he found himself in.

The wood beneath his fingers. The wind rushing by. The birds chirping in the Shimmering Tree and in the air.

How she felt about him.

With a roar, he was spurred into action once more. He wasn't done. Not yet.

He stood tall, unafraid to be seen, brushing his hand across the bark of the handrail as he carried on speaking to the Shimmering Tree. Even as it started to fall to the dark forces arrayed against it, he felt its spirit resist, even as its ancient consciousness knew they were likely doomed. A fiery golden-green embrace enveloped him, and he felt at one with the tree.

He wove tales. Created stories. Conjured weapons with his words.

He told of the magnificent Golden Aurics that appeared to raze the hordes of corrupted beasts and attack the figure in the cloud among them.

Magnificent birds flashed their golden feathers as wings beat down around him. They disrupted the advance of evil, sending the Unwritten army spiraling away into the skies. Arturo walked among those marvelous creatures, feeling connected to the tree, to magic itself, watching as his allies cleared a path toward Suttaru, before they finally attacked the figure himself.

The ash cloud billowed as they swooped and dove into it. There were flashes of fire, as many did not make it out again, but Arturo did not allow himself time to grieve. He knew they were all making a stand here. For Adscendo. For every realm. While their words were here, he would use them to defend their world and his friends.

Touching the wood again, he spoke of the birds of water. How they flocked together to dampen Suttaru's fire.

This they did, returning from the skies and swarming around the Shimmering Tree. They swallowed the figure in the cloud, smothering him with water.

A fine mist grew as Suttaru fought back with flame.

Still Arturo kept on toward him.

"And then the bridge itself took the fight to the evil in its midst," he called. "It bucked and rolled, impeding the villain's advance. It swayed and shook, trying to rid itself of him. It grew in new, weird, twisting ways, grew knots and branches. Whenever he burned through them, more would appear to slow him down. To tackle him. To stop him."

The bridge rumbled as it came to life again, bringing truth to the story Arturo was narrating. The path beneath Arturo's feet held steady, but ahead he saw everything he had asked for as the branch rocked and transformed, doing everything asked of it.

"The bark beneath his feet grew soft, like sap. It sucked him in, holding him fast . . ."

Suttaru was on to him though. As he felt himself losing his footing, Suttaru reached out and was grabbed by a passing bird, corrupting it to his will even as it carried him up and over the danger, dropping him on the other side.

More and more, Arturo let his imagination run wild, allowing Robin's power to give him strength, speaking with grand gestures of his arms and hands, spinning vocal theatrics as he strode toward Suttaru, directing his incredible ally in the aid of a storyteller's cause.

Arturo felt the stories emerge through the bark beneath his feet as he kept walking. He knew he was winning, because the bastard's featureless face was fixed firmly on him and not the airship escaping behind him.

He was finally using his words to effect change.

The Unwritten scarabs and bats and birds continued to fall from his path, carried by those he had called to help.

The bridge continued to buckle and twist ahead of him. Alive. A raging river of wood, bucking off any who dared get close to him.

The Golden Aurics continued diving into the ash cloud to try and deter the figure in its midst.

Arturo had guessed Suttaru was too powerful for such magic to defeat him. The birds were quickly incinerated. The newly grown knots and twists of branch were burned away. But it all took time, and so still he walked toward him as fearlessly as he could.

Rosa would be proud, he thought.

Suttaru could light him up at any moment, but he didn't. Arturo figured he'd irritated him enough to warrant the villain wanting to deal with him in person. Good! Let him come. He knew what lay ahead of him on this bridge. The manner of how it would happen was almost inconsequential.

They both kept walking toward each other. Evil toward good. Good toward Death incarnate.

Inevitably. Impossibly. Lured by fate and the promise of the greater good.

Arturo's lips moved, telling his stories. He knew simply speaking of Suttaru's demise wouldn't work. Nor would conjuring things out of thin air. That's not how it worked. He could only use the world around him. And right now there was so little world around him, only the retreating bridge beneath his feet and the magnificent birds of Adscendo, that it was only a matter of time before he ran out of help.

Still, he used it all. Everything at his disposal, he wielded through words. He spoke stories using everything he could see and feel and hear, bending them to his will. Asking this realm to help him protect Rosa back in the Great Library. To keep her safe. For she was everything to him, and he would gladly give himself to Adscendo if only the realm could help do that.

They just needed to distract the evil a little longer, enough that his friends could escape with Haruto and the fragment. To take it back and use it to stop Suttaru for good.

"Just a little longer," he pleaded, knowing his last moments were almost here.

Until, finally, he had no words left to give.

CHAPTER FORTY-FIVE
THE GREAT LIBRARY FALLS

Mwamba hurried through the Atrium. His protégé, Triss, walked alongside him, doing her best to help extract evacuees from the battle raging across the Great Library.

"Where is the Book now?" he asked Canopus, the Orb skimming the air just ahead of him. Trails of people followed behind, but he had no need of discretion right now.

Trapped in the Haven, Canopus said.

"Shielded though? Did the cage protect the Author in time?"

It worked. She is safe, but we cannot reach her.

Mwamba paused to calculate. His understanding of the Library and its inner workings were second only to the Book herself. He decided that the protective system they'd crafted since the last attack had worked. The cage would ward off the darkest magic they knew about, at least for a time, and he just hoped it would last long enough for the Sages to figure out a way to reclaim the Library and reach her.

"We should have prepared more," he said.

"You did your best," Triss signed. "Nobody could have predicted they would be let in."

"I should have seen the possibilities laid out ahead of each mission though. The probability this could happen. The way in which they're so easily taking over. It's as classic a tale as the Trojan horse."

The cloud had been a masterstroke by Suttaru. Mwamba didn't know how the man was still alive—or how he might have returned to life—but he still was shocked by just how strong the magic he wielded was and the cleverness of his approach.

The mass of smoke that was creeping through the Great Library was the perfect weapon because it had no mass and could not be fought. It moved independently, seeking out life and dissipating when challenged by the Library's defenses. Its victims fell to the ground, alive, but stunned and unable to walk. None of the Sages still free, including himself, had managed to fight it with magic. Only a well-rested Veer could have had a shot at trying to manipulate the air to shepherd it back out through the portal into which it had been poured by Suttaru. Yet Canopus had advised him the Author had seen Veer captured. They'd likely designed this attack in advance, knowing he was in their hands already.

So now the cloud was filling the Great Library, smothering those unlucky enough to have run into its path. What's worse, though, was that they'd heard through the other Sages that there was something living inside it.

Mwamba had seen the fear etched in the faces of his friends and colleagues who had run from it. He had heard the screams of those who had been caught, their cries suddenly muffled and silenced.

He didn't know if the vile intruder was damaging the hallowed halls themselves. Perhaps it was leaving everything untouched as it made its way through the city. But it didn't matter. The people *were* the Great Library. Which meant that Mwamba's entire focus right now was getting as many of them to safety as possible.

"We need to get to the Holds," he muttered.

"Do you think they'll be enough to protect us?" Triss signed.

"They were built to withstand an earthquake, or even our discovery by the rest of our world. They should be strong enough."

"But will they keep out that cloud?"

Mwamba frowned. "We can hope."

The Holds were twenty huge chambers that had been converted from the cavernous natural spaces under the mountain range that ran the length of the Library itself. They were deep inside the rock, deeper even than the First Cave. They were each an island within the island, gigantic caverns crafted with vertical walls of thermal water infused with the same magic that now protected the Book of Wisdom. Built collectively to hold the entirety of the Great Library's population of tens of thousands in dire circumstances. Mwamba was very aware this had never been tested.

Over the centuries, their existence had become largely irrelevant, woven into the many myths about this wondrous place.

Yet Mwamba had sought them out after the last attack. And, once inspected, he had set about making sure they were as full of supplies as possible. Ready to house the Library's tens of thousands of inhabitants at a moment's notice.

You started the evacuation, Canopus's patterns said, as if reading his mind. Perhaps Canopus was, in a way. Centuries together lent itself to a tight bond between Sage and Orb. *You are getting people to safety. More would be taken otherwise.*

Mwamba nodded, not wanting to spend what little breath he had left as they continued to the end of the Atrium and then took a spiral staircase down into the rocky halls of the North Wing. Canopus might be right. He *had* warned the community leaders that something could be coming and to lead their kin down to their assigned Holds if they heard the alarm.

The Orbs, too, had been busy.

"Any word from the Volare Machina, Canopus?" he asked. The tiny machines that assisted the Sages around the Great Library had been assigned emergency roles by the Orbs to ensure the entire city was being watched. In truth, the Volare had been tasked for months now to keep watch for portals where there should be none. Unfortunately, nobody had foreseen the Sage of Strength being the one to let them in straight to the heart of the Great Library, right into the Haven. Now they had been directed to ensure their "eyes and ears" were everywhere, to chart the direction of the invasive force.

The cloud has reached the reading rooms.

"It's gaining, then. Come on, Triss, everybody. We need to move quicker."

Mwamba stepped up his pace, taking the steps two at a time as he led his group down to the next level. Triss followed closely behind, making sure to sign, "Faster!" for those behind them who might be hearing impaired.

Then she turned back to him.

"Arturo's daughter?" she asked.

Mwamba had been concerned about her too. "She's with Eldra, off exploring the Great Library. All we can do is ask the Volare to keep an eye out for them."

"What if they get into trouble?"

"Then I'll go back for her myself," he said. He owed Arturo that.

They were hurrying through the Underhall that sat below the North Wing when he saw another group pouring from the other end of it. At first he was glad to see other escapees. Then he saw the smoke drifting after them, reaching out, forming bodies that chased and grabbed. One man was dragged back by his hair, swallowed whole by the cloud. Then another group was overwhelmed and fell to their knees, choking as it swept over them.

Mwamba caught sight of Amin, Sage of Loyalty, in the midst of it all. The handsome Sage pushed as many people as he could past him before he stuck his hands into the rock face to manipulate it into helping him.

"Go, go!" Amin yelled to the others as he went to work, making the rock form a barrier to block the smoke in the staircase. But soon enough wisps crept around his rock and wove around his arms. He cried out as he lost his power. The barrier disappeared in the smoke, and then so did he.

Then a river of water swept over their heads and punched a hole in the cloud. Mwamba knew it must be Jin, Sage of Creativity, pulling the moisture from the air and channeling it into a weapon. But even with her skill and ingenuity, the river wasn't enough to do much to the evil blanket that was filling the Underhall.

"Jin, you can't stop it," he called. "Leave it and join us!"

"No, let me hold it back!" she said, standing her ground.

"It's too strong. We need you in the Holds."

But she stood her ground, determined to hold it up as long as possible while Triss waved the woman's group over to join Mwamba's. He set his jaw and moved on. There were more of his people to save now, and he could not let them down.

"Mwamba, wait!"

Maïa pushed herself through the crowd toward him. She was a mess—pale, exhausted, and her usually dazzling eyes were dull and bloodshot. She carried a half-conscious Paix with her, who was still somehow channeling her Orb's strength into her own power. Weak bolts of electricity shot out and burned the fringes of the cloud now gliding toward them.

"Veer was captured," Maïa said, stumbling along beside him.

"I know. The Book is protected, but she saw what happened."

They pushed on. Along a corridor, then down and down again, into the depths of the Great Library. Down past the thermal pools, past the Nest, where Amare had brought Helia to safety after Xavier's death. Down below everything, into the ancient and secure caverns of the mountain island. Toward their Holds.

Maïa wouldn't let it go though; the guilt was plain to see in her anguish.

"I'm sorry, Mwamba. It was a trap."

"I know."

"They led us to believe we were safe to open the portal. The pages were a ruse to get us to follow Payne. It was their plan all along."

"It's okay, Maïa. It's not your fault. We have to focus now on escape—retreating and saving as many as we can. There is no time for the past, only our future. Are you still with me?"

"Always," she said.

Yet her revelation provoked a question that now raged within his head as they ran.

How did I not see that as a possibility?

He went over his decisions again and again, replaying the outcomes in different ways, and he tried to analyze where he might have done things differently to avoid this happening. Perhaps he should have ignored Arturo's disclosure of the journal pages. Nor sent his Sages chasing the rest of it, and that fragment, in such a dangerous place. Perhaps he could have spent the time fortifying the Great Library even more.

That way, the evil might have remained on the outside, causing problems remotely, but not putting the Great Library in danger directly.

No choice, Canopus said.

"You're being kind," Mwamba replied. But he knew the Orb was right.

A choice to ignore evil was a choice to be compliant in its growth. One could not simply stand by and let men like Payne and Suttaru go about freely, murdering poor folk like Densi and robbing the world of the hope it so badly needed.

He had made the logical decisions to try to stop the evil. Now was not the time to reflect on what he could have done better. All he could do was orchestrate the escape, to ensure as many people as possible would survive.

He just had to keep leading by example and not give up.

Helia's face came to him. Always kind. Forever optimistic. She was no longer here, but her legacy lived on.

Hope persists, even when life does not, she had once told him.

It was hard to keep that in mind now, given what was chasing them. The void she left behind meant the Great Library was more vulnerable than when the collection of Sages was whole. The new Sage of Hope would have completed them once more, but Payne had prevented that.

All part of their plan, Mwamba thought sourly as the roar of fleeing footsteps filled the tunnel. A group of not-enough survivors who were nearing safety.

A towering iron door, arched and carved with ancient symbols of protection, came into view. "We're there," someone yelled, and there were a few whoops among them, but the rest were focused on not falling and not being left behind to be taken.

Canopus flashed brightly, causing many to shield their eyes. The symbols in the door lit up, and one side of it creaked open.

"Quickly now," Mwamba called. Canopus amplified his voice to ensure everyone could hear, and Triss signed for those who couldn't. "Keep your feet, keep your heads. If you are able, help those who are tired. You are close to safety, I promise you. One last push!"

As he skidded to a stop beside the open door, he urged the people rushing through to keep going. Maïa and Paix stood on the other side of the tunnel, Paix still weakly wielding her power against the rushing smoke.

There were so many people, but they made quick work of getting inside, and soon the crowd thinned.

Mwamba watched the smoke growing closer.

"Quickly!" he urged the stragglers. One woman fell, and he knew she would not make it. He pushed past the last couple of people and ran to her aid, pulling her up and over his shoulder. There was movement beside him, and a dark figure appeared in the smoke, featureless and menacing. It reached for him, only to burst apart with a chime as one of Paix's bolts of electricity blasted through it.

"Move, Mwamba!" Maïa yelled, dragging Paix inside the Hold and getting Thebe to speak with the door. It began to close. "We can't let it in here!"

Mwamba stumbled as fast as he could, the woman struggling on his shoulder, trying to avoid the wisps of smoke that were still reaching for them. More bolts shot past them, weaker and weaker. Paix was almost spent.

The door was nearly closed.

"Hold it," Mwamba pleaded. "Hold . . . it . . ."

He slipped through and collapsed, just as the door shut with a rumble of permanency.

Ahead of him, the long trail of survivors walked through a towering wall of water that lay just inside the door, their bodies creating little ripples through the liquid magic as they traveled into the Hold. Canopus nudged Mwamba's shoulder as he slumped on the rocks, telling him to get up and to follow them through the shield.

With a gasping sigh, Mwamba got slowly to his feet, helped the woman up, and listened to his Orb.

"Are you okay?" he asked Triss.

She gave him a thumbs-up as they passed through the water to the island at its center, where several thousand people were already making camp. Their tearstained, panicked faces greeted him as they rested among the rudimentary rock-carved seats and sleeping nooks or dished out the rations he had stockpiled over the last few months.

As he sat down next to a family of three, the little girl looked up with naive wonder at the elder Sage. A banging started on the iron door behind them.

"Don't worry. It can't get through," Triss signed to the family.

The children all understood. One of them signed back. "Okay."

Triss looked to Mwamba and smiled reassuringly.

He returned it as best he could, then closed his eyes and began the seemingly impossible task of trying to figure out how they were going to get out of this.

CHAPTER FORTY-SIX
HOPE, LOST

Edwin Payne stood in the center of the Haven holding the four pages of journal entry the Sages had taken. He'd hoped by reading the pages again it might help alleviate his growing distrust of the strength of Suttaru. He needed to see the moment Adi had chosen, for himself, to take the step toward the darkness after trying to fight it.

It didn't help.

In the distance, cries and screams could be heard. The Limniss Cloud had won the war, but smaller battles still continued. He had finally let some of the Unwritten through from Penumbris because they wanted their flesh, and Edwin was happy for them to take it.

But his already addled mind remained troubled.

The scribbles in the journal detailing the mechanics of Adi's experiments with the Maksus Stone's energy had helped him revive his liege. That had been the goal, so he'd not needed to keep reading.

Except he found he could not stop. Because something inside continued to push him to learn more about the man Suttaru used to be. To understand on a deeper level what he had written in there, besides equations and theories surrounding the dark magic they both now wielded.

Now Edwin knew.

For Suttaru had once been a very normal, very human man named Adi. A clever scholar who possessed not only a heart and compassion but courage too. A willingness to sacrifice himself to stop the very evil they both now served.

His old journal had not simply served to present his scientific findings. It had inadvertently laid bare his humanity.

Suttaru was once willing to risk himself to save someone else. To give himself for the greater good. The fact he had eventually turned, through a twist of fate, was irrelevant. The core of his being had been good, and there was every chance he still contained slivers of Adi within him. Buried deep, but still potentially dangerous to Discordia.

He could yet be a weak link in the darkness's plans.

Edwin suddenly felt a disturbance in the otherwise empty chamber. His eyes flickered to the Book of Wisdom beyond the impenetrable cage, but the tome remained shut for now.

The disturbance was something equally powerful.

He knelt just in time, as there was a horrendous tearing sound at the center of the chamber. The air rippled, then split, like a knife through skin. As it was pulled open, a figure stepped through.

Suttaru.

"My liege, the Great Library is ours. They were not prepared for the Limniss Cloud, as you knew they would not be. Now we may finally enact our revenge against them all!" He bowed his head. "What would you like to burn first?"

The Sages are bound and guarded in the reading rooms, as I requested?

Edwin had not expected that. He thought the first order of business here would be to destroy as much as he could. After the betrayal by the Author, the Great Library deserved nothing less.

He cleared his throat. "Myrtilus has informed me that is the case, yes. With those we captured, anyway. I have kept them alive, although I am unsure of why. I would have thought the necessary and pressing issue at hand was to remove these tiresome obstacles and their troublesome nature from our path. Alive, they may yet present a problem to our plans."

The figure held still, silent for a moment.

You dare to question my decision?

Edwin had overstepped the mark. No matter what he was thinking right now, he could not afford to suffer the consequences of appearing to doubt his leader.

"I do not, my liege," he replied quickly, bending his head and leaning over his knee. Trying to appear small, ignorant, weak. "I am just eager for revenge. These Sages deserve to die after taking your life and imprisoning you for so long. I'm sorry. I spoke only out of my need to please you."

His sniveling worked. He knew it would. It had worked in the army long ago. Fragile soldiers who stepped out of line were thought to be stupid, not worth bothering with. The ones who were executed were those who maintained eye contact in their defiance.

He was not ready to do that. Not yet.

Revenge shall be ours, of that you should have no doubt. The Great Library has been captured. You have played your part, and it shall not be forgotten. Now, rise.

As Edwin did so, another voice crept into his mind now, less distinct than Suttaru's, as though it was coming from a distance. The words were sticky too. That was the only way to describe it. Sticky. Hungry. Evil. A voice that gnawed at every fiber of his being.

Bide your time, said the other voice.

Edwin shivered and nodded, though not to the figure standing in front of him.

CHAPTER FORTY-SEVEN

AN ENDING

Robin leaned so far over the railing that Nu was terrified she was going to fall. Yet she expected nothing less from her friend.

Robin's arms were outstretched, her face like an ocean of concentration—seemingly calm, but with strong, deadly currents underneath. The flows of power that sprang from her hands wove across the skies to the retreating bridge and Arturo. The airship was dragging them farther and farther away by the second, but Nu could see the love pour into the writer. He almost glowed as he strode along the bridge toward Suttaru.

It was the bravest thing she had ever seen.

It was also just like in her vision.

It all made sense now, after months of glimpsing puzzle pieces. Arturo had always been the one who would stand against evil for the greater good.

She wanted to stand out here on this wind-blasted balcony, offering whatever support she could in these last moments. To be with him for as long as possible, until the end.

But he was making a sacrifice for a reason. If they did not honor that, they did not honor him.

"Robin," she called as the winds buffeted her and the engines of the *Golden Oriole* continued to roar around them. "We have to get inside. Rascal is going to jump, and we can't be out here."

Suddenly, a figure rushed past them.

"Just hold tight. I'll get him!" Wilx called as he leaped onto the railing and then swan dove over the edge. Nu's insides leaped from horror to hope as he first disappeared into the chasm beneath them, before he reappeared, swinging by one hand on the claws of a giant bird. As it lifted its wings and caught a current, soaring higher, he somersaulted over its ducked beak and landed on its back.

The acrobat and his companion ducked and weaved through the sky in ways Nu couldn't even believe were possible.

Then a streak of white-hot fire exploded from the cloud of ash. It was so fast and sudden it singed the wing of Wilx's bird, disintegrating the feathers. They heard the cry as it spun out of control.

Wilx had no movement in the air now, besides gravity. And he was unable to resist its pull.

As he fell, arms outstretched, still trying to save Arturo even at the very end of it all, another blast of fire emerged from the cloud.

There was no cry this time. Only a distant, barely perceptible snuffing out of life as the acrobat disintegrated in midair, leaving his ashes to scatter across the bridge he had so nearly reached.

Robin moaned in horror and redoubled her efforts, throwing everything she had toward Arturo now.

Nu could only swallow back her remorse and try to focus on what mattered. There was no time to mourn the fallen. That would have to come later.

"We have to go now," she said, leaning into Robin and placing a hand on her shoulder. "There's no more we can do."

"But he needs me!"

"No, what he needs is nobody else to die today. He needs us—*you*—to leave this realm and ensure Haruto and the others reach safety. He needs us to get back to the Great Library with the fragment so we can fight back. He saw the Truth in *me,* Robin. He knew without me saying it that this was the only way for us to get out."

A yell came from within the airship.

"Blue sparks and blasted fire, girls! Get in here! We're leaving!"

Fighting the wind as the *Golden Oriole* flew faster, readying to jump, Nu maintained her grip on her friend's shoulder and tried to pull her back. Robin resisted, shoving her away, but Nu wasn't going to mess around. There was no time to waste. It was now or never.

She pushed a strand of her own power across her friend.

They both saw the truth of the moment. Suttaru's fire could destroy them instantly. It was already setting the Shimmering Tree ablaze and the isle he had crashed the tree into. The *Golden Oriole* would follow, if they did not leave immediately.

Robin turned her head to Nu, horror in her eyes. Nu tugged at her again, and this time the other Sage relented. She continued to send her power to Arturo as best she could, even as Nu dragged her into the cabin. The strands of love still wove out of the airship and across the bruised skies of Adscendo. Centauri flashed weakly beside her, but continued the bond with Robin, ensuring they gave Arturo whatever they could, while they still could.

Another yell emitted from the increasingly panicked pilot.

"We're out of time!" Rascal cried as the realm outside the airship grew darker still. Billows of evil flashed across the windshield. "Three . . ."

"Strap in," Nu urged Robin, pushing her into a seat.

"Two . . ."

Nu fell into the seat across the aisle and wrestled with the safety belt.

"One . . ."

"No," Robin moaned, sending out one last burst of love.

Rascal glanced over her shoulder to check they were in, then slammed the lever forward, and they jumped.

The ash fell thickly around Arturo now.

It was almost comforting, how it muffled the chaos of the realm. He was glad he didn't have to look on the destruction and death all around him, at the perversion of such a wonderous and magical realm. Such was the silence that enveloped him, he was immediately taken back to the last Sunday morning Rosa had stayed over at his apartment. The quiet of the dawn. Getting up with her and having his coffee, and then the pair of them reading their books until they got hungry enough to go out for breakfast.

They hardly spoke that morning. But just sitting there in his chair, occasionally looking over to see her sprawled on the sofa, engrossed in whatever story she was reading, he had felt such a moment of fatherly pride.

How he missed her.

Suttaru stood opposite him. The ever-retreating bridge had brought Arturo within striking distance of the man. Brought him within the drifting ash that smelled of death. Or rather the absence of life. Even in death, you could sense the energy that had once been. But fire was unforgiving. It left nothing but dust.

Arturo didn't fear that now though. His purpose here gave him strength. He waited for the inevitable with a smile on his face.

Suttaru was intent on killing him—of that he was sure. Arturo couldn't tell it from his featureless face, but he could feel the anger blistering off the hideous man in waves. Suttaru knew he'd failed. Nu and Robin had rescued Haruto and the fragment. They would escape and figure out a way to stop the evil from spreading and perhaps defeat it altogether.

Arturo's grin widened. Suttaru gave no indication he cared, but the heat around Arturo grew even fiercer. Arturo didn't care. Rosa was going to be saved from what might be. He trusted the Sages to beat this son of a bitch and save his little girl. Beautiful little Rosa, who he could remember cradling in his arms as a baby, who was now on the verge of her teenage years.

"I love you, Rosa," he said quietly, hoping that if the Shimmering Tree survived this day, the words may grow here for eternity. Perhaps Rosa would one day return and see them.

He liked the thought of that.

Taking a step toward Suttaru, he found the other figure did the same. They approached each other until they were only feet apart. Then they stopped.

Arturo waited to be struck down, to be incinerated as so much in this realm already had been. "You lost," Arturo said, wanting to have the last word. "People like you will always lose. Those driven by hate cannot win. That is not the way of things. Evil cannot triumph, because it can never extinguish good completely. There will always be another shoot of life in a burned field. A ray of light through the clouds. A drop of rain after a drought. Good cannot die, as long as life remains. You lost."

Suttaru's head tilted.

So have you, he said.

Then Suttaru's hand raised, and a shimmer of heat spewed from his fingers.

Arturo expected it to be the last thing he felt, but it wasn't. The evil didn't touch him. The heat came up against the wall of love still surrounding him. Robin's love was a shield, a barrier, a dam holding back the fire. He could have sworn he felt her speaking to him within it, whispering words that filled him with the kind of love he'd only read about in books.

For a moment Suttaru seemed shocked, helpless even. His scarred face crinkled in a horrifying manner as he pushed harder, trying to burn straight through the magic protecting Arturo. But Robin was still in the realm, and her wall held, enveloping Arturo within its embrace. And for one hopeful second, Arturo thought they'd done it. They'd beaten the evil figure.

Then the love flickered and went out.

The *Golden Oriole* had left the realm and taken Robin with it.

The wall fell.

The sudden rush of heat was agonizing, overwhelming, burrowing into him with a thousand tendrils of fire. Arturo could feel the white-hot agony in his very soul. In the essence of his being.

It flayed him alive from within, but not just his body. His everything. He felt his skin crawl with pain as though someone were carving him with a knife. He felt it in his head too. In his heart. He felt treasured memories being stripped away, cut from the flesh of his recollection. Then came the fire, the burning letters an alien presence on his body and in his mind. It seared his memories as it burned his flesh. His first love, ripped away and turned into something dark and painful; the first copy he wrote that made it to a major campaign, before he lost the taste for it—gone, the words burned from his mind and turned to blood, dripping from a page. The warmth of holding Robin in bed, just hours ago, turned to searing pain, until he asked himself: Who *was* Robin? And finally, his daughter's face, happy and joyful, sad and tearful, brash and sarcastic, as only a daughter can be to her father . . . turned to ash in his mind. And still the letters burned through him, and just when he felt he couldn't bear a moment more, the pain gave way to emptiness and utter loss, the absence of himself, fading away until the pain returned, and after a while, it seemed like only the pain remained.

All Arturo's stories—the stories that made him who he was—were being lost to the new evil stories covering every inch of his skin.

He threw back his head and screamed.

And he felt himself unravel.

CHAPTER FORTY-EIGHT
ASHES ON THE WIND

The *Golden Oriole* exploded from its leap between realms and fell into relative calm, drifting through a strange green cloud outside. Nu sat in the blissful silence that followed, wishing it might continue for a moment longer after so much noise and chaos and death.

But as she got out of her seat to console her friend, all too quickly the peace fell apart.

"You let him die."

Robin's words were calm, and perhaps that was the worst of it. Even in her utter grief, she was still a Sage, strong and wise and capable of holding herself upright when many others would collapse in on themselves. Yet her gaze, too, contained none of its usual warmth or sense of mischief. She simply stared at Nu, unblinking, through the strands of hair that stuck to her ash-streaked cheeks.

"I'm so sorry, Robin." Nu was stricken. She'd made a terrible, unthinkable choice, but it had worked. They'd escaped with Haruto and the fragment, but Arturo had fallen. She'd hoped it wouldn't be this way, but she'd known, deep down, that this could happen. And she'd been too scared to tell Robin in particular. She's seen their love, the truth of it, and knew it would blossom, and that love might in turn save the day.

Robin just kept staring, waiting for something more.

"I had no choice," Nu said. And that was the thing. It was true. She'd had no choice in the matter. She could have warned Arturo the moment she'd first seen him and known he had to come. She could have given him the choice then. She could have told Mwamba, the oldest of them, and asked his opinion, or simply put her feelings to the Council of Sages, or given Arturo a chance to stay in Silvyra, safe at the Great Tree. Now there was no regret over her decision, no wondering if she'd done something differently, could things have worked out. This was how it was meant to have happened. She'd seen it, and it had come true. It echoed through her even now, the memories of the vision. Her deliberate silence, seeing Arturo had been cut off from the others, but then seeing he'd made his choice—and it had been the right one. His stand against Suttaru had saved them all—on this airship and probably beyond. They'd shared a moment as pure as anything she'd ever known, and he'd accepted it. He'd given her his blessing. But how could she tell Robin that? Robin, who had been a mentor and a friend since she'd first picked up Xavier's battered Orb as it rolled toward her in the Great Library. Robin who had quietly encouraged her.

"I couldn't—"

"I see," Robin said, cutting her off.

"Robin, please listen! I saw Arturo was probably our only chance. He looked me in the eye, before he chose to stay behind. He knew it. He accepted it." Her voice was pleading now, but the other woman was silent; she wouldn't even look her in the eye. Nu glanced around, and the others wore their expressions like masks. Rascal was angry, but not, it seemed, at Nu. Haruto seemed resigned, sorrowful even, his head cast down in what might have been a prayer.

But *Robin* . . . The lack of anger, passion, any kind of furious retort left a void in Nu's head that was suddenly filled with thoughts she'd been trying desperately to avoid.

What if I'd just ignored the visions though? Left him behind to protect him?

Nu didn't dare give voice to these doubts. Perhaps she could have done just that, but what then for the rest of them? For the mission?

The visions were her power. Some might see them as a curse, but that's not how the magic of the Great Library worked. It was a struggle to accept she'd been thrown into this role at a time of great challenge. By rights, she should have had the chance to properly champion truth in a universe that was not falling apart. When evil was not running amok throughout the many realms. When she was not forced to worry about what could happen to those she cared about.

But this was the role she had been given. She would fulfil it to the best of her abilities, come what may.

She took a step back but kept looking at Robin. In truth, she wanted nothing more than to run away from the damage she had helped bring about. But there was nowhere to run to. She, Robin, Rascal, and Haruto were trapped aboard the airship. In what realm, she didn't even know. The escape had been fast and furious—only Rascal knew where the four of them had ended up.

She knew running never did any good anyway. It only left the problem for another day. And unresolved problems tended to fester like wounds. Better to address it now than risk irrevocable harm to their friendship.

"Robin," she began softly. The words almost caught in her throat, but she forced them out as best she could. "There was no choice. I promise you, there was *no* choice. Arturo was meant to do what he did. He knew he had to stay and protect us as we left. Had he not, we would have been blown out of the sky."

"How do you know for sure?" Robin asked. The words were wisps on the wind, devoid of life. "We might have made it."

Nu just shook her head.

"You saw this, didn't you? You knew this was coming."

"It came in waves. At first I didn't really understand it, and even when we left for Silvyra, I wasn't really sure. It just seemed vital that Arturo was with us. I . . . I knew he needed to be there. Then it became clearer, the closer we got, and I didn't know what to do. I didn't know if mentioning it might ruin everything. I'm so sorry . . ."

"So you knew enough," Robin said.

Nu heard the sound of Rascal's chair twisting around as she heard Robin's accusation. In the background, Haruto, who had been sitting groggily in his seat, collapsed to the side with his head on the porthole window, now sat up.

Nu straightened. "Not all of it." Even to herself, saying the words for the second or third time, she hoped it wasn't true. But she of all people knew the truth of things.

"But some of it, Nu. Be honest. I know your power gives you the opportunity to witness the truth of things that haven't yet happened. You saw this."

"Yes. Some of it. Enough to guess what it might mean. I saw a man standing against the darkness. Brave and alone. I didn't know for sure it was Arturo. I couldn't. I only had a feeling that might be his path, and it could be the truth of what needed to happen. And when he said what he did, I knew he felt it too. He sacrificed himself to save us. To protect the greater good. Sometimes that's what any of us can hope for."

"So you let him sacrifice himself? You knew what awaited him, and you led him straight to his death."

"That's not what happened, Robin. You know I would never!"

But was that really true?

Nu wasn't sure anymore. Perhaps Robin was right. Perhaps Nu *had* led Arturo to this moment for the greater good. To ensure that their mission would be a success, and they could retrieve Haruto and the fragment. That was the goal, was it not? To get the artifact they needed to prevent Suttaru from spreading his evil destruction to all the realms.

They had done that, but maybe she had still failed. Maybe there had been no way to win this one, because the cost of success had needed to be paid regardless. If she had told Robin, they may well not have succeeded. If she had told Arturo, he may have sacrificed himself anyway so they definitely would.

Either way, Rosa would have been left fatherless, and Robin, the Sage of Love, was incandescent with heartbreak and fury. They were alive but broken. And there was still no guarantee they could get the fragment out of Haruto.

Robin continued staring into space, cradling Centauri in her lap.

Nu left her alone and went to slump in a seat near the front of the cabin. She put her head in her hands. What had she done? *Should have told him*, she thought. *I should have told them all. I killed him.* What would Triss think of her, when she found out? Would she still love her? Was Triss even still alive, if the Library was under attack? Her heart was breaking, and there was no truth that could comfort her.

Antares nuzzled her head, and she saw Haruto go gently to sit beside Robin. He resisted the need to take her hand or physically comfort her in any way. He just sat there in silence with her, so she wasn't alone.

Meanwhile, Rascal shifted seats to move next to Nu.

"Did you really know, Nu?" she asked. "Did you know Arturo was going to do that?"

Nu closed her eyes. "I wasn't sure it would be him."

"But you thought it could be?"

"Rascal, I didn't know what to do. Should I have told him . . . or even Robin? Should I have warned them about what I was seeing?" She shook her head. "I couldn't. My interference might have changed things, altered what was meant. And I cannot believe Suttaru is meant to win. So, I have had to go along with this path I have seen set before us. I have had to follow it until now and must follow it until its conclusion. We might not make it out of this alive, but if Suttaru is defeated, then it will not have been for nothing."

Rascal reached over and put a hand on her shoulder. "That is a heavy burden, girl. I'm sorry you've had to carry it." She sighed loudly and leaned back in her seat.

"I do miss the time before I knew what true responsibility was," Nu said, with a sad smile.

"We all do. But it doesn't matter now, Nu. Please search inside yourself and try to understand that. What you knew or didn't, it was Arturo's choice in the end. His free will. And he did it for us, so that we would be safe. Which we are. Let us be grateful for that and take advantage of what he has given us."

"I know. And Robin will understand that in time."

"I think Robin will realize it was the only way we could have left. It's awful, but Arturo sacrificed himself as a distraction so we could get out of here with"—she looked up at the man with Robin and narrowed her eyes—"well, I'm assuming that's Haruto. It better bloody well be him, after all that." Nu nodded, and she continued. "Arturo. Wilx. Zavia. They all gave their lives to let us accomplish what we set out to do. There is something to be said for that, when your friends give up themselves to ensure you could continue with your journey in life. The question now is: What's next?"

Can't go back, Antares flashed.

Nu closed her eyes and nodded. That's right. The news had been passed on just as Suttaru had arrived in Adscendo.

"Nu?"

"I'm sorry, Rascal. Antares had just reminded me that we can't return home. We were told the Great Library was under attack, just before we suffered the same." She looked up to her Orb. "Have you heard anything since?"

Nothing. The Author sent warning. Then communication was lost.

As Antares vibrated beside her and Nu leaned over to rest her cheek against the Orb's warm metallic surface, she listened to what the Orb had learned before it had all gone silent.

It seemed the Rogue Sage, Payne, had somehow commandeered Veer's portal back from Penumbris. It had been a trap, so Antares said, one that had been carefully planned this entire time. The journal pages, deliberately left with Arturo, provoked the Sages into splitting up—one group to locate the Maksus Stone for Suttaru, the other to embark on a pointless journey that would sap their strength and lead to an orchestrated escape, allowing Payne to lead the Unwritten through a portal of the Sages' making.

It was the only way they could possibly have returned to attack the Great Library.

"What of the other Sages?" Nu asked, her insides cold, feeling suddenly lost, cast adrift in the universe, alone and afraid. "What of my family? What of Arturo's daughter?"

Antares had not had much of an answer for any of those questions. It seemed some might be holed up in a secret place in the depths of the Great Library. But there was no specific news about any of them. Only the confirmation that many had died trying to fight back.

She wondered if her parents were among them. Or Triss. Or Rosa.

"What do you want to do now, Nu?" Rascal asked.

Nu blinked, unable to think straight. She tried to clear her head.

"We cannot return and fight Suttaru. Not as we are. We came to get the fragment of Maksus Stone, and we did that. But the truth of it . . ." She sighed at the cold irony of what she was saying. "The *truth* of all this is that I do not know what comes next. The piece is still in Haruto, and he has suggested it could kill him if we extract it. I've no idea how we may even wield it against the darkness once extracted anyway, especially if the other pieces are now lost."

A small, weak voice answered her.

"There is something we could try," Haruto said.

Nu and Rascal turned to the man. He looked haggard and beaten, but there was a glint in his eyes that spoke of hope.

"There is a realm I have heard of—one created entirely of melody and sounds, where they have perfected the art of sonic healing techniques. Surgeries, in fact. I contemplated visiting them, long ago, to extract this cursed stone from my body and end my unnaturally long existence. But I was too scared to leave my sunlight and risk the piece being found."

"A risk we can see was worth the concern," Nu said. "What's the realm?"

"Melodia."

Nu glanced at Robin, and there was the briefest, subtlest nod.

"It is known as a strong and powerful kingdom," she said. "If any realm can help stand against the darkness, it might be Melodia."

Nu mouthed the name silently, remembering what she had been taught of that realm; she had that feeling of knowing, and she suddenly realized this was where they were meant to be. They were still on *their* path, despite the horror of what it took to get there.

Rascal didn't need to ask Nu to understand the decision had been made. The ship's captain turned back to the dashboard to ready the *Golden Oriole* for another jump.

Nu looked back to Robin. Their eyes met again. But she was met with an uncomfortable truth that no matter how much time they might have on their side, the damage had been done.

The Sages of the Great Library had been fractured before this, rendered weaker by Helia's loss and then Densi's. Not only had hope suffered its lack of a champion, but the Book of Wisdom and the Library itself had been made more vulnerable because of it.

But as the ship shuddered and the light exploded through the cabin as they traversed the realms to a new destination, Nu could not help but feel that the unity that had once bound the Sages, protecting Earth and the vast realms of Paperworld for so long, had now been ruined in ways that could not be repaired. It had been burned away, becoming ashes on the wind.

And without unity, all was lost.

CHAPTER FORTY-NINE
REVENGE

The Haven was silent.

Edwin waited with his hands clasped behind his back, staring through the bars of the protective cage at the Book of Wisdom. It was smaller than its reputation suggested. He had always thought so. A book of such power should be huge, dwarfing other books, commanding attention from whomever dared stand before it.

It was pitiful, really, that such trouble could stem from such an insignificant object.

"You have lost," he said, allowing himself a gloat. "Everything you have stood for, all this time, is at an end. We have the Library. And we have you. It is over."

He wondered where the Limniss Cloud was now. Suttaru had bade it to continue through the Library, sweeping up the stragglers. Choking them, trapping them, growing larger with every soul it held within its magic. Keeping them for whatever punishment Suttaru would decide on later.

Suttaru himself had gone to find the Sages who had escaped. Yet now the door blew open in swirls of ash, and the faceless figure strode across the cavern in its midst to stand before the book.

"Did you find them?" Edwin asked.

They remain out of reach for now, Suttaru replied, the words crawling like spiders through Edwin's mind. *The magic protecting them is strong, and it will take time to break it down and gather the remnants of this city from the holes in which they cower. But it will be done.*

"Yes, Suttaru."

Step aside now. There is someone with whom I must speak.

Edwin hesitated only momentarily before realizing what was about to happen. Then he quickly backed up, allowing Suttaru to glide over to the caged Book of Wisdom unimpeded.

He held his breath, waited.

Fairen.

Suttaru's voice vibrated through the Haven, through Edwin's bones, and rattled inside his skull. And somehow it passed by the protection of the cage, because the cover of the Book lifted a little, as though letting out a breath. The pages fluttered momentarily.

"I am the Author," came her voice, echoing through the space. At once as powerful but different as could be from Suttaru's. Strong yet calm, gentle yet firm. If she was rocked by her precious Library being overrun, there was no hint of it in her tone. "Fairen is a name I have not gone by for a long time. As you know, *Adi*."

Suttaru shifted on the spot, his finger flexing and clenching into a fist.

You may shape-shift, pretend you are something you are not. But you forget I knew you. Before you gave yourself away like this. Hid yourself inside your own creation. I knew you in the beginning.

"You did. Once. But I'm afraid even then you failed to see me."

How dare you—

"What is it you seek from me?" the Author asked, cutting him off. Edwin stiffened, waiting for Suttaru's wrath to explode around them. Yet it did not come.

I only sought to speak with you one last time. For this is the end, Fairen. Your betrayal has been long in catching up with you. But it is finally time to pay for all you have done.

"And how did I betray you? By finding love with another man? For daring to dream of hope, and family? You are going to destroy me now? As you have sought to destroy all else?"

I am. And not because of your cretinous ship captain. He meant nothing to me. Or you, it seems, or you would not have imprisoned yourself in this gaudy relic of a book.

"Love comes in many forms, Suttaru. Once even Adi would have known that. For myself, I chose to send my love, my future, away and become the thing that would ensure its survival. But even then you were beyond my help."

You talk in riddles, Author. But not for much longer.

"And what will that bring you, Adi? Peace? Contentment at my demise? For whatever ills you think I have bestowed upon you?"

You did this to me.

"You did this to yourself," she said calmly.

Lies!

Now the anger exploded, and the room shook with the fury of Suttaru's response. His palms erupted in flames, and he held them stretched out, as if ready to burn away everything and anything around him.

You lie, Fairen. This—he gestured to himself, his face, the glow from the flames in his fingers casting his pale skin in crimson hues—*was your doing. You set a barricade I could not cross. You trapped me where* this *was inevitable. No matter our time together, you knew what would happen, and you locked me out there anyway.*

"You were already lost, Adi," she said, softer this time, though Edwin detected a hint of doubt in her voice. "Even before you went through the portal, you and I were no more. We hadn't been for some time. You had just failed to see it. Ignored what was right in front of you, so consumed you were with your work."

More lies. I did what I did for you. And you discarded me.

"That was your excuse then. It rings even more hollow now."

It was not an excuse. How dare you accuse me of such—

"No!"

Edwin had never heard ire from the Author in all the years he'd been a Sage here. Yet there was bite to her voice now. Frustration and anger. He felt Myrtilus buzz in acknowledgment of what they were witnessing.

"No, Adi. You have rewritten your own story in your mind. Changed your narrative to play the victim. The truth of the matter is that you made your decisions back then. And I made mine. Those choices took us away from whatever we had, and I am glad of it. Look at what you have become. It was always there, the potential for *this* inside you. That's what Discordia sought in you. It was already there, and you allowed it out. There is no one else to blame but you."

Suttaru's arms raised above his head, the fire growing in his hands until the two sets of flames became one. Edwin waited for the destruction, the excitement in him building, eager to witness the end of the blasted Author and her Book.

Then . . . laughing.

Suttaru was laughing, a sound so horrifying Edwin's guts twisted upon themselves.

Fairen still exists, I see, he said. The flames went out, and his arms dropped to his side. *It was good to talk one last time, my love. But now the time has come.*

He turned to Edwin.

Leave us now. I would do this alone.

"Of course," Edwin said, fighting a surge of frustration. Hadn't *he* led the attack on the Library that had led them to this moment? Hadn't *he* been the one to trick the Sages into coming to find him and then allowing them into the Haven in their haste to escape? Suttaru hadn't bothered to kick him out for the conversation with the Author. Maybe it was to show him she was still weak or could be riled. Even so. If this was to be the end of things, Edwin deserved to be here for it. To witness the final destruction of the cursed book.

And yet.

There was something more important. The matter of what he was owed. If he was going to miss this glorious moment, he should at least collect what Suttaru had promised him.

Suttaru sensed his hesitation.

Speak your question and do it quickly. Do not delay me any further.

"My nightmares, Suttaru. We have achieved what we needed. It is now time for you to rid them from me, as you promised you would. I will be able to serve you far better when they are removed."

The man laughed again. A tormenting vibration that continued for longer than it rightly should have.

And yet you have served me so well already!

The fury was simmering beneath Edwin's skin now. His Orb mocked him within his eye socket, and it took all his strength not to pluck it out with his fingers and crush it within his grasp.

He took a breath, steadied himself.

"We have the Library. I did that for you. Now, please, you must do this for me. That was the bargain."

Do you doubt my word?

"No, but—"

There was a burst of light in the room, and a blinding agony shot through Edwin's right foot. When he looked down, he moaned quietly, seeing it ablaze. The flames slowly began to spread up his leg.

"I'm sorry," he gasped. "I did not mean to voice my doubt."

If you wish me to stop, you must do better than that.

Edwin gritted his teeth, trying to dampen the pain as he humbled himself, dropping to his knee even though it brought tears to his eyes to do so.

"Please, my liege. Forgive me. I did not mean to question your word. Your word has seen us victorious this day. *I trust you implicitly.*"

His last few words came out in a rush as the fire reached his knee and began up his thigh. But it must have been what Suttaru wanted to hear, because there was a *pffffft* noise of the fire being snuffed out and a relieved gasp escaped Edwin's lips.

"Thank you, my liege."

I do not require your thanks, just your unquestioning loyalty. To listen and obey, without question.

Edwin bowed his head, as much to project subservience as to hide the snarl curling his lip.

Good, Suttaru continued, assuming he was being understood. *There is work still to be done. Haruto remains elusive. He escaped. To where, I do not yet know. Until I do—and can tear him apart to retrieve what he stole from me—we must remain alert. The Author will help us. She knows the location of the last piece, for there were three parts, the two fragments and the broken sphere itself. We have plenty of unwilling sacrifices at our disposal now. She will give it up soon enough.*

"I understand, my liege."

It is good that you do. Rest assured, you will have your revenge when the Maksus Stone is united and in my hands. We will burn it all down. Paperworld. The Library. Earth.

"The Sages and the Book too?" Edwin said hopefully.

Of course.

It was such a casual answer that the Edwin of old would have accepted it as a given. A certainty. Yet he had read the journal and knew that a beating heart had once sat within this monster. There was a sliver of doubt now as to what Suttaru would do when it came to the moment of action.

Edwin hesitated a moment longer, trying to figure out what to do. But he was interrupted by the sound of uneven footsteps coming through the door to the Haven.

Ah, my latest acquisition.

There was such pleasure in Suttaru's words that Edwin turned around more eagerly than he would have wanted. But he couldn't hide his shock as he caught a glimpse of a figure he recognized, with his beard partially scorched and dark words burned into his skin like all the other Unwritten souls.

Parade him before the prisoners, Suttaru told Edwin. *Show the Library's people a glimpse of their future. Perhaps they will be more helpful when the need arrives. Can I trust you to do that for me?*

Edwin let slip an easy smile as he looked into the lifeless eyes of the very same man who had prevented him from taking the Library the first time. A man who was now under their control.

Perhaps revenge would be his after all.

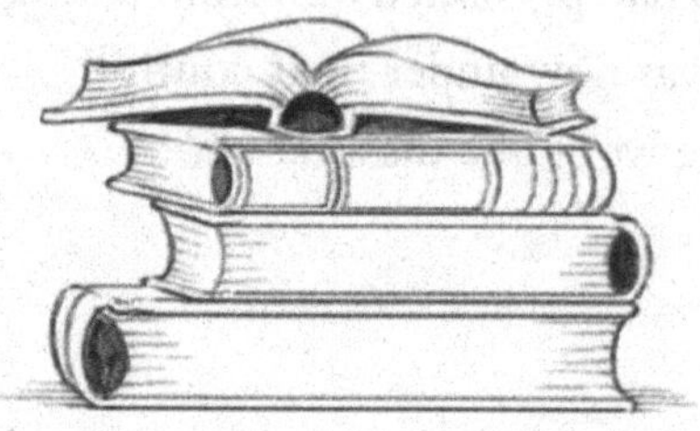

EPILOGUE

They were hidden in a small room.

The Cradle, Rosa had heard Eldra call it. And it had one, too, a cradle, like the kind of place you put a baby. Except she'd already seen that this one held something very different.

An Orb.

"Eltanin?" Eldra whispered beside her toward the ball of silver, resting within the strange nest. Hiding from the invasive force, as they had been. "Eltanin, wake up."

Eltanin stirred. A wary sliver of azure spun like a hair caught in the wind across his surface. A question, Rosa thought. That's what it felt like, though she did not know what he'd said.

Eldra translated.

"He's asked if it's time," he said to Rosa. The Sage put his hand gently on the Orb. "Yes, little one. It's time."

Rosa felt the excitement light up Eltanin's surface as he rose up, preparing himself. She knew a little of what had happened before she'd arrived at the Great Library. That Eltanin had been searching for a new Sage of Hope, but that the man had been killed. And Eldra had said the Orb had since then been searching for a new candidate. One who would unite the Sages once more.

It seemed like that was needed now more than ever.

"Have you found the person we need, Eltanin?" Eldra asked. The Orb made some fascinating shapes as he responded, and the Sage nodded. "Well, some is better than none. If you're sure the one is among them, you should depart immediately. Seek each out until you are sure. Do you understand?"

Rosa felt the strength of Eltanin's beaming light as he responded. She didn't have to know how to speak with the Orbs to understand he'd said yes.

Eldra looked to his own Orb. "Ask the Author to get us a portal."

"You can do that?" Rosa asked, surprised.

The Sage nodded. "The Great Library is full of magic. The Haven is where it's strongest, where the main portal to Paperworld is. But there are other places here that are conducive to such things, where the boundaries between realms are not quite as distinct. The Author can use the Book of Wisdom to draw on the magic held within these very walls to create Eltanin a way back to . . . Ah, here we go!"

There was a gust of wind from nowhere, before suddenly there was a shimmer in the air and light appeared. Rosa covered her eyes against it for a moment, too used to the half dark of the Cradle. Until her sight adjusted, and she was able to look.

Hanging in the air, at the center of the room, was an image of a city across a bay. Neon lights burned brightly, reflected in the water. Indistinct noise drifted across to the spit of land where the doorway lay.

Rosa could see all this contained within a small patch of air where it shouldn't rightly be.

"The portal," she breathed.

Eldra gestured to Eltanin. "Quickly now. Seek the one who will unite us. Bring us hope."

The Orb was lit up once more, its eagerness reflected in the complex bright blue patterns on its surface. Then it floated over to the portal, bobbed before it momentarily as though taking a deep breath, then it swept through.

"Do you want to go home too?" Eldra asked. And Rosa realized he was talking to her.

"Home?"

"Yes. It isn't safe here now. I don't know what's going to happen, or how we're going to free the Great Library. Perhaps it would be best for me to take you home to your mother."

There was a part of Rosa that wanted to say yes. To let Eldra lead her through the portal, back to Earth, to find her mother and sleep in her own bed and try to forget the bad things she'd seen today.

But her father was still out there in the realms somewhere. And her new friends were in trouble. This was their home, and it had been taken over. She couldn't just leave. Who would do such a thing?

"No, thank you," she said. "I'd like to stay. I want to help."

Most adults would have argued. Told her they knew best. Explained how dangerous it was and that she was better off staying out of the way.

Eldra didn't do any of those things. He smiled gratefully and then glanced at his Orb.

The image of the city quickly dissipated as though it had never been.

"Well then, Rosa," he said, standing and brushing himself off, preparing to depart. "We have some work ahead of us to save our friends, and it won't get done if we're stuck hiding in here. Are you ready?"

She stood, too, giving the Sage a look usually reserved for her father when he said something especially idiotic.

"Of *course* I'm ready."

GLOSSARY

Adi (now Suttaru): One of the original scholars who worked with Fairen, who later becomes corrupted by Discordia and transforms into Suttaru, also known as "the Ash Man."

Adscendo: This realm has a unique magical property that allowed its major cities and regions to rise (and stray) into the air. It is also believed to be the place of origin for the magical great bird Amare, whose children, the Golden Aurics, have a revered status across the realm.

Advisor: A senior position in the hierarchy of the community at Mother, the Great Tree, on Silvyra. An Advisor serves as one of the Chief Scientist's closest and most important councillors.

Amare: A large, miraculous, magical bird from Paperworld. Amare has multicolored feathers, golden aspects, and fierce intelligence. She can carry a full-size human on her back and can travel magically to anywhere in Paperworld and beyond by opening a rift in time and space and flying. She has a special relationship with the Sages of the Great

Library of Tomorrow, who can call upon her in times of great need. She can, however, only carry one passenger at a time.

Amicorum Spectaculum: A fabled troupe of performers across musical, acrobatic, and mystical disciplines who exist across multiple realms and, on very rare occasions, come together for a spectacular performance. They are rumored to engage in other, more clandestine roles when called upon.

Amin, the Sage of Loyalty: A former architect born in Jordan, he came to the Library in the 1990s. His aptitude for sustainable living has translated into an affinity for his surroundings, allowing him to become part of the physical landscape he inhabits.

Arcadiana: One of the key islands in Adscendo, this walled city is home to the five main Guilds of Adscendo: the Birdsingers, the Windriders, the Ateliers, the Weavers, and the Laborers. Each plays a vital role in the city inside the walls, which cover the entire perimeter of the island. The city is heavily populated and a hive of activity. From the bustling marketplaces, like the Mire, near the airship docks to the south, to the revered space of the Aviary, where the Birdsingers commune with the realm's flying inhabitants. Overlooking all this is Mount Nest, a large mountain where the Windriders and their airships are housed.

Arturo: A middle-aged man from Mexico City, Arturo has worked in marketing as a copywriter for most of his adult life. He is divorced, with a daughter named Rosa, and feels increasingly unfulfilled in his job, until he happens upon a magical gateway to the Great Library. Once there, he discovers that he possesses the magical ability to write things into reality.

Assembly Room, The: This is the largest reading room in the Library, reserved entirely for the gathering of the ten Sages and their Orbs. At its center is a large circular table with ten chairs, one for each Sage. The table has intertwined legs like the branches of a tree and is polished to a high shine, while the tabletop itself is made from a multicolored glass patterned like the wings of a dragonfly.

Atmosphere: Situated on Jaele's Mount, a volcano on Centonis, the largest island in Adscendo, this city is a place of celebration and entertainment. From the permanent city built into the exterior slopes, with its tall, many-floored towers and canals fed by water fountains, to the ever-shifting and changing interior of the once fearsome volcano, its gaping crater a sight to behold and a place for death-defying acts of skill and bravery. Above all this, airships of various sizes and people sporting customized wings fly about like bees around a nest.

Auditorium, The: Located off the Main Concourse, this is where Sages and scholars give lectures and answer questions from the audience. The Auditorium is a cavernous space, with high-arching ceilings and curving, dark wooden walls. It is arranged like an inverted cone, with semicircular rows of seats descending one after another, with a raised podium at its center. Atop the podium itself is a pillar of brass and steel, with a ring of crystalline lenses mounted around a concave mechanism at its top.

Author, The (see also "Fairen" and "the Scholar"): This is an honorific given to Fairen, often known simply as "the Scholar," who first discovered the portal to Paperworld and built the Book of Wisdom. During a time of great danger, she became one with the Book of Wisdom, becoming its voice and operating consciousness. While the Book of Wisdom is considered one entity, it speaks with the Author's voice.

Birdsinger: Birdsingers, named for their Guild, have a special affinity for the birds of Adscendo and can communicate and channel with and through them the same magical energy that allows the islands to remain in the sky.

Bloom: Located in the western region of Silvyra, the Land of Flowers, which includes Aedela (its capital), Lake Arroya, and many smaller towns and communities. It borders great forests and mountains to the east, where the Rose Garden is located, the stewardship of which the people of Bloom are dedicated to.

Book of Wisdom, The: The Book itself appears as a humble, moderately sized tome with a gilded red cover. Hidden beneath its bindings, interwoven, the secrets of its construction are only known to the Scholar (also known as "Fairen" and "the Author"). The Book rests on a grand pedestal that dominates the center of the chamber, a podium fashioned from wood taken from the island trees.

Bluefruit Tea: A popular beverage in the Great Library of Tomorrow.

Bravadier Blossom: A famous pilot and former first captain of the Silvyran airship fleet from many generations ago. He commanded the *Wanderer*, a vessel almost as famous as himself.

Captain Finesse: The former captain of the *Golden Oriole* and now retired. A longtime friend and companion to Rascal.

Centonis: The largest island in all Adscendo, it covers a vast area that includes farming, mountain ranges, a great ravine, and desert regions. It is best known for the location of the volcano Jaele's Mount, where the famous city of Atmosphere is located.

Chief Scientist: The Chief Scientist is the appointed ruler of the community living within the borders of the Maze in the First Forest and at the Great Tree in the realm of Silvyra. Typically a woman, the Chief Scientist is often a former Runner with great scientific curiosity as well as a deep affinity and knowledge of horticulture.

Chronologist: A title given to Silvyrans who dedicate their lives to the maintenance and preservation of the Rings of History and its secrets.

City of Forever, The: The City of Forever is a sophisticated and magical city located in an unnamed and sparsely populated realm. Although uninhabited, it serves as a repository of memory from across Paperworld. The scholars and Sages of the Great Library are currently working to uncover its secrets.

Clockwork Mountain, The: A very large, artificially manufactured structure consisting of three giant tiered cogs that serve as living space for a city ruled by an individual known as the Raptor Prince. The origins of the Mountain are mysterious, but it is believed to date back to before the Age of Spirits, when raw elemental forces controlled the realm.

Codex: This is both the catalog and operating system of the Great Library of Tomorrow.

Conjunction, The: This event occurs once every five seasons in Silvyra during the harvest season, when the realm's two moons and sun line up together and cause the natural life of the realm to prosper and renew. Various cultures in Silvyra celebrate this event with a great celebration and consider it to be the most important event of all the seasons. The timing of the Conjunction is somewhat random, with the people of Silvyra sensing and observing its coming by both their reaction to its effect on nature but also by observation of the moons and sun.

Densi: A young man chosen to be the Sage of Hope after the death of Helia, but he was tragically killed before he was able to begin his role.

Discordia: The Realm of Dark Stories, it is believed that Paperworld constructed this place to house and keep separate the very darkest of stories. It was first discovered accidentally by scholars from the Great Library while studying the portal to Paperworld.

Dzin: One of two orphaned brothers, he suffered from anxiety yet overcame those obstacles to help defeat Suttaru at the City of Forever. He now serves as Advisor to the Chief Scientist in Silvyra.

Edwin Payne, the Dark Sage: A former British army general from the time of the American War of Independence, after losing an eye during battle, he turned his interests to the development of electricity, eventually becoming the Sage of Creativity. On learning the history of Suttaru, he eventually abandoned the Library with his Orb, Myrtilus, to join Suttaru in his quest for power.

Eldra, the Sage of Harmony: Eldra was born in the first half of the twentieth century and pioneered the study of marine biology. He is accompanied by his Orb, Zubin, and has a black cat named Hocus.

Elixir of Life, The: The most precious resource of Silvyra, the Elixir is a paste created by Runners from unique recipes. Its creation is a gift given generations ago by Mother, the Great Tree, and is a potent remedy for ailments, both spiritual and physical.

Fairen (the Scholar; the Author): An early scholar—often referred to as "the Scholar" in histories of the period—and contemporary of the Founder, Fairen was responsible for creating the Book of Wisdom. When the realm of Discordia threatened the safety of the Library, she joined her consciousness to the Book and became known as "the Author."

First Forest, The: This large and diverse forest surrounds Mother, the Great Tree, and is home to a multitude of plants, animals, and people.

Forest Everlasting, The: An undying and unchanging forest in the realm of Solernia, it surrounds the realm's world tree, the Tree of Eternal Flame. The forest itself was made up of smaller white-leafed trees. After the fall of Solernia, the forest becomes known simply as the Burning Forest.

Formula (also Recipe): The Formula (or Recipe) is the formal name given to the ingredients a Runner chooses and combines to create their own unique batch of the Elixir of Life. The Runners go through the Maze and into the realm to collect eight ingredients that have special meaning to them, one being the petals of the Cerulean Rose, and typically the final combination is written down on a ceremonial scroll.

Founder, The: The originator of the Great Library of Tomorrow. Little is known of his early life, not even his given name, but he was an avid collector and appreciator of books and knowledge. When drawn to a mysterious, secluded island during his travels, the Founder decided to build a place to celebrate humanity's values, stories, and knowledge. The Founder was lost to the portal before the construction of the Book of Wisdom.

Fountain, The: An ancient floating mountain with an impressive natural waterfall, which captures moisture from the air and recycles it to other islands that pass underneath it.

Foyer, The: This is the oldest part of the Great Library, built upon the carved stone rotunda that the Founder discovered at the base of the mountain when he first arrived on the island. There is a grand circular chamber with a high ceiling and a large classical-style mosaic mural that celebrates the many forms of storytelling that the Founder brought together in his collection.

Gateways (Silvyra): These are the entrances to the Maze that surrounds the First Forest and Mother. They are placed roughly north, south, east, and west of the Great Tree.

Gallery of Sages, The: The Gallery of Sages is a grand space where ten marble statues of the Sages stand larger than life.

Golden Aurics: The children of Amare herself, these magical birds are large by any standard (although smaller than Amare herself) and have golden metallic feathers. Dropped feathers are prized in Adscendo above all other things, and the metal properties of donated or found feathers help the Ateliers Guild fashion improved flying machines for their realm.

***Golden Oriole*, The:** A magnificent airship made of wood and brass, the *Golden Oriole* is one of the rare vessels from Silvyra that docks at Mother, the Great Tree, and can travel to other realms to deliver the Elixir of Life.

Gumpf Stalks: A primary food source for the flying squirrels of Silvyra. They eat the stalks and use their droppings to line their nests.

Hall of Finding, The: A vast and cavernous space in the Great Library of Tomorrow, filled with high shelves of bound atlases and travelogues in a seemingly endless array of cartographical information about Earth and the realms beyond. It also houses the Orrery.

Haruto: A former scholar of the Great Library of Tomorrow and friend to both Fairen and Adi. Little is known about him, as he disappeared shortly after Adi became corrupted by Discordia.

Haven, The: Perhaps the most important room in the Great Library, the Haven is the very center of the Library, where the Book of Wisdom and the original portal to the other realms reside. It is a place of sanctity and magic, a place that students whisper about as they pass its doors, slowing to wonder about what astonishments lay beyond.

Heartwood, The: Located near the trunk of Mother, the Great Tree, it contains a collection of every floral species the Runners have ever found.

Helia, the Sage of Hope: Originally from Italy, where she escaped one of Mount Vesuvius's eruptions, Helia had been the Sage of Hope for several centuries and was the second-longest-serving Sage after Mwamba before giving her life to help defeat Suttaru at the City of Forever. She was supported by her Orb, Vega, and was romantically involved with Xavier, who died in the original attack on the Rose Garden.

High Eyrie, The: The oldest known floating island, it is home to the Shimmering Tree and serves as a roost for the Golden Aurics. It has ancient chambers built within the mountain, suggesting untold stories from much earlier in the realm.

Holds, The: These emergency safe zones are located on the cluster of islands, shaped like a butterfly, that house the Great Library on the left "wing." Deep tunnels run from under the main Library to the Holds on the right "wing," where there are several self-contained safe areas for people to shelter.

Huffbop Seedlings: A delightful and aromatic flower from the west of Silvyra.

Isle of Ulm, The: A small island in Adscendo and the birthplace of the acrobats Wilx and Zavia.

Jaele's Mount: The name of the volcano on the island of Centonis, the largest island in Adscendo, upon which is located the city of Atmosphere.

Jin, the Sage of Creativity: Originally from a small town near Beijing, Jin had always been an activist and champion for good. She had started out designing and building inventions to help mitigate her country's water crisis and then graduated into a climate scientist of much renown around the world. Such was her commitment to helping solve the environmental problems facing the world, she became a Sage in the 1990s and is accompanied by her Orb, Cor.

Joining, A: The Silvyran term for marriage and the ceremony.

Junic: A Silvyran airship captain and the romantic partner of Yantuz, Dzin's brother.

Kestrine: A large and very intelligent bird native to Adscendo. They are often used as messengers and are fiercely protective of their human friends.

Limniss Smoke: A magical creation of Suttaru, it can be deployed as a weapon to render its targets unconscious, presumably through suffocation. It appears as a foggy smoke that moves at will and seems to contain within it living or constructed beings of some kind.

Lyvanda: The current Chief Scientist of the Great Tree of Silvyra.

Maïa, the Sage of Integrity: Before becoming a Sage, she was a circus acrobat in late nineteenth-century France. As a Sage, she possesses incredible physical skills due to being "one" with her body and is capable of feats unmatched by normal humans. Her Orb, Thebe, is her constant companion.

Maiden, The: An ancient floating island thought to be from the same era as the High Eyrie (although smaller) and the Fountain. It has mountainous cliffsides, upon which grow a multitude of wildflowers.

Main Concourse, The: Beginning with classical architecture, evoking the cathedrals of the Middle Ages, then slowly changing to reflect the different ages of the Library's construction, this is the main thoroughfare of the Great Library. It contains towering shelves on both sides above marble floors illuminated by sunlight from outside the mountain, shining in through shafts bored through the stone itself and redirected throughout the area by a series of mirrors. There are balconied galleries leading to the arched roof far above, and all through the Concourse is the sound of bustling activity, from those who live and work here to visiting scholars and the machinery of the Library itself. The Concourse provides access to the other important areas of the Library, with the Haven at its center.

Maksus Stone, The: A gleaming black-and-ruby ball, much like a blend of obsidian and lava, with a fire visible within the stone itself. It is a relic from the early days of the Great Library, named by the scholar Adi after discovering it within a meteorite of exotic metal that had crashed on the island possibly many hundreds of years before it was discovered.

Matilaux: A boy of unknown age from the realm of Penumbris.

Maze, The: A creation of Mother, the Great Tree, the Maze encircles both herself and the First Forest and acts as a security barrier. Only the pure of heart can safely navigate the Maze while wearing a blindfold (or similar). If one is not worthy, the Maze will devour the traveler.

Morpho: A magical dragonfly and a living part of Mother, whose origin story goes back to a time generations ago, to the first Chief Scientist. He serves as a guide and protector to the Chief Scientist and appears as a treen tattoo on their arm until such time as he is needed, at which point he takes on his physical form, which is made up of parts of the living forest.

Mother (The Great Tree): She is the Mother Tree, the representation of the circle of life not just on Silvyra but in all the realms of Paperworld.

Indeed, each realm has a descendant of Mother unique to its environment that acts as its realm's Tree of Life.

Mwamba, the Sage of Knowledge: The oldest-serving Sage in this era, Mwamba has the ability to absorb, understand, and retain information from any book at incredible speed and the experience to put his knowledge to practical use in the service of the Great Library. Consequently, he and his Orb, Canopus, rarely leave the Great Library, where they can be of the most use.

Nu, the Sage of Truth: A young woman with a talent for "knowing" the truth of things, she was born in the Great Library of Tomorrow to her Australian mother and Burmese father, who found the Great Library in their twenties and became permanent citizens. After the defeat of Suttaru at the City of Forever, Nu becomes the Sage of Truth.

One World Bridge, The: A name given to the roots of the Shimmering Tree, which unfurl to connect with nearby islands and airships in order for them to dock with the Shimmering Tree. This, in effect, becomes an interconnected pathway around the connected islands. Words of love and unity, spoken into the bark of these root branches, appear as words, as though carved there.

Orbs: Originally designed by Fairen, the Scholar, there are ten sentient Orbs at any one time, and each is bonded to a Sage, whom they have selected on behalf of the Book of Wisdom. The Orbs have exotic materials in their makeup, and they can communicate fluently with their Sages, each Orb using a specific color and unique patterns displayed on their surface, combined with a strong psychic link and in a more limited way with other Sages and non-Sages. The Sages' Orbs can alter their size to hide and boost the Sages' power and are the mechanism by which Sages can travel through the portal safely.

Observatory, The: The Observatory is a special room where one can see events on Earth through an ingenious mix of technology and magic. The device is slightly bigger than your average crystal ball, and it is like watching a film, but one that makes the user feel as though they are really in the place being viewed.

Orrery, The: Located in the Hall of Finding in the Great Library, this great machine dominates the room—a complex assemblage of brass, steel, and crystal filling the vast space around it, a multitude of concentric rings that spin and twist on individual axes and orientations. Its purpose is to help the Sages find new realms in Paperworld and to track the Sages' Orbs while in Paperworld.

Paix, the Sage of Joy: Born in Brazil, she appears to be in her late twenties but has in fact been a Sage since the early 1900s. She is a talented pianist, and her powers are literally electrifying.

Paperworld: A metaverse of realms, Paperworld is the parchment patchwork of all stories ever told, where the River of Letters flows freely along endless channels, branching off into both physical and metaphysical streams, forming into words, sentences, and ultimately stories, which can each turn into a unique world of their own.

Penumbris: A dark and shattered realm, home to Suttaru and the Rogue Sage, Edwin Payne, and their creatures. Formerly known as Solernia.

Perennia: Silvyra's dragon protector, Perennia's origins are shrouded in mystery and much folklore. She lives in and guards the Rose Garden and can be seen soaring above the mountains west of Mother, keeping watch over the skies.

Pianna D'alatra: A Silvyran delicacy, comprised of salted leaf wraps with the most divine frosted center baked in Pianna nectar.

Portals: First discovered in the Great Library by Fairen (also known as "the Scholar" and "the Author"), it is a magical doorway to the realms of Paperworld. It is unique to the island where the Great Library is located and can be regulated and controlled by the Book of Wisdom. There are also portals from Earth to the Library, usually traveled by visitors to the Library, who emerge in the Foyer. They are also regulated by the Book of Wisdom.

Rascal: A former Runner from the Great Tree on Silvyra and now First Captain of the Silvyran airship fleet and the *Golden Oriole*, which is the flagship. She is full of vitality and seeks adventure in all aspects of her life, including having metal wings fitted to her back that allow her to glide through the skies of her world.

Ravager: A monster from the realm of Penumbris. It is made from red mist in humanoid form, with arms that are far too long, ending in clawed fingers that are as long as swords. And from the head, antlers jut out like upside-down lightning strikes. It is unrelenting and can read the minds of its prey.

Reading Room, The: This is a place for the Sages to research and converse. It is a beautiful, enormous space housing large numbers of books—tall, small, thin, thick, of all colors and decorations and designs—stored up against the walls three stories high and even somehow held across the ceiling too.

Refinery, The: Located at the lower levels of Mother, the Great Tree, the Refinery is a huge complex of wood, bark, and copper machinery, with giant brass containers where the Elixir of Life is manufactured in large quantities. Destroyed by Edwin Payne, it has now been rebuilt.

Rings of History, The: A sacred and secret chamber within the trunk of Mother herself, it is a repository of knowledge from across Paperworld, made possible by Mother's unique metaphysical connection across the realms through her offspring, the world trees.

River of Letters, The: This is the source of all magical stories and life that make Paperworld. It flows freely along endless channels, branching off into both physical and metaphysical streams, forming into words, sentences, and ultimately stories, which can each turn into a world of their own. It is constant change and creation.

Robin, the Sage of Love: A former special needs teacher, she is Indian British and has a mischievous, infectious smile. She is a relatively new Sage, but still considerably older than one might think. Her powers allow her to touch the emotions of all people, often appearing as waves of golden light. Her Orb, Centauri, shares her upbeat manner.

Rosa: "Rosa" is the diminutive (or pet name) of Rosalia, the daughter of Arturo Aguilar and Josephine Solace.

Rose Garden, The: Once known simply as the Hidden Vale, the Rose Garden is located in a secluded space between the mountains to the west of Mother, the First Forest, and the Maze. It is the home of the Cerulean Rose and to Perennia, the dragon protector.

Runners: These are the very best of Silvyra's horticulturists, who have studied and committed to searching out a unique formula for the Elixir of Life. Typically, only a small number of Runners are chosen for every cycle of seasons, and they must be brilliant, brave, and pure of heart. They spend several seasons researching, traveling, and navigating Silvyra on a personal quest to find eight meaningful ingredients for their unique formula for the Elixir. This includes passing through the Maze and traveling to the Rose Garden, where they must obtain a petal of the Cerulean Rose.

Sages: The Great Library of Tomorrow has ten Sages, a position created by the Book of Wisdom to watch over humanity's core values and its stories across all worlds. The Sages are a fundamental part of the Library's leadership after the Scholar joined with the Book of Wisdom. An Orb selects each Sage under guidance from the Book of Wisdom, and once selected, they bond for life. The Sages' natural affinity for their core value—hope, truth, strength, knowledge, and so on—manifests in magical powers related to nature and their specific value. This becomes an innate power for the Sage, which the Orb can also enhance by channeling energy from the Library. Sages can live a very long life—sometimes many hundreds of years—but are not immune to physical harm or accidental death.

Seed of Life, The: Connected to the Flower of Life, the Seed of Life is a central philosophy for the people of Silvyra and reflects the need to find balance and unity with nature and respect the cycle of life.

Scholar, The (See "Fairen" and "the Author"): A formal name given to Fairen, who discovered the portal in the Great Library and built the Book of Wisdom, for the period before she became one with the Book.

Scholars: A general term for residents or visiting researchers at the Great Library of Tomorrow. For citizens of the Library, this honorific places them as part of the research, librarian, and archivist careers within the Library.

Shimmering Tree, The: The world tree of Adscendo, located on the High Eyrie in Adscendo, resembles a circular ball of light. Its spear-like golden metallic leaves reflect the sun and offer a shining beacon to all. Located on a rocky island, its roots unfurl to create anchors for those passing islands and airships, bringing them together as a united whole.

Silvyra: This is the realm of plants and flowers, home to Mother, the Great Tree, the Elixir of Life, and the dragon Perennia. It is a large and varied world with continents, islands, oceans, rivers, lakes, and even deserts. Across all these terrains, there is an abundance of flora and fauna, as well as thriving communities, from large settlements to smaller communities. Silvyra has twin moons and a bright yellow sun, which align once every five seasons to create new life and prosperity.

Solernia: This is the original name of the realm that fell to Discordia and became known as Penumbris. Little is known about the realm, except that it featured dual suns and was known for advanced organic biomagical techniques.

Spirit of Death and Decay, The: Known as "the Sere," it was an ancient spirit, representing the cycle of death and decay. It is the opposite number to "the Verdant," the Spirit of Life. Together, they represent the circle of life.

Spirit of Life, The: Known as "the Verdant," it was an ancient spirit, representing life and the opposite of "the Sere," the spirit of death and decay. Together, they represent the circle of life.

Sugarweave: A sweet plant from the realm of Silvyra.

Suttaru: Formerly known as Adi, once a close friend and colleague of the Scholar Fairen, he is the corrupted remains of that man, shrouded in a cloak of burning ash and servant to Discordia, the realm of Dark Stories. In the Great Library of Tomorrow, he is known as "the Ash Man," a title given to him mostly in jest to scare naughty children.

Terropus: A large, many-tentacled creature found on the wastelands of Penumbris. It was once potentially a domesticated agricultural beast used to plow the ground by burrowing underneath the soil, but it is now a deadly predator.

Tree of Eternal Flame (also known as "the Tree of the Unwritten" and "the Burning Tree"), The: Located in the Forest Everlasting, the world tree of this realm is larger than the surrounding forest trees, but her unique aspect is not in her size. Her trunk can transform into a humanoid figure, and her leaves burn with golden flames. Her powers extend to the forest itself, and she uses biomagic to write the natural world around her into simple, undying perfection. During the fall of Solernia, she was overwhelmed by the might of Discordia, transforming her whole form and the forest into a burning nightmare. The darkness subverted her powers, and she was forced to develop the technique of Unwriting.

Triss: She is a gifted young, deaf scholar and Sage Mwamba's protégé and is being trained by him for a future senior position in the Great Library. She is also Sage Nu's romantic partner.

Underhall, The: A series of passageways underneath the North Wing of the Great Library that leads to the Holds.

Veer, the Sage of Strength: Veer was born in the first half of the twentieth century, and before becoming a Sage, he worked on the development of early wind power for NASA. His powers, amplified by his Orb, Lynx, echo his former profession, and he can command the air and wind itself.

Vernassia: A magical Silvyran word that allows the speaker to seek permission from Mother to open the secret door that leads inside her trunk to the Rings of History.

Volare Machina: These are the messengers and workers of the Great Library, a variety of mechanical and magical flying machines of all shapes, designs, and roles. Some have wings, others rotors, but all use a sprinkle of ancient magic in their workings.

Vortex: The name of the performance space at the center of the volcano on Atmosphere, where death-defying stunts, acrobatics, and acts of artful bravery are performed.

Unwritten, The: These are the victims of Suttaru and Discordia. They are helpless people and creatures whose personal stories have been rewritten, turning them into obedient servants of their new masters. The Unwritten can be identified by the burning script that appears all over their bodies while being controlled. It is written in a language unknown to the rest of Paperworld or the Great Library.

Wilx: A famed acrobat and member of the Amicorum Spectaculum, based at the city of Atmosphere. Brother and performance partner to Zavia.

Windcatcher: A type of wind and sail-powered ground transport vessel from the realm of Solernia (Penumbris).

World Tree, A: Each realm has its own unique descendant of Mother, the Great Tree, seeded across the metaverse of Paperworld. These world trees are symbols of life and unity in their realms.

Xavier, the Sage of Truth: A true embodiment of the Sages, he was selfless in his duty and deeply in love with Helia. His powers of truth and foresight, however, were not enough to stop him from being struck by Suttaru during the assault on the Rose Garden. He died heroically and is survived by his Orb, Antares.

Yantuz: Brother to Dzin and partner of Junic.

Zavia: A famed acrobat and member of the Amicorum Spectaculum, based at the city of Atmosphere. Sister and performance partner to Wilx.

ACKNOWLEDGMENTS

First, a huge thanks to all of you wonderful readers, who have embraced *The Great Library of Tomorrow* and followed the adventures of Nu, Veer, and the other Sages in this second part of the Book of Wisdom Trilogy. As this story reveals how I first encountered the Great Library of Tomorrow and Paperworld, its magical realms, and the heroes and villains who cast their light and shadows across the metaverse, it holds a special place in my heart, and I'm grateful for your support.

Thanks also to the creative team at Tomorrowland: Their inspirational ideas and magical world-building made it all possible. And to the writing and editing teams from Tomorrowland and Blackstone Publishing: Dan Hanks, Michael Rowley, Daniel Ehrenhaft, David Baker, and Rebecca Brewer. A huge thank-you for your wisdom and all-around support. And to Jamie-Lee Nardone from Black Crow PR and Marketing for joining our adventure.

To Paul Lucas and his team: Your continued belief in the project and support have meant bringing these books to life across multiple territories and languages.

Thank you all for your creativity, passion, and love, which have made these stories not just possible but come to life!

ABOUT THE AUTHOR

Rosalia Aguilar Solace grew up in Mexico City, the scion of a long line of writers. Finding Rosalia can be a challenge, as she splits her time between her hometown, where you might catch a glimpse of her writing in a bookshop café, and the Great Library of Tomorrow. But whether she's at home with family or researching future work, you can be sure of one thing: magical stories follow.

The Sky of Sacrifice is the second volume in the Book of Wisdom Trilogy.

www.thegreatlibraryoftomorrow.com

ABOUT TOMORROWLAND

Established in 2005 by Manu and Michiel Beers, Tomorrowland is one of the most beautiful music festivals in the world, famous for its fantasy themes, magical worlds, and unique feeling of global unity, with visitors from every country in the world. Located in the wonderful town of Boom, Belgium, the summer festival sells out in minutes and welcomes more than four hundred thousand visitors across two amazing weekends every year.

Tomorrowland's motto is "Live Today, Love Tomorrow, Unite Forever." "Live Today" stands for living life to the fullest; "Love Tomorrow" means having respect for oneself, including one's mental and physical health, others, and nature; while "Unite Forever" celebrates unity, diversity, equality, and freedom for all.

Yet Tomorrowland is so much more than just the summer festival. With new events landing each season in fabulous locations around the world, from Tomorrowland Winter at the magnificent Alpe d'Huez to the beautiful Itu with Tomorrowland Brazil, it is truly a global phenomenon.

Tomorrowland also connects with the People of Tomorrow all year long via One World Radio and its own record label, Tomorrowland

Music, while projects like the Tomorrowland Academy DJ and producer school help mentor the next generation of musical talent. Meanwhile, the Tomorrowland Foundation builds music and art schools around the world, giving vulnerable children the opportunity to express themselves creatively, with schools currently running in India, Nepal, and Brazil.

With Tomorrowland Fiction now adding another layer and sharing unique stories full of magic to a global audience, Tomorrowland continues to spread its messages of love and unity around the world.

REVISIT THE GREAT LIBRARY OF TOMORROW
WITH BOOK ONE OF THE BOOK OF WISDOM TRILOGY:
THE GREAT LIBRARY OF TOMORROW

www.thegreatlibraryoftomorrow.com